HIDE and Keep

A. MARIE

Editing: My Notes in the Margin
Proofreading: Judy Zweifel, Judy's Proofreading
Cover Design: Okay Creations
Formatting: Champagne Book Design

PLAYLIST

You can find the full playlist on Spotify

Hide and Seek—Klergy, Mindy Jones
Running Away—Genevieve Stokes
Eulogy For Nobody—Debbii Dawson
Scatterbrain—Emei
Other Boys—Marshmello, Dove Cameron
Better On Mute—Sophie Powers, Chandler Leighton
Cheerleader—Ashnikko
Drama Queen—Sueco
Poison - Perplexus Remix—Rita Ora, Perplexus
jealousy—FKA twigs, Rema
Dying Star—Ashnikko, Ethel Cain
The Night We Met—Haley Klinkhammer
Tell It to My Heart—Paris Paloma
INTIMACY ISSUES—Lilyisthatyou
Got Me Obsessed—Jade LeMac
Sacrifice—The Weeknd
Monster—Haven Madison
Fly—Nicki Minaj, Rihanna
In Silence—Janet Suhh
tear myself apart—Tate McRae
Broken—Palaye Royale
Miss YOU!—CORPSE
Shackles—Steven Rodriguez
Panic Attacks in Paradise—Ashnikko

Grenade—Bruno Mars
Vicious—Bohnes
Devil in a Dress—Teddy Swims
You Are The Reason—Calum Scott
If God Knew This Girl—Taylor McIntosh
ok on your own—mxmtoon, Carly Rae Jepsen
i wish you cheated—Alexander Stewart
The Things I Do For Love—bludnymph
Death of Me—WizTheMc
Butterfly—Bryce Fox
Die With A Smile—Lady Gaga, Bruno Mars

This book is a 168K-word enemies-to-lovers romance standalone intended for audiences 18+.

It contains content that may be triggering and/or disturbing to some readers, such as, but not limited to: foul language, alcohol use, graphic violence, explicit sexual situations, bullying, anxiety, depression, physical abuse, stalking, theft, talk of suicide, attempted suicide, talk of sexual assault/rape, attempted sexual assault, food poisoning, swallowing/exchanging of bodily fluids, public play, raw sex/sex without a condom.

Any on-page sex between the main characters is consensual.

For the dreamer:
Don't let anybody cut your wings.
Envision landing somewhere better than you are,
then fly high and hard until you get there.

HIDE and Keep

PROLOGUE

I READ THE EMAIL AGAIN, MY HEAD SWIMMING, MY BODY temperature skyrocketing more than it already was.

He said I had four years. Four measly fucking years to get the full college experience. Or as close to one as I'm allowed.

Does he know I left?

Even if he figured it out, he doesn't know where I am…right?

Every year, the Saturday after Halloween, our local corn maze gives college students the place to themselves for a night to run amok. Originally, it was meant to be an opportunity to decompress with peers, but under the anonymity costumes provide, it quickly became a hunting game of sorts, and now it's legend among the entire Northeast, not just the state of Connecticut. For everyone outside the maze, life continues as usual, but for everyone inside…time comes to a standstill. For one night only, all bets are off. Responsibilities cease to exist. Relationships are put on pause.

You can do anything you want, be anyone you want, and most importantly, be *with* anyone you want.

That's the whole point of Hide and Keep now—you run, you hide, but once you're found, that person gets to keep you until the first light of dawn appears, then everything goes back to the way it was before you stepped into the maze.

Every high schooler dreams of finally getting to attend Hide and Keep, myself included, but me being…well, me, I wasn't sure I'd get the chance.

After high school graduation, when my father informed me of my new future, I decided I would. I *should*. I've been planning for this event ever since, going to great lengths just to experience a night of total anonymity while I still can.

I change my phone to selfie mode, trying to see myself through the dark of the backseat. Thanks to a lacy black mask covering half my face, heavy makeup, orange contacts, and my hair hidden under a long amber wig with artificial monarch butterflies clipped to the wavy strands every few inches, I don't look anything like I normally do.

I don't feel anything like I normally do either. Or at least I didn't until this email appeared on my screen, reminding me not only who I am but who I have to be.

Not even a full three months into my freshman year and my father's already changing the terms. I thought four years was nothing compared to the lifetime he's demanding from me. Now he's cutting it down to only one. Less than one really.

"If it's all right with you, I'm gonna wait in this line so I can drop you off near the front?" the rideshare driver says from the front. "Even though I'm technically supposed to, I won't charge you. I just don't feel comfortable leaving you on the side of the road out here."

I can't help the incredulous huff that leaves me before I thank him. This man sounds more like a father than my own.

Money determines my father's every move, even the emotions behind them. Everything in his world is so incredibly fucking dire, while everything in mine is trivial, including my happiness.

Including me.

The thought makes my stomach churn.

The only thing Arthur Munreaux cares about is money. His entire personality is based on the balance of his bank accounts.

Which I have access to and could do anything I wanted with… as long as my father approves.

I study the driver's profile. He sounds like a father…

"Ugh. My father's gonna kill me," I complain under my breath.

Feeling his stare, I frown at my phone, my eyebrows scrunched together painfully.

"For coming here? You're old enough, aren't ya?"

I meet his weathered eyes through the rearview mirror.

I used to hold that same belief, that once I was eighteen, that was it—the end of my father's reign over me—but that was back when I was too naïve to understand age is the only number on this planet my father doesn't give a shit about.

"No, that's not it. I was supposed to do something for him before I went out tonight and I completely forgot," I lie.

"Uh-oh."

"Yeah."

After a moment of sitting in the long line of cars waiting to turn into the parking lot, the driver asks, "What was it?"

"I was supposed to go into the bank and transfer some money for him."

"If you have the app, you could probably do it right now."

"I don't."

"You could download it."

I bob my head slowly, noncommittally. "Or I could try calling?"

Inching forward to a cacophony of thumping sound systems, the driver's shoulders do a little shimmy, and he mumbles something about it being after hours, probably unaware that people like my father don't have any real limitations.

And for tonight, neither do I.

When my father's financial advisor answers, he does it already knowing who I am even though I've never called him directly before.

"Good evening, Miss Munreaux. How may I assist you?" His smooth, professional tone doesn't hold a trace of irritation at being inconvenienced at nine p.m. on a Saturday.

I think about how I'd word the request if my father were right next to me.

"Some funds need moved around."

"Absolutely. I'd be happy to assist you with that. Which account are you wanting to withdraw from? And how much?"

"Three hundred thousand taken out of the money market account."

The line goes silent, meanwhile the driver begins choking. Or at least that's what it sounds like.

"I'll need to call your father to get approval for that amount," the advisor says finally.

"Oh, no need. He's right here."

As soon as the driver whips his head over his shoulder to gape at me, I mute the call and start begging.

"How do I know your dad would approve of you taking three hundred grand from him? You're just a kid!"

I try not to bristle at his words. I am not a kid. I'll be nineteen in a couple of weeks.

"It's not *that* much," I say, because to me, it's not. To most people, I'm sure it's inconceivable to even have three hundred thousand dollars readily available.

"Not that much? That's more than my house is worth!"

"I'm not taking any money out. I'm just moving it around, I promise. My father, Arthur Munreaux…" I let that marinate for a moment. Everyone in this state knows that name. They teach it in state history classes in high school. "He told me himself to do this. Please. I wouldn't ask if it wasn't an emergency."

He eyes me skeptically. "What kind of emergency?"

What would he consider an emergency? He thinks I'm just a kid.

Kids need school.

"My college career," I blurt. "This money is for my tuition. If it's not in the right account when the check my father wrote the university goes through, I could be dropped."

When the silence stretches so long I know he's going to decline, I pop out my bottom lip.

"Dang it. I can't believe I'm doing this. What do I say?" He keeps one hand on the steering wheel and extends the other out to me, but I keep the phone in my hold.

"Just that you approve."

I tap mute again, then the speaker button.

"Here he is."

"Mr. Munreaux, how are you this evening?"

"Uh, good. You?"

I cringe. My father would never ask anybody that.

A tight chuckle drifts through the speaker. "I'm doing all right. Mr. Munreaux, I apologize for the inconvenience, but I must ask, what's the password?"

I mouth "Milan" to the driver and he repeats it out loud.

"Fantastic. Speaking of Milan, aren't you getting ready to head there soon?"

My head almost nods off my neck. Milan is where they hold the largest motorcycle exhibition every November. Of course the founder of Munreaux Motorcycles will be there.

"Uh-huh."

"Got any fun surprises up your sleeve this year?"

I mime twisting a key between my lips.

Following my lead, the driver says, "I guess you'll have to tune in to find out."

Another chuckle, this one easier.

"Fair enough. Now that we've gotten that out of the way, can I get your approval for transferring three hundred thousand dollars out of your money market account?"

"I approve."

I take the phone off speaker to ask, "Is that all you need from him? He's running out the door."

"Yes. Thank you for your patience."

Turning my face away from the phone, I yell, "Bye, Father!" adding to the confusion of the driver.

"What account would you like the money transferred to?"

"High-yield checking."

"You got it." There's some typing. "Okay, three hundred thousand has been—"

"Oh crap! Actually, it was supposed to go into the high-yield savings account."

"Not a problem, Miss Munreaux. Bear with me just a moment." More typing. "Three hundred thousand dollars from the high-yield checking into high-yield savings. Is there anything else I can do for you?"

"Umm… Maybe? I'm kind of confused now. I can't remember if he did want it in high-yield savings or if I'm just getting confused by the names."

"Checking. That's where checks come out of," the driver whispers, reminding me what I said this money was for.

"Would you like to call and ask him, then call me back?"

"No, that's okay. I'll just buzz him on the intercom. He's probably still in the garage, deciding which car to take." After putting the advisor on "hold" for thirty seconds, I get back on and say with faux embarrassment, "Okay, so…apparently, I did confuse myself. I had it right the first time. It's supposed to go in high-yield checking."

After a brief pause, he says, "All right, that's all finished. Three hundred thousand dollars have been deposited into the high-yield checking account. Now, because of your father's preferences for getting alerted anytime there's a withdrawal from an account, he will be receiving three separate texts. Please let him know not to be alarmed, they're just in reference to the transfers done tonight between different accounts."

I let myself smile as I say, "I will," before hanging up. I may have only shuffled three hundred thousand dollars around, but my father will think I withdrew nine hundred thousand and that will ruin his night. Just like he ruined mine.

The rest of the wait is so full of questions about my father and our garage, specifically how many motorcycles it must contain, that by the time we reach the front of the line, I'm dying for fresh air. It's always the same once people realize who I am. All they want to talk about is my father and his company. It's never about me. I'm only a bridge to Arthur Munreaux, not my own destination.

After adding a three-hundred-dollar tip to the electronic payment, I thank the driver again and get out.

Taking in the fifteen-foot-tall twin scarecrows with scary jack-o'-lantern heads and bodies wrapped in flickering orange lights, giving the illusion of being ablaze, I allow myself the first full inhale since I snuck out earlier.

Thick woodsmoke clings to the air, hinting at the bonfires I'm looking forward to seeing in person. Leaves flutter off shivering tree branches, relocating their coverage to the ground where piles are already gathering.

Slowly, I walk through one, smiling at the way the leaves crunch beneath my soles. A gust of wind suddenly picks up, swirling them around me like I'm inside an autumn snow globe.

My smile grows as my eyelids fall closed, committing it all to memory.

Somebody lets out a scream, making my eyes fly open. When no one appears next to me or calls my name, I find my way into another long line, this one for admission.

What feels like an hour later, I'm getting my hand stamped, then with the twin scarecrows towering above me, their features welcoming in the most sinister of ways, I enter the maze. Immediately, a weight slips off my shoulders, my hands lifting on their own, high into the night sky dotted with twinkling stars.

I made it. I'm here.

Bringing them down to shoulder height, the orange and black silk attached to my wrists spread my wings out wide. Before I know it, I'm breaking into a frolic. I drift through the maze, weaving around people who have no idea who I am. For once, nobody's scrutinizing my every move. I'm just…free. Free as a butterfly.

I don't know how long I float, but it's not long enough before the foghorn is blowing and everybody scatters from the well-groomed path into the cornstalks, hiding, laughing, squealing in excitement.

The hunt begins…

Careful to keep my steps light over the vegetation, I make my way through the tall stalks, my skin tingling, my heart thundering.

Rustling to my left has me freezing in place. Whoever finds me can't know it's me. My hair and eye color may be different, half of my face concealed, but there are other identifiers about me, like my voice. I didn't think about that. I didn't think about the kept part at all, only the hiding.

Really, that's the only part that appealed to me. If I could be this—a butterfly—forever, I would.

I can tell it's a person making the noise beside me, not a critter, because they're…panting? Sounds like it's two people.

Someone else's moan creeps up my own neck and into my ear, flooding my cheeks with warmth.

Definitely two people. And they're already going at it.

Peering through the foliage, I catch sight of them. A man dressed in Ghostface is hammering into a pirate, her fishnet-covered thigh pulled up to his ribs as he pumps into her mercilessly. The scene causes a fire to ignite in my core, my pussy clenching. Both of them are in full costume, Ghostface's mask still in place. They probably didn't even speak to each other before getting right down to fulfilling that basic need everyone's here to satisfy.

I watch them for another minute, my mind wandering, imagining, before I move on, quietly leaving the couple in search of a new hiding spot.

It's not long before somebody charges right past me. While I'm still in the stalks, he's out in the open. Cloaked head to toe in black clothing, he's in some sort of tactical gear, like a soldier or military police. Instead of diving into the cornstalks, he positions himself where the path leads into a corner and waits, his head on a swivel as it rotates back and forth, glancing both directions. A hood is pulled over his head and he has a fabric mask covering the bottom two-thirds of his face. I can't make out any of his features, yet I can't stop looking at him. His approach is…interesting. Confident. He's not actively hunting anybody. Like a spider sitting atop its web, he's set a trap and now he's waiting for someone to come to him.

My eyes fall down his body to his heavy-duty boots, then back up, coming to a stop on his hands. In fingerless gloves, they're twitching at his sides like they're trigger-happy even though he clearly has no weapons, at least none that are visible.

His head begins another rotation, so I quickly crouch down.

What if he finds me this early?

Do I even want him to be the one to find me?

I...don't know. Maybe? It'd help if I could make out anything about him.

But that's the point of tonight. The allure of the unknown. And the freedom to explore it without judgement.

A newly formed couple—a meticulously detailed Medusa and a creepy clown in haphazard makeup—passes by him and he gives them a nod, his stance still alert as he continues his watch.

As soon as he's focused elsewhere, I sink backward to put some distance between us, hopefully muffling my movements as I approach him from the side. Something about him has me intrigued enough to stay a little longer. He isn't behaving like the men I know, the ones I've grown up around.

I think it's the way he holds himself. He's confident but not arrogant. He's choosy, not desperate like the guys currently stomping through cornstalks, grabbing at anyone they can reach.

Who, exactly, is hidden beneath all those layers?

Not that I can actually find out, but I can wonder. I can study from afar.

"Are you going to say something or just watch me all night?"

I scan the area, searching for who he's talking to, but find no one.

Me? Does he mean me?

My chest locking up, I work to control my breathing but it's coming out of me in fitful spurts.

After a tense moment, he turns his head, giving me his profile, and says, "Your breath gave you away." Pulling down his mask, his lips form an O to blow out a cloud of steam.

I knew it'd be cold out here, but a coat doesn't go with this costume. Teeming with adrenaline, curiosity, and anticipation since I left my house, the temperature hasn't registered once. And I'm in a minidress and thigh-high boots.

No, what has my entire body feeling absolutely electric with goose bumps are his full lips. They look downright pillowy, more so from being pursed.

I remain quiet, still unconvinced he's talking to me.

Replacing his mask, he finally looks at my exact spot, his eyes piercing mine through the darkness.

I've been caught.

Without breaking eye contact, his expression turns expectant, but I hesitate, unsure what to do. Do I run and take my chances being caught by somebody else? Do I wait until he seizes me?

Does he want to?

A loud crash behind me solidifies my decision as I rush forward, spilling out from the stalks and into muscular yet gentle arms.

"Do you want to be kept?" he asks, his gaze penetrating.

I shake my head without hesitation.

With a nod, he guides me behind him as he faces the oncoming noise.

He's really tall, at least a foot taller than I am, so he easily blocks my entire body with his.

I hear him mumble a few words to whoever just pushed through after me. As soon as that person leaves, another takes his place, then another, an entire line of guys filing out from my previous hiding spot. I would've been found—and kept—a half dozen times by now.

I focus on my savior's shoulder blades at my eye level. Beneath the tight black fabric, they move and flex as he gestures the group away from us.

One of his gloved hands reaches back to me, grabbing my hemline to pull me closer, out of view. My body obeys with hardly any coaxing at all, my forehead fitting between those shoulder blades. I rest my face there, releasing a full, contented exhale.

His hand doesn't release my dress, the chilled fingertips awakening the skin underneath the fabric as they graze my thigh.

Warm breath pours in and out of my mouth, making a damp spot on his shirt.

Safe. That's what I feel in this moment.

When was the last time I felt safe?

Have I ever?

I became a cheerleader soon after learning to walk, a flyer in preschool. I was being thrown into the air with only one to six hands below to catch me before I could recite the alphabet. My body's in constant danger.

As for my sanity… Being a Munreaux feels just as perilous these days. Impossible expectations. No real safety net. And through it all, a smile plastered on my face because we at Munreaux Motorcycles know it's presentation that truly makes the sale.

Tears cloud my vision, so I close my eyes before any can fall and ruin my expertly applied makeup, instead choosing to focus on the scent of this newfound safe haven. Salt water and some sort of tree. Fresh. Outdoors. Amazing.

The line of guys finally ends, but neither of us makes a single move. We just remain locked together in this unconventional pose. Unconventional to humans. Monarch butterflies stay embraced for up to sixteen hours when they mate.

Not that we're mating but… This somehow feels more intimate than mating. More meaningful, at least to me. I've always envied monarchs for that ritual. Now I kind of pity them. After feeling this for myself, sixteen hours doesn't seem long enough.

"Are you ready to come out yet?" he eventually says.

Releasing a private smirk, I shake my head, the edges of my mask snagging on his shirt.

"Can I come to you?"

That makes my smile grow and I nod. It's not just that he asked for permission, it's that he asked *me* for permission.

Slowly, like he doesn't want to scare me, he pivots around to face me. To look up at him, I have to crane my neck back.

"Why'd you come tonight if you don't want to be kept?"

Unable to answer, at least not verbally, I shrug a shoulder.

He lets out a husky chuckle. "Okay…" His attention shifts from my face to the raised shoulder, then down my arm. Lifting my hand with his out to the side, he murmurs, "Butterfly."

Maybe because I do feel safe with him and because he asked me for permission and because I'm not me, not tonight, I thread my fingers through his and pull.

His gaze snaps to mine.

"Um…" Shaking his head, he swallows and glances around us, but my hold on him tightens, bringing his attention back to me. "This is…uh… You don't…"

One small step toward him and our bodies are flush against each other. My skyward chin doesn't even graze his, so I push up on my tiptoes.

"Butterfly…" His voice sounds strained, like he's in pain. "You're…" He gestures at me. "And I'm…not."

Not? That's exactly why I'm drawn to him. *Because* he's not. He's not like anyone else I've ever encountered. He's not asking me about my father. He's not looking at me how *everybody* always fucking looks at me.

I go to pull his mask down, but his free hand catches my wrist, stopping me.

"It's not…" Again, he shakes his head. "Worth it."

What isn't worth it?

One hard tug and the mask comes down—his, not mine.

At first, I maintain eye contact, but when his drop, mine follow. Except while he's staring at the ground, I'm studying his face. His stunning, unique face. Stunning because he has light eyes, full lips, a razor-sharp jawline, and just enough hair on his chin to qualify as a goatee. Unique because of the half-moon scar under his left eye, which I'm assuming is what he didn't want me to see, what "isn't worth it."

It does nothing to detract from how hot he is. If anything, it makes him hotter.

But obviously he doesn't feel that way.

He's not as confident as I thought. He might not be confident at all.

If I could speak, I'd squash any insecurities he has by telling him how beautiful he is, how much of a disruptor he is to the current stale beauty ideals. Goddess, if I were scrolling through fifty selfies, his is the only one that'd stop my thumb from swiping. I wouldn't just pause either. I'd zoom. I'd take a screenshot. I'd keep him, and not just for one night.

Palm to his cheek, I run my thumb over the groove, a gentle smile playing on my lips to show him it doesn't bother me. I *like* it.

He tries to shake me off, saying, "Butterfly—"

But I hold firm, molding my hand to his face and pulling him down a few more inches until his lips touch mine. Thanks to the mask, they're not the slightest bit cold. They part instantly, letting my tongue right in and giving me the freedom to do as I please. The way nobody ever has.

The way nobody ever will.

I kiss him with all the conviction I wish I could voice, all the affirmations I can think of.

You are worthy.

You are attractive inside and out.

Your imperfections make you beautiful.

You don't need to blend in.

You're perfect exactly the way you are.

Sliding my hand to the back of his head, I tilt him for a better angle, pouring more energy, more desire into him.

Something about it sets him off, like a match to a fuse, and on a growl, he grabs an ass cheek, tugging my body flush against his as he finally gives in completely, kissing me, not just back but ravenously, like I'm the first taste of something he's had in days. Maybe longer.

It takes all my effort not to release my own sound of appreciation at the feel of his growing erection between us. My mind flits back to the couple I saw in the stalks and the carefree way they fucked each other out in the open. Raw, like animals.

I want to be like that. I want to do that, with him, now.

When I reach for his waistband, the rest of him locks up before he breaks the kiss to say, "Sorry, uh…." With a backward glance, he gives our surroundings another scan.

He's used to hiding himself.

I keep his hungry gaze as I back up, toward the vegetation, the coverage.

"Where are you going, butterfly?" he asks with a trace of humor to mask the worry his feet give away by following immediately after me.

Leaves tickling my back as I continue walking backward, I crook a finger at him with one hand while lifting my dress with the other. As long as I don't pull it up past my stomach, I'm fine.

"Fuck," he grits as he reaches for my hips. "You're gonna get me—"

A helicopter appears overhead—flying too low and way too slow to be coincidence—cutting him off. Anything loose on the ground becomes airborne, creating a cyclone of dirt and debris around us. My savior curses as he spins around, shielding my body with his once again. His face to the sky, he's trying to get a look at our intruder. Only the bottom of the helicopter is visible, but I don't have to see the sides to know whose name is on them.

Impeccable timing, Father.

After one final glance at that spot between his shoulders, I put my dress into place, turn, and disappear into the cornstalks. When I emerge out the other side, my father's chopper is just touching down on the front lawn, letting everybody know exactly who he is, and now, who I am. He doesn't get out, just waits oh so fucking patiently for me to come to him.

He's only patient when it suits him.

I try to keep my attention out ahead of me, but extended fingers pointed at me from every direction spear my periphery. My spine straightens on its own, my posture as confident as if I were at the top of the pyramid.

Yeah, I made an appearance at Hide and Keep. My costume was too good not to. But finding the game juvenile and the selection lacking, I called my father to pick me up early.

That's what I'll tell everyone, and nobody will doubt me. Why would they? I'm Ever Munreaux, sole heiress to Munreaux Motorcycles. I get everything I ask for.

Except a single shred of autonomy.

Before climbing into the helicopter, I let myself look back, but I don't see the man I kissed.

Look for me…

Inside, my father tosses a headset onto my lap. When I don't rush to put it on, he reaches over and pinches the side of my hip until I cry out, scrambling to get it over my head.

As soon as the seals are over my ears, his voice booms, "A million fucking dollars!"

We're off the ground in the next instant, the speed making my stomach drop. I focus on Long Island's scattered lights in the distance, my eyes watering. Sounds like his night did get ruined.

Good.

"I can't believe you made me chase you down here. Here. This is not somewhere you should be. This is not where you belong!"

I don't react whatsoever, gazing aimlessly out the glass…until I feel another pinch at my hip, then I gasp. That one was deeper than the first. What is happening? He's only pinched me a handful of times before, always where no one will see, but he just did it twice in a row.

"You can consider that million dollars your signing incentive. And your money allowances? Those just got lowered. Significantly. A million dollars…"

I've been such a good, quiet, *demure* daughter. This is the first time I've even attended a public outing that didn't directly benefit him in some way and I had to sneak out to do it. But what did any of it get me? More of the same. It'll always be more of the same.

Right now, I don't feel the same. I don't even feel like me.

I tear my eyes off the horizon to glare at my father, shouting into the mic, "I didn't take a penny of that *three hundred thousand dollars I moved around three times!*" I stick three fingers up to emphasize my point and brace myself for a third pinch.

Except my father does something uncharacteristic and laughs. It's *not* humorous. It's full of malice and mockery and makes me want to rip the headset off my ears just to make it stop.

"I guess you carry some of my genes after all."

He says it like he's proud of me, but I know that's impossible.

Up until this point, I've done everything to try to make him proud, but nothing's ever worked.

Why bother anymore? I only have five months until Nationals—apparently the last one I'll ever get to compete in—and six months before my duty to Munreaux Motorcycles catches up with me, and my adult life will officially begin.

Six months to live how I actually want to.

Six months to live.

CHAPTER 1

Crue

Five months later

THE EIGHT-FOOT-TALL MONOGRAMMED WROUGHT IRON gates swing open and I pull through, slowly climbing up the winding driveway bordered on both sides by dense woods.

Finally cresting the hill, the mansion comes into view, along with the lavish grounds around it. The driveway breaks off into three separate paths, left, right, or straight through two identical-looking hedge mazes.

"This is fucking insane," I mutter under my breath.

There're no signs telling me which I should take, but since the house is where the interview is being held, I decide to go straight.

Past the mazes, I find a helipad. Automatically, I seek out the accompanying helicopter. Ever since Hide and Keep, I can't help but look over every helicopter for clues. Five months of wondering if that's where my butterfly disappeared to, into the helicopter that flew directly above us, ruining what was shaping up to be one of the most memorable nights of my life. She was there, right in the palms of my hands, but I took my eyes off her for a second, one fucking second, and she slipped out of my grasp. I didn't get a name, a number, a single way to find her…except the helicopter she may or may not have left in.

It's probably just wishful thinking.

It's not wishful thinking. It's worse. It's delusion.

Private helicopters are common in this type of neighborhood, so the chances of someone living like this going for someone like me is ludicrous, outlandish, so beyond comprehension, I should stop. Stop looking, stop hoping, stop wasting my goddamn time.

There's also the fact that I didn't see her leave in it. She *could've* left with anybody, at any time. With her inquisitive gaze, soft yet demanding touch, and bold-as-all-hell kiss, my butterfly was…enchanting.

But she isn't actually mine. Even if for a brief few moments, it felt like she was. Whoever she was.

No helicopter in sight, I focus on the mansion before me. It's as tall as it is pretentious. The massive, detached garage off to the side hides two more buildings only seen from aerial footage I pulled off the internet during my research for today's interview. One is a pool house with what appeared to be an indoor/outdoor pool, but the other was harder to identify. Definitely too small to be another garage, even for motorcycles.

Those two other parts of the driveway lead here, too, obviously wrapping around the mazes' outer perimeters, so I park my Bronco in front of the stairs leading up to the front door, not entirely sure I'm supposed to but not knowing where else I should. There aren't any fucking signs. Do they not get guests very often? This property is way too big not to have signage for first-time visitors.

While I'm taking stock of the front of the Georgian-style stone house, and struggling to find a single security camera, a man who is older—but not the man who founded the most well-known motorcycle company in history—comes down to greet me.

"Mr. Brantley, I presume?"

Instinctively, I pull my baseball hat a little lower over my face.

"You can call me Crue."

Ignoring my request, the man asks, "Mr. Brantley, is there anything I can get you after the long drive? A refreshment perhaps?"

I give him my full attention again and a more thorough once-over. He may not be the homeowner but he's acclimated to this lifestyle in his time working here. Although the drive here wasn't long in distance, this area feels a world away from the one I live in.

"No, thank you. Is my car good here or should I move it?"

"Leave the keys in it and one of the techs will park it for you."

Techs. They have technicians onsite.

As soon as I drop my keys on the driver's seat, he tells me, "If you're ready, Mr. Munreaux will see you now."

"Mr. Munreaux is already here?"

He cocks his head. "Yes."

"I just thought…" I glance behind me at the helipad with the giant M in the middle of it. Facing forward, I say, "I didn't catch your name."

"I'm Mr. Munreaux's valet. Now, if you'd—"

"But what's your name?"

After a brief hesitation, he says, "Edwin, sir."

"Nice to meet you, Edwin." I hold a hand out to him that he eventually takes with one of his.

"Pleasure's all mine."

"I was kinda hoping I'd get to see Mr. Munreaux land his helicopter."

Edwin's gaze barely sweeps over the monogrammed slab of concrete, saying, "Private aviation contributes to the current global crisis."

"So do motorcycles." And his boss mass produces those.

With a raise of a wiry eyebrow, he says, "For the time being," but doesn't elaborate.

I gesture for him to lead the way, then follow him up the staircase that has a motorcycle statue on each side, into the cavernous foyer with two-story-high cathedral ceilings, and through a hallway to a solid, probably hand-carved, door. He knocks once before announcing my name.

At a voice on the other side replying with, "Enter," he opens the door to let me in.

The first thing I see is a fireplace I could step inside of without needing to bend down. It's gotta be at least eight feet tall. Next to it is a painting of the man who definitely founded the most well-known motorcycle company in history. He even posed on one for the portrait so there's no fucking confusion.

"What was the delay?"

My eyebrows plummet as I turn to face Arthur Munreaux. "Delay?"

"You're a minute late," Arthur informs me, his eyes noticeably narrowing on my face, on my scar.

I dip my head just enough that I can still see him while hopefully casting shadows over the top third of my face with my hat's bill.

"Mr. Brantley was inquiring about your *helicopter*, sir."

Arthur frowns at his valet, then me. "Helicopters are terrible for the environment, and we're moving toward a cleaner, greener world, aren't we?"

There's an unmistakable bite to his tone that leads me to believe he's not entirely happy about the progression.

I'm just about to mention the plan his company announced back in November to roll out an electric motorcycle but has yet to produce when Edwin speaks up, saying, "Yes, sir. Sooner than anticipated."

Arthur smirks. "Much sooner."

"If that's all, sir…"

Edwin waits for his boss to dismiss him, giving a half-bow before leaving us alone.

"Take a seat." Arthur gestures vaguely, so I take one of the two plush chairs in front of his desk, my back to the door.

A document I'm all too familiar with in his hand, he says, "Your résumé is…colorful. You were a straight-A student, yet didn't further your education beyond high school."

I don't make a sound, waiting to see if he'll ask why.

"It also says you have experience in martial arts and combat. Is that how you got that scar?"

"Um…" I hesitate, his directness catching me off guard. Most people focus on it while acting like they're not. No one usually asks me about it. They don't really have to. It's pretty well known how I got it. "I was a wrestler," I say, not exactly answering his question. If he doesn't know, that's on him for not doing his research. Or more accurately, making someone he pays do theirs.

He sets down my résumé, giving me his undivided attention.

"Any good?"

"State champ."

"You've worked security at a lot of places, yet you've never been let go, so you jumping from job to job is your own doing…"

Finally lifting my head enough to meet his eyes directly, I tell him honestly, "I like to be challenged."

"You'll be challenged here. All day, every day."

"*All* day?"

Sitting forward, his gaze narrows on mine. "The position I'm looking to fill, it's around the clock, twenty-four hours a day, seven days a week. From the moment you're hired, your shift begins and you get no breaks. And I mean none." His flattened hand makes a chopping motion. "And that's not for everyone, especially someone with a wife and kids to go home to every night. You got any rugrats running around?"

"Not that I'm aware of."

He huffs out something like a half-laugh before focusing on my scar again.

"Married?"

"No."

"Girlfriend?"

"No."

"Good, because there is no going home. This will be your home for the foreseeable future. Understand?"

"Yes, sir." Spotting the device on the window behind him, I add, "But if you were to make some upgrades to your home's defense system, even just installing cameras outside, I'm not sure you'd need a full-time guard."

Arthur sits back. "You won't be guarding the house. You'll be guarding my daughter."

"So, you're looking for a bodyguard?"

"That's such a crude term. It implies a meathead with very little skill. I prefer executive protection agent. Someone smarter, faster, able to blend in a little easier."

I consider his words, my head beginning to move into a shake.

I've never done that kind of work. It sounds…public, at least more than the security jobs I'm used to. It also sounds like babysitting.

The motorcycle mogul holds up a hand. "Before you decline, let's talk numbers. Once moved in, all living expenses will be covered, making your salary of fifty thousand a month more than sufficient."

Fifty thousand? A month? Damn. I could do a lot with that much money.

As far as I know—as far as *everyone* in Sea Haven knows—Arthur Munreaux only has one daughter.

"It'd be for Ever?"

"You know her?"

"Not personally." Luckily, I've never met the princess of Sea Haven. I've heard plenty about her though. And like I said, *luckily* I've never met her.

"So, you've done your homework then."

I bob my head slowly.

Ever Munreaux, star student at the most prestigious college in this country and social media influencer for some kind of dance team bullshit. At least that's what it showed on the only social media account I was able to find for her. She could have another private one.

"Look. I'll cut to the chase. I need someone to start right away. Today. Now. And because it does require a bit of…let's say…hazard pay, how about I tack on an additional five-thousand-dollar sign-on bonus if you make it past your first day?"

If I make it past the first *day*? How much danger is she in?

"What exactly does your daughter need protecting from?"

Without blinking, he says, "Herself."

I have no idea how to take that. Is she suicidal?

"She—"

The door behind me bursts open, causing Arthur's posture to stiffen.

"Father," I hear behind me but don't take my eyes off Arthur just yet. Most people become more relaxed, happier, loving when they encounter their offspring. Arthur looks like he's none of those things.

"Speak of the devil," Arthur drawls.

The steps behind me falter for a moment before resuming. A body to my right breezes by, a faint current of honey and sunshine floating past.

"We got first place. As expected," Ever tells her dad.

There's a long stretch of silence, then Arthur says, "You look pleased with yourself."

"I am—"

"Imagine how it'd feel to get first in a real sport."

I let my gaze drift over to the back in front of me. Ever's spine straightens, making the muscles in her back flex, her dimples of Venus visible thanks to her crop top and skintight booty shorts.

It's a hell of a body to guard, I will say that.

"Cheerleading is a sport," she argues.

That's what her feed must've been full of—cheerleading…which is absolutely not a sport.

"Is that the uniform you competed in?"

Confused, I drag my eyes back to Arthur. His are locked on his daughter's, the disapproval palpable.

Ever puffs out a laugh. "No, I got this after. It's a joke."

The tense stare-off between the two continues until Ever shakes her head and spins to leave. Spotting me, she freezes.

And unfortunately, so do I.

While her shoulder-length hair is black, her eyes are far, far from it. They're azure.

I have dark hair and light eyes, too, but the contrast between hers is much more significant. Seeing it in photos online is striking. Seeing it in person is…different. Very, very different.

I could tell from her pictures she was pretty, but face to face, she's absolutely fucking gorgeous. She's also really short. Short enough to be my butterfly.

Beneath furrowed brows, that blue gaze touches every inch of my face, lingering on my—

Shit. I forgot.

I tuck my chin down, cutting off her view.

Only able to see as high as her neck now, I notice a couple hickeys there, one fainter than the other. Below that is her black crop top, so short it barely skims the bottom of her gray sports bra, with the words "I got wet" scrawled in white cursive across the chest.

I feel my expression settle into a frown. What a dumb fucking shirt. Reminds me of high school when everyone was so goddamn desperate for attention all the time, they'd embarrass the fuck out of themselves to get even a shred of it. This girl graduated though. She *should* be mature enough to behave better, but obviously, she's still seeking attention. Probably always will.

Spoiled brat.

I'm not expecting her to duck down, catching my eye, but she does. She fucking does. And I...freeze. Again.

What the fuck is wrong with me? It's not like she is...the butterfly...is she?

Our eyes locked on each other's, she says, "What—"

"Never, meet Crue Brantley...your new executive protection agent," Arthur announces confidently even though I didn't accept the position and have no intention to, especially after coming face to face with Ever. There's no way this girl isn't out and about all the time. That's so many people to encounter. So many gazes to avoid.

Those sea-glass eyes wince briefly before leaving mine altogether.

"You're shitting me. Another one?"

"Don't use that expression. It makes you sound as common as you currently look."

Arms out at her sides, she yells, "It's funny!"

"Do I look amused?" Arthur asks her with a chilling tone before saying, "You did this to yourself, Never."

The first time he said it, I thought I must've misheard him, but now there's no mistaking him purposely calling his daughter Never.

"You were given ample time to get your act together and conduct yourself like a Munreaux. Instead, you've chosen to make a mockery of my good name and I won't have it. Not anymore. Too much is at stake, more now than ever."

"Father, I—"

"If you're going to act like an insolent child, you will be treated like an insolent child. If you need to be watched day and night, then you will be watched—"

"Father?"

"—day and night."

"Ugh!" Ever spins my way again, practically spitting, "I wouldn't get too comfortable if I were you. I'll have you back out on the streets by the end of the night like I did the others he tried putting on me."

"I'm not from the streets," I say, shoving to my feet before I know what I'm doing. I don't even attempt to hide my scar. I know she's seen it anyway. Let her look.

Closing the gap between our bodies, she does exactly that but with an added lip snarl to say, "My bad. I get my levels of poor confused when the stench of destitution becomes unbearable." Then she plugs her nose and pushes past me.

Fuck. You. Bitch. I may not live like the Munreauxs but I've never been destitute in my life.

I twist to watch her leave, those back dimples prominent as her hips sway aggressively, and conclude with absolute certainty that there's no fucking way she's the girl from Hide and Keep.

"Take your shirt off."

Ever pauses at her dad's voice, then shakes her head, sneering, "Like I don't work out in my sports bra every day anyway."

To keep up those abs, all eight of them, tight and toned to perfection, I'm sure she does work out every day. This girl's in better condition than I am. She's fucking *cut*.

"Not you," Arthur says as she grabs the high-ass hemline of her shirt.

I turn to face her father, finding him looking at…me.

"As of yesterday's competition, cheerleading's over."

"But we have—"

"It's over!" Arthur finally loses his composure, shouting the last word at his daughter.

I don't really like it, him yelling at her, even if she does deserve it, but I bite my tongue, counting down the seconds until I can leave this place. Rich people are weird as fuck and not for me.

"As is your excuse for not wearing enough clothing." Arthur gestures to me, ordering, "Give her yours."

Grateful I technically have on two shirts today, I start unbuttoning my flannel. What does it say about the pauper literally giving the princess the shirt off his back?

"I'm not wearing his off-brand rags."

"Cover up or so help me, I will strap a chastity belt to you," he warns.

Although I've seen this man show zero humor, I hope to God he's just joking.

I walk my shirt over to Ever. As she goes to grab it, her nails sink into my wrist, but I don't give her the satisfaction of a reaction—good or bad, because while she's wanting bad, my cock thinks it feels good. Really fucking good.

Peeking up at me through thick black lashes, she juts out her bottom lip, and whispers, "I'd rather wear a chastity belt than your ugly hand-me-downs. At least then I could run your dick through it like a meatgrinder."

I rip my arm out of her hold, those fake nails leaving angry lines in their wake, then I fit the flannel over her shoulders, making sure to button it from the top down.

When I'm on the last one, I bend down so I'm next to her ear and, grazing the inside of her bare thigh with a fingertip, whisper back, "Good luck getting it hard enough to try. I've put my dick in glory holes more attractive than you."

I'm full of shit of course. Not only have I never even seen a glory hole in person, I'm currently fighting a hard-on. She was attractive before she marked me, but now... As long as she didn't talk, I'd have no problem wetting my dick in Ever Munreaux.

Her breath tickles my ear as she says, "Quit now or when I'm finished with you, the only job you'll be able to get is manning a glory hole..." She pulls back to look me in the eye. "...swallowing so much cum, sperm will shoot out of your tear ducts."

The corners of my eyes itch from that graphic visual.

"That's not how it works."

"Whatever you say, cum fountain."

Snapping to my full height, which is at least a foot taller than hers, I keep sperm-free eye contact with her while telling her dad, "I accept the position."

I don't have to be her bodyguard forever. But after the challenge Ever just laid at my feet, that five-thousand-dollar bonus is as good as mine.

One brow arched, Ever mimics a blowjob, then spins and leaves.

"Well, that went better than expected."

Finally peeling my eyes off the doorway Ever disappeared through, I return my attention to Arthur. Did it? She threatened both my dick and my livelihood, and I can't decide which I should be more pissed about.

"As you can see, my daughter is acting out. She's struggling with..." His gaze drops. "...her mother's death."

I mumble out an apology for his loss that he shrugs off. Although no one ever really saw Alette Munreaux when she was alive, everyone heard about her tragic death. But that was several years back already.

"I've given her ample time to come to terms with her new reality, but her behavior continues to worsen. And while we all were a little rebellious at her age, she's meant for more than being some frat bro's chew toy. She's important. Necessary. The future of Munreaux Motorcycles depends on her. Do you understand?"

I give a nod even though I don't know what the hell the girl I just met could possibly offer Munreaux Motorcycles. If Arthur's plan is to hand his daughter the reins one day, that day is *far* off. Ever's not fit to intern at a multi-billion-dollar company right now, let alone run one.

Is there literally no one else to take over?

"Recently, she's been on a bit of a tear. Sneaking out at all hours of the night, showing back up with fuck-marks on her neck from God knows who. Now that her little cheerleading competition is over, I fear she'll let her studies slip and lose her exemplary academic standing as well. She only has a few weeks of classes left for her freshman year. I need her to finish her time at college strong. Your job is to ensure she does."

She's a freshman. That means I'll be babysitting her for the next three years. At least. She could major in something that requires even more schooling.

I remember who we're talking about. Three years is being generous. Ever Munreaux isn't going for something like a doctorate.

Three years of fifty grand a month though…

It's not forever, and it'll give me enough money to actually do something, go somewhere, be…someone. Someone *else*.

"So, her education is the priority?" I question.

"Her reputation is the priority. That's why you will be with her at all times, tirelessly working to keep what's left of it intact. You're… what?" He glances down at my résumé. "Twenty-five. You're considerably younger than the other guards I tried out. So you're close enough in age to her you should be able to think like her, and hopefully, get ahead of her to nip destructive behavior in the bud."

"You mentioned wanting me to start today—"

"Not wanting. Needing. And you did start. You started the moment you accepted. Unfortunately, while we've been talking, she's already got the jump on you."

After tapping the screen on his computer with some sort of electronic pen, he points it at a TV mounted on the wall to his side, instantly summoning live video feed.

So, they do have one camera on the property.

The gray-and-white image on it is unmistakable—Ever flipping off the camera as she takes a left out of the driveway. In my shirt, but also…in my Bronco.

"Shit."

"Now's a good time to make your peace with whatever God you believe in. My daughter's about to put you through hell."

CHAPTER 2

O NE OF THE LANDSCAPERS GIVES ME A LIFT TO MUNREAUX Motorcycles' headquarters. I tried to think like an immature, nineteen-year-old, spoiled rotten cheerleader, which was about the complete fucking opposite of how I usually think, and came up with this place. She stole my vehicle, and with a top-of-the-line garage at her disposal, she could get anything she wanted done to it, without question, without a wait, and without payment.

Her pushing my Bronco off a cliff did cross my mind but I quickly crossed it off the list of possibilities. As threatening as Ever tried making herself seem, she came across more petty than ruthless.

That's exactly what I'm hoping for as I charge through the entrance, demanding to know where she is.

"What's your business with Miss Munreaux?" The woman behind the counter barely even glances at my scar. Of course she notices it. Everybody does. At least she's professional enough not to fixate on it.

"She brought in my Bronco."

"For servicing?"

I give a stiff nod, trying not to imagine the engine ripped out, the tires removed, the sound system's settings all reset. Jesus fuck, not the equalizer. It took me forever to get that shit just right.

"Miss Munreaux was just in here telling me the good news. First place in Florida." The older woman beams. "But she didn't say anything about why she was here. I assumed it was…" Her features scrunch together as she appears to mull something over. "I suppose you may be correct about the nature of her visit. I'll put in some calls and see what we can find out, okay?"

After a couple minutes, she sets the phone down to inform me, straight-faced, that my Bronco's in the process of getting new paint.

"A paint job?" I almost snort. That's the best she could come up with? Petty. "What color?"

She claims she doesn't know, but while pointing me toward which hall to take, her lips press together like she's trying to keep from smiling.

Fuck. *Fuck*. So much for that bonus going toward anything useful.

I find the bay with my Bronco already in it, the hood and sides taped up and painted with flames. *Pink*. Mother. Fucking. Flames.

Not giving a single fuck whose last name is printed on the back of his uniform, I storm inside and confront the asshole with the spray gun. He didn't seem to care *my* name's the one on the goddamn title of the Bronco he's currently giving a custom paint job.

"Hey!" I shout over the noise, shaking both my head and hands at him to get him to stop.

His bloodshot eyes meet mine through the goggles he's wearing and crinkle at the corners as he nods a greeting at me. Is he smiling? With his lips hidden behind the respirator, I can't tell for sure. Either way, he's so fucking unconcerned by the sight of me, I have to wonder what Ever told him. That I *wanted* pink flames?

Who *wants* pink flames?

The pink she chose doesn't necessarily clash against the carbonized gray. The shades actually look good together. It's just that I don't fucking like them going together on *my* ride. I'd never get something so girly or gaudy.

Rich bitch.

The technician holds up one finger and continues spraying.

"What the fuck?" I bark, my voice evaporating much quicker than the VOCs in the paint.

This close, it's clear he's almost finished, and despite the space being well-ventilated, the fumes are still strong, so I stalk over to the corner, folding my arms over my chest as I watch my Bronco become unrecognizable.

Paint can be fixed. It's nothing in the grand scheme of things. I did the math on the way over. In three years, I'll leave the Munreaux estate having earned close to two million dollars. After taxes, I won't have that much in my account, but I should still have around a million, especially with living expenses covered.

With one final horizontal stroke, the technician turns off the gun. Just as he's heading my way, a door to my left opens, and Ever appears, a mirror and sink behind her.

She pauses when she sees me but is quick to recover, pasting on a fake smile. Down to her crude baby tee again, she has my flannel balled in her hands.

She gives it back to me with a sweet, "Thanks."

I feel myself scowl even harder as I turn it over in my hold. It's all wet.

"Didn't have any toilet paper," she answers without me even asking.

Clogging my nose mid-inhale, I immediately spread my fingers and let the shirt fall from my grip. Son of a bitch. I'd demand she wash it but doubt she even knows how. People like the Munreauxs have staff for that.

The flannel pooled at my feet, I debate whether the money's enough to handle someone else's bodily fluids or not. Technically, I'm not being paid at all yet. Not until tomorrow.

As long as I don't strangle the fuck out of Ever before then.

I kick the material away from me. These motherfuckers are already on Arthur's payroll. Let them clean up his daughter's piss.

Pulling his mask down, the tech says, "I just stocked that bathroom with toilet paper this morning."

Ever shrugs unapologetically and glances at me with more of that challenge.

I glare at her, tempted to pin her ass to the floor in a wrestling move called the banana split until tomorrow morning.

My dick jolts at the fucking prospect of having Ever in that compromising of a position, legs spread as wide as they can go, pussy in the air.

I shake the image away before I get any harder.

As soon as I do though, more images filter in. Worse images. Images of other positions I could put her in because as much as I'd like to think I could, there's no way I'd keep her in a banana split the *whole* time. She's a cheerleader. She's gotta be flexible. I could twist her body into a fucking pretzel and—

Fuck.

I shove past her into the bathroom and wash my hands under scalding water before turning it to freezing, the piercing cold waking me the fuck up. I only met the girl a couple hours ago and she's already insulted me, scratched me, defaced my car, and pissed on my clothing. The last thing I should be thinking about is stuffing my cock in her. Creatively. And repeatedly.

Ever comes up behind me, her eyes on mine as I track her approach.

"It doesn't have to get worse. Quit now and it won't," she says quietly.

I don't remove my gaze from hers until after I dry my hands and spin to face her, my ass pressed to the counter's edge to create as much distance between us as possible in the cramped bathroom.

We regard one another for a few tense moments, those bruises marring her otherwise flawless skin pulling my attention away.

"Is slutting yourself out really that important to you?"

The muscle in her jaw twitches as her azure eyes fill with flames brighter than the ones on my hood.

"Yes."

Damn. I didn't expect her to cop to it so easily. Most women wouldn't.

It's actually a turn-on that she did. Another one.

Goddamn it. This is going to be a long, painful three years.

"Men have been making sex a priority since the beginning of time. Why shouldn't I?"

I actually agree that women should be able to like sex, want sex, and have sex without repercussions. But Arthur Munreaux doesn't. Or he might, I didn't inquire about his exact stance on the matter, but he doesn't want the fact his daughter's a fuckgirl broadcasted for the world to know and ultimately judge because those repercussions do exist. Women can't like sex, want sex, and have sex without being ridiculed for it. No matter how much change there is in the world, society is still, and will probably always be, biased.

"I'm not here to stop you from getting dick," I make myself say, not loving the way the words taste on my tongue but not stopping to examine why. "I'm here to make sure getting dick doesn't derail your future."

Unfolding her arms and dropping them like they suddenly weigh a thousand pounds each, she lets out a scoff. "As if there was *anything* that could derail that. You have no idea what you're protecting."

"I'm protecting *you.*" It's for her father's sake, but *she* is my assignment.

Something unreadable flashes across her face, but she doesn't say anything, prompting another long pause.

"You can tell yourself that tonight, in your own bed, at whatever little slum you call home because you won't be staying at mine."

"You're very sure of yourself."

"I have to be. I'm a flyer. And I always, *always* land on top."

My eyes shoot to her rib tattoo. *My soul is in the sky.*

I don't know what the fuck a flyer is or why she's so certain she's going to get rid of me. A million dollars on the line? An actual shot of getting out of Sea Haven? I wouldn't give that up for *anything.*

"Flyer? Is that some sort of cheerleader lingo?" Better learn it now. I'm gonna be around it for a while.

"Mm-hm. And here's some more." She shuffles closer. "Eat." Another step puts her face within inches of mine. "My."

If she says what I think she's about to say, I'm not sure I'll be able to stop myself from doing it. I would eat her fucking—

"Ass."

Before I can process *that,* she rips my hat off and drops it in the toilet.

Fucking bitch!

My hand latches on to her bicep the next instant, then I'm dragging her out of the bathroom.

Tight quarters. Tight body. Tight—

I force a headshake.

Tight fucking deadline. There's a reason Arthur's offering a bonus for making it past the first twenty-four hours. Nobody else has. Ever said as much. She made everyone else quit before they could.

She's gonna throw everything she's got at me today. Tomorrow…

I'll deal with tomorrow when I get there, because I *will* be getting there. Short of Ever killing me herself, there's nothing that'd make me not show up for work tomorrow.

"Get in the fucking car," I tell her even though I forcibly sit her in the passenger seat of my Bronco and buckle her myself.

"Yo!" the technician calls out.

I prep my fist, ready to throw blows over how I just treated his boss's daughter. It wasn't right to handle her like that, I know that, but…

God, she pisses me off.

Surprisingly, he just says, "You gotta pull the tape off in two hours. Exactly two hours, man. Don't wait any longer than that or it'll fuck your shit up."

I stop myself from gesturing to the emasculating design on what was a very masculine SUV—*my* very masculine SUV—and snarling, "More than you already fucked it up?"

"Two hours. Got it," I bite out instead. Because that's what'll eat at me driving around in my blazing pussy on wheels—how perfect the paint lines are.

When I get in, Ever's waving to the guy with a genuine smile tugging her lips.

I force myself to look away from it, my gaze falling to her legs instead. They're not long but they are smooth and sun-kissed. Her phone's wedged between toned thighs that I wouldn't mind feeling clenched around my head as I ate her—

"You ogle glory holes the same way?"

"It's too cold to be dressed like that," I snap, tearing my attention away from her to start the engine.

"Have any other clothes you'd like me to *use?*" She chuckles at herself. She thinks she's so funny. She thinks she won.

"Once we grab some from my *slum*, I will."

My words shut her right the fuck up because she hasn't won shit. I'm moving into Chateau Munreaux and her ass is gonna help.

CHAPTER 3

A GOLF CART CROSSES THE FOUR-WAY INTERSECTION IN front of us, the older couple in it gawking at Crue's Bronco, probably admiring its lovely new paint job. Crue pretends not to notice, continuing to drive one-handed through the neighborhood full of small houses so tightly packed in no one even has side yards.

It's too early in the year for the hydrangeas to be in bloom, but every front yard we pass features their bright green bushes, already awakened and preparing for the months ahead when they'll charm everyone with both their calming colors and pleasant scents. Our property has hydrangeas, too. In Sea Haven, everyone's does. Mostly in blues and purples, but occasionally you'll find one with white flowers, which bloom later, usually toward the end of summer and into fall. While ours are professionally manicured, these are all wild and overgrown, blocking entire windows, even parts of people's crushed-shell driveways. Nobody seems to care about the imperfection. They just live with it. They just live.

Swallowing hard, I tear my eyes away from a quaint farmhouse with a welcoming red door and focus on the man to my left. Without that annoying baseball cap covering his face, I can make out all of it right now, including those moss-green eyes with slight brown central heterochromia near the pupils. And that scar he's constantly trying to hide? I like it more in its entirety. I haven't been doing it nearly the justice it deserves. He has a diamond earring in his ear I suspect isn't real, and every couple seconds, he bites the corner of his bottom lip using his top fang before quickly releasing it. If I could kiss that lip again, I'd bite it, too. It looks delicious. *He* looks delicious. And since I tasted him for myself, I know he is.

Ignoring me altogether, Crue's taking in our surroundings, just like he did at Hide and Keep. He was working security then, too. After spending countless hours analyzing his every breath from that eye-opening night, I'd already pieced together as much. He wasn't patiently waiting for somebody to find him like I assumed. He was doing his job. Which makes what we did that much more…forbidden. He wasn't supposed to be paying me special attention. And yet, that's exactly what he did.

I get preferential treatment everywhere I go, to the point it feels stiflingly commonplace, but his was different. Crue didn't know what my last name was. He didn't care. He just wanted *me*, enough to risk his job.

The only way someone in my real life would be willing to do the same is with the knowledge I'd be assuming the financial loss. Not even the hope that I would, but the surety.

Crue was willing to lose his job to be with me. He hesitated at first, but he'd just conceded when my father crashed my very first party.

All the questions I wish I could ask him play through my head.

Is this where you grew up?

Did you love it?

What was the best part?

Or did you move here recently?

Do you…live by yourself?

Do you walk to the beach I can spot at the end of the road?

What do you do once you get there?

But I don't let myself ask any of them because that'd make him the guy from Hide and Keep, not the prison guard assigned to my cell, and I have to lose the latter.

What I wouldn't give to keep the former, just for a little while, just until…

Why did it have to be him? For months, I've clung to the memory of this man, his lips, his touch, the way he protected me like it was natural for him. That memory was the one thing, the one beautiful, perfect thing in my life that my father couldn't take from me.

But now he has. Unknowingly. It has to be some sort of cruel cosmic coincidence. There's no way my father found out who Crue is…to me. And judging by the lack of recognition on his part, I don't think Crue knows either.

So our first meeting is still my secret. It's just going to haunt me now, like everything else my father gets his hands on.

When Crue pulls up to a Victorian colonial with an enclosed front porch, I tell him I'll wait for him out here.

After making a show out of pocketing his keys while keeping my gaze, he says, "You're my responsibility now. Where you go, I go, and vice versa."

I can't. I *can't* go inside with him. It'll be too much. This next part is hard enough without seeing where Crue spends his free time.

"I'm not going into your dumpy little shack." I flutter my fingers at the house dismissively.

Those light eyes narrow. "Just because it's not a mansion, doesn't make it a shack."

"It looks infested."

"You're such a…" He shakes his head but doesn't finish as he gets out.

Not that he needs to. I know how I sound. It's not that hard to pull off the snob routine when it's all I've ever been around, ever known. Back in the corn maze, I hid this side of me so far out of sight, he probably wouldn't have even believed me if I tried telling him who I was.

Opening my door, he props a forearm on the roof and leans toward me, saying, "Look, I gotta go in there and I don't trust you enough to leave you out here by yourself, so you can either walk or I'll carry you. Either way, you're coming inside with me."

"Despite what my father wants you to believe, I'm not a fucking toddler."

"Until I see the proof for myself, I'm gonna have to defer to his word."

"Fine. I can't believe I have to actually show you this, but…" I pretend I'm getting something out of my shoe, then flip him off as if I found my middle finger in my size-six-and-a-half lululemons. I glance from it to him with a *would you look at that* expression.

He shoves off his car. "Carrying it is."

I scramble out of the seat, pushing his middle out of my way, noting the defined abs beneath his shirt. "I'll walk. I'll walk. Goddess. Nobody can take a joke anymore?"

"Like your hilarious shirt?"

"Exactly," I mumble while approaching the door. I point at it. "It's purple."

"Good job, Ever," he says with a voice full of mock praise, then pats my head like one would an actual toddler's. "Maybe tomorrow you can share what numbers you know."

My middle finger aches to meet his perfectly chiseled face again.

"Was it like that when you moved in or did you paint it?" I ask, pointing at the front door.

"My mom," is all he says.

"Your mother painted your door?"

"No, she painted her door. This is her house. And my dad's."

"You still live with your parents?" I ask without even trying to hide my disbelief. He's older than me.

"So do you."

"But I'm—" I cut myself off.

"What? Rich?"

"Obviously," I snap. What other reason could there *possibly* be? Certainly not that my father won't let me move out.

With a headshake full of incredulity, he unlocks the deadbolt and motions for me to go in first.

One look inside and the bitchiness starts flowing from my mouth. "It stinks."

It smells delicious, like basil and broth and some kind of bread I'm dying to sink my teeth into.

"It's dirty."

It's lived in.

"It's cold."

It's warm and inviting.

"It's ancient."

It's the coziest house I've ever seen up close and all I want to do is curl up with a soft blanket inside it and just…breathe.

Instead of arguing a single point, Crue bends at the waist and picks me up, carrying me over both thresholds into the living room.

They don't have a foyer?

"Help! Help! I'm being kidnapped by your son!"

Crue closes the door, then sets me on the carpeted floor, not just hardwood with a carpet rug but actual wall-to-wall carpet.

"Yell all you want. No one's here." After doing something on his phone, there's a series of beeps somewhere in the house. "The alarm is set, so if you open a door or window, I'll catch you before you can step foot outside."

"You have an alarm on this place?"

"Yeah. We don't use it anymore really, but it's there…just in case."

"In case of what?"

With a shrug, he says, "People."

Before I can ask what kind of people, he leaves. Literally. He just leaves me here, all by myself in the middle of his parents' home.

As much as I'd love to follow him and see his bedroom, I plant my feet and call to his back, "Where are your parents?"

"It's the middle of the day. Where do you think?"

"The food bank?" With him gone, I cringe at myself, my shoulders shuddering from my own insensitivity. My high school team had a tradition of volunteering at the food bank at least once every December. Luckily, they scheduled the visits at the same time as our practices, so I got to go, too. It was a very humbling experience. Obviously, my father's never done it.

"Work," Crue replies. "Not like you know what that is."

Despite the last part being muttered, I still pick up on it, mostly because I'm used to that insult.

People assume—correctly—that I don't *have* to work, but what they fail to realize is I'm not *allowed* to work. My future is set. My purpose predetermined. My father barely let me cheer at the collegiate level. And even that is being taken from me.

Tears blur my vision.

One quick glance around the room and I bring my hands to my face, covering my eyes with my fingers and plugging my nose with the edges of my palms, forcing myself to breathe through my mouth. I don't want to commit a single thing in here to memory.

As soon as my eyes are closed though, every detail I just glimpsed is shown in vivid clarity, like my brain already did.

Damn it.

"What's the matter?" I hear sometime later.

Dropping my hands, I grit, "It. Stinks." The tears hopefully helping my case.

Brows furrowed, Crue looks around from his spot on the other side of the sectional. "Like what?"

He's wearing another black, non-descript hat. I got rid of the other one for a reason.

"Like…" I follow his lead until I spy a dog bed in a corner. "Dog."

His expression turns thoughtful. "Could be. Zeus is out back right now but he's in here a lot." He rounds the couch. "We must be nose blind to him. Is it bad?"

"Terrible," I mumble as I stare at the bag hanging off his shoulder. "You don't need any of that. I told you you'll be back tonight."

"This…" Using his thumb, he tugs on the thick strap. "…is just to get me started. We'll come back and get more some other time."

I chuckle. "*We* will not."

"Yes, *we* will. For the next three years, *we* will be going everywhere together."

"Three years?" I can't keep the hope out of my voice. Did my father tell him that or did he just assume?

"Until you graduate. Your university is a four-year, isn't it?"

He assumed. Of course.

One year of college—just enough to boast about, not enough to derail my father's plans.

But Crue doesn't know how temporary his job is. He should.

"I'm not graduating, Crue Brantley. You might as well walk away now."

He doesn't respond right away, just focuses on his phone, pressing a button that disarms the house's alarm with another set of beeps. When he's done, he looks up at me through dark lashes, and says, "I'm not walking away, Ever Munreaux. I will do everything in my power to make sure you fucking graduate."

I have to swallow three times to get all the emotion clogging my throat down.

"You don't have enough power to make that happen." If I don't, he definitely doesn't.

He gives a huff of humorless laughter. "What makes you so fucking sure? You don't even know me."

Because power wraps its insidious limbs around people, changing them, poisoning them from the outside in, but your outsides match your insides which I know firsthand are pure because you asked for my permission, and the corrupt never, ever do.

"Because power stems from money, which clearly…" I hold out my hands, infusing a large dose of disgust into my expression. "…you don't have."

"I don't need a dime to get you to graduation."

I scoff. "You could certainly use it."

"You know, I heard about you over the years…"

My chin lifts on its own. Blood, sweat, tears—I wish those were all it took to be as notorious as I've become. It wasn't even the countless insane routines pulled off flawlessly in public. It was the sprains, the concussions, the bone bruises and breaks, along with the perfected smile accompanying it *all*. I've worked too hard not to be notable. If people are talking about me, I've either done something incredibly right, incredibly wrong…

"Awful is too nice a term for you."

Or I was born to a man who did. My father's influence is a perversion on my life. I hate it. I hate him.

And I hate myself for having to play into the perception, especially with Crue.

"You don't know me either," I let slip, some of my own frustration infusing my tone.

"I know enough." He gives me an inspection that is nothing like the time he did it at Hide and Keep. "You hate me…just because I'm not rich."

I don't hate you.

I don't want to hate you.

Please don't make me hate you.

Please.

"I hate you because you want to help my father ruin my life." *That* is what I need to remember, what I need to hold on to. My short run at freedom isn't up yet. As soon as I ditch Crue, I can get back to it.

"Jesus, you're *so* fucking dramatic. Nobody's trying to ruin your life. Everyone has rules, responsibilities, obligations. Why the fuck do you think you're so different?"

It's not that I can't handle rules, responsibilities, obligations; I already have plenty. It's that I don't want *those* rules, responsibilities, obligations. Each one is a shackle around my entire existence, chaining me to a life I didn't agree to.

"I need to use the restroom."

"Again? Didn't you *just* go?"

"What am I, back in middle school, only allowed to pee between classes?"

"You look like it with that shirt."

"You look at a lot of middle school girls?"

"What? No. I just meant—"

"Mm-hm. Sure. Where's your bathroom?"

Crue studies me for so long, my hands find themselves behind my back, my fingers twisting together roughly.

"Or can you not afford indoor plumbing? Do you have an outhouse out back or something?"

With yet *another* headshake, he points at the hall, telling me, "It's the door on the left. I'll be watching the alarm system."

"Like you'd catch me," I mumble once I'm out of earshot. Lifting weights doesn't necessarily translate to stamina. Sure, Crue's muscular, but I bet I could still outrun him, probably on the worst day of my period.

"What was that?"

Whoops. He heard me.

"You're poor," I call out sweetly before slamming the bathroom door shut.

Sitting on the edge of the tub, I stare down at my phone, my thumb hovering.

Don't overthink it. Don't even think about it. Just…do it.

Do it.

I do it. I dial.

CHAPTER 4

"WHAT DO WE HAVE THE REST OF THE DAY?" CRUE ASKS while driving, his left hand gripping the top of the steering wheel, his right elbow on the center console as he plays with his bottom lip.

He's obsessed with it, always fidgeting with it.

"*I* have hair, nails, and makeup," I rattle off even though I don't. It's what he expects.

"Do *we* have enough time to drop my stuff off at your house before your appointments?"

"They come to me."

"Who?"

"Everyone. Stylists, designers."

He frowns. "They can do that?"

"For the right amount, you can get anyone to do anything you want."

"Not anyone."

"You." Obviously.

"I'm not like that."

"If you say so." I divert my attention out the passenger window because I'm obsessed with that lip, too, and staring at it isn't doing me any good.

Sucking on it probably would though.

"I meant don't they need special equipment?"

"We have it all."

"Must be nice."

"It must," I whisper. My mom…suffered. I'm sure there was a diagnosis for what exactly was wrong—it just wasn't shared with me—but to me, it seemed like depression. When she had her good moments, she was amazing. Really fun. They just never lasted that long. And in between those, when she refused to leave the manor, my father still expected her to look good. Even in her own home, around her own family. So, he put a salon in our house and called in professionals.

Presentation, presentation, presentation.

Blue and red lights appear in the mirror a second before the siren sounds.

I fight to keep my expression neutral as I glance at Crue.

He lifts his hand to look at his speed. "What the fuck? I'm not even speeding."

"Maybe your tags are expired."

That earns me a scathing side-eye.

"They're not."

As he's pulling over, he tells me to open the glove box.

"Is that where you keep your gun?"

"I don't carry a gun."

"Why? Isn't that what bodyguards do? Carry weapons?"

"I don't know. Just grab my registration and insurance."

How doesn't he know that? It's his job.

I slide the contents around. "They're not in here."

He rips his gaze off his rearview. "What do you mean? That's where they always are."

I shrug. "It's your car. You can look for yourself."

He does, only to get the same results.

Where could they possibly be?

"Did you take them?"

I half-scoff, half-laugh. "And do what with them?"

"Wipe your ass with them."

"I would've given them back to you if I had."

"You're unbelievable."

"You're poor."

"Come up with better insults."

"You're ugly."

Crue doesn't respond at all. He just lowers his head so that the bill of his hat casts shadows over his face.

I'm sorry, I'm sorry, I'm sorry, I'm sorry.

I clamp a hand over my mouth to keep the projectile apology vomit in. I didn't mean it, and if I could, I'd take it back. He's never going to take his hat off now.

"We can't change what we're born, only what we become."

Crue's words play on a loop in my head, searing themselves into my memory.

Just as the cop's approaching, I rush out, "Good luck keeping up that optimism when you're someone's prison bitch."

"What?"

Crue twists his head to look at me wide-eyed, but the knock on the driver's window saves me from having to explain myself. In a few more minutes, I won't need to anyway.

As soon as the window lowers, I hear, "Crue Brantley…no shit? I thought that was you."

The cop *knows* Crue?

"Ronny Veen," Crue greets. "What's up, man? What've you been up to?"

Crue *knows* the cop?

"Oh, you know." Ronny takes a step back to let us marvel at his uniform. "Stopping crime."

"Just like your old man, huh?"

"Much to his relief." With a chuckle, Ronny's posture relaxes a fraction and he grips the door with both hands. "Remember that time in high school when we found those forged hundred-dollar bills and tried using them in the school's vending machine?"

"We didn't try. We did use 'em."

"That's right. I was on my fifth bag of chips when the principal came into my classroom to pull me out, my dad already out in the hall waiting for me."

"If it wasn't for him, we would've got in a lot more trouble than we did."

"That's for sure. What about you? Where are you working these days?"

"Uh, all over really, but I just started working for Munreaux Motorcycles."

"Munreaux?" Ronny whistles and ducks his head, catching sight of me in the passenger seat. "And your friend here… She's…"

At the same time Crue says, "Not my friend," I stretch my arm out, my hand in front of his face as I shake Ronny's with more friendliness than I've given Crue all day.

"Ever Munreaux. You've probably heard of my father, Arthur Munreaux, founder of Munreaux Motorcycles and Crue's new employer." Make sure to put that in the paper. It'll embarrass my father as much as he's embarrassed me by repeatedly forcing "guards" down my throat.

Ronny doesn't take his gaze from mine as he asks Crue, "So… your boss's daughter?"

The corners of Crue's eyes tighten but he only nods in response.

"You always did like mixing business with pleasure, didn't ya?"

"It's not like that. She's just a kid."

Ronny releases my hand instantly.

"I'm nineteen."

"Nineteen." Ronny grins, and so do I. "And *very* pretty."

"I didn't notice."

Crue doesn't even look my way, just squints at passing traffic. He is so over me.

He really thought he could last three years with me.

Maybe he would've. Like I said, for the right amount, you can get anyone, including Crue Brantley, to do anything.

My smile widens. "He noticed."

This gets Crue to look over at me, his eyes narrowed to slits.

We hold a heated stare-off with one another, neither of us willing to blink first.

Eventually, Ronny clears his throat, gaining Crue's full attention again.

"I am gonna need to see your license, insurance, and registration."

"What for?" Crue asks without moving. "I thought—"

"That this was a social call? Afraid not. We received an anonymous report of reckless driving. The vehicle described was a Bronco, freshly painted, with your license plate number. Seemed someone was concerned the driver…well, you…were intoxicated, which I guess you'd have to be to paint your car like that." Ronny gestures to the hood, then to Crue. Shifting on his feet suddenly, his features scrunch like he's in pain. "That's not to say—"

"All I have is my license." Crue leans to the side and reaches into his back pocket. "I don't know where my insurance and registration are."

"Did you look in here?" I drum the center console with my fingertips, my lips stretching ever so slightly.

Crue freezes. "I did."

"You didn't."

"They're not in there."

"But how do you know unless you check?"

"Ever." Those canines of his flash as he bites out the last syllable of my name, his bottom lip popped.

I only lift my eyebrows at him. I warned him. He had an opportunity—two to be exact—to get out. He chose not to.

"Hey, Crue? It'll make things a lot easier if I can get all the information from ya now, so if you don't mind going ahead and checking real quick, I'd appreciate it. I already know you're not drunk."

Ronny's chuckle is strained and has the corners of my smile faltering. How does he know that?

After handing his ID to Ronny, Crue opens the center console, his face losing all its color at what he finds.

His eyes close briefly as air pours from his nose.

Is he an alcoholic?

I didn't even consider that when I asked my father's tech to buy the rum for me earlier.

I don't want to ruin Crue's life. I just don't want him to have a hand in ruining mine.

My heart pounds inside my chest, the sound like a train scaling up my neck into my ears.

"Crue," I vaguely hear myself say. "I'm—"

"Man, I hate when people make me a liar," Ronny says, his gaze locked on the half-empty bottle. I didn't drink any, just poured out enough to be believable. "I thought you gave up drinking senior year."

Senior year? Crue was already drinking enough by then to have to give it up?

"Unless…is it hers?" Eyes relocating to me, Ronny pulls out a small notepad and flips it open to a blank page.

"Yes," I say at the same time Crue gives a firm, "No."

I grab his bicep, but he yanks his arm out of my grasp, twisting in his seat to face Ronny and telling him, "It's mine. I relapsed. But not today. It was a while ago."

He's taking the blame? For me?

"But…you admit you were drinking and driving recently?"

"No." Crue shakes his head. "Never."

Ronny looks from Crue to me, then back, I swear his eyes are locked on Crue's scar though.

"I didn't think you would. Not after what happened to Yasmin."

Nothing on Crue moves.

Who's Yasmin and what happened to her?

"But…I didn't think you'd ever pick up the bottle again either. I'm sorry to do this, I really am, but I need you to step out of the vehicle."

"It's all a misunderstanding," Crue says while stepping out.

"You have an open container in the front seat."

"But I didn't touch it today."

"Someone called you in, Crue. Speeding, swerving, generally erratic behavior."

They go around to the front of Crue's Bronco. Thanks to the open driver's window, I can still hear them.

"Who?"

"It was anonymous."

"Okay, well, when did it come in? I wasn't driving my car earlier."

"Who was?"

Crue looks directly at me and Ronny follows his gaze. Shaking his head, he mumbles something to Crue I can't make out.

Then he calls out, "Miss Munreaux?" A hand beckons me forward. "Why don't you join us out here?"

Crue steps in front of his old friend, his hands up between them.

"No, it was me. Just leave her out of it. She's innocent."

That's twice now he could've thrown me under the bus but only threw himself under instead.

Ronny studies Crue long and hard before asking, "Are you drunk right now?"

"I take full responsibility for being distracted while driving. You can write me a ticket for that, but I'm not drunk. I told you I haven't had a single sip, not today, not…today."

"Hmm, yeah, I guess I can see what had you so distracted," Ronny says as he eyes me through the windshield. Turning to Crue, he points at him. "All right. Okay. But you gotta pass the sobriety test."

Crue gives a stiff nod. "Whatever you need."

For the next several minutes, Crue performs various tests from eye tracking to standing on one leg while counting. I keep my phone up in front of me, acting like I'm watching the screen but in reality I'm glued to Crue's every move. Just like in the corn maze, he's impossible to look away from.

By the time he gets back in the Bronco, I've shaken off the momentary regret for planting the rum. I don't want Crue gone from my life, I *need* him gone.

I do, however, still feel bad about the ugly comment.

There's nothing I can do about it now though.

"So no jail time?" I ask.

He ignores me to start up his car, then waits for Ronny to pass.

After a wave to his friend, he says, "The flames, the liquor…" He gives me an unimpressed look. "That shit was pathetic. What else you got?"

"Guess we'll have to wait and see, won't we?"

"*We will*," he says before pulling back out on to the road.

The rest of the drive I have to bite my lips together, trying my hardest not to ask Crue any personal questions because there are so many just waiting to break the tense silence.

Don't ask.

Don't ask.

Don't ask.

"Who's Yasmin?" tumbles from my mouth.

I sit on my hands while I await his answer.

Crue's fist clenches the steering wheel until his knuckles turn white. I don't think he's going to, but then finally he does, saying, "My ex."

A scalding pain slices through me.

"When did you guys break up?"

"We didn't."

"How is she your ex then?"

"She died."

"Oh." My voice low, I tell him, "I'm sorry."

"It was a long time ago."

"How long?"

"Eight years."

"My mother died five years ago. It doesn't feel like it's been that long."

Crue glances over at me, but my gaze is set straight ahead.

"Your dad said that's why you're…" He lifts his fingers off the steering wheel. "This. Because you're having a hard time with her death."

This. My father is the reason why I'm *this.* Not my mother. And not her…death.

"My father's a liar."

"So the apple doesn't fall far from the tree."

I wish I did. I wish I fell far from both my mother's and father's trees. Or branches. Or… What does that saying mean exactly?

"I've been upfront all along with what I want."

"And what is it exactly that you want, Ever?"

To see if you kiss as good in the light as you do in the dark.

"For you to quit."

"Not happening."

"If this is about the money, I can pay you. Not as much as my father, but I can pull out some cash to give you."

"You're surrendering already? I was kinda hoping you had a little more fight than that."

"I'm not surrendering. I just…" *Don't want things to get uglier. What tops trying to send someone to jail?* "Have a lot going on and don't want to deal with you."

"I don't know what it was like with your other guards but I can keep up. You don't gotta worry about me. Just live your life, and I'll be right here alongside you, making sure you're not doing anything to put it, or your future, in jeopardy."

"My future?" I can't hold back my laugh. "You mean my father's legacy."

"That's his concern."

"It's not yours?"

"No."

"What is your concern?"

"I told you. You."

Another laugh, one much sadder, bubbles up because as much as I don't want to believe him, I think I already do.

Why does it have to be Crue?

And why, if I'm so spoiled, doesn't anything ever go my way?

CHAPTER 5

Crue

"WHERE ARE YOU GOING?" I CALL TO EVER'S BACK AS SHE practically bolts from my Bronco.

"For a run."

"I thought you had beauty shit to do."

This finally pulls her attention to me, and over her shoulder, she says, "I just got back from competing. All that 'beauty shit' was last week."

I frown. Like I fucking know. She's the one who said she had appointments to get that shit done. Liar.

Bitch.

God, I've never disliked someone so much, so quickly.

I sigh. "Give me a minute."

"For what?"

"So I can go with you."

"I'm not—"

I dip back into my Bronco and grab that rum she planted, keeping my head in here for longer than necessary. She may just be the literal fucking worst. She almost got me arrested. If it hadn't been Ronny who pulled me over, I'd probably be in a cell right now. With my history...

"What are you going to do with that?" Ever's voice is closer than it was a second ago.

When I glance over, I find she's backtracked several feet.

Something about her tone rubs me the wrong way. Something about *her* rubs me the wrong way.

Everything about her rubs me the wrong way.

"Why? Hoping I'll get drunk on the job?" Giving Arthur an excuse to fire me, no doubt.

Her gaze falls momentarily before moving to my right, toward the outer wall of one of the hedge mazes, her eyebrows lifting fractionally.

"More like worried you'll waste perfectly good liquor. I went through a lot of trouble to get—"

Ignoring her, I walk over to that same bush, then empty the bottle into the crushed white shells below, the splashing not quite loud enough to drown out Ever's outraged gasp.

My lips spread on their own.

"Such a waste."

Ever huffs while putting her hair into a ponytail. With her hair being so short it doesn't all go up, but enough of it does, so her face is visible. Her smooth, flawless, beautiful face.

"Anyway, champs wait for no one so…" She flaps her fingers at me, her glossy fake nails catching the sunlight. "Bye, loser."

Without another word, she spins on her heel and takes off toward the woods.

Gritting my teeth, I toss the empty bottle back in my car, shut the door, then bound after her. Thankfully, I catch sight of her just inside the tree line.

"Ever! Wait!"

"I thought you said you could keep up!" she shouts into the air, scaring a pair of birds.

I can keep up. I just…wasn't prepared. I will be going forward because this shit can't happen again. I'm already losing her. Fuck.

I increase my speed, my legs pumping faster than they have in… Shit. Months? I haven't had a reason to do cardio in a long time.

Ever's small form passes behind an oak tree before disappearing from view altogether.

How the fuck is she so much faster? My legs are probably twice as long as hers.

I continue running in that direction for a few more minutes before pausing to listen. She only has her phone on her, stuffed…somewhere. I don't fucking know where she's keeping that thing. All I know is it wasn't in my car after she got out.

She has her phone on her.

Before I left to go track her ass down the first time, Edwin gave me some info about the Munreaux estate, including the necessary phone numbers. Hers was one of them.

Taking out my cell, I call it. The second I hear the ringtone echoing through the forest, I pivot and sprint that way.

"Shit," Ever says, narrowing down her position for me.

I charge right toward her, full steam ahead, eating up the distance between us in seconds. I'm going too fast to stop when she suddenly steps out from behind a massive tree. Busy trying to remove her phone from the back of her shorts, she doesn't see me until my arms are closing around her and…then we're falling.

Fucking shit!

We go sailing through the air, time suspended as we both tense for impact. At the last second, I twist us so only my body hits the ground, hers in the safety of my arms creating a cage around her. One hand cradling her head, I hold her to my chest so that even as we roll from the force, she's protected.

It feels like minutes but it's probably only a few seconds before we come to a complete stop, me on top of Ever, my arms still holding her.

I immediately lift myself enough to look down at her, scanning for injury.

"I'm sorry. Fuck. I'm sorry."

When the visual evidence isn't enough to placate me, I sit up all the way, my hands joining the search, touching everywhere I can. They're shaking but still have feeling.

"Are you okay?"

"What the hell's wrong with you? You—"

"Ever!" I shout, silencing her. Coming in close again, I run my hand along one side of her jaw, chin, throat, and ear before doing the same to the other. I feel her swallow the same time I hear it.

Her eyes shut instantly, her nostrils flaring like she can't stomach my close proximity.

I don't give a shit. I just need to know if she's hurt. Not all injuries are visible. The worst usually aren't.

"Are you okay?" I cup the back of her head, feeling for any wetness but luckily find none.

"No," comes out ragged between her clenched teeth.

My gaze flies to her closed eyes, her long black lashes quivering, and my heart lurches. I missed something. Again. I fucking missed something.

I start my inspection all over again.

"Tell me where you're hurt." I could only protect her upper half, her most vital half, so her bottom half was exposed.

Slowly, her eyes open and she shakes her head. "I'm not hurt."

"You could be. If you're in shock—"

Her hands clamp down over mine as she sits up, forcing me back on my heels.

"Crue, I'm not hurt. You made sure of that."

"I'm sorry."

Her expression is unreadable as she regards me. "Yeah…you said that already."

"I'm really fucking sorry." I shove to my feet. "That." I point at the tree where we collided, then Ever still on the ground…several feet away. We didn't just fall hard, we fell far. "And this. I'm sorry for all of it."

"Uh-huh." She glances around us.

There're broken branches, pinecones, rocks, twigs. It's not asphalt, but still dangerous.

Her focus sharpens on me again. "Are *you* hurt?"

"No," leaves my mouth automatically.

"You didn't even check."

"I don't need to. As long as you're fine, I'm—"

"Let me take a look." She gets to her feet.

I take a step back. "Don't pretend like you care."

"I'm not." She halts for just a moment before resuming her

approach. "If you're injured, I need to know now so I can call for help. I'm not dragging you out of here myself."

Lifting my arms for me, she makes a show of inspecting each of them before shuffling around to my back.

Her fingers move my shirt, their tips brushing over my shoulders before coming to a rest between their blades. Even through the material, I sprout goose bumps from her gentle touch.

I get a weird sense of déjà vu as the forest seems to come to a standstill. It's like Hide and Keep all over again, except not. Not the place, not the girl. Not the fucking same.

"Wouldn't you rather call your dad and have me fired?" I say to break the silence.

Leaves crunch under Ever's feet as she circles around to my front again.

"He wouldn't fire you for this."

"For putting you in danger? That's exactly what I'm supposed to be preventing."

A soft chuckle leaves her lips. "I've had five concussions, several bruised bones and sprained ankles, two broken wrists, muscle strains in my hips, back, and legs. You could name any position on the football team and I can guarantee you I've been hit by at least one of them on the sidelines. I've been dropped from eight feet up, fourteen feet up, higher, in more hospital rooms than movie theaters, and busted my nose on more faces than I've kissed or will ever hope to kiss in my lifetime. If physical pain, *my* physical pain, was my father's concern…" Her eyebrows plummet before she arches one. "He would've stopped it a long time ago."

"Cheerleading?"

Busy searching my face, she only nods.

Damn. I didn't even get hurt that much from wrestling.

"Why do you do it?"

Those azure eyes lift from my chin, connecting with mine as she whispers, "Because the only time I'm free is when I'm flying."

Her rib tattoo.

"That small amount of time is worth the risk?"

She steps away, her gaze falling to the ground between us.

"Every second." Turning, she points, and says, "The house is back that way."

"I'll follow you."

"I'm not done with my run."

"Then neither am I."

Glancing down at her bare wrist, she smacks her lips. "Would you look at the time. It's been exactly two hours. You got tape to remove."

"My rig has pink fucking flames on it, you really think I give a fuck if the lines are crisp?"

"Look, I just want to get a run in, then I'll go back to the manor. I need to unpack anyway."

"I'll come with you."

"Are you scared I'm going to fuck someone out here?" Her arms out at her sides, she spins in a slow circle. "There's no one *to* fuck. Believe me. The neighbors on both sides of us are in their sixties and seventies."

"I don't believe you."

"Go meet them for yourself."

It's not that I don't believe her neighbors are that old. It's the part about no one being out here. A fuck in the woods? Ever doesn't *look* like the kind of person who would resort to that, but she's got the feral behavior for it.

"I've got three years to meet them. For now, let's just run."

Her jaw shifts off its hinges for a few seconds before she informs me, "I'm not slowing down for you."

"Did you hear me ask you to?"

Without another word, she passes me at a pace she obviously assumes I can't match.

I can't.

But that sure as fuck doesn't stop me from trying.

Minutes in, my calves are on absolute fire. I ignore the pain, instead focusing on Ever's back, flexed above two round globes accentuated nicely by her tight shorts. Despite being ridiculously gassed, I don't let her get more than fifteen feet ahead of me. Unable to keep up maximum speed forever, she eventually slows, then I give her about ten feet. I don't know shit about being a bodyguard but I meant what I told her. I don't have to be a huge interruption in her life. I'm only one right now because she's fighting me every step of the way, like oil and water in the same bottle. Give it a little shake and we can blend together temporarily, too.

Just because we're complete opposites in every regard, doesn't mean we have to be enemies. Once she mellows the fuck out, she'll see that.

"You're out of shape," she states calmly, matter-of-factly, with zero strain in her voice. "You're young and you *look* fit, so why are you so out of shape?"

Poor and ugly, I already knew. But out of shape, to this extent... honestly, it's a surprise to me, too.

"What do you *do?*"

My eyes drop to her shoes barely touching the earth, like she's gliding over it.

What do I do? I work jobs I have zero attachment to so if they were to all of a sudden disappear, I wouldn't be too torn up about it. I occasionally fuck girls, never more than once, never with emotion. And I live with my parents, the only two people on this planet who have never turned on me.

There. That's me summed up. I get through each day, not putting too much thought into the next, not when it's not guaranteed. Nothing in this world is, so I don't bother putting much stock into any part of it.

"You probably only lift weights," Ever says, comfortably carrying the entire conversation for the both of us since I don't trust my voice enough to respond. This is already embarrassing as fuck. I got gapped by a teen girl, and I know for a fucking fact that if I were to let up the slightest amount right now, just for a second, she'd do it again.

It's not true though—what she said. I don't even lift weights.

I guess it shouldn't be a surprise I'm this out of shape. I don't *do* anything. Not anymore.

Despite slowing down, Ever doesn't rub it in, just falls quiet, so I finally let my eyes stray from her.

All around us, trees are showing signs of spring, their tops sporting billions of green buds stretching toward the sky. I spy a box on one trunk, high up near the branches, then another a couple minutes later.

Trail cams? They look kinda big for that though. If they are trail cams, why are they so high up? Soon the branches will be filled in completely and blocking any visibility of the trail below.

I glance back down. I've been so focused on Ever—and not dying—that I failed to notice there isn't even a trail.

If I could talk, I'd ask if she knows where she's going. She sure acts like she does. There's been no hesitancy in her strides whatsoever.

We run together in silence for at least another thirty minutes until we come to a break in the trees, revealing a cliff with the sea far below. The water looks endless but isn't. Somewhere out in the haze is Long Island.

Approaching the edge, Ever doesn't slow. If anything, her speed might be increasing.

Automatically, I speed up, too, just to check, and yeah, she's fucking all-out sprinting now.

"Ever, stop," I warn, not giving a fuck how winded I sound—how winded I *am*—but still, she maintains the breakneck pace. Fear tears through my body, giving me an adrenaline boost, enough to shorten the space between us, and I reach out to wrench her shoulder, which jumps in my grasp as she pulls up short, making me run into her from behind.

I wrap my arms around her to steady us both, and she cranks her head up at me like she forgot I was here.

Her eyes are glassy, too. I don't know if it's from the wind or… something else.

"You okay?"

The confusion melts away from her features, irritation taking its place.

"Goddess, Crue, murder much?"

My arms drop to my sides, the adrenaline evaporating in an instant.

"I've never murdered anyone."

"Says the serial killer to his next victim."

"I haven't."

Her eyebrows lift. "Okaaay."

"You're the one running at a goddamn cliff. What the fuck was that about?"

Gazing out at the water, she says quietly, "I wanted to see if I'd fly."

"What?"

When she doesn't answer, I shake her and repeat myself.

A break in her reverie, she studies me but doesn't follow suit. Not that she needs to. I heard her the first time. She considered jumping.

If I wasn't here, would she have followed through? It seemed like she was about to even with me here.

Maybe she did forget I was here.

Or maybe she just didn't care.

"What exactly does she need protecting from?"

"Herself."

"Working for your dad is that bad?" I ask. Enough to kill herself? It's a fucking motorcycle company. It's not like she's set to be the next mafia don.

"That bad?" She scoffs. "Do you have any idea what it feels like to have someone take *your* future away?"

Without waiting for a response, she jogs off. I don't follow immediately after, staying a moment longer to watch the waves coming in.

"Yes," I answer. Except Ever's future consists of her running a multi-billion-dollar company. Mine was going to consist of…

It doesn't matter because mine was taken away from me and now I'm stuck babysitting the unqualified, undeserving, bratty little shit who'd rather throw herself off a cliff than run a multi-billion-dollar company.

I turn and head in Ever's direction.

CHAPTER 6

Crue

"**R**IGHT THIS WAY, MR. BRANTLEY."

"It's Crue."

"Of course, sir."

Following close behind Edwin, duffle bag bouncing against my hip as he leads me to the pool house out back, I shake my head at his deeply engrained manners. I wonder if I'll be able to get him to break protocol before my three years are up. If I got him drunk, I probably could. Although that means I'd have to drink, too, so probably not. I can drink. I just choose not to. I haven't chosen to since homecoming night, senior year.

Edwin stops on the fieldstone terrace and gestures for me to go up the outdoor staircase first. After filling out a shitload of paperwork, the valet offered to show me where I'll be staying.

Inside, directly over the pool, is almost an exact replica of the main house, just on a much smaller scale. While the exteriors are light and more in line with most homes in this area, both interiors are far from traditional. Decorated with dark, masculine colors, different woods, copper accents, and live plants, it's more Gothic in style and feel. If it weren't for the paneled windows everywhere, it'd be too dark in here. Without any window coverings whatsoever, the natural light keeps it from leaning outright sinister.

"This is where guests stay?"

"The manor does not get many guests; however, there are many lodging options to choose from on the property."

"All of them look like this?"

His mature eyes take in the guesthouse before saying, "Aesthetically speaking, yes."

"Are the others less…" I wave a hand at the full kitchen with its own farmhouse sink.

"Less, sir?"

"Smaller."

"Rest assured, Mr. Munreaux has made the proper arrangements for you to have the largest accommodation during your stay."

Stay. Three years is more of a residency than a stay.

Although the guesthouse is way too opulent for my taste, it will be nice to have my own space away from Ever, especially during times like this. My body's sticky with dried sweat, and I can smell something gross. I caught a whiff of it the moment I followed Ever out of the woods, and it's been with me ever since. I'm pretty sure it's me.

I finally did something to work up not only a sweat but a stink, too.

I did something.

Edwin leads me through the guesthouse, giving me a thorough tour while showing me where I can find literally fucking everything from bags of tea to hand towels.

When we reach the living room, there appears to be a giant unfinished portion of the hardwood floor but it's actually transparent glass set directly above the indoor half of the pool.

"Whoa."

Coming to an abrupt stop next to it, I run the toe of my shoe over the smooth transition.

"It's structural glass."

I look at Edwin. "Safe to walk on?"

"Yes, sir," he says with a confident nod.

Just as I press one foot on it, the water below ripples. A moment later, Ever's body slices through the surface as she does the butterfly across it. There's a glass wall partition that stops a few inches above the water, separating the indoor half and the outdoor half. She dives under it, resurfacing on the other side, then continues on.

"Why doesn't Ever live out here?" I ask once she's out of sight. This seems like the kind of arrangement she'd want for herself. It'd make sneaking out that much easier. Not that she should have to sneak out. She's old enough to live on her own.

"Even if I were privy to that type of information, I would not be at liberty to say. Discretion, in all manners, is of the utmost importance here at Munreaux Manor. It'll do you well to remember that."

There's another long pause that I use to imagine all the ways I'd tell Edwin, Ever, and Arthur to fuck off. These people are something else. Something I could've gone my whole life never interacting with.

"How am I supposed to protect someone if I'm not allowed to know anything about her?"

"The same way I can predict what the Munreauxs will require without them even needing to ask…by watching."

Ever returns, still doing laps.

"If that's all, Mr. Brantley?"

Without taking my eyes off Ever, I nod.

Watching. Watching.

"Edwin?" I call him back.

"Yes, sir?" He reappears instantly, like he knew I'd need something else.

Watching.

"I saw boxes on some of the trees around the forest. What are they for?"

"Conservation."

"Mr.—"

"*Miss* Munreaux has a proclivity for things that fly."

Birdhouses.

"Are you supposed to be telling me that?"

There's a long pause before he says, "Perhaps not. However, I would be remiss not to warn you to keep your distance from them. I'm told their inhabitants are extremely territorial."

What the fuck am I gonna do to a bunch of birdhouses? They're high up anyway.

"What about the other building on the property? The one with the glass roof. Can you tell me what that's for?"

"Same purpose. Conservation."

"Let me guess, the inhabitants of that are territorial, too?"

"Not that I'm aware of, no. Nonetheless, I strongly advise staying away from it as well."

"Why's that?"

"Because while the inhabitants themselves may not be territorial, their caretaker is."

Ever? Is that why she's so against my presence here? I don't want anything of hers, only a small fraction of her father's fortune.

"Is there anything else I may assist you with?"

"No." I shake my head. "I'm good. Thank you."

He disappears without another sound.

Ever pushes off the side of the pool, heading for the outside half, when I notice movement from the pool house's doorway. Assuming Edwin's just checking up on Ever on his way back into the main house, I head to the bedroom, shedding my shoes and clothes on the way to the en-suite bathroom. Down to my boxers, I'm just about to turn on the water when the image replays in my head. The pants. They were that pale red color rich people love so much. Edwin was wearing black slacks with a crisp white button-up.

I spin on my heel and beeline it back to the glass floor. No matter what angle I look from though, I can't make out anything higher than the pants of the person still lingering in the doorway. They're not Edwin's and they don't look like they belong to Arthur either, so whose are they?

Ever's just coming back in from outside when the person moves suddenly, shifting their weight and dropping their arms enough for me to catch a diamond-encrusted watch on one wrist.

Did she invite someone over?

Motherfucker.

I'm out of the guesthouse in the next breath, charging down the stairs. I have to hike around to the other side of the pool house, and by the time I reach it, the doorway's empty.

He's in there with her. I know it. Probably already balls deep in her just to fuck with me. Like I'd quit over seeing her fucking someone. Or someone fucking her.

I shake both scenarios from my head, the discomfort tightening my back muscles as I throw open the door.

"Ever!" I roar, my voice echoing.

The splashing in the center of the pool doesn't stop, only sloshes higher, and I jump in without thought, ripping Ever away from…

No one. There's no one here. It's just Ever…swimming. Was she speeding up to get away from me?

I scan the pool house, somehow not finding anyone else in it.

How'd he disappear so fast?

"I didn't do anything!" Ever screeches suspiciously—because who just says that when they haven't even been accused of anything yet?

It's not until she shoves me that I realize I'm still holding her. I don't release her, only cock an eyebrow at her.

"Where is he?"

Ever searches around.

"Who?"

"Who? You know damn well who." She wouldn't be seeking his ass out right now if she didn't.

With a mumbled insult, she tries to swim away but I stop her with one hand under her stomach, pulling her back to standing.

"Where do you think you're going?"

"In case you haven't noticed, this is water we're standing in. And since I'm not a washed-out old man like you, I'm trying to utilize it to get some exercise."

On top of everything else, now I'm old. As for being washed out, I may be. I don't know. I don't pay attention to shit anymore, least of all me.

"Tell me where he went."

"Where who went?"

"The little boyfriend you got hiding in here."

"If your job *isn't* to stop me from getting dick, why do you seem so fucking pressed about me getting dick?"

It's not like I got a clear outline of what all my job entails. I'm just making it up as I go. One of the things I've decided on is that I won't be watching Ever get fucked by someone else, and not because I turn a blind eye to it, but because it's not gonna fucking happen on my watch. Sure, she can fuck all she wants, I don't care, just as long as she does it when I'm not around.

It just so happens I'm gonna be around for the next three years.

"Stop stalling and tell me where he is."

Some of the tension leaves her body.

"I don't even know what you're talking about. I'm not allowed to have guys over."

I let the validation for refusing to leave her alone in the woods wash over me. I knew it was to meet up with her fuck buddy.

"Why? You're nineteen," I ask, genuinely curious.

"That doesn't matter to my father, hence why you're here." The last half of that sentence is said so fucking snottily I almost wipe her goddamn nose for her. Fucking brat.

"I'm here because you're sloppy as fuck. Not every guy that sticks his dick in you needs to mark you up."

I look at her neck, at those fucking hickeys marring her skin, and feel myself grow hot.

"I know that." She drops her gaze, her long, wet lashes draped over her cheeks, and for a second, I feel bad. Maybe I took it too far.

But then she looks up at me through them, saying, "But it feels so much better when they do," and I clench my teeth together so hard my jaw aches.

I didn't take it far enough.

With my hand around her arm, I jerk her body to be in front of mine.

"Let's take a look outside, shall we? See what we find."

If that fucker isn't in here, he's probably out there somewhere.

"Help yourself. I didn't get all my laps in yet so…"

Ever tries her bullshit again, but I catch her one-handed…also again.

"You just got done running a mini marathon. You'll survive missing a couple laps."

She fights me the entire way to the partition, but she's short and the water makes her weightless, so I drag her over by her bicep, all while exerting minimal effort.

"Twenty-six laps."

I snort. "That's excessive." Anything more than a few curls to lift her pom-poms would be.

"Just because you're out of shape doesn't mean—"

"I kept up with you the whole time."

"Barely."

I battle the urge to shrug or react in any way that'd make her think she won. Doesn't matter how ugly it was, I still kept up. A few more runs together and I'll be gapping her ass instead.

Probably. Her legs are pretty short.

They're toned though. Like fucking jacked. I don't know why the guys she fucks with waste time on her neck. If it were me, I'd be feasting on Ever's thighs all night long.

But. It's. Not. Because she hates me, I hate her, and she's my… client? Is that what bodyguards call them? Or executive protection… whatever Arthur said. Agents? I don't know the official jargon yet, but bottom line is I'm her guard and she's my responsibility. I'm being paid—well—to be around her, so regardless how tempting her thighs may look—or would probably taste against my tongue—I will not be sinking my teeth into either of them and sucking until the only sounds coming from her mouth are incoherent screams of pleasure.

Although…shutting Ever up does add another layer of appeal.

"Go under," I tell her at the glass. There's not enough space to fit one head under, let alone two. We'll both have to go underwater.

"No. You want to go out there, go ahead, but I'm staying—"

I fit my palm over her mouth and plug her nose with my thumb and index finger before tugging her below the surface. Holding my breath, I go with her, and the second we're under, without any sound or distractions, we end up just staring at each other. Surprisingly she's not fighting anymore, only studying me curiously as I slowly move us sideways.

Ever's not so bad like this—silent and compliant. And the way she looks at me… It's different from how other people do. They either shamelessly stare at my scar or they make it so insanely obvious that they're trying to look everywhere but directly at it. Ever doesn't do either. She just meets my eyes.

Except for now as they trail down my body, widening when they reach my waist. I follow her gaze, making sure my swim trunks—

Shit. I'm still in my motherfucking boxers. I didn't consider my attire before coming down here. I just fucking ran.

So what? They cover as much as swim trunks do, they're just a different material. And have a hole in the crotch…that's currently gaping wide open. Fuuuck.

Ever's hand enters my vision as she hesitantly reaches toward that opening. The water's stinging my eyes the longer I keep them open, but I ignore the pain, riveted on Ever's slim hand going right for my—

Pain erupts in my palm from Ever's teeth biting into it. And that hand I couldn't look away from? It becomes a fist with one solo finger sticking out from the rest as she flips me off. Her foot collides with my stomach next, making me release her and allowing her to shoot backward out of my reach.

We surface at the same time.

"You bit me!"

Sure enough there's a complete mouth imprint of each and every one of Ever's teeth wrapped around my palm where she clamped down on the middle and side of it. If she'd bit me under different circumstances, I'd be pretty fucking turned on right now.

As it stands now, I'm…still kinda turned on. She bit me. It hurt but…not in a bad way.

Ever's voice pulls me from the sight. "You tried to drown me!"

"I warned you and I plugged your fucking nose." *You're welcome.* Not that she'd ever thank me.

Red colors Ever's cheeks.

"You exposed yourself to me."

I rear back. Not this shit again. "By accident. I was about to get a shower before I came down here."

"To catch my boyfriend?" she mocks before shrugging, all feigned innocence. "Well, where is he?"

Ripping my eyes off her because I can't stand the mere sight of her right now, especially in a bikini top that's a size too tight, mashing her small tits together into a mesmerizing display of cleavage, I turn in a circle, surveying our surroundings. Obviously, there's no one at the end of the infinity pool. If there was, he'd be dead. RIP. So I focus on the grounds, only finding a really fucking nice setup. All around the pool are enough tables and chairs and loungers to host forty people, at least. There's nobody out here, yet every umbrella is open. And clean. And new? Not a cobweb or sunspot in sight, they gotta be brand new.

Beyond those is an expansive yard with gardens everywhere—every bit of it professionally maintained, of course.

This is how people *live*? It seems almost like a waste. So much money being dumped into a yard nobody even uses.

"Find him yet?"

I give up on my perusal.

"Where'd he go? In the woods?"

"Uh-huh," Ever says with an exaggerated nod. "You should get out right now and go chase after him. Preferably over the cliff."

"And give you the satisfaction? Never. I'll stay here, with you, instead."

"I doubt you've ever given anyone satisfaction judging by that acorn between your legs." She makes a grimace and lowers her eyes down me even though the bottom two-thirds of my body is underwater and not easily visible. "Don't even try to blame it on the water either. It's not *that* cold."

The pool is heated but it still has a *slight* chill to it.

"It was your hand coming closer that made it shrink in horror," I reply, despite being ninety-nine percent sure she didn't see my dick.

She did get one thing right though. I am circumcised.

"Oh, you thought…" She covers her mouth, a laugh escaping through her spread fingers. "That I was…gonna…"

Grinding my teeth, I turn away from her and dive under the water so I don't have to hear her annoying fucking voice. No, I didn't think she was actually going to grab my dick.

Maybe for a second, but…

Look where that got me. A kick to the gut, exactly what I deserve for assuming in the first place.

A million dollars. A million dollars. A million fucking dollars.

A swarm of bubbles pass by me, and at first, I slow to let Ever go ahead, but then all her insults about me turn to liquid fire, propelling me forward until I'm neck and neck with her, racing toward the opposite end. When we reach the wall, there's a moment's hesitation from both of us.

"Twenty-six, you said?" I ask in challenge.

"Try to keep—"

I kick off the wall before she can finish, gaining myself only a *slight* head start because Ever's on my heels instantly, her presence quickly moving to my side for the entire way back. I don't let up once, going as hard as I can, until the thirteenth lap when I gas out completely and have to float over to the side to catch my breath. Ever doesn't miss a beat though, continuing on without me. Sitting on the pool's edge inside, I alternate between looking at her and the fading bite mark she left behind on my palm.

One of the times she dips under the partition, I bring my hand up to my mouth and fit my teeth to the impression of hers and bite down. I let my lips relax against my palm, sucking the flesh.

Nothing. No trace of her whatsoever. The pool washed it all away.

All at once, I release my jaw and drop my hand to my thigh.

I watch Ever swim, sometimes sneaking glances at my palm, the only place our mouths will ever meet, sometimes imagining biting Ever back. I wouldn't go for her hand though. The inside of her thigh, right below her pussy, so when she started leaking, she'd drip right on my cheek, her pussy juice rolling down into my mouth.

When she finishes her laps, she's not even panting.

I could get her to pant. I could get her to pant a lot.

"Are you going back to the house?"

Staring at her back and ass as she ascends the steps, I watch the hundreds of tiny drops gliding down her tight body. My cock already at half-mast from imagining her pussy being inches from my mouth, the sight only pushes more blood to it.

"Nuh-uh. Off to let my *boyfriend* fuck me against a tree," she mutters as she climbs the rest of the way out.

"Hilarious," I say, but she doesn't respond, only grabs a towel off a hook.

When she twists to drape it over her back, I spot more hickeys.

Are they hickeys? Both above and below her bottoms, they're on the sides of her hip bones. It's a weird place for them but…they look like hickeys.

I guess they *could* be bruises, but what would they be from? Her pom-poms? They have handles…I think. I've never seen one up close.

I'm on my feet in the next instant, walking over to grab the towel next to hers so I can get a better look.

Drying herself off, Ever's moving so quick it's hard to see her hip bones clearly.

"You don't need shoes?"

"Nope. No protection of any kind for me." Her follow-up wink grates on my last nerve.

"I'll escort you inside," I tell her shortly.

She pauses with her towel clutched to her front, throwing dagger after dagger at me using only her eyes.

"I was messing with you. I'm going to my room."

"Then I'll walk you to your room."

After tying the towel around my waist, I gesture for her to go first.

"I'm surprised your legs still work after the last two hours," she quips.

I can make yours stop working in two minutes.

Out loud, I say, "Like your mouth, they don't quit."

"Except that they literally did," she says, her wet hair dripping onto her shoulder. "On what was it? Lap three? Four?"

"Thirteen," I correct in complete monotone, making her break into laughter.

I roll my eyes and am immediately reminded of the skylight into the guesthouse overhead. Could the guy in here see me? Is that why he took off?

I wait until I'm at the door—right where he was—to see for myself. It's transparent from both sides, but from this angle, it's difficult to know what I'm looking at exactly. I should've looked when I was in the pool.

When I turn back around, Ever's stopped to watch me, guilt radiating off her.

Her poker face being so fucking terrible will work in my favor, so I don't call her on it.

"Hope you didn't bother unpacking that dusty bag you brought."

"I did," I lie.

She studies me for a moment longer, looking for…something before spinning to cross the terrace.

"Mm," she says like she isn't bothered but I know she is. "At least I know where to send your belongings after your body's been discovered."

"You kill me, you'll never fucking sleep again."

"Why?"

"Because I'll haunt every waking second of your life and I'll make sure you're awake for all of them."

Another rumble of laughter rolls through her just before she says, "You'll be in good company."

"Whose? Yours?" I ask, holding back laughter of my own.

At a set of French doors, she spins to face me.

"Father didn't tell you? This house is haunted."

"Good thing I'm staying in the guesthouse."

"You could stay at your own house."

"Then how would I keep an eye on you?"

"Leave one behind. The rest of you doesn't need to be here."

My fucking eye? Jesus, she's morbid.

"Your father would disagree. Now get inside before I throw you over my shoulder again."

She tries arguing, so I reach past her and turn the handle myself, pushing her inside. Edwin didn't give me a complete tour of the main house yet, so I don't know where her room is, but I keep prodding her, hoping she'll just go there herself.

Thankfully she does. I know when we reach her room because her entire body goes rigid as soon as we're a few feet away from the door.

"Okay, I'm here. You can go."

"Go into your room first."

"Am I a prisoner already?"

"Some prison," I murmur as I drive her forward. Whoever thought herding cats was hard never worked with Ever Munreaux.

She lets out a little growl that would be amusing if I didn't find everything she does annoying as fuck.

Before I can touch the handle, she shoots ahead of me and opens the door herself, only keeping it cracked slightly as she slides her body through the thin opening.

It feels a little date-ish, walking her to her door, so I give her an awkward nod and turn to leave. Her calling my name stops me though and I twist to look back at her.

"Yeah?"

"You might need this tonight." Careful to keep herself wedged between her door and the jamb, she reaches behind her to get something. I can't make out anything in the room, just that it's as dark as the rest of the house.

Preparing for her to pull a fucking Taser on me or some shit, I start to move toward the wall her room's on, but all she does is brandish yet another middle finger for me, except this time she mouths the words, "Fuck. You," along with the display of hostility.

"Go ahead and hold on to that one," I tell her. "Considering I ruined your fuck earlier, you'll be needing it more than me tonight."

Her door slamming shut ends the conversation but brings a genuine smile to my face. Peace at last.

Back out in the guesthouse, I decide to put my clothes away

first thing, even before that much-needed shower, just to prove Ever wrong. I am staying and there's nothing she can do to make me leave. Not willingly.

The first drawer I open, I drop my stack of shirts in without looking, and somehow set off a…mousetrap? Luckily, the sound has me jerking my hand back in time to keep all five fingers intact.

"What the *fuck?*" I pull out the trap. Who the hell sets a mousetrap *in* a drawer? This place is spotless. There aren't even any traps on the floor.

Ever's words come back to me.

"You might need this tonight."

I yank open every drawer of the dresser, only to find the same thing—a fucking mousetrap in each one just waiting to catch some unsuspecting fingers. *My* unsuspecting fingers.

Ever.

Eyeing the bed, the comforter isn't as pristine as the rest of the guesthouse. Instead of being smooth and tucked around the mattress, it's lumpy and laid haphazard. One hard tug on it triggers an entire legion of mousetraps.

A chuckle leaves my lips. Climbing into bed wouldn't have killed me, but it's gonna kill Ever when she finds out she didn't so much as get one of my fingers.

Just as I move away, my foot kicks something, setting off another one. I drop down on all fours and lift the bed skirt, only to discover a shit-ton more traps underneath.

It's gonna be a *very* long three years.

CHAPTER 7

NOT ONLY HAS THE INTERIOR OF MUNREAUX MANOR BEEN completely renovated several times since it was first built in the 1700s, but my father increased the square footage with a massive addition to the back of the house. He also added his garage to the side, turned the carriage house out back into a pool/guesthouse, and for one of my mother's birthdays, he had the atrium built. The only thing that hasn't changed over the centuries is the original building's façade, which lucky for me, is where my bedroom is located, making it easy to wedge my feet between the granite blocks in my descent.

I didn't use to sneak out. Truthfully, I never even considered it before… Before my father handed me a contract instead of a graduation present. Even then, doing this was just that—a thought. One I eventually followed through on for Hide and Keep. After that I started sneaking out more and more frequently. Now it's almost a regular occurrence.

If I were any other nineteen-year-old, I probably wouldn't have to resort to such measures. Most nineteen-year-olds can come and go as they please, hang out with whoever they want, do whatever they want, *be* whoever they want.

While my fate has never been open-ended, it didn't have an exact end date either. Discovering that it does set off a countdown only I can hear.

Ticktock. Ticktock.

Overwhelmingly loud, sometimes I can't focus on anything else, can't even *hear* anything else. And it's not just my ears. I feel it in my throat, a constant strangling sensation like a noose around my neck, tightening with each of those ticks.

How am I supposed to live like that? How is anyone?

Sometimes I just need something, anything, anyone to distract me from that choking feeling. Since those kinds of distractions aren't allowed at Munreaux Manor, at least not for me, I have to go offsite to find them.

I'm not sloppy like Crue said. I'm thrashing. Cut off anybody's air supply and see what they do. They'll thrash, kick, fight, scream, anything they can to draw in air. It's not a choice—attempting to prevent asphyxiation. Self-preservation is natural, built into every living being. If I were a man, my behavior would be applauded, promoted without hesitation. Because I'm a woman, I'm judged for it. Ridiculed. Labeled.

Slut.

Out of control.

Risky.

Tainted.

Regardless of behavior, girls everywhere are constantly repressed. If I'm already getting screwed, I might as well indulge in the little bit of pleasure I can find while I can, where I can.

On the ground, I'm just coming out from behind a dogwood bush, rubbing at that invisible rope, when headlights flash on, blinding me. Automatically, I book it toward the maze straight ahead. What the hell is this? No one's ever out here at this time. Edwin's interest is limited to what happens inside the manor. As for my father, sleep's way too important for him to miss a wink over something as trivial as me.

This has to be another "bodyguard."

How my father managed to replace Crue so quickly, I don't know.

Hopefully, this one's in worse shape than the last one. One thing's for sure, he won't be sexier. It's impossible for anyone to be. Crue is—

"Ever, stop!" he shouts somewhere behind me.

Here? Crue is here?

I almost bite it.

How? I filled the guesthouse with enough mousetraps to send him to the hospital. Did he not go into the bedroom at all? Did he even sit on the couch? What has he been doing this whole time? Just waiting in his car for me?

I was too busy researching him on my phone to notice what was happening out front. While he did tell the truth about Yasmin being dead, Crue wasn't entirely upfront on the details. For one, she was *not* his girlfriend, and two, he was partly to blame for her death. Apparently, he'd been drinking and driving the night of his senior homecoming, so when another drunk driver came at him on the wrong side of the road, his abilities were too impaired to avoid a head-on collision. The other driver sustained serious injuries that he was expected to make a full recovery from before being carted off to jail. Crue's were minor, mostly cosmetic, but his passenger's were fatal. Yasmin—his passenger—eventually succumbed to hers a few days later at the hospital where she died surrounded by family and friends…excluding Crue because, again, he was neither.

Another confusing tidbit about the situation is that Crue didn't get in any trouble for his part. The other driver was clearly more at fault, but Crue was not only drinking while underage but also driving under the influence. Only one of the articles I found reported him being cut from the wrestling team he'd been captain of as a result of his infraction, otherwise he served no jail time whatsoever, not even in juvie, or community service. I'm guessing Ronny Veen's father had a lot to do with that.

Hearing my bodyguard enter the labyrinth, I pick up the pace, quickly taking the turns that will eventually lead out the other opening. There are a couple dead ends in here, not many, but I envision him winding up in those, buying me time.

I can't believe he has the energy to chase me again. I pushed myself to the point of exhaustion today. I mean, I wasn't exhausted but he should've been. He's not a runner, or a swimmer, or a… I'm not sure what Crue is. Or was. Regardless, he's supposed to be passed out, preferably under the covers of the bed I took over an hour to prepare for him. It was so hard to position the blanket over the traps without triggering them.

When Crue's steps grow closer, I halt and slow my breathing as I wait for him to pass on the other side of the evergreen wall. At over six feet tall, they keep the maze's occupants hidden from view while inside. I can only see the pathways closest to the house from my bedroom windows, but the rest of the maze is obscured, even from the elevated vantage point. The walls are tightly packed, too, but knowing what I'm looking for makes it easier to pick out the movement of Crue's body charging past.

I picture him running right into a dead end, frustrated and helpless, and smile. It will be too easy.

Quietly, I resume my previous pace until I exit the maze, practically skipping out. I knew it. He didn't stand a—

"I know you fucking heard me!"

I glance back to find Crue jogging through the same opening I just did.

Oh my Goddess. How'd he make it through so fast? I don't think he got lost once in there.

Spinning around and running backward—still faster than him, by the way—I taunt, "I can't hear anything past your wheezing."

Unsurprisingly, he doesn't respond, probably because he can't. He really should work out more often.

I turn and sprint into the woods. Once I'm sure there's enough distance between us, I twist and press my back up against a tree trunk, the bark snagging my sweater. The risk, the fear, the *thrill* of being caught takes me right back to Hide and Keep, and I can't help but smile even bigger. It was fun while it lasted.

This isn't exactly like that, but close. The rush feels the same.

Flapping noises pull my attention skyward. Some of my nocturnal friends have returned from their winter roost.

Welcome home, I tell them in my head.

What will happen next month? Will all my conservation work just stop? Will I get to have any hobbies at all?

Of course I won't. I'm already being forced to give up cheer.

That choking sensation reappears, and I roll my head forward as I gasp out loud. Hot tears fill my eyes, burning.

It isn't fair. It isn't fucking fair.

A twig snapping nearby has me on the move again, darting from tree to tree, only stopping long enough to gauge which direction Crue's coming from. Each time he gets too close, I perch down and bear crawl away. Because he's already taller than me, and probably not expecting me to be on all fours, the significant height difference allows me to escape without discovery time and time again.

Suddenly, the forest goes eerily silent, and with how hard my heart's pounding in my chest, I'm surprised the sound alone isn't leading Crue directly to me.

I close my eyes and concentrate on my hearing. The Sound to my left, clicks overhead, and…music? I tilt my head to the right, picking up a few words. "What it means to be a girl" by EMELINE.

My ride is here.

The moment I open my eyes, I shrink back. A tall, dark form is in front of me, latching on to my shoulders. His mouth opens and I imagine him repeating what he asked me that same night. *"Do you want to be kept?"*

My answer now is the same it was then. No. I don't. I want to fly.

But he doesn't ask that. He asks what the fuck is wrong with me.

Does he mean in this moment? Or in general? Neither is easy to explain.

"Eighty-seven."

I give him a blank stare.

"That's how many mousetraps I found in the guesthouse."

Oh. He missed a few.

"You wanted to know what else I was capable of."

"Is that it? Is that all you fucking got?"

Trying not to look at the silhouettes swooping over our heads, I lazily shrug a shoulder.

His green gaze narrows. "Are you high?"

"Drugs are strictly prohibited in cheer. And unlike you, I actually respect my team enough not to jeopardize my spot on it."

"Unlike me?"

I shake him off and step forward to say in his face, "Unlike *you*."

Understanding dawns, but it's not nearly as satisfying as I'd hoped it'd be.

"I see. You think you know me because you looked me up." Those eyes ping back and forth between mine. "You don't know shit."

"I know I'm leaving and there's nothing you can do to stop me, murderer."

With one arm out to the side, he stops me when I try to pass. "What'd you say?"

I regard his arm against my waist, then his profile. The muscle in his jaw jumps as he stares straight ahead.

Is he really going to make me say it again? I already regret the word leaving my lips once.

"Murderer," I repeat, shame eating away at my insides until I feel like I might puke.

Crue lets out a humorless laugh as he rotates his head to finally meet my eyes, and I see the pain he's working to conceal. All I want to do is take his face in my palms and apologize, not just for calling him a murderer but for everything I've done and said to him today. *I'm sorry. I'm so fucking sorry, Crue Brantley. If you'd just leave, it would all stop.*

For him. I'll still be in my own personal hell. But at least he won't be here with me.

My hands find themselves behind my back, my fingers writhing against one another. *Don't do it. Don't touch him.*

"No, not the name," he says a little too dismissively. "The part about me not being able to stop you."

That arm at my stomach hooks, then Crue's hefting me off my feet and carrying me—*one-armed*—back toward the house. The closer we get, the fainter the music from Paris's car becomes. She's waiting for me.

I buck in his hold, but he brings me against his front, wrapping his other arm around my chest, too, restricting my movement. If I were taller, he wouldn't be able to carry me like this, my feet would be dragging, but since I'm about a foot shorter, my toes don't even skim the ground.

I eye his bicep flexed next to my face.

"If you even think about biting me, remember you're not the only one with teeth," he warns.

A shiver runs up my spine. Would he bite me back? Where? The only place he could reach right now is my face…or my neck.

Warmth floods my pussy, making me ache between my thighs.

"If you do that, I won't need to go out and find someone else."

It could be my imagination, but it feels like Crue's steps falter for a split second.

"You're not going anywhere tonight." His voice is hoarse and low, maybe from the strain of carrying me, maybe not. Maybe it's because he wants to bite me as much as I want him to.

If that's the case, I could trick him into releasing me right now, no physical exertion needed.

I angle my head to the side, opening my neck up to him. "So do it. Give me a reason to stay. Bite me."

Halting, his breath fans across my skin, igniting the surface into goose bumps. He quickly readjusts his hold on me, his arms like steel bands around my body, keeping me locked in place. Not that I want to be anywhere else right now.

My pussy tingles in anticipation.

He lowers his head until his lips are just below my ear, making my heart hitch in my chest. What if he does sink his teeth into my neck? Will he stop there? Will I let him?

I can almost guarantee I won't want to stop him. I'm already putty in his hands and his mouth hasn't even touched me yet. But I remember when it did. Vividly. It's practically all I've thought about since.

If he kissed me on the mouth again, he might remember, too, and *that* I don't want.

Hovering there like a spacecraft, Crue rasps, "I'd rather eat glass," then he's on the move again.

I'm equally offended and relieved. That was a stupid plan.

Unfortunately, this next one isn't much better.

I tangle my legs with Crue's, causing him to trip and both of us to fall. I'm crawling away in the next instant until two hands on my calf pull me backward, my nails leaving gouges in the earth. *No.*

"Eat this!" I send my free leg out, kicking at his perfect jawline, but he just grabs that, too, before flipping me over onto my back. He comes down on top of me, pinning me to the ground, a sharp rock digging into my back and tree root wedged up my ass. The harder I struggle, the more everything hurts, so I force myself to go limp. It's pointless to fight anyway. He's a former wrestler.

"How is this any different than what I want to go do?"

At least Crue still sounds out of breath when he says, "Penetration, Ever, that's the difference."

"I'm being penetrated from so many different angles right now I could be a heroine in a why choose novel."

"What's that?"

"A why choose novel?"

He jerks out a nod, his lips bitten between his teeth.

Goddess, he is *really* out of shape.

If I had any feeling left in my body, I'd use it to feel embarrassed for him.

"Instructional manual for men that don't know how to please women. You should pick one up sometime. Maybe learn how to use your acorn better. I've heard not *all* women care about size."

"Fuck you. My dick's not an acorn."

"Why are you trying so hard not to let me feel it then?"

He's purposely angling his body so the side of his hips are between my legs, holding me down, not his crotch. I lied in the pool. I didn't see anything. However…I did feel it in the corn maze and it was not even remotely close to the size of an acorn.

"I'm trying to keep things semi-professional."

I attempt to bark out a laugh except with the pressure of another, larger body on top of mine it comes out a wheeze.

"You're so immature."

"You're so unprofessional," I counter.

My bodyguard just shakes his head.

"I'm taking you all the way back to your room, where you're going to spend the rest of the night."

More wheeze-like laughter ensues.

"I'll just do the same thing all over again," I admit.

"Then we'll do *this* all over again."

"Aren't you tired?"

"Fucking drained."

"When are you planning on sleeping?"

"In three years. After you graduate."

"I told you," I groan. "I'm. Not. Graduating. You're better off letting me leave now. At least you'll get a full night's sleep."

"That's not what I was hired for."

"My father doesn't have to know I sneak out."

"Like *I* told *you*, you're sloppy. Your father already knows."

How does he know?

The hickeys. I guess I *could've* been more inconspicuous.

"The second you walk through the front door, you'll set the alarm off and wake up the whole house. Once the alarm's been activated, my bedroom window's the only way in or out." After Hide and Keep, I paid a girl to disengage the sensor so I could open and close it without affecting the manor's security system. "And I'm not going back in," I add sweetly because he can get fucked if he thinks I'm climbing back up there right now.

"Then you'll sit in my car until someone gets up. You're not leaving the property."

Crue pushes himself up in one smooth motion, but I don't move a muscle. If he wants to carry me anywhere, he'll be doing it without my help.

He does exactly that—carries me to his Bronco while I lie limp in his arms, making myself complete dead weight. He basically drops me in his passenger seat in a boneless heap before slamming the door shut.

Professional.

Sitting up, I admire Crue's side profile as he rounds the front end.

In another life, he might be here for an entirely different reason. He might be here because he likes me. He'd pick me up to take me somewhere or climb up to my room so we could spend the night together.

Past Crue, movement on the second floor catches my eye, and I swear I see my curtain flutter, but then I strain my eyes, and everything's as it should be—completely still.

"The paint job came out nice," I chirp once Crue's seated next to me.

Sometime in the last several hours he must've removed the tape on his hood. Because he waited so long, the flames did turn out a bit shoddy, but they were never supposed to look good. They were meant to humiliate, enrage, spark any emotion that'd get Crue to overreact and either quit or get himself fired. Sadly, neither happened.

All of today's plans have failed.

Crue only mutters an equally insincere, "Thanks," as he pulls out his phone and opens it to a screen full of text.

I have to admit, it's hot that Crue isn't intimidated by the uber-feminine flames. A lot of men would be.

"What are you reading?"

He turns his phone away from me when I lean over to sneak a peek.

"*The Babysitter's Guide to Taming Unruly Children*," he deadpans.

"Good luck with that." I chuckle while retrieving my own phone to check Paris's location. Paris is…gone, already at the party. She didn't even text me to ask what was taking so long, she just left.

What if something happened to me? Would she even give a shit?

Would anybody?

"Is that your ride?" Crue's voice makes me jump, and now I'm the one hiding my screen.

"Yes. I told him to circle the block. As soon as you get tired reading about your future kids and pass out, I'll meet him at the bottom of the driveway so we can finally begin our night of debauchery."

"How do you get over the gate?"

"I fly over it," I lie.

Obviously, Crue hasn't explored the outer perimeter of the

Munreaux estate yet. Yeah, near the driveway we have tall wrought iron fencing to give the illusion of security, but like a lot of residents around here, we use the property's original stone walls as our border. Hand-built by farmers back in the late 1700s and early 1800s, stone walls aren't very high, only like two and a half feet tall usually. Covered in moss and algae nowadays, they're historic and charming, which New Englanders love. Robert Frost even wrote his poem "Mending Wall" about a New England stone wall.

Yawning, I notice how dirty my hands are and flip them over to find a bunch of filth caked under my nails, too.

"Do you have anything in here I can use to clean my nails?"

"No, but I'm sure your room does." He doesn't even look up from his phone, his forehead creased as he reads.

Using my pinky nail, I start digging out the grime, then drop it right onto Crue's floormats. Crue gives me a nasty side-eye but doesn't say a word. We sit in silence for I don't know how long, me picking my nails, him reading, until somewhere around finger eight or nine, my eyelids prove too heavy to lift again.

CHAPTER 8

Something's burning my eyes. I crack one, instantly blinded by a ray of sunlight streaming through the passenger window of Crue's Bronco directly onto my face. *Ow.*

I roll my head to the left and find Crue fast asleep in the driver's seat, one hand still around his phone, the other holding…mine. He's holding my hand?

Both my eyes snap open.

Crue's holding my hand. Purposely. It's not like "oops, my hand fell on top of yours." No. His arm is stretched over the center console, his forearm resting on my thigh, while his hand visibly envelops mine.

I don't know when he took hold of my hand. Or why. But I'm not rushing to get out of it. I've never held a boy's hand before.

Technically, he's holding mine because his is so much bigger but I've never had a boy hold my hand before either. It feels nice.

What a way to wake up. With the plumpest set of lips I've ever seen, or felt, contradicting the unforgiving jawline that appears to be clenched even during complete relaxation, Crue's the perfect male specimen. Under his crewneck is a full sleeve of tattoos that had me losing my train of thought more than once in the pool yesterday. That arm is too far away from me to explore right now but the phone he's holding with it is aimed my way with his thumb on the glass, keeping the screen lit up…and revealing what he was looking at before drifting off.

"Bodyguard Requirements" is in bold letters.

Has he never been a bodyguard before?

Below that's a list. There are a lot, making most of the words too small to make out but I do see "high stamina, excellent combat and defense skills, and strong communication skills" at the bottom. In parentheses, directly under that last one, is "do not engage with Protectee unless prompted."

All Crue's done is engage with me so far.

The hand on mine tightens suddenly as my novice bodyguard sits up in a rush, asking, "What's wrong?"

I immediately throw his hand and arm off me, anger filling my voice. "Other than you molesting me in my sleep? Nothing. Can't you keep your filthy hands off me for—"

"You're the one that had filthy hands."

Had?

I stop to assess my hands. They're clean, even the nails. Didn't I pass out before getting to all of them?

I did. So how are they clean? And my hands? How'd they magically get clean without any water in here?

"Did you clean my hands?"

Rubbing his face, Crue shrugs and mumbles, "I didn't want to get my hands dirty, too."

He did. He cleaned my hands *and* my nails for me.

"You could've kept them to yourself. Or did you skip over that part in your *Bodyguarding for Dummies* handbook?"

He glances down at the phone abandoned on his lap and makes a noise in his throat.

"I needed to know if you tried to leave."

That's why he was holding my hand? Not because he wanted to?

Something crashes against my ribs from the inside.

Nothing he'll ever do while being on my father's payroll will be because he actually wants to. Not talk to me. Not protect me. Nothing.

"What did you use? To clean my hands."

"Spit with a little bit of elbow grease."

"You *spit* on my hands?"

Crue doesn't answer.

Why doesn't that gross me out as much as it should? Truthfully, it doesn't gross me out at all.

"How'd you clean my nails?" I ask quieter, genuinely curious.

"Same way you did."

Our eyes both fall to his hands just as he curls his fingers into his palms.

"You don't have long enough nails." He probably couldn't even scratch me with those nails, they're so short.

Again, I'm met with silence.

How did he clean my nails? And why? Nothing under my nails would've gotten on him from holding my hand.

"Alarm's off," Crue says, nodding at Edwin shaking out a rug at the bottom of the staircase.

I don't move, just watch the hundreds of pieces of dust spring off the rug as they float through the air in all different directions.

"Do you have classes today?"

I nod without taking my eyes off the airborne particles, wishing I was one of them.

"I'll walk you inside."

Getting out, he heads straight for the manor, his back entering my vision and stealing all of my attention…until he turns to face me and catches me staring.

Hardening my features, I point at the passenger door.

"What?" he mouths.

"It's not working!" I yell with more hand gestures.

He pulls out his key fob and begins the trek back to his Bronco.

The locks click into place, then unlock again.

"Try it now," he instructs from the other side of the window.

I pretend to yank on the handle and give him an irritated look like he's the one doing this to me. *Quit fucking around, Crue. It isn't funny.*

He gives it a try, opening the door right away.

I hop out.

"So you do know how to get the door for women?"

"Fuck…" he mutters with a shake of his head and a flare of his nostrils.

I strut by him, but when I look back, he's not admiring me the same way I was him. He's glancing all around, at everything but me, surveying the area for some sort of threat.

His research is kicking in. He's full bodyguard now.

Does that mean he's going to stop engaging with me?

I veer away from the manor.

"Where are you going?"

"For a run."

"You just—" he starts to say before cutting himself off.

After shutting his door, he follows wordlessly.

I break into a steady jog, not going as hard as yesterday. I guess I can ease up on him a little bit. He did clean my nails for me. And he held my hand.

I squeeze that hand into a loose fist, pretending his is in it for the rest of the run.

When we make it back to the manor, instead of following me up to my room like yesterday, Crue lingers in the foyer and says, "I'll be right here when you're ready to leave, miss."

I freeze halfway up the stairs. Miss?

"I need to talk to Mr. Munreaux," he tells Edwin.

"Of course, sir. May I ask in regard to what?"

"My accommodations."

He's going to rat on me, tell my father what I did to the guesthouse.

"Were they not to your standards?"

"Uh."

I can feel both men's eyes on me, so I resume the climb to the second story with my head held high. I don't care if he tattles on me. What could my father possibly do to me that he hasn't already?

I'm just coming out of my room when I practically run into Edwin.

"I'm…uh…" At a loss. I can't remember the last time I saw someone in this wing of the manor.

I spy Crue behind him.

Ah, now I remember. It was yesterday, when Crue escorted me to my door.

But before that, I honestly don't remember. I don't even see the maid when she cleans my room.

It had to have been my nanny when she still lived here.

"Miss Munreaux, Chef Koch had to run out but he left some breakfast items on the counter for you and Mr. Brantley."

"Is that why you're up here?" I can't keep the suspicion from my voice. Why is he here right now? Why are either of them here?

"No, I was just showing Mr. Brantley to his room."

"His room? He's staying in the guesthouse."

"Not anymore," Crue says smugly. "It's too far away."

"So put him in another guest room," I tell Edwin, ignoring Crue altogether.

Crue's the one to respond first. "This is the closest to yours."

"But it isn't available."

"Miss Munreaux, do you have a guest I'm unaware of?"

I look between Edwin and Crue, both their expressions souring by the second.

"No, but that doesn't mean I want one either. That room's off-limits. There are six guest rooms in this house. Give him one of those."

"Five now." Shit. That's right. I'm not used to any of them being occupied. "Mr. Munreaux believes this one is best suited for Mr. Brantley's needs. The close proximity will provide—"

"The close proximity will provide a stranger direct access to me," I fucking hiss.

"I'm not a stranger. I'm your executive protection agent."

"You're not my anything, and I'm not an executive."

"You will be soon enough."

I glance at Edwin for the briefest of seconds, but he's back to being as stoic as ever.

"If you'd prefer, you can call me your personal protection ag—"

"I'd *prefer* to call animal control to come fetch this fucking stray trying to make himself at home outside my bedroom!"

I can't *believe* I took it easy on him this morning.

Ignoring my mounting hysteria, Crue just says, "As your personal protection agent, I need direct access to you in order to keep you safe."

"If you want to keep me safe, get me a lock for my door!"

"Your door doesn't have a lock on it?"

He eyes my doorknob with a scowl.

"I didn't think I needed one…" My gaze drops. "Until now."

"I'd never go in your room unless it was for your protection," Crue says quietly but vehemently.

I don't acknowledge him, only continue staring at the floor. It's not like anyone would believe me anyway. My room's never felt as unsafe as it does now.

Edwin breaks the tense moment with a forced cough. "If you'd like, Miss Munreaux, I can make the proper arrangements to have one installed while you're at school."

"*I'll* install one myself," Crue tells him. "I need to make sure no one else can make a copy of the key."

That has my gaze rising.

"Shouldn't *I* be the one to install it?"

Neither man responds, making my blood boil. Is it because they think I can't manage such a task or because they don't trust me to be the only one with keys to it? After all, it is *my* private sanctuary.

Crue gets between me and Edwin, telling the valet, "I'll personally take care of the lock," before ushering me over to the room next to mine. "If you don't mind, I'd like Miss Munreaux to show me my accommodations this time. Make sure there aren't any surprises waiting inside for me."

He was just calling me Ever last night. I hadn't even realized how much I liked him using my name until he stopped.

"How could I leave any surprises if I didn't even know this would be your room?"

I'm shoved inside without an answer.

Crue closes the door on Edwin still standing in the hallway, staring after us but doing nothing to stop this. *Thanks for the help.*

"Pull back the comforter."

With his focus solely on the bed, I check the spot beside the headboard. Not finding any noticeable seams, I sigh in relief.

"There aren't any mousetraps under it."

"Show me."

I cross my arms over my chest.

When I don't make a single move, he finally looks at me. I keep my eyes locked on his and lift a brow.

"Does your dad call you Never because you never do what he asks?"

The arrow slices through me, making my shoulders curve inward. I quickly drop my arms to my sides.

"You didn't ask anything, *murderer.*" And neither does my father. It's all commands, all the time.

Two large hands grip my shoulders, then I'm sailing through the air. I land on the mattress with a hard bounce.

He threw me on the bed. Without knowing for certain if it was covered in mousetraps. What a dick.

"What the fuck?" I screech as I scramble up to sitting. "My outfit—"

"Is fine. Everything except your skirt."

When I turn a glare on my bodyguard, his face is hard as marble.

"What's wrong with my skirt?"

"It's too short."

"Long enough to conceal this." I pull a middle finger out from under it.

Ignoring me, he says, "Now check the dresser."

"Check it yourself." It's not like he can throw me on it.

But he does drag me by my elbow over to it, which I do not appreciate one bit.

I yank each drawer open with way more aggression than necessary, then go over and open the closet before he can drag me there, too. I even walk inside it and wave my arms around, proving there's nothing in it.

"See? I told you."

"What about the bathroom? You put traps under the toilet lid last time."

I internally snicker. I forgot about those.

"Do you really think I'd pull the same exact shit?"

All he does is shrug. He does. He believes I'm that uncreative. *Thankfully.*

We go through the en-suite bathroom, getting the same results—no traps whatsoever. I did absolutely nothing to welcome my new room neighbor. Had I not been blindsided by this turn of unexpected, not to mention unwanted, events, I would've given him a reception to remember.

I think I still will.

Under the pretense of an eye roll, I scan the top of the room where the walls meet the high ceiling.

"Well, I don't want to be late to school, so…" I'm already walking backward.

"You still have thirty-five minutes before your first class starts," he says as he disappears into the bathroom.

Someone must've given him my schedule. Father.

"The drive there takes me seventeen minutes alone, then I have to find a parking spot and walk—"

"It won't take me that long to get us there. Just give me a minute, then we'll leave."

He wants to drive me to school? But then he'll see the clones. He'll see me *with* the clones.

Disgust dripping from my tone, I say, "A minute won't help you. You need a shower."

"I'm aware, but we don't have time for that."

He steps out of the bathroom.

I consider his all-black outfit from the long-sleeve V-neck to the jeans to the boots. It's not that he looks like a bodyguard per se, but he is giving off major danger vibes.

Major Danger. I almost laugh at myself. That sounds like the name of the costume he was wearing at Hide and Keep.

"Is that what you're wearing?"

"Yeah." He glances down at himself. "Why?"

"You're about to walk onto one of the wealthiest campuses in the country and you look…" Hot. The clones will be throwing themselves at him. "Poor. Wear a suit or something."

Suits are almost trite in my world. Nobody bats an eye at a suit, but everyone will be batting their eyes at Crue looking like a piece of forbidden fruit.

"I don't own a suit."

"I'll have to fix that," I blurt before reminding myself I don't want him as my bodyguard. I don't want anyone as my bodyguard. "Give Edwin your measurements and he'll have some made," I tack on to make it sound less personal.

"I don't know my measurements."

"Because your body's changed recently or…"

"I've never been fitted."

"Never? Not even for that homecoming?" He knows which one I'm talking about.

Darkness settles over his features as he shakes his head. "I borrowed my dad's wedding suit that night."

"That's the only one he has?" My father's closet is almost entirely suits. Suits for every occasion, even Sunday dinner when people are supposed to be at their most relaxed.

"Had. It got ruined."

Because of the accident.

My eyes find the scar on his cheek.

"That got ruined, too," he says.

So that's how he got the scar.

It doesn't ruin his face at all. I'd tell him, if I could, that pristine art never sells as well as the messy, chaotic pieces because perfection isn't real, it's manufactured, then replicated. People settle for replicas, but what everyone really desires is an original. Crue is a true one of a kind.

And he's about to find out that I'm not.

I sigh. "Let's get this over with."

Outside, Crue automatically heads toward the driver's side of his Bronco before stopping suddenly, backing up, then veering left. Without a word, he opens the passenger door and waits for me. I get in with a frown on my face but a smile on my heart. Major Danger opens my doors now.

CHAPTER 9

Crue

DESPITE EVER'S COMPLAINTS, IT DOESN'T TAKE ME LONG TO find a parking space. Littoral University is extravagant but smaller than I expected. The campus consists of a handful of Gothic buildings clustered around a large lawn area. All are made of stone. Some have stained glass windows. And the center one, the tallest, has a tall clock tower I've only seen from afar.

Ever doesn't move to get out right away, just gives me an expectant look, reminding me Her Majesty requires certain assistance when exiting a vehicle. Allegedly. Suddenly. Yesterday she didn't have such demands. Yesterday she was a pain in my ass. Today she's a royal pain in my ass.

Visibly sweeping the area while walking over to her side, I open Ever's door for her. She gets out without thanking me. Or acknowledging me.

I assumed her outfit was some sort of school uniform, but looking around at the other students in the parking lot, either everybody else is in violation of the dress code or there isn't one.

In addition to the high-waisted hunter-green plaid skirt, she's wearing a cable-knit sweater with a turtleneck underneath, the white collar doing a good job of hiding the hickeys on her neck. Her high heels make her look more woman than girl as do her taut calf muscles.

Needless to say, Ever pulls off the schoolgirl outfit well. Very fucking well.

Even if her skirt is still too short. She might've pulled it up higher since I told her so. I can't be sure. I'm trying very hard not to stare at her hemline.

I wish I would've thought of that *before* I threw her on a bed.

"I'll meet you right here after," she says, eyeing the hat now on my head.

I could let her walk in by herself. It'd be easier. There's gonna be a lot of people. There already is.

But…that's not what's best for Ever.

With shaky hands, I close her door, then grab my coat from the backseat. I have to jog to catch up with her but what's new? At least this time, I actually do.

I stick to my protectee's right, no less than an arm's length away… just like I read how to do last night.

Ever stops in her tracks the moment my coat touches her shoulders. "What did you put on me?"

"My coat. It's cold out and you're not wearing…a lot."

With a flick of her middle fingers, my coat falls off her shoulders to the ground.

"I don't wear that brand."

She doesn't know what brand it is. I don't even know what brand it is. I think my dad got it for me a couple Christmases ago, and the thought to check the tag never even occurred to me. I don't give a shit about those kinds of things.

I scoop up the coat with a tight, "Fine."

Neither of us moves.

"Well… Leave."

"I can't. I'm accompanying you to class."

"Why?"

"Mr. Munreaux wishes to ensure your studies remain a priority."

"I'm here, aren't I?"

I remain silent. Arguing is pointless. She doesn't have to wear my coat, but I'm walking her to class.

"Ugh." She resumes her strut. "Also, you sound like Edwin and you look lost."

I feel lost. The last time I was on a campus was the summer before senior year when my parents and I started touring some of the colleges that were trying to recruit me.

We cross the quad, Ever's heels clacking against the concrete, drawing every eye in the vicinity our way. Is this how it always is for her? Everyone constantly watching her?

Or is it me?

Instantly, I tuck my chin.

The stares don't stop.

I hang back several feet as a test, but my proximity doesn't seem to affect anything. It's not my presence that has people fascinated. It's hers.

Not that she notices.

I fall into step with her, causing her to groan as she increases speed.

I duck my head even lower, tugging on the bill of my hat. I know why she's embarrassed to be seen with me. I don't want to be seen either, especially not here. This is the upper echelon of Sea Haven.

Right in the center of the lush landscape is a cluster of contemporary art sculptures shaped like…snakes? They're long and rope-like. While a couple of them appear to be coming out of the ground, others are mid-slither. Lounging against one of them are some people dressed similarly to Ever.

Not similarly. Identically.

Both girls look like her carbon copies and all three guys are in dark suits, stark white button-ups, and ties.

I take in the rest of the student body. Jeans, leggings, hoodies, puffer coats—all clothing you'd expect to see on any campus in America. I can tell by the stiff fabrics and bright colors, the brands are more expensive than what I'm used to, otherwise, everybody looks…normal.

That's why Ever had everyone's interest as soon as she stepped foot on campus. She's one of the elites. These six are probably the wealthiest and most influential students here.

One of the girls gets to her feet the second she spots Ever and points in our direction, demanding, "What is that?"

Immediately, I check over my shoulder for the threat. Seeing none, I return my attention to Ever. She's doing the same thing I just did, but jerks back when our gazes collide like I'm the last person she was expecting to find. Like she forgot I was here.

Again?

Unless she has amnesia, there's no way she could've forgotten that quickly. She *just* tried outrunning my ass.

Her sky-high heels are the only reason she couldn't.

"Goddess, why are you so close?" she asks me loudly, obnoxiously. "Can you back up? You're ruining my aesthetic."

Her aesthetic? She didn't… She didn't just fucking say that shit.

Scowling, I lace my hands together in front of me, not backing up so much as an inch. Fuck her aesthetic.

She huffs before turning to her friends.

"Father has a stalker, and out of an abundance of caution, he's burdened me with a bodyguard until authorities can apprehend the madman," Ever says, lying through her impeccably straight teeth.

So she doesn't want her friends to know she's out of control.

It is pretty fucking embarrassing. I'd lie my ass off, too.

"I want one." Her double pouts, looking me up and down like I'm in the window display of her favorite boutique.

All at once I realize she was talking about me. I'm the "that" she was referring to. And she didn't ask *who* is that. She asked *what* is that. I'm nothing more than an object to these people. A tool for hire.

"No. You. Don't," Ever bites out like I'm the biggest inconvenience anyone could possibly be saddled with.

For the next several minutes, I have to stand here and try to ignore every vapid word coming from Ever and company's mouths. Some topics are easier to tune out than others. Yachting. The Masters. Charity auctions—that shit might as well be another language to me.

A gala though, that's just another word for party, and that piques my interest. Not for my sake. For my protectee's.

Taking place this Saturday, Ever's friends couldn't be more excited for the gala. "The event of the season," they keep calling it.

"What time will you be making your grand entrance, Munreaux?" the blond guy asks lazily.

"I'll have to let you know. I have something beforehand."

He perks up. "Pregame?"

"Without us?" the first girl, Paris, practically whines.

Ever mumbles, "That's rich." Then louder, she adds, "It's for cheer."

The group, minus the blond, erupts in groans.

"Didn't you already have your little show?" Paris asks.

"You mean Nationals? It's a competition, the biggest one of the year. And yes, we competed on Saturday. We won fir—"

"So then why is it still going?" the blond interrupts to ask.

"It's not even football season anymore," another guy says.

The third one adds, "And basketball ended weeks ago."

"The season is over, it just…"

I thought she told Arthur it wasn't over.

When Ever doesn't continue, I twist imperceptibly so I can see her fully. Ignoring the double takes her friends give my face now that it's on display, I focus on Ever. She's lost in thought and standing in a way I've seen her do a couple times now, with her hands behind her back.

Nervous habit maybe? What is she nervous about? Is it something with cheerleading?

Or is it these people?

They bother the shit out of me.

"So you can skip it?"

Ever releases her arms back by her sides. "No, I can't. We've been asked to perform our winning routine at the Flower Fest this year."

No one says a word, making Ever's scoff hard to miss. They all act like they do though.

"I'll let you know when I'm on my way," she tells them with a shake of her head.

There's a collective sigh of relief.

I return to my previous stance of my left side facing away from the elitist group, grateful I don't have friends because what the fuck are these people?

After that, the discussion turns to fashion, specifically what everyone's going to wear to the gala, so I zone out until Ever passes me, then I'm hustling to keep up with her again.

She stops in front of the tallest building to face me. "You're not going into my class with me, are you?"

I shake my head. I wasn't planning on it.

"Are you just gonna sit out here and wait?" Her tone isn't as cunty as when she was around her friends, but it's still got a superior note to it.

"I'll be right here when you get out, miss," I assure her.

Her face screws up in irritation.

"This class is three hours long."

I nod, already aware.

"So, what are you going to do the whole time?"

"I'll figure something out, miss."

More annoyance.

It's ironic, how worried she is about public perception when her disregard for it is what led to me being here in the first place. What does she think, I'm going to be out here holding up a goddamn sign broadcasting who I'm here for? I may be new to this gig, but I'm not that fucking inept.

"Here." She hands me a keycard without making eye contact. "This is for the library. You can go in there and stay warm."

One of my eyebrows cocks all on its own. Is Ever Munreaux concerned about my wellbeing? After shitting on me for caring about hers?

"Thank—"

She disappears through the double doors before I can finish thanking her. I wait until the line of students heading inside thins out to ask someone where the library is.

Two and a half hours later, I'm just leaving the library when I spot Ever coming right at me.

"What are you doing? Why are you here?"

She jerks a thumb over her shoulder. "I got let out early."

"I said I'd meet you where I left you."

"Yeah, but you weren't there. I checked the parking lot first, and when I didn't find you there either, I figured you took my suggestion."

She walked all over campus without me? What the fuck? She could've just left. Or been fucked in a broom closet. There're probably hundreds of guys around here wanting a taste of Queen Ever.

"You should've called me." My voice comes out more strained than I intended.

She studies me carefully before shrugging. "Next time I will."

I open my mouth to argue, then realize she didn't fight me. She…agreed…with me.

"What?" I ask, needing her to repeat it to be sure.

"Next time I get out early, I'll text you."

"I said call me," I argue because it feels right. Better than us getting along. Are we getting along right now?

She rolls her eyes and chuckles, the sound light and twinkly as she approaches. I open the door wider for her, spinning to follow her back inside.

"Nobody calls anyone anymore."

"My mom calls me all the time," I admit, then regret it.

"She does?" Ever stops to face me. "Why? Don't you live with her?"

"Yeah…but that doesn't stop her from caring about me whenever I'm not at home."

"What is that like?"

Students try to get by us since we're posted directly in the middle of the aisle, so I grab Ever's elbow and guide her over to the side.

"What is what like?"

"Having someone care about you."

My lips spread into a smile until I realize Ever's don't. She's serious.

"Uh. A little overwhelming at times. Mostly nice, but…" I smooth out my left eyebrow with my middle finger. Twice.

Ever pulls my arm down and meets my eyes. "But what?"

I glance around just to break the tension. She's so intently focused on me, it's like there's no one else on earth except me.

"You know, it's like with all nice things, you kinda forget to appreciate it."

Those azure eyes drop to my chest, then the floor, her eyebrows scrunched over them.

"I don't."

"You don't…what?"

"Know. You said, 'you know,' but I don't. That's not something I'd ever forget to appreciate."

"Seems like you already did with your dad—"

"My father only cares about Munreaux Motorcycles," she says with a noticeable bite. Glancing at me again, she plasters a smile on her face to ask, "Are you hungry?"

Before I can even answer, she immediately follows up with, "Did you try out the café?"

I shake my head, making her eyes widen.

"You have to. My treat."

She latches on to my arm, the act taking me by complete surprise, then almost runs into one of her look-alikes. Her hand falls from my forearm instantly and her spine elongates.

"Okay, spill. Where were—"

"Where were *you?*" Ever counters, getting in Paris's face. "You just took off without me last night."

Paris blanches. "You were taking forever and I wanted—"

"You didn't even text to see if I was okay. I could've been hurt."

"Well, you have him to protect you, right?" Ever's friend gestures at me.

"Yes," I say at the same time Ever says, "No. I have him to make sure I'm not kidnapped and held for ransom. I can still go to a party if I want to."

Um, no, she can't.

Paris tilts her head. "I'm sorry, okay?" She doesn't sound sorry. "It was—"

Ever singsongs, "Major, can you escort me to the café?"

My head on a swivel, I'm scanning every face around us. Who the fuck is Major?

But when I return my gaze to Ever, she's blinking at me expectantly. Me? I'm Major?

"Sure…right this way, miss." I lead her away from Paris with a mumbled, "Excuse us."

What the fuck is happening? First, Ever is nice to me. Now, she's calling me Major and asking me to escort her somewhere.

"For the record, I'm not a major," I tell her once we're clear of her friend. "I didn't even serve."

Ever keeps her eyes straight ahead. "I thought I read that most executive protection agents were soldiers."

I don't remember that being on my phone's screen this morning. Did she read that somewhere else?

"Are you sure it's not because you want your friends to think I'm more qualified than I am?"

With a scoff, she peeks at me out of the corner of her eye. "Those aren't my friends."

"What are they?"

"Clones."

They certainly try to be. None of them come close though. Even dressed alike, Ever stands out among her clones.

Getting in line, we study the menu.

"It's my treat, so get whatever you want."

When I side-eye my protectee, I find her grinning at me and feel myself return it. Three years of this won't be so bad.

What's got her so happy?

"Did you catch some dick in a broom closet or something?"

"Not a broom closet, no. My professor prefers we use his office."

There goes my good mood.

And my plans to let Ever attend her classes without me.

"You better be fucking with me," I grit, but she only shrugs innocently.

We don't speak again until we reach the front of the line.

The cashier is already talking when we step up, his gaze locked on the tablet on the counter. "One unsweetened matcha lemonade… And what can I get you?"

I wait for Ever to speak, but the cashier looks up at me.

"What would you like?"

"She's first—"

"I already got her usual," he says.

Must be good then. If the queen orders it.

"Then I'll have what she's having."

The cashier says, "Of course," but not in a professional way, in an apologetic way.

Ever's lips pull down at the sides as she taps her credit card on the tablet, then presses the button for a custom tip. She types so fast I only catch her entering two zeroes at the end, in front of the decimal point. She tipped at least a hundred dollars on a fourteen-dollar order.

"Maybe you're not so bad after all," I tell her when we make our way to the other end of the counter. The pickup area clears out almost instantly.

"Or maybe I'm worse. Maybe I'm trying to give my father a heart attack," she deadpans, without an ounce of emotion. Or humor.

Even though no one's within earshot, I drop my voice to ask, "Is that why you act out so much? To get Daddy's attention?"

"I act out because letting someone's son make me speechless is a lot more fun than talking about my feelings in therapy."

Speechless myself, I study her profile for a full minute until our drinks are set in front of us.

"You're the horniest chick I've ever met. You're basically a guy."

She swirls her green lemonade vigorously.

"It doesn't sound like you've talked to any of the women you've ever met. If you had, you would've learned they're probably all just as horny as I am. Guys aren't hornier than women, they're just more open about it because society expects them to be."

"That's..." Somewhat accurate. I know from experience the part about society not only allowing but expecting men to be super sexual at all times, is true, but the first part is...not inaccurate. I don't talk to anybody enough to get to know them like that.

Maybe Ever's sex drive is normal.

Still, she should be able to go a day without getting fucked. Right?

Unless her professor's the one I saw in the pool house.

"Are you in a relationship with your professor?"

Ever barks out a laugh, making the entire café go silent.

"I doubt her husband would like that very much."

"Her? But you said *'he* prefers *his* office.'"

"Maybe I'm trying to send you to an early grave, too." She chuckles again, her blue eyes sparkling. "You make it too easy, Major. I was annoyed by your insinuation that I can't go three hours without having someone's dick in me, so I bit back." One of her eyebrows quirks as she glances down at the hand she bit yesterday. "This time verbally."

"Brave considering I told you I bite, too."

"You did when you compared me to a man. Worst pain I've ever felt."

"I thought pain was nothing to you," I counter, feeling some of that block of ice between us melt. Actual honesty but some joking mixed in there, too? I can do that.

But then Ever says, "Physical pain," and I'm not sure which category that falls into.

"If I've caused you any pain, physical or…otherwise, I'm sorry."

Her eyes search mine before she whispers, "Thank you. And same."

She didn't hurt me, but I appreciate the sentiment.

"Can we start over?"

"I'd be okay with that."

"Yeah?"

The corners of her lips pull in opposite directions, and she nods.

For a moment, I forget my surroundings, my job, my name. Her genuine smile's so goddamn hypnotic, it could stop traffic. Or my heart. Am I dead? And she's my angel?

I blink and reality comes back into focus. Café. Bodyguard. Ever Munreaux, head bitch on campus and flyer, whatever the fuck that means because I passed out before I could look it up.

Shit. I need to build up a tolerance to her soft side and fast.

Clearing my throat, I tap her cup with mine, rasping out, "Cheers."

Cheers? What the fuck?

I'm about to send myself to that early grave.

I quickly gulp lemonade like a dehydrated man before it almost comes back up, a whole-body shudder rolling through me.

"It tastes like seaweed water," I somehow choke out.

Setting her drink on a nearby high top, Ever pulls out her phone and says, "Yeah." Her expression matches how my taste buds now feel. "It's not good."

"Why do you drink it?"

"I don't. Matcha's disgusting and I hate citrus," she says without looking up.

"Why do you order it at all?"

"Because that's what the clones like to drink. It's the moment." The last sentence is said with a tone meant to imitate the clones but sounds similar to how Ever spoke with them this morning.

"But why do *you* have to order it?"

"If I don't…" Her eyes lift to mine. "…then they won't."

I think back to their conversation this morning, the bits I actually paid attention to. It's true. Ever's their leader. They rely on her for everything.

"Even when they're not with you?"

She fans her fingers out around us, at all the eyes aimed our way. "I'm always on duty here."

That cashier didn't even ask Ever what she wanted, didn't even give her the opportunity to say, just assumed.

"If you weren't, what would you order?"

"Doesn't matter because I am."

"Red peppermint mocha? Lavender…uh…cappuccino?"

Her head shakes as she tries to hold back a smile. I release mine though. I don't know all the names.

"Come on. If we're gonna start over, you gotta let me get to know you a little bit."

Even focused on her phone again, I catch her rolling her eyes, but she says, "Iced chai latte with almond milk and three pumps of pumpkin brown sugar."

I seek it out on the menu board. The chai latte is one of the few options with a picture next to it. I examine the green liquid in our cups, an idea forming.

"How long have you known the clones?" I ask her.

"Since preschool. Except Paris. She moved here in middle school."

"None of them have figured out you hate citrus yet?"

"They haven't figured out much about me," she mutters.

"Do you drink the lemonade around them?"

"Only when I have to." She looks up at me suddenly. "Ready?"

"Where are we going?"

"Shopping."

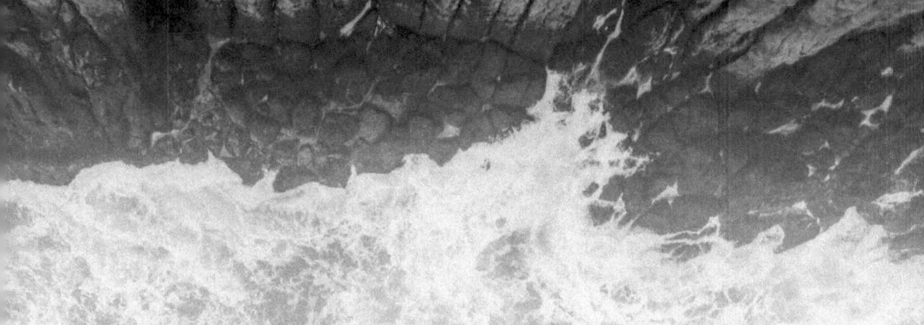

CHAPTER 10

Ever

"WHAT'S WRONG WITH YOUR SHOES?"

"What's *wrong* with them? Nothing is *wrong* with them. They're off the runway, chosen straight from this year's summer collection."

Crue grimaces, making me realize I've done it again, acted like *them*, this time not on purpose but out of pure instinct.

"They hurt my feet," I admit in a softer tone.

"I believe it. They hurt me just looking at them. Did you bring another pair to change into or do we need to stop by the manor first?"

I shake my head and gently set both high heels behind the driver's seat. "I'll put them on when we get to the store. I just don't want to wear them any longer than I have to."

My bodyguard continues to stare at me like I have three heads, and with an arrogant claim like the one I just spewed, I'm sure I sound like I do.

They are fantastic shoes though…even if I do hate them.

"If they hurt your feet so bad, can't you just wear shoes without heels?"

"No?" Like, hello.

"Why not?"

"The aesthetic."

"Yours?" He looks me up and down, his expression bordering on…mocking? "What about it?"

"Flats would clash."

"But they would make you more comfortable."

"Comfort isn't the objective." It's *never* the objective.

"Do you wear heels when you're cheering?"

A chuckle tickles my lips. "No."

Crue starts up his Bronco and pulls out of the parking lot.

"When exactly *is* cheerleading season?" he asks after I give him directions.

"It depends."

"On what?"

"Mostly what team you're on, but for a lot of people, cheer is year-round."

"Obviously you cheer for Littoral…"

"What makes it obvious?"

"The photos of you in a Littoral uniform all over your socials."

My eyes skate over to his hand on the steering wheel, light and loose as he confidently drives one-handed.

"You follow me?"

"I don't follow anyone."

"You just stalk them online?"

"It's not like that. I don't go on social media at all…usually. I only did when I was researching this job. Not that I knew what this job was." The last part is muttered, then louder he says, "All right, what else do I need to know?"

"About?"

"Cheerleading."

"Why the sudden interest in cheer?"

"Because it's important to you."

My eyes fly to his but they're focused on the road ahead.

He clears his throat and shifts in his seat, not looking quite so confident anymore. He even adjusts the hat on his head.

"And you're my job."

Yep. His job. I'm his job. I'll only ever be *just* his job.

"So, what other kinds of cheerleading teams are there?"

I launch into a detailed explanation of how cheer works, along with the different types of teams and competitions there are. He doesn't say much, only listens as he drives, but it's more than what most people do the moment I start talking about the sport I've lived and breathed since I was a toddler. I'll never understand why it's so divisive. Just because it's mostly female doesn't make it less—less physically demanding, less entertaining, less powerful, less of a damn sport. Golf is less of all those and it gets far more respect than cheer.

"Are you on an all-stars team, too?"

"No, not anymore. Father made me quit when I started at Lit U. He believes collegiate teams are the only ones worth bragging about."

Crue checks out the driver's side window.

"Were you on any sports teams in college?" I ask.

"No," he practically bites out.

"Did you…go to college?"

"Why the sudden interest?" he throws back at me. "And shouldn't you already know everything about me from doing your own online stalking?"

"I didn't…" My seat suddenly becomes uncomfortable, too. "I didn't look into you *that* much. I only read about the accident. The rest of your life wasn't—"

"The rest wasn't worth bragging about. Not according to Arthur Munreaux's standards…or to anyone else's."

The car comes to a stop, then he's saying, "We're here, miss," while jumping out before I can say anything else.

I press my thumbs together as he rounds the front end, over to the passenger side to open my door. He doesn't say a word or even look at me as he waits for me to get out.

So that's it? He's back to hating me again? I wasn't even trying to offend him this time.

I need his walls to be lowered before we go inside, or this won't work.

None of it will.

I retrieve my shoes from the back. While putting one on, I say, "Nobody meets my father's impossibly high standards, not even me." *Especially not me.* "Yeah, I'm on a collegiate team but it's for something he doesn't consider brag-worthy. If it was fencing, or crew, or…" I sit back and throw my hands up momentarily. "Golf even, then maybe he would."

That's a lie. Nothing I do will ever make that man proud.

With a sigh, I lean forward again to continue with the other shoe.

"I was going to say the rest of your life wasn't relevant, so I didn't bother looking it up. Whether you went to college or not, you still ended up working for the wealthiest man in Connecticut. Maybe you don't meet anybody else's standards because you're too busy setting your own."

When I'm finished, I peek up through my lashes, finding Crue watching me. This is how I wish I could talk to him all the time. No snobbery bullshit. Just real-life conversation.

After a moment, Crue holds out his hand for me, palm open.

"Your school has its own rowing team?"

I grin and slide my hand into his.

"Two. Men's and women's."

We go into the store together—Crue opening the door for me—but cross paths when he goes to the women's side and I head for the men's.

"Oh. Um." He kind of hesitates in the middle, his hands clasped in front of him as he pivots to keep an eye on me.

He's so adorable. If spoiling him is half as fun as fighting him, then I'm in for a real treat.

"Miss Munreaux, we've been eagerly awaiting your arrival," the store manager, Thierry, comes right up to me and greets. "Your messages stated you're looking to update some wardrobe staples. Will your companion be joining us or do you happen to know his measurements?"

Even out of the corner of my eye, I catch Crue's shoulders squaring at the mention of my *male* companion. *Always assuming I'm after the dick.*

As much as I do like dick, it doesn't rule me.

"He's right here."

Thierry's eyes sweep the store, glossing right over Crue, who dips his head, clearly wanting to be missed.

"He is?"

"Yes, he is." I walk over to Crue myself.

Crue looks behind him like a puppy who lost sight of his tail.

You, Crue. I'm talking about you.

How is anyone else going to take Crue seriously if he doesn't even take himself seriously?

"I apologize for the confusion—"

"That's quite all right, Miss Munreaux. We can wait until your—"

"—in my texts. I'd like him to get an entire new wardrobe, not just pieces."

Despite the dollar signs lighting up his eyes, Thierry still refuses to so much as glance at Crue, so I rest my hand on my bodyguard's forearm, forcing him to.

"This is Crue Brantley. He'll need to be measured, then anything he wants—"

"Me? I don't want anything. I thought we were here for you."

Of course he doesn't want anything. The price tags are too high for him to even allow himself to.

I glance from Crue to the manager. "Anything we choose for him, put it on my tab."

"Absolutely." He attempts to whisk Crue away. "If you'd allow me, Mr. Brantley."

But Crue stays rooted, his arms now folded over his chest.

"It's Crue, and no, I don't allow you. Ever?"

He said it again. My name.

I can't keep the smile off my face as I say, "Yes?"

"This isn't…" His arms fall limp. "I don't need…"

"You're going to be by my side for the…" Just because he believes this assignment is for the next three years doesn't mean it will be. "Foreseeable future, correct?"

He gives a stiff nod.

"Then I need you dressing the part. Besides, my father already gave his approval," I say while waving my phone at him, its screen blank, its history completely void of any such communication.

Father should've given Crue a clothing allowance anyway. His own valet wears sixteen-hundred-dollar Valentino poplin shirts to putter around the manor. If Crue's to acclimate to my lifestyle, accompany me to all aspects of it, then he can at least look like he belongs in it.

Goddess knows he doesn't act like it.

All out of objections, he's ushered toward the back of the store, allowing me to grab things I think will look good on him. He's so handsome, and could probably pull off literally anything, that I end up with several armfuls of options for him to try on.

I meet the manager outside the dressing rooms.

"When you say entire wardrobe…"

"I mean entire wardrobe, down to his underwear."

"Any preferences on style?"

"What's wrong with the ones I'm wearing?" Crue asks from behind a partially closed curtain.

"If they're anything like the pair I saw you in, they're fraying at the edges, baggy, and faded." I truly loathe boxers. They reveal nothing.

Lowering my voice, I tell Thierry, "Boxer briefs. Dark. No visible branding."

The fifty-year-old trying to look thirty gives a knowing head bob, his glossy lips puckered. "Understated, yet sophisticated."

"Exactly. Classic. In addition to the everyday staples I grabbed, he'll also need several suits. Two-button, single-breasted. Black, *possibly* navy. Nothing flashy or colorful. No brown."

"I have him trying on one right now you might like. The only thing I wasn't sure of is if you'd want a tie or bowtie."

"I don't know how to tie either," Crue says as he yanks the curtain to one side.

Both Thierry and I press a hand to our chests.

I barely hear him mutter an aghast, "Those are basic skills every man should possess."

In a black suit and crisp white undershirt, Crue looks like he could waltz right into any ball, festival, or luncheon, no questions asked. He has a timeless quality about him. Drop him in any era and he'd fit right in. The fifties, nineties, today…he just fits.

Without looking away from him, I tell Thierry, "I can show him how."

"If he's going to wear a jacket, a semi-cutaway will sit properly with or without a tie."

The invisible line between me and Crue grows tighter, drawing me closer to him even though I'm completely immobile, unable to move anything other than my head as I nod to Thierry.

"I'll need an actual coat, too. Ever, can you pick one out?" Crue asks, causing my eyebrow to rise. I'm picking everything out.

"One coat, got it. Any accessories?" Thierry asks me.

"He doesn't need any."

"Agreed. However, a watch will make a nice point of interest while still giving an air of nonchalance."

"I have a watch," Crue argues.

Ignoring him, and that ugly thing on his wrist, I tell Thierry, "He'll need two. One for casual, one for formal."

"I'll go pull some options."

Thierry lingers a moment longer before disappearing from my periphery.

"You're insane," Crue says with a scan down his outfit.

"You're worth it."

He stops his perusal to look up at me, his eyebrows knitted together.

"Were you… Did you…" He shakes his head. "You didn't go to Hide and Keep…did you?"

The line snaps, causing reality to come crashing down over me, and I stumble forward a step. That was stupid. So fucking stupid.

I give my own head a shake. "Hide and what?"

"Hide and Keep. You know, the thing down at Knot's Family Corn Maze, where they give it over to college kids after Halloween, basically so they can fuck whoever they want while wearing a costume."

"Sounds desperate. You went to it?"

"Not exactly. I worked security at it."

Did you keep anyone? I yearn to ask because I have no idea what happened after I left. He could've.

Instead, I force a chuckle. "Goddess, look how far you've come." I gesture at him, then me. "Now you're Ever Munreaux's bodyguard."

After a long pause, he scoffs, saying, "Personal protection agent."

"Whatever title you use, *Major*..."

Shaking his head at the nickname, he turns around to face the mirror, a small grin curving his lips.

"You represent the Munreauxs now. And with that, comes the expectation to be your best at all times."

"What if I don't know what my best is yet?" he asks while tugging on his sleeve.

"Then do what I do and settle for looking it."

His eyes once again find mine in the reflection.

That was stupid, too. Or genius, if it lowered his defenses a little more.

"Well, at least you're succeeding at that."

"So you did notice?" I whisper, making us both laugh.

Crue's the first to sober, saying seriously, "I'd have to be dead not to."

Everyone assumes it's credentials that open doors, and while they do most of the time, looks and charm can get you just as far, sometimes farther. Now that Crue has all three, he could get hired anywhere after this.

That's what I tell myself as I sign the thirty-one-thousand-dollar bill. If I can't save my own future, at least I can help his.

CHAPTER 11

I'M JUST WALKING EVER UP TO THE FRONT DOOR WHEN "NEVER!" booms from the other side. Forgetting about the bags of clothes in my Bronco, I head inside with her.

Standing in the grand foyer, red-faced and slightly sweaty, is Arthur, glass half full of amber liquid in hand.

"My advisor just called. You spent thirty-one thousand dollars this afternoon."

Thirty-one *thousand* dollars? On me? She didn't let me see the total. I had no fucking clue that's how much it was or else I never would've accepted all that shit. I mean the watches… They were pieces of art on my wrist. And the underwear… Those felt like they were made for me. But the tailor-made suits, and the shirts that felt like butter, and the…

Fuck. I can't believe I let her spend over thirty thousand dollars on me. She made it feel like it was nothing though. She made me feel like I was…I don't know. Worthy? For once. The way she looked at me… No, not looked at. Marveled, like I was someone worth marveling at. And the way she treated me. I felt like I was her equal, not the piece of shit people in her tax bracket tend to treat people in mine like.

For a split second, it felt like she could've been the girl from Hide and Keep.

Unfortunately, she wasn't.

"I got a new dress for the gala," Ever surprises me by saying. She did? I didn't know that. I didn't know she even glanced at the women's side. She was in the men's section or with me the whole time. Not once did I lose track of her whereabouts in that store, fully fucking aware she might slip out if I did.

"What about the dress you bought last month?"

She shrugs. "I didn't like it anymore."

"You didn't like…" Arthur scoffs. "So now I'm out forty grand because you had to have the perfect dress?"

"I don't have to go at all," his daughter singsongs, her chin rising.

Eyes bulging, he sticks a finger in Ever's face, making her flinch.

I automatically take a step in her direction, my hand at my side gravitating toward her elbow so I can yank her out of the way in case… In case…

Arthur Munreaux wouldn't hit his own daughter…would he?

"You know how important this meeting is. You're going."

Meeting? I thought it was a gala.

Ever doesn't blink, just stares her father down, that chin still lifted.

"Then I'll go wearing whatever I want."

"Mr. Brantley?"

"Yes, sir?"

"Tell me about this dress my daughter just had to have."

Uh.

"She likes it a lot." Right? Otherwise she wouldn't be throwing such a fit about it.

"Will *others* like it?"

I don't know why the fuck he's saying others like that, but I didn't see any fucking dress to know what anyone would think of it. Still, Ever could make a potato sack sexy.

"I'm sure everyone will love it, sir."

"Everyone?" he parrots before leaning into his daughter's space and saying much quieter, "Is that true?"

"Of course. They'll *all* want to fuck me."

In an instant, the motorcycle mogul's spine becomes ramrod

straight. "I'd sew your lips together if I thought it'd keep you from being so vulgar."

I *really* dislike when he talks to her like this. It doesn't sound like a real threat, yet it doesn't exactly feel empty either.

"And kill me before the gala?" Ever beams like the prospect excites her.

Dying. Dying excites her. She's basically a peppy Wednesday Addams.

"Don't be dense, Never. A feeding tube could easily fit under a dress."

"So could a man's head."

"Not while your executive protection agent's around." He gives me a stern look that I dip my head at.

I'd like to see a motherfucker try.

"He can't be around all the time."

"Given the new sleeping arrangements, he most certainly can."

Ever takes an audible inhale, but exhales silently.

"You two will have to have dinner without me tonight. I have business," he says, completely moved on from the insane amount of money Ever blew in a matter of hours.

"I'm tired. I'll just eat in my room."

As she attempts to pass him, Arthur does something that halts her in her tracks. Grabs her wrist maybe.

"Chef Koch is a world-renowned chef, not a fast-food fry cook. You will eat where he can see you enjoying his cuisine."

"He cuts up fruits and vegetables for me. It's really not that serious."

"I don't care if he serves you a single speck of salt, you will sit at the dining room table and eat it with a grateful smile on your face."

With that, he storms out of the foyer.

Ever's wincing when I step forward but is quick to school her features.

"Are you okay? Did he…" It didn't look like he hurt her but…her body was blocking my view. Any man that can threaten his daughter with a chastity belt and a feeding tube, I wouldn't put it past him to grip her too hard—accidental or not.

"It's my shoes. They're killing me."

"Here. Take them off." I hold my arm out for her to grab on to.

She bypasses me and my arm. "Not until I get to my room."

"Why not right now if they're hurting you so bad?"

"Haven't you been paying attention?" She spins and walks backward with her arms out wide. "It's all about presentation!"

The last word echoes off the walls and high ceiling, closing in around me like a boa constricting the life out of me.

Turning around, she mutters, "See you at dinner," then glides up the stairs.

I wait until she's gone from sight to go back outside and unload the bags, making sure to check each one. None of them contain a dress.

I'm the only one in the formal dining room when Ever enters. Edwin seated me with an explanation of how Chef Koch operates, then disappeared. Whether he's lingering nearby or if he went somewhere else entirely, all I know is I've been alone ever since. There's music floating through speakers set in the ceiling, so at least it hasn't been silent.

Smiling tightly, Ever takes the seat across from me, her eyes stuck on the table between us.

Is she embarrassed? Because of her own behavior? Or Arthur's?

To even the playing field a little, I glance around and ask, "Do we put in our order or…"

One small chuckle escapes her lips as she finally looks at me directly, amusement illuminating her face.

I don't really care about making a fool of myself. As long as Ever looks at me like that, I'll do it every fucking day.

"No, Major. Edwin should've taken your preferences when you were hired. That's what the chef uses to plan each day's menu."

He did.

"I was pretty busy yesterday chasing after a car thief."

"Thief? I was planning on returning your precious car."

"You took it without permission. That's a thief."

"I never ask for permission. Only for forgiveness."

Based off Arthur's reaction earlier, I already suspected she lied about getting his permission for today's shopping spree, but now I know she did. And she definitely didn't ask for his forgiveness.

Or mine.

"I don't remember you asking for my forgiveness."

"Would you have given it to me?"

"I think…" I think if Ever asked, I'd forgive her anything. I shake my head. No wonder she's so fucking spoiled. "We'll never know unless you try."

She tilts her head one way, then the other, either sizing me up or weighing her options.

Come on, Ever Munreaux. Bend for me.

The door from the kitchen opens into the dining room, ending the moment.

"Hopefully you like whatever the chef prepared for tonight," Ever whispers just as Edwin steps through and lets in a man wearing a chef's uniform and carrying two plates.

I shrug and unroll my napkin, draping it over my lap. "I'm sure I will. I'm not picky."

"Only when it comes to matcha lemonade?"

Another involuntary shudder rolls through me, making Ever chuckle. That wasn't me being picky. That shit was gross. There's a reason sugar exists and I'm pretty sure it's to make matcha lemonade palatable.

Standing at the end of the table, the chef silently eyes both of us. Since I ate what was in the guesthouse's fridge last night, and he wasn't around this morning, this is my first time seeing him. Wrinkle-free black pants, pristine white chef's jacket, and ash-blond hair cut and styled in an Ivy League, he looks like he's in his late twenties, maybe a year or two older than me, but completely at ease in this world— more than I ever could—so he was most likely born into it.

A tic in his jaw, he waits until Ever's quiet to set one plate in front of her, droning, "Grilled chicken breast with a side of black beans."

I also spot some sliced kiwi on her plate, the only real color on there. All she had this morning was a banana, so at least she's getting some protein now.

My plate's next with a much livelier description of, "Bourbon pecan chicken with roasted grapes, smashed potatoes, a sprinkling of rosemary sea salt, and a drizzle of truffle oil."

Jesus fucking Christ, that's the fanciest shit I've ever heard. Who roasts grapes?

"Uh, thanks."

"My pleasure, Mr.—"

"It's Crue."

"Mr. Crue. I'm Ryan Koch. If there's anything I can make for you, day or night, please don't hesitate to come find me."

"It's just Crue. No Mr. So, you live here, too?"

"I do. I was out in the guesthouse up until yesterday."

"If you miss the guesthouse so bad, I'm sure Father would let you move back out there. Crue's already vacated it."

"I'm finding I quite prefer the new arrangement. It makes me more accessible should you all require my assistance during the night for…anything."

After a shrug, he returns to the end of the table while I try to figure out if there's more to that last word. Is Ever fucking around with the chef?

He's a handsome guy. Not exactly my type, considering he has a dick, but he's the kind of guy I could see Ever go for.

His hands behind his back, he remains planted, staring at us soundlessly.

What the fuck?

I've eaten at restaurants before, none as upscale as the Munreauxs frequent I'm sure, but I've never seen one of the cooks leave the kitchen, especially not to watch me fucking eat. Taking her fork, Ever spears a single bean and bites it off the tines.

"Mm. Delicious." Her tone is just as dry as Ryan's was about her meal.

She could be trying to throw me off by intentionally being an asshole to him.

Or she could just be an asshole to everybody. Her actions so far have been extremely assholish.

Except today.

I cut off a piece of chicken, add a pecan as well as a wrinkled grape below it, then slather the whole thing in sauce before shoveling it in my mouth, my expectations high. Every single one of them is exceeded the second the flavors burst on my tongue, the different textures a whole other experience than what I'm used to. What *is* this?

"It's amazing," I mumble out before my mouth is even empty, earning a grin from Ryan.

He turns his head to Ever. "Now that you don't have to stick to such a strict diet, Miss Munreaux, hopefully you'll allow me the honor of feeding you some, um, more."

Feeding her? Does he mean cooking for her?

"So I can sound like Crue, moaning around a mouthful of food?"

"I didn't moan," I shoot back even though I have no idea if I did or not. I hope I didn't. If I did, it'd be understandable. This guy's skills are undeniable. Ryan Koch can cook.

"You moaned."

I hold Ever's eyes for a beat. I thought we called truce earlier. Why is she calling me out like this? The moan was obviously involuntary.

Those azure eyes drop to my mouth, making my throat go dry.

I have to clear it to tell Ryan, "It's really good. Thanks, man."

"Thank *you*. I'll leave you two, uh, to… Yes. To it."

With a clumsy half-bow, he leaves the room.

Maybe he's not as comfortable as I assumed. Maybe he's awkward as hell, his words even more so.

"What kind of diet are you on?"

"The kind that keeps me in the air and off the ground. I'd rather eat this…" Ever gestures to her bland food. "…than ass."

I almost choke on my five-star food. I thought she was going to say mat. *I'd rather eat this than mat.* Not ass. That's the second time she's said something along those lines, but what does eating ass have to do with cheerleading?

"Probably helps you fit in dresses without trying them on, too."

"What are you talking about?" Ever asks between bites.

"You didn't try on any dresses today."

"Yeah, I know. So?"

"You told your dad you bought one."

"Oh, that dress. I special ordered it."

That explains why I didn't see it and why she feels so strongly about wearing it…but not why she just forgot all about it.

"Without getting fitted?"

She waves me off. "Thierry has my measurements on file."

"They don't change?"

"Not really. I have to walk around at a hundred pounds or less all the time."

"A hundred fucking pounds? Just to look good in your uniform?"

"It has nothing to do with that. At least not for me. Flyers have to worry about the amount of weight we're putting on our base's wrists."

"What's a base?" She went over the different kinds of teams with me but not the positions on those teams.

"Have you ever seen cheerleaders perform?"

"Yeah. Everyone has."

"No, I mean really watch them."

"I've watched them do their high kicks and—"

"Oh my Goddess. You mean you glanced over at them on the sidelines throughout sports games. Let me guess, to look up their skirts, right?"

I shrug. "Maybe. I don't know." *I definitely do because I definitely did.* "Look, boobs. Belly buttons. Short skirts. Pom-poms. Clapping. Shouting chants. That's what comes to mind when I think of cheerleaders. I don't know anything about flying or bases."

"That's like saying all wrestlers do is lie on top of each other."

"That's mostly what we do." We? "But they're not just lying there," I say, taking myself out of the equation. I haven't been a wrestler in a long time. "They're working simultaneously to get a pin and to not be pinned."

She eyes me another moment.

"Well, that's not all we're doing either."

"Really?"

"Clapping, shouting, and short skirts, yes. The rest, no."

"No boobs?"

"Some girls have those, but I don't. Most flyers don't. Our body fat's too low."

My eyes find her chest. She's got enough to fit my mouth around.

Jesus. I stuff a potato in that mouth, making damn sure I don't moan out loud because I could. I swear to God the inside is as fluffy as a cloud.

"Okay, so what's a base? And while you're at it, what's a flyer?"

"I'm a flyer."

"Obviously."

"So, I'm at the top of the pyramid. The one basically doing acrobatics in the air. A base is the person that puts me in the air. They lift me, throw me, and hold my stunts."

"Does it hurt?"

"If I land hard, yeah, it can. But mostly when I fall."

"How often do you fall?"

"Never."

"Is that why your dad calls you Never?"

"No. That'd require him to actually know something about me." She scoffs through a headshake. "He calls me that because I'll *never* stop being a disappointment to him."

"I'm sure that's not true."

"Ask him yourself." She shrugs like it doesn't sting, but how could it not? That's her parent, the only one she's got.

I take my time eating some more. I don't know what I'd do without my parents' support, especially these past several years.

"If you don't fall, how'd you get so many injuries?" She listed a fuckton yesterday and I'm guessing that's not all she's suffered.

"Being dropped. Other people falling. Being tackled by football players. A basketball bouncing off my head."

I crack up.

"What?"

"A basketball? That kind of shit doesn't happen to people like you." Perfect people don't have embarrassing moments.

"I swear. I'm surprised during all your online stalking, you didn't come across videos of it. It was posted from, like, twenty different angles."

"Remember, if I'm a stalker, so are you." She fucking looked me up, too. What she read wasn't even the whole truth but I'm sure she thinks it is. Everybody else does.

She's quiet for a while after that, then softer, she asks, "What about you? Did your weight yo-yo? When you were a wrestler?"

"A bit. I did my fair share of cutting, but I wrestled in a class close enough to my natural weight that I didn't have to go to the extremes some guys did to make weight. Because of that I never really gorged afterward either."

"Were you any good?"

"You should know—"

"I didn't look up everything. I'm not actually a stalker."

"Neither am I."

"Okay." She drops her fork on her empty plate and leans back, crossing her arms. "Fine. Neither of us are stalkers."

"Great. Glad we cleared that up."

I go back to eating.

"And..."

I look up. "And...what?"

She rolls her eyes. "Were you any good?"

"Yeah. I was." Really good. But one bad call and my entire wrestling career went up in flames. I've been sifting through the ashes ever since.

"Are you any good at cheerleading?"

I'm about to take a bite when she repeats my answer, just much quieter.

"Yeah. I was."

My hand freezes partway to my mouth.

"You have another performance for this season, right? The Flower Fest?"

"Right. One more." She covers her widening mouth with the back of her hand. "I'm gonna head upstairs to bed."

"I'll walk you up." I stand before my plate's even clean.

"I'm not going anywhere, Major. I really am tired. You can stay and finish your meal. I'll see you in the morning."

"I'll walk you up," I repeat. The best chicken in the world couldn't stop me.

When we reach her door, she pulls out a key to unlock a different knob than the one that was there this morning.

"Where'd that one come from?"

Ever looks from the key to me. "Edwin didn't tell you? He went ahead and had a lock installed after all."

"No, he didn't." I don't like that he didn't. I don't like that he went behind my back either. I said I'd do it. If I hadn't been so busy earlier, I would've.

"Well, goodnight."

Once again, she barely cracks the door before sliding through.

I stop her from closing it though, my palm flat on the thick wood.

"Just so you know, I removed the sensor off one of my windows, too."

Do I believe she's tired? Fuck yeah. We both slept like shit last night. But that doesn't mean I believe she won't try sneaking out.

"You planning on going somewhere tonight, Major?" While her tone is light, her expression is murderous.

"Only if you are," I promise, then head next door.

I go straight to the window I took the sensor off and open it a few inches. It smells musty in here anyway. I noticed it when I got back from shopping, too. Probably from no one staying in it. Arthur told me it used to be Ever's nanny's room but that nobody's been in it since Ever's eighteenth birthday. That was a year and a half ago.

Butting the side of the armchair up against the corner of the window, I fall into it, the last couple days catching up to me. I hope to fuck she's as tired as she says. Even if she's not, I'll be right here, watching for her. From this angle, I can't see her window, but I can see if someone tries scaling the wall below it. I'll be out mine and after her before she can reach the ground.

Ever Munreaux's days of sneaking out are officially over.

Something is moving. Something is close. Something…isn't right.

My eyes pop open.

Open? They were closed?

Shit! I must've dozed off.

Heart racing, I push to standing and wrench the window up the rest of the way. Sticking my head out, I see Ever's window still closed. A scan below reveals no one. Nothing on the driveway either.

If it wasn't her, then what was it? I sensed…something.

Lowering the window halfway, I settle back into the chair and scrub a hand down my face.

I *thought* I sensed something. I could've sworn I did.

Was it just a dream? Could've been.

Must've been.

When I pull my hand away, I catch movement out of the corner of my eye and look over to see a small…something…flying around the room. A bird? I squint through the darkness, straining to see it better. Its flight pattern isn't like any bird I've ever seen and its wings… They're almost like a bat's.

My eyes lift, then the rest of my head. The ceiling is fucking moving. It's *moving*.

It is a fucking bat. And it's not alone.

One dips down close to my head.

"Fuck!" I run through the room, out the door, almost knocking Ever over.

Ever?

"What's wrong?"

"What are you doing out here?"

"I heard you yell and came out to see if everything was okay. You look like you've seen a ghost."

"Not a ghost. Bats."

"Bats?"

"My room is full of them."

"You're sure? How would they have gotten in there?"

"I don't know," I tell her.

"They might've already been in there. No one goes in that room anymore, so they could have a whole roost."

I gag, that fancy dinner threatening to make a reappearance. A roost. But wouldn't I have noticed? It's unlikely. I didn't spend very much time in there today. And bats are nocturnal. They do all their activity at night.

"Shit."

"What?"

"They could've got in through the window. I left it open."

"Is it still open now?"

"Somewhat."

"Maybe they'll fly back out of it," Ever offers.

"But how long will that take? All my shit's in there." My phone. All the new clothes Ever just bought me. Everything.

"We could try to guide them out."

"What?" She would do that for me? I shake away the idea. "No, you can't go in there. What if one bites you? I'll go. Just…" I glance past her, down the hall. "I need something long. A broom, maybe."

"You can't use a broom," Ever's quick to say. "That could hurt them."

"Hurt *them*? Ever, they're in my fucking room."

"It's not their fault they got lost, *Crue*. They could be on the endangered list."

"My ceiling wouldn't be fucking crawling with them if they were endangered."

"Well, they could still be on a special concern list."

"Special concern list?" She's more worried about the bats?

"What? If they are, that'd look bad for my father."

It's not like I *want* to hurt anything. There are bats in my goddamn bedroom.

"Whatever. What about one of those skimmer tools for the pool?"

"It'd be in the pool house. But we'd have to turn off the alarm and I don't know the code. I could go out my wind—"

"No." I do not trust her to leave this house.

"Okay, well, I saw Edwin taking a net down to the basement once. I don't know what it's for but it had a long handle."

"Show me."

"I can go get it myself if you want to go open your window all the way and see if any will fly out on their own."

"All right, yeah." As long as she's in the manor, she can't go anywhere.

I face my bedroom door. With a warning to be careful, Ever turns to leave. After taking several deep breaths, mentally and physically preparing myself, I open the door and dart through to the other side, my head ducked low. I get the window open, then return to the hall, no Ever in sight. I wait for her for several minutes before going in search of her.

I saw Edwin taking a net down to the basement once.

That doesn't mean he left it down there. Even if he did, she might need help locating it. If the basement's anything like the rest of the manor, it's huge.

Before I reach the stairs though, I'm intercepted by a silk-pajama-clad Edwin.

"Can I help you, Mr. Brantley?"

"Have you seen Ever?"

"No, sir. I'm just headed to the kitchen for a glass of water. Is… something the matter?"

"I woke up to bats in my room."

"Bats?" He gives me a quizzical look but not a worried one. Bats are *in* the manor and the only person freaking out is me.

"Ever went to get the net."

"The net?"

"Yeah, do you know where it is? She's taking forever, so she must be having a hard time finding it."

"The only net I'm aware of is the one in the pool house."

"What about the one you put in the basement?"

"I apologize but I have no idea what net you're referring to."

"No, no, no, no, no." I take off, back up the stairwell to our rooms, going to Ever's first. I bang on her door, demanding, "Ever, open up."

I try the handle with no luck because, of fucking course, it's locked.

"I see you got her a lock."

I glare at the valet wisely giving me several feet of space.

"What do you mean? She said you did."

"I would've been happy to but it was my understanding you intended to."

"Then who…" I glare at Ever's door and pound both fists on it. "Ever!" She fucking lied about the lock. She lied about the net. What else did she lie about? Probably that special concern list bullshit.

It doesn't matter. I don't care what list those bats are on because they just made my shit list.

"You got a broom, Edwin?"

"Yes…" he drawls, the first bit of worry entering his tone since I ran into him. "May I ask what the broom will be used for?"

I thrust a hand toward my room. "There are bats in my room." How many more times do I need to fucking say it?

"I'm afraid I'm unable to fulfill your request. Miss Munreaux would be very upset."

"That you gave me a broom?"

"That I gave you a broom with the intent to harm her bats."

"*Her* bats? They're not her bats. They came in through the…" That odor. The one I smelled before I even opened the window. It wasn't there this morning but it was there after I'd been gone all day. Which Ever was with me the whole time…except when she wasn't. When she was in her three-hour long class. That she got out of early.

I poke my head in my room and flick on the light. Among at least twenty dark, white-tinged-fur creatures are slim wooden boxes, the very ones I saw in the woods yesterday, now nailed to the top of my black walls, high enough up that I wouldn't easily notice them unless I was actively seeking them out. Fuck!

Crossing the room over to my window, I spot her immediately. In the middle of the driveway, like an apparition herself, is Ever fucking Munreaux. She raises a hand to her mouth, kissing it maybe, but when she goes to send it my way, all her fingers curl until only the middle is up and she's flipping me off. Twisting around, she takes off down the driveway, disappearing into the dead of night.

"Fucking bitch," I mutter before climbing out after her.

By the time I make it to the front gates, she's long gone.

"Motherfucker!"

Today everything Ever did, everything she said, every single interaction that transpired between us was a complete ruse. I can't trust *anything* about her, not her words, her actions, nothing.

Ever Munreaux is a liar, a manipulator, and a cock-fiend.

And I fucking hate her guts.

CHAPTER 12

Dressed in one of his brand-new outfits, Crue's waiting outside my bedroom when I emerge the next morning. From the neck down, he looks absolutely delectable. From the neck up though, my bodyguard's looking a little worse for wear if I do say so myself.

His bloodshot eyes don't lift any higher than my knees as he sticks out a hand, suggesting I go ahead of him.

That's it? He's not going to chew me out for what I did last night? I went to great lengths to sneak out unnoticed. I went to even greater lengths relocating those bats to his room.

I stop and wait for him to let me have it.

Not so much as a nibble, I throw him a bigger piece of bait, asking, "Rough night, Major?"

Still, his mouth remains an angry slash.

"Hmm. That makes two of us." I smooth out my tan-and-black plaid bodycon skirt. "I don't know if I'm drunk still or just really hungover." It's not that bad. I didn't feel like running this morning, but I could've if I made myself.

Crue's temples pulsing is the only reaction he gives.

I consider telling him about the guy I let feast on my neck like a newly turned vampire.

He'll see the evidence for himself soon enough…now that he sleeps right. Next. Door.

Father's already seated at the breakfast table in the kitchen, a pile of documents in front of him, his steaming breakfast next to those.

"Father," I chirp as I take the seat on his right.

"Never." He doesn't look up from his reports.

Crue sits to my father's left, directly across from me, but doesn't let his gaze wander past the table runner between us.

Opposite Father is a wall of glass with an unobstructed view of the sea. Dinner's always in the formal dining room, the walls the only thing to look at, but breakfast is served in here where we can focus on something other than each other. I lock my eyes on the thick fog clinging to the water. I've always liked the fog. Some people find it eerie, but to me, it's comforting.

Instantly, Chef Ryan appears tableside to serve both of us. His foot bumps mine under the table and I have to stop myself from standing up and slapping him across the face. The only reason I don't is because then my skin would be touching his.

After getting his coveted first reactions to his creations, Chef Ryan excuses himself.

My father doesn't ask Crue about his first night in the manor because that'd require him to act like he cares, which he truly does not, so the three of us eat breakfast in complete silence, my small plate of diced cantaloupe and strawberries the first to disappear while Father and Crue take a bit longer to eat their eggs Benedict, home fries, and whatever else Chef Ryan made for them. I stopped listening once I heard the chef's voice. His over-the-top descriptions always sound so self-congratulatory.

I wait until Crue has just enough left that he can't finish it in one bite to get up and announce, "Off to school." I'm not sure how much sleep he got last night, if any, but he doesn't deserve a full breakfast either. He would get both sleep and full meals if he'd stayed in the guesthouse.

Without complaint, my bodyguard stands from the table, leading the way out to his Bronco. While he does still open the passenger door for me, he does it pretending I don't exist.

The ride to school is void of sound but full of tension so thick I'm practically choking on it when we pull into Lit U.

This time Crue literally escorts me to each of my classrooms, waiting at every threshold until I'm seated inside before turning to go…somewhere. Wherever he goes, it's close by because his face is the first thing I see whenever the door's opened at the end of class.

At the end of the day, he meets me at the door holding two drinks, one green, one tan.

The gesture makes me smile.

Until he holds the green one out to me, and after taking a small sip, my joy wanes significantly at the familiar flavor.

"What'd you get?" I ask him, hoping he'll answer but not expecting him to.

He takes a long swallow. Just when I think he's not going to respond, he says, "Iced chai latte with almond milk and three pumps of pumpkin brown sugar."

His first words of the day to me and they're to gloat about enjoying the exact drink I would love to have but can never actually order for myself.

Staring him down, I walk over to the nearest garbage can and toss the matcha lemonade in. Without taking his eyes off mine, Crue comes right up to me and throws his out, too. He didn't even want it?

He ordered it just to spite me.

I seethe all the way back to the parking lot, my heart thundering so loud I almost miss him catching up to me in time to get the door.

Inside the Bronco, I practically rip my shoes off my feet and blindly toss them into the backseat. Crue cranes his neck to glare at them, then does the same thing to me, the muscle in his jaw twitching the whole time, but again, he doesn't say anything. Not one fucking word. Not during the drive, or at the manor when we pull up. So, before he's even stopped, I reach back and grab my shoes, making sure to swing them wide when I bring them up front and whack Crue in the face.

And when he looks at me, clearly wanting some sort of apology, I give him the same treatment by keeping my lips zipped shut. I'm not sorry anyway. Not for any of it. Not for the bats. Not for sneaking out. Not for the thin line of blood blooming from the new slice across his cheek.

My heels did that? I wasn't trying to—

I mean, good. Serves him right.

He can impose on every part of my life, even my sleep, but he can't talk to me?

The bats didn't have any interest in him anyway, only bugs, so why is he so damn butthurt?

Because he was bested by a girl? He should get used to that now. I've done it before—we're sitting in the pink-flamed proof—and I'll probably do it many, many more times before his stay at Munreaux Manor concludes.

Or was it because said besting made him look like an incompetent idiot? Well, he is. And technically, he did that himself when he researched how to be a bodyguard his first night being a bodyguard.

Now at my door, Crue's waiting for me to exit.

"I need help putting my shoes on," I say.

His gaze drops to mine, incredulity written across his features without him even needing to open his mouth.

"What? I'm serious. I can't get it. They're…" I act like I can't reach the right foot, then do the same thing with the left one. "Ugh. My skirt's too tight."

"Go barefoot."

He returns his attention elsewhere. Anywhere but near me.

"I can't do that."

He gives no response, as if I didn't even speak.

"It's your job to protect me, isn't it? What if there's a screw on the ground?"

Crue examines the driveway halfheartedly but doesn't budge.

"Then I guess you're carrying me inside, *all* the way up to my room."

Shaking his head, he breaks posture to snatch a shoe from my grasp.

My triumphant smirk dies the moment his hand wraps around

my right ankle and yanks my foot off the floor, forcing me to rotate in the seat toward him to accommodate the odd angle. My left leg stays where it is though and I don't rush to close my legs, so I'm as spread eagle as my tight skirt allows, my panties rubbing against my suddenly aching center.

Crue either doesn't notice as he jams the expensive stiletto on my foot, his eyes glued to the ankle strap like it's some sort of puzzle, or he's pretending not to.

"Second hole."

That gaze flies to my crotch before slowly rising to my face, his nostrils flaring with each labored exhale.

He was pretending.

And I'm wet, picturing him looking at my pussy without the barrier. Admiring it. Flicking it with his tongue, his lips, his entire fucking face as I hold him to—

"What?" he snaps, breaking the fantasy before I soak my underwear straight through.

"The prong goes in the second hole on the strap."

It takes him several tries and even more curses, but he finally gets the shoe secured before moving on to my left foot, except I don't lift my leg for him, so he has to reach over my lap to get it himself. The side of his face only inches from mine, I spy a bead of sweat rolling down his temple.

The temptation too strong, I catch it with the side of my thumb.

Suddenly, there's a great pressure just under my palm.

"Don't. Touch. Me," Crue grits out, his hand squeezing my wrist.

I hadn't even noticed. I was so absorbed.

Sticking the thumb in my mouth, I suck it clean.

"Mm," I moan around the tiny blast of salt against my tongue, my eyes fluttering closed. "If your sweat tastes this good, I can only imagine what your…" I open my eyes to find Crue's locked on mine. "Tears taste like. You might just make a worthy opponent after all, Major."

Crue releases my wrist like it caught fire.

"I'm not your opponent, miss. I'm your personal protection agent.

And crying's for pussies." He nods toward my lap, his top lip curled. "Like yours is doing right now."

She's crying all right, absolutely pleading for Crue's touch, the one he gave so freely five months ago but looks revolted to have to give now… Now that the cloth mask's been replaced by a less visible yet much more permanent one.

Is it jealousy that has him so worked up today? You can admire a waterfall without ever considering taking a dip. The only thing Crue Brantley seems interested in is becoming my dam.

I watch him work on my other shoe, my thumb still up to my mouth as I repeatedly drag it back and forth across my bottom lip.

As soon as he's done, Crue drops my foot.

"Goddess, your bedside manner could use some work."

"How can I ever be at your bedside when you're never in it?"

"Touché."

"Also, you locked your fucking door."

"And got both keys," I add, quite proud of myself.

"I would've given you both."

He actually looks wounded that I didn't give him the opportunity, but he would've needed to go inside my bedroom to install a new handle and that's a risk I was unwilling to take.

Now that he's talking to me, at least somewhat, I inquire about the bats.

"They're out," is all he gives me.

"How'd you get them out?"

"It doesn't matter."

"It does to me. Remember that whole speech you gave? What's important to me is important to you?"

"If they were so important to you, you shouldn't've stuck two dozen in my room before skipping off into the night."

An unladylike snort rips out of me before I can stop it. "I didn't skip anywhere. You saw me."

"I saw Satan's spawn returning to the hell she belongs."

"If that's where I belong, why are you trying so hard to keep me here?"

"Because it's my job."

"Do you have to be such a dickhead while doing it?"

"No." He drops his gaze.

Right as I expect him to offer up another apology, Crue looks at me, and says, "But it feels so much better when I am," throwing my own smartass comeback in my face.

"Move," I bark as I pass him, my left ankle buckling almost instantly. *What?* I glance down to see Crue fastened the strap wrong. He did the first hole, not the second. And if the partially smothered chuckle behind me is anything to go by, it wasn't accidental.

Dickhead.

I need space. Privacy. I need color and hope in a dull, depressing world. I need to know flight's still possible even if I'm not the one in the air.

"I'll meet you in the dining room for dinner," I call to him.

"Where are you going?"

"I'm staying on the estate."

"Where?"

Crue's voice is closer than it was. Than it should be. I told him where, so why is he following me?

"I'm going for a swim."

"Where's your suit?"

"Don't need one. You saw for yourself, my panties are already drenched. A little pool water's nothing."

"Miss, you can't swim in your underwear," he gnashes in warning.

I ignore that as I round to the back of the manor because it's *not* my name. Also, what's the big deal? My underwear covers the exact same things my swimsuit does. He just did the same thing the other day.

"Ever," comes out in a growl that sends a shiver up my spine, not in fear, but in…something else. Something that makes my panties even wetter.

"I'm not going off property. Isn't that good enough?"

"No, it's not, and you fucking know it. Stop being so difficult."

"You asked for it," I mutter because he literally did. More than once.

When I reach the atrium, I pause outside the door and face Crue. He approaches me like a bull in a ring, all snarly and pissed off.

"This isn't the pool."

I pat his head exactly like he did mine. Well, I try to. Even in heels, I'm still shorter than him. It doesn't help that he bats my hand away with one easy swipe.

"Good job, Crue. Maybe tomorrow you can—"

"I need to see what's in there."

"No, you don't."

"It's my fucking job to protect—"

"There's nothing in there that can hurt me. I promise."

"You're a pathological liar. Your promises don't mean shit to me."

We hold a stare-off, neither of us willing to back down.

"Don't follow me inside. I mean it. I'll stab you."

He laughs. "With what? Your fucking high heels? You already tried that—"

I stomp on his foot, making sure the sharp heel lands on his toes, hopefully piercing at least one.

"Shit!"

I close the door on his doubled-over form, then lock it. After a couple calming breaths that fill my lungs with the balmy eighty-degree air, I turn around and go through the second door, a genuine smile splitting my face. Dropping my head back, my eyes lift to see hundreds of butterflies flitting about overhead. It's mostly silent in here, but if you listen closely, you can hear the light fluttering of wings.

Hundreds more hide in plain sight—on tree branches, the floor, the walls, rocks around the koi pond set into the center. There are fewer than thirty indoor butterfly atriums in America, this being the only one in Connecticut. Housing both tropical flora and butterflies from all over the world, these three thousand square feet are not just the butterflies' sanctuary, but mine as well. I don't have to be anything other than myself in here. I don't have to say anything I don't want to. I don't have to *do* anything I don't want to. It's one of the few places that I feel free.

A common birdwing lands on my sleeve, using its two front legs to taste me.

"Hi."

Even though I don't have nectar, the black-and-golden-yellow butterfly remains where it is, content to hitch a ride for a while.

Tears fill my eyes as I'm suddenly overcome with an enormous sense of gratitude for this insect's trust in me. Aside from making outfit choices, nobody trusts me with anything.

Without jostling my stowaway, I carefully remove my shoes, then watching where I step, I start checking each feeder, removing any rotten fruit peels and making sure there's enough sugar water to keep the sponges wet. Weaving between the plumeria tree and some pentas shrubs, I breeze by the garden of wildflowers, slowing next to a Queen Anne's lace to watch a black swallowtail emerging from its chrysalis.

Since the atrium's creation eight years ago, I've had over six hundred different types of butterfly species in it. With my nanny's help, I used to order chrysalides from a supplier that imports them from a number of other countries, but I cut back after she left, and now most of the butterflies flying around were laid by their own mothers. From egg to caterpillar to chrysalis to butterfly, I've witnessed thousands of life cycles in this atrium.

For the most part, I'm the only one who gets to. Even if I did have friends over, I wouldn't share this with any of them. They wouldn't get it. Other than snapping some selfies for their feeds, they probably wouldn't even care. It's a secret I hold close to my heart.

Crue used to be another. I guess, technically, he still is. Well, our first meeting is. The night he protected me because he wanted to, not because he was being paid to. The night he saw me as something other than my last name. The night he touched me, held me, kissed me, and…cherished me. That's how Crue's attention felt. Like I was a treasure all on my own, no price tag required.

And now, after catching a glimpse of that expensive label, he'll never look at me the same way again.

I'd rather him look at me with hate in his eyes than the same dollar signs I detect in everyone else's. At least hate is complex, not one solitary emotion but a combination of several.

I've never gone hungry a day in my life, yet since my nanny's "retirement," I feel just as starved as if I had. If I'll never so much as get a taste of love again, what other choice do I have but to gorge on hatred? Desperate people take desperate measures, and at this point, I'll accept anything to fill the bottomless pit in my stomach.

All the chores taken care of, I sit on the bench near the pond. The three-foot-deep pool has its own small waterfall trickling into it, adding oxygen to the water for the fish as well as ambience for… me. Now. More people used to come in here. My mother, for one. And my father when she'd make him. He had this atrium built to not only cheer her up but also get her out of the house. It worked. Until it didn't. My nanny, Winnie, and I took on the upkeep. Nowadays, it's just me, unless I'm out of town, then I have to rely on Edwin to check on things.

The common birdwing on my arm flew away at some point, making me stowaway-free. Next to me is a dead owl butterfly though, its large wings open, making it appear like a set of owl eyes eerily tracking me. A butterfly's lifespan after they eclose from the chrysalis stage is usually only about three to four weeks, so every time I come in here, I find at least a handful of dead ones. While it's completely natural, it doesn't make the discoveries any easier. Whenever Winnie and I would stumble across a lifeless carcass, she'd share a different meaning behind seeing dead butterflies. It wasn't until recently that I learned she only told me about the positive premonitions, hiding the bad omens from me. Once I found out deceased butterflies also symbolize feeling trapped, suffocated in your own cocoon, that's the one I think about most. It's kinda hard not to given my current predicament.

A trio of blue morphos flap right past my cheek, their brilliant blue wings spectacular. For how eye-catching they are, they're nearly impossible to physically catch. After many failed attempts to catch the fast butterfly myself, now I just wait for one to take a rest near me to admire it up close. I have yet to be lucky enough for one to land on me.

The owl butterfly tugs my attention back to it. A sign of re-pressing your creative side is another meaning for coming across a dead butterfly. I haven't sketched anything in over a week, since before Nationals. I haven't drawn an owl butterfly with both wings showing yet. The huge eyespots would look good in charcoal.

I clean up a little more, then head out the way I came, making sure to lock the door behind me. For the first time all day, Crue isn't waiting for me and I don't know how to feel about it. It's positively stifling, having him around all the time. But it's also…less lonely. As much as I hate to admit that, it's true. I didn't have siblings growing up, but I did have Winnie, and I guess my mother—sometimes—so I've never felt true loneliness until this past year. The day I turned eighteen, my father let my nanny go, a severance check in one hand, a restraining order in the other. When I asked about the restraining order, he shrugged, like it was commonplace to give them to loyal, longtime employees. Winnie was my sole caretaker from the moment I was brought home from the hospital. Eighteen years later, she was ripped from my life. Poof. Gone. Like she was never even here.

When I begged him to let me call her, just call her, he told me I was an adult and it was time for her and I both to move on.

I wasn't ready to move on. I still very much needed her. If I'm being completely honest, I still do. My eighteenth birthday wasn't some special day where I woke up magically knowing everything. Even at nineteen I find myself wishing I had someone to go to for advice, guidance, or just…a hug, a hair tuck and gentle smile, any sort of tenderness whatsoever.

My father wants me cold, hard, a professional with her eye on the objective.

I'm not a sniper. I'm a nineteen-year-old student athlete with interests and needs and wants and…dreams? Once upon a time I had lots of dreams. Dreams of putting some of our fortune to good use. Not anymore though. Now I know better. The only good thing about Arthur Munreaux was his wife, my mother, Alette Munreaux. With her died any humanity my father might've had, leaving behind an unhinged version of the man I grew up around. He used to be somewhat decent, but like Winnie once said, "Even butterflies need gravity, otherwise they'd drift into space." My mother was his gravity, the one thing keeping him grounded. Without her, he's drifted. After Hide and Keep, I forced myself to stop looking for glimpses of redemption in him. He's eternally lost to me.

No sign of him, or my bodyguard, I go straight upstairs uninterrupted. The door to my bedroom is locked, yet the moment I step inside, I can feel another presence. While my body freezes in place, my eyes begin moving—rapidly. Searching every square inch of the dark room, I finally land on an outline of a head and shoulders sticking out above my oversized armchair.

Poking my keys between my fingers, I warn, "I won't make it easy for you."

A soft puff of humor dances between us until it reaches me, obnoxiously tapping its feet on my chest.

5, 6, 7, 8.

"You don't make *anything* easy..."

Crue?

"Except making you drip." That head shadow quickly tilts, then rights itself. "I did that without even trying."

Crue's voice somehow makes the tempo over my ribs increase. He's *in* my room.

He's in my room?

"But, just like your stamina, it was short-lived. I'm all dried up now," I inform him.

Relaxing my grip on my keys, I spin around and study the surface of my dresser...and all the crap on it.

"You don't know shit about my stamina."

"Is that why you're sitting in my bedroom? Alone. In the dark. So you can prove your stamina to me?"

He's not here to rape me. He's one of the good guys. Unfortunately, I have to treat him like a bad one, otherwise...

Otherwise.

I light one of the candles with thick drips down the sides, not only to see better but also because beeswax candles cleanse the air by releasing natural ions and Crue's negative energy is practically palpable. I'm not sure I would've sensed him so quickly if it wasn't.

"No. I'm in here for other reasons."

"Which are?"

Using the low light, I sweep my dresser's contents, searching for anything embarrassing. I already hid the mask from Hide and Keep, so there shouldn't be anything incriminating out. Clusters of crystals, more candles, several sets of tarot cards, my most recently pulled oracle cards, a stack of books, a moss-covered fairy door. The door itself isn't embarrassing but the story behind it is. I used to take it out to the woods and pretend it opened to other places. I'd mentally escape to fantastical worlds with kind princes, skies full of dragons, oceans you can go right up to and touch. I don't know why I kept it. Maybe as a sign of hope? Looking at it now, it only makes me sad. And yes, a little embarrassed. Not because I used to have an active imagination, but because I ever believed there was a way out of the world I was born into.

"To figure out what's in that building that made you threaten me."

Now my humor escapes me. It wasn't just a threat.

"How are your toes, by the way?"

I turn back around to face him, my palms on the dresser behind me, the candle to my side flickering out a nice hazy glow, enough to highlight Crue...and the object in his possession.

Any trace of humor evaporates in an instant, that tiny dancer on my chest turning to a hundred-pound boulder, making it difficult to draw in air.

"Where did you find that?" I choke out.

Crue doesn't blink. "It's a conservatory. A butterfly conservatory."

"Where. Did. You. Find. *That?*"

"Oh, this?" My bodyguard lifts my sketchbook off his lap and regards it like he forgot it was even there. "It was lying around."

"It was under my bed," I snap.

He nods. "It was lying around..." His head stops moving. "Under your bed."

I was worried about a childish fairy door, meanwhile my floor held one of my worst secrets of all. He was never supposed to make it inside this room. The lock on my door—

The lock.

"How'd you get in here?"

"Same way you do on the nights you sneak out. Through the window."

I…never considered that. I never considered the possibility of someone other than me coming through my window.

I'm lucky it was only Crue.

Although, this feels like a different kind of invasion. That's *my* intellectual property and I did not consent to him so much as touching it, let alone…seeing it. Did he look inside? He must've to know about the butterfly atrium.

He looked inside. But how much?

"I thought you'd be happy finding me in here?"

He saw it all. Oh my fucking Goddess. He *saw*.

"Why's that?" I ask, playing dumber than dumb.

In answer, Crue opens the book to a sketch of his full torso, his head turned to the side, a hand on his rock-hard abs, and I let my shoulders droop, my breaths finally coming easier.

It's the newest sketchbook. The one before this had sketches of him in his costume from Hide and Keep. After a while though, that got old, so I started focusing on different parts of him, trying to see if I could imagine what he looked like without the costume.

He starts flipping the pages, lingering momentarily on sketches of butterflies, the atrium, and the sea, all between every angle imaginable of Crue.

I drew *all* parts of him, which is mortifying, yes, but not incriminating. Nothing in this sketchbook puts me at Hide and Keep. I can act like I crossed paths with him somewhere else.

Eyebrows nearly touching as he continues perusing my private artwork, he questions, "How are there *so* many? Is this all you do once you close your door?"

He thinks these were all drawn in the last couple days.

I don't date my drawings. That's my one saving grace here. I don't care if he thinks I'm a manic stalker. It's better than him knowing the truth.

I force my feet to move in his direction.

The sputtering flame the only noise in the room, Crue hears my shoes against the hardwood floor and lifts his head to watch my approach.

"I'm sure you've noticed…" I gently slide the book out of his grasp and start thumbing through the pages myself, his gaze from below merciless. "…that I have a fascination with the underprivileged."

I snap the book shut, and using both hands, slap him across the face with it, making his head whip to the side viciously, his cheek already looking as inflamed as mine feel.

Without righting his head, he says, "It must kill you."

That I'll never know if you'd like me for me?

That I'll never know if anyone likes me for me?

That my father will never let anyone like me for me?

That I can't grab your face and kiss you until my lungs give out?

Yes. It kills me. It all fucking kills me.

"What?" I ask, staring at the lips I'd give anything to feel on mine again.

Slowly, he rotates his head back to look at me. "To know you'll never actually be able to see what my cock looks like hard."

"Because you're impotent?"

He shoves to his feet, putting us only inches apart. I have to crane my neck way back to meet his gaze, but I do it, because I refuse to be intimidated by him.

With his eyes flicking between mine, he says, "Only around you," then brushes past me.

"That's gonna make for a dry three years," I mutter just to rub salt in the wound while I can.

"For both of us."

I can't help my chuckle at his arrogance.

"Not for me. I—"

"No longer have a way to sneak out and get dick." Crue doesn't break stride, only sticks an arm out to his side, pointing at the window he came through. "That was another reason for being in here. I put sensors on both your windows, along with your door. You so much as tap one of the surfaces and it'll alert my phone."

He drums his fingers on the door on his way out, then holds his phone up over his shoulder for me to see the screen light up with a notification.

With a screamed, "Stay out of my fucking room!" I throw my sketchbook at the back of his head. Unfortunately, it hits the closed door a second too late before falling to the floor, sheets of paper strewn all around it.

"Ugh!" I stomp into my bathroom and grab the edge of the granite counter with both hands, pulling like I'm able to rip the whole thing off. Strange noises gurgle in the back of my throat as I attempt to keep it all in.

I am an animal.

This is my cage.

I'm being herded exactly where he wants me.

I don't have a choice. I don't have any choices.

I never have.

I never will.

This is my life.

This is my life.

This is…

I bow my head and sob as silently as I can, that boulder from before so heavy it's hard to stay upright, making the floor seem like a really, really nice place to rest.

If I let myself though, even for a moment, I will never get back up.

Slowly, I lift my head, then my eyes, all the way up to the top right corner of my mirror, to the sticky note there. I mentally repeat the affirmation…

We can't change what we were born, only what we become.

Then I move to the next note, reciting that one…

I deserve good things to come to me.

And each one after it…

I'm doing my best, and that is enough.

I stand up for myself.

I am inherently worthy of love.

I will live in the moment today and not stress about my past or worry about the future.

My needs matter.

I matter.

…until I've read the entire frame of affirmations.

With my breathing regulated, my grip on the counter relaxes enough for my hands to fall away, limp at my sides.

I can't focus on what's coming, only what's happening right now. In this moment, I need to relax.

I turn the handle for the bathtub to Hot, then light white beeswax pillar candles and place them around the rim. Something…off… catches my eye and I look down to see the water becoming whiter and thicker?

Bubbles?

It's not foaming.

Epsom salt?

But mine smells like lavender. This smells like nothing really. Maybe a hint of cardboard. Kind of papery.

I drag my hand through it, noticing something's definitely wrong. The water's not even liquid. It's more of a…paste.

Ew.

I turn the handle back the opposite way with my clean hand.

"What the…" I mutter while studying my mush-coated fingers.

Semen?

No. This is way too dense, not to mention it just appeared. Semen, especially this much of it, would've been here before I started the water and it would've gotten thinner, not thicker. Nothing was in here before I turned on the water.

I don't think…

I didn't inspect the bottom of the tub, but I would've noticed *this*.

Bringing it closer to my nose, I inhale again. It's almost like…

Against every ounce of good sense in my brain telling me not to,

I stick my tongue out and taste it. Oh. My. Goddess. It's potatoes. Bland but creamy, mashed fucking potatoes.

But why? How?

Crue. He didn't specify how many reasons he had for sneaking into my room, just left out putting dehydrated potatoes in my bathtub being one of them.

That…

Genius. I wish I would've thought of it first.

Damn it.

CHAPTER 13

Today, Ever's clones don't seem as insufferable as they did yesterday. Probably because I finally got some sleep under my belt. I can't help but smirk as I think about the instant potato flakes I sprinkled in Ever's bathtub last night. I heard her running the water shortly after I walked out, then her banging on the wall between our rooms, letting me know she didn't appreciate my present. I'm just wondering at what point did she figure it out? Did she notice right away? Or was it when she was naked, her bare legs slipping beneath the surface?

She hasn't said a word about it, not even to bitch me out. I don't know what she did with all the mashed potatoes because she didn't leave her room once and she wasn't carrying anything extra on her this morning. Probably washed it all down the drain.

Or left it for the cleaning lady to take care of. Edwin told me she's at the manor every other day.

I sneak a glimpse over at my protectee. Face to the sky, she's leaning back against one of the sculptures that are supposed to be American eels, and according to the plaque next to me, they are technically freshwater fish and only go out to the Atlantic to reproduce, which is news to me because I was under the impression all eels were saltwater fish. Apparently, they're endangered, so this monstrous art piece placed in the middle of the nation's wealthiest quad is supposed to bring awareness to their declining numbers. Pretty sure I'm the only asshole to even realize there's a sign describing the giant metal water snakes and only because I'd rather read the same paragraph about eel migration until my eyes bleed than hear Ever's friends discuss the merits of their families taking their yachts out before versus after the gala this weekend.

"What do you think?"

There's a pause in the chatter and not in a comfortable way like previous ones, so I make myself glance around at Ever's cheap knock-offs, finding them focused on me. All of them except Ever, who's been silently raging all morning.

Only giving them my right side, I ask, "What do I think about what?"

Instantly, Ever's head twists my way.

"For the gala?" Paris answers. "Would I look better with a tan or—"

"Why would you lower yourself to ask *the help?*" Ever spits, her aversion for me clearer than her friend's desperate need for a compliment. She's standing now, her arms crossed over her chest. Just a second ago, she couldn't be bothered to contribute, but now, she's got a *lot* to say.

She draws naked pictures of me, "the help," but her vapid little follower isn't allowed to even engage me in conversation? Because I'm not worthy of having an opinion? My body's worthy of her imagination, time, and energy though. With how much detail Ever puts into those drawings, I know she's spent a lot of all three on me.

About me. Jesus Christ.

If she spent any of those *on* me…

It was hard not to pull her on me the moment she walked in her room last night. After seeing page after page of what her hands are capable of, I wanted to. She's a really good artist, very talented, but the way she draws me…it's as if I'm a god or something. A superhero. Someone much better than the real me.

Which is why I didn't actually pull her to me. Because she doesn't want *me*. She wants a cleaned-up version of me. She wants another clone to add to her collection.

"I'm just curious, you know, from a guy's perspect—"

Ever cuts her off, saying, "Bradford's a guy. Why didn't you ask him?"

The blond glances around, his eyes glazed like he's not really seeing anything in particular, just…above this topic, and says, "Because she knows I have to see the ensemble in person to judge it."

"I think you'd look good no matter what," I tell Paris honestly. As hard as she tries, she's still got nothing on Ever, but that doesn't mean she isn't a pretty girl. She is. Just kind of pales in comparison. Paris is like a star. On her own, she stands out, but put her with the millions of other stars and she becomes forgettable. Ever though… she's the sun. Once the sun enters the sky, every other star disappears from sight.

No one's forgetting the sun.

Speaking of lethal balls of fiery energy, several shoot from Ever's eyes as she stares me the fuck down.

I shrug. *What?*

She asked. I answered. What's the big deal? Ever said it herself. I'm going to be by her side everywhere she goes. Did she honestly think I'd ignore someone speaking to me?

I save that special treatment for Ever.

My protectee's trajectory switches from me to Paris.

Paris smooths her hair with her palms, her attention suddenly required on the ground between her feet as they begin shifting restlessly.

"I'll see you later," Ever announces, then storms away without another word to her clones.

I escort her to class, giving her professor a nod when she greets me with a warm smile.

At the sound of my name on Mrs. Flemming's tongue, Ever's gait slows significantly. She doesn't stop or acknowledge either of us, just sort of lingers.

"Good morning, Mrs. Flemming," I reply with a nod I don't rush to lift all the way.

Yesterday, I took the liberty of going around and introducing myself to all of Ever's professors.

"Oh, please, everybody calls me Johanna. Besides, Flemming is my ex's last name and I'm counting down the days until I go back to my maiden name."

"I just figured with the Mrs...."

"I'll change to Ms. once I drop the last name. And the emotional baggage." She laughs.

"Okay," I say, having no idea what else to say. "Well, then, good morning, Johanna."

Even with my head bowed, I catch Ever surreptitiously shake hers. I knew she was listening.

"Any news regarding Mr. Munreaux's stalker?" Johanna whispers to me.

I also let Ever's professors know about Arthur's "stalker." Along with giving each of them my number, I stressed the importance of being informed immediately if Ever were to suddenly go missing. After all, it's a matter of life and death.

"I'm afraid not. With the perp still at large, all efforts to keep the family safe are to remain in place," I say, trying to sound as official as possible.

Ever's scoff tickles my ears but she's the one that led with that lie. I'm only going along with it.

And using it to my advantage.

Now if she tries ducking out again, I'll be right on her ass.

"Would you feel more comfortable sitting in on today's lecture? I don't typically allow just anyone in, but I'm willing to make an exception."

Momentarily forgetting about my scar, I scan the auditorium. Attending a real college class? I gave up on that dream years ago.

I guess I could, just to see what it's like.

Or maybe I shouldn't. It might be better to not know what I'm missing.

The professor leans *very* close to add, "In the name of safety, of course."

"Right..."

My eyes land on Ever, now sitting front row, innocently chewing on a pen tip as she not-so-innocently spreads her knees a few inches apart, not enough for me to make out what's under there, but enough to drive me fucking crazy imagining what could be. If she's wet again… For me…

I shake my head and clear my throat. I won't be able to focus on anything but Ever.

"No. That's not necessary. I should be, uh…" I jerk a thumb behind me. "I'll be fine out here."

"Are you sure?"

I nod way too hard, my throat feeling like it's clogging up all over again. I hate Ever—fucking *hate* her—so why does she affect me like this? Not only do I hate her, but as her personal protection agent, I shouldn't be so goddamned turned on by the thought of her soaking her panties again. And yet all I want to do is bend her over that table and stuff my cock in her right this fucking second. With or without the rest of the class watching, I don't care, I just want to feel Ever's tight cunt squeeze the fucking life out of me until I fill her with so much cum that even if she did manage to sneak out again—which she won't—no other man would even consider putting his dick in her.

"Oh, okay. Well, it's an open invitation. Feel free to stop by… anytime really."

I drag my gaze away from Ever to her professor, finding her cheeks turning pink. She spring a leak for me, too?

Why doesn't that knowledge affect me the same way? I don't feel any deep desire to fuck Johanna here and now. I would. I totally would. But it's not a *need*. It's more of a mild want. A curiosity. Like Paris, she's also attractive. I'd guess she's about a decade older than me and with that, comes experience. She's divorced, or about to be, so she's looking for something new, something fun. Hopefully nothing serious. She'd be the perfect fuck for me.

I can't bring anyone back to the manor. And I don't have any time off to meet with someone elsewhere. My only shot at getting laid in the next three years might just be during Ever's classes, especially if the person's already on campus. Even better if they have their own private office…

"I will," I tell her with my own implication.

I send one last look at Ever, her thighs pressed together as tightly as her lips. She pulls down her turtleneck, revealing a dark hickey, then smirks.

Bitch got a new one when she was out.

I force myself to exit the auditorium.

Yeah, it'd probably feel like heaven sinking into Johanna.

But thrusting into Ever? My money's on it feeling more like the unquenchable flames of hell—hot, dangerous, stupid to even consider, and...

Irresistible as all fuck.

Before Ever's even settled into the passenger seat, I get to work removing her high heels.

"What are you doing?" she yelps, but I don't respond. She attends one of the most prestigious schools in the country but can't figure out when someone's taking her shoes off for her?

Her nasty green drink in hand is untouched, and she gapes at me as I round the front-end, climb in my own seat, then carefully set her heels on the floor of the backseat. She lost the privilege of wielding sharp objects around me.

And because I'm still upset about the toe gouging, slap, hickey, and...everything else this woman's put me through, I pick up my pumpkin-flavored cinnamon roll in a cup and take a long drink, almost draining the entire thing in one continuous pull...all while maintaining eye contact with Ever.

I even sigh audibly when I finally release the straw. *Tasty.*

The next time she speaks, I'm already on the road, and all she says is, "I need to go to the store."

"For what?" Chef Ryan does all the shopping.

"Cheer."

"I thought cheer was on Saturday."

"Our performance is on Saturday. Tonight's a potluck to celebrate."

"You're trying to take a dish?"

"Why? Do you have more of those disgusting dehydrated potatoes you need to get rid of?"

I fight a laugh. "How do you know they're disgusting? Did you eat them?"

"No, but my vagina did and now I have a yeast infection."

The laugh slips out. So she didn't notice until it was too late.

"It's not funny. Yeast infections are the worst."

"What's a yeast infection?"

"You don't know?"

"No, I've never had one."

"Of course not. You're a guy. Guys can stick their dick in a bee's nest and be fine."

My cock shudders. "First of all, that's not true. Second, what's a yeast infection?"

"It's where your vagina itches so bad you consider sticking a bottle brush up it just to get a few seconds of relief."

"Potatoes gave you that?" Shit. "Is there medicine you can take?"

"Yeah. I need you to buy it for me."

"Me? Why me?"

"Because you're the one that caused it."

"That's…" Fair. I didn't know it'd affect her like that. I sigh. "Where do I get it?"

"There should be some at the grocery store."

"Why didn't you just ask your chef to make you something?"

"Because lemongrass-fed beef and truffle-oil pressed potatoes aren't really potluck food."

I eye Ever, the road, then Ever again. "Lemongrass? It's grass-fed." I wasn't raised on that shit, but even I know it's just regular grass the cows eat. What I don't know is what the hell lemongrass is. Or what a pressed potato is. If it's anything like the smashed potato I had the other night, then it's delicious, which potluck food typically isn't.

"You actually listen to those long-winded descriptions?"

"Yeah, I do. It's called common fucking courtesy. I know Ryan's 'the help,' but he is a person, just like me and just like you."

"He's obnoxious," she argues, the reference to her earlier insult going right over her head.

"The man's proud of his work."

"Chef Ryan's absolutely *full* of pride…among other things." She whispers the last bit as she turns to peer out the window.

"Like what?"

Still looking between Ever and the road, I see her posture change.

"What else is Ryan full of?" I prompt when she doesn't answer because I'd really love to hear this.

"Oh, you know."

"No. I don't. Spell it out."

She better not say anything even remotely sexual, I swear to fuck.

Glancing my way again, she smiles a hair too pleasantly, and says, "Shit, like every other person at Munreaux Manor."

"Including you." I don't pose it as a question because I don't need to. It was very much a statement. Ever is full of shit. All she fucking does is lie.

She's probably lying right now. A potluck to celebrate first place? Shouldn't the school host something special for them? In wrestling, we had a banquet at the end of every season, where there was an entire buffet for both the team and their families, a full bar for the parents, and individual awards handed out to the athletes.

That was high school though. I don't know how things work at the collegiate level. Or for cheerleading. Just because Ever considers it a sport doesn't mean everyone else does.

I don't.

Enough time passes I think the topic is dropped until Ever mutters, "Including me," surprising me even more, and possibly making those two words the first truth she's told me so far.

First and probably last. I'll never make the mistake of trusting her again. Never.

I'm pretty sure I just figured out why Arthur calls her that.

Thankfully, Ever helps me find which yeast infection treatment she needs but makes me carry the package through the store.

Examining the box gets confusing, specifically the picture of the applicator.

"You gotta put more stuff up there? I thought that was what made you…sick in the first place."

Ever snorts. "I'm not sick. My vagina is."

An old lady walking by gasps and clutches her chest.

Neither of us acknowledges the possible heart attack in process.

"Um… Don't you think that seems counterproductive though?" I ask.

"I don't know. You can ask my gynecologist at my next appointment," she says while beelining it over to the pickle section. "I'm sure he can do a much better job explain—"

"Wait. What's a gynecologist do? Your…" I gesture at her lower region, not all that familiar with the word she's using. I've used a lot of terms for a pussy, none of them technical.

"My vagina? Yeah. He's a vagina doctor basically."

"You have a male…" More gesturing. "Doctor?"

"Dr. Robbins."

"He goes…in there?"

"Goes? Like it's space exploration? And 'in there'? It's my vagina. Literally."

"He touches your…"

"Not really touches but he does probe me for the pap smear."

Jesus Christ. Jesus fucking Christ.

"What the fuck does he probe you with?"

"With the…probe thingy. I can't remember what it's called, but it's a tool he inserts in my vagina that spreads my walls so he can inspect and swab my cervix."

What kind of fucking job is that? He gets paid to do *that* to women on a daily basis?

"Then what does he do?"

"Then he takes it out and… Oh, I guess there is touching. I forgot at the end he puts in two fingers and presses down on my stomach to—"

"No." I shake my head. I've heard enough. Two fingers? *In* her pussy?

"No what?"

"None of that sounds right. He shouldn't be fingering you."

"He's not. He's checking my organs for changes."

"I don't care. Your organ doctor can do that."

"The vagina is an organ."

I knew that.

Kind of.

"Just… You need a female gyna…whatever."

"Gynecologist. And I can't." She returns her attention to the pickled cucumbers. "My father won't let me go to another one. He knew Dr. Robbins from school. Says he's the best."

"That's…" Twisted as fuck. "Also, no." A bigger no. A huge no. I don't like any of what she just said. Or the sweat gathering on my back. What the fuck is happening to me? Am I having an allergic reaction or something?

It's just this applicator is going to be inside her pussy but right now it's in my hands and—

"Fuck." The box slips from my slick grasp as I struggle to keep hold of it.

Why did I put those instant potatoes in her bath?

Ever half-twists to face me, deadpanning, "Are you okay?"

"Fine," I grit through clenched teeth, finally getting a good grip on the now damaged package.

After picking out an obnoxious-sized jar of pickles, along with a strawberry rhubarb pie, we head to a park along the Connecticut River. Both times we exit the car, I put Ever's shoes back on for her. I don't look anywhere near her plaid skirt either time though, focusing all my energy on the task at hand.

Twice, I catch my eyes wandering up to her ankles but stop myself from going any higher because I know if those toned thighs come into view, I won't be able to stop at all.

She's sick right now. Or her…pussy is.

My hand's no bottle brush but I'd let her use it like one.

What the fuck? What's wrong with me thinking that kind of shit? She's my protectee.

I drop her leg without warning and she lets it fall, no effort to catch her weight whatsoever, so her heel lands on the ground between my feet, nearly impaling me again.

Fuck, that was close.

"You should be more careful, Major," she tsks while getting out.

Holding the door tightly so I don't "accidentally" let it shut on her, I glance around at the other people heading toward a gazebo with a banner on it.

"That's your squad?" I ask without looking away. I was half-expecting everyone to be in their cheerleader uniforms, but they all look like they just rolled out of bed. Everyone's in sweats and has messy hair. There's not an ounce of makeup to be seen.

Until Ever steps forward.

"Team, yeah," she says, her tone holding a healthy dose of pride.

"Hey, Zero." A girl breezes by and knocks Ever's shoulder, causing her to teeter on her high heels in the grass.

Automatically, I reach out to steady Ever. She doesn't need it though as she's already diving into some drawn-out handshake that isn't limited to just hands with the girl. They're kissing cheeks, bumping hips, tapping the sides of their feet. At the end, they even hug each other.

"Missed you, Scoops," Ever tells her.

I watch the interaction with the same amount of fascination. This is not how Ever acts with the clones. This is not how she acts with anyone. For a split second, she's not the trainwreck of a human I fucking despise, but a cute girl I'd enjoy having under me for a night.

Or two.

Just one. They're all just one.

"Missed you, too." Her friend pulls away to pin her with a serious expression. "It's been hell since I got back."

"That's right. The new stepfather moved in."

"And stepbrother." The friend trembles dramatically.

"Oh, yeah. What's his name again?"

"Khaos."

Ever giggles. "It sounds more like a warning than a name."

"Consider me warned. I plan on staying as far away from him as possible." Another shiver.

"Uh-huh…" Ever exaggerates the last part of that, not sounding the least bit convinced.

The girl's cheeks turn a shade of pink that makes everything she just said that much harder to believe. "Anyway, did you get the pickles?"

"The biggest jar I could find."

"Good." The blonde eyes me but asks Ever, "Did you get a new stepbrother as well?"

"No. Ugh." The sound she makes sounds like a gag. A gag I'd find pretty fucking offensive if I didn't already know what she keeps under her bed. "After carrying this team on my back all season, I had to hire someone to do all my heavy lifting."

"Oh, God."

They both break into laughter.

"Putting the ol' family fortune to good use, I see."

Ever drawls, "I try," then sticks her hands behind her back, her fingers tangling together.

"Who is he really?"

As Ever regurgitates the stalker story, I lock eyes with a hot brunette. She's a bit more put-together than the others, but not to the degree Ever is. I'm convinced Ever and her clones are the only people on earth who walk around looking like actual models. She is still imitating Ever by wearing a shirt similar to the one she was wearing the day I met her. While not a crop top, it does say "I got wet" across the chest in the same exact font Ever's did.

"That's so scary. Are you okay?"

"It's fine. I'm just looking forward to not having a chaperone every waking moment."

I ignore that jab, too. I'm busy anyway. The brunette's doing some serious eye-fucking that I'm having a hard time not returning. I am on the job but that job is starting to give me blue balls. I'm only human.

"As far as chaperones go, yours is hot—"

"He can hear you," Ever says as if that's ever stopped her from talking about me in front of my face. It does make me tear my eyes away from the brunette though. Eye-fucking isn't gonna make my balls any less blue.

There's an awkward pause where both girls peek back at me and I have to pretend not to notice, lowering my gaze to the ground, the bill of my hat blocking my face from view.

Do they *both* think I'm hot? Or just blondie?

Ever's friend asks, "Well, did they say how long it'll be?"

I'm about to answer for her with some vague answer that three years could easily fall under but Ever beats me to it, saying, "Less than a month."

Her friend saves me from voicing my thoughts by parroting, "A month?"

How did she come up with that answer? And why? Won't that make my presence harder to explain when this next month comes and goes and I'm still by her side?

"That's so long."

Ever scoffs. "No, it's not. It's *nothing*."

I don't understand. She been acting like every second I'm in her presence is a colossal inconvenience. She didn't even want me under her roof for a single night. She tried sending my ass to jail just so I couldn't. But now she's saying a month with me around is *nothing?*

It's not nothing, not even for me. I've only spent a few days with Ever and I'm already sick of her.

Out of nowhere, she releases a laugh unlike any previous ones, so much throat in it, that has my attention snapping up to see some motherfucker hugging her from behind, whispering something into her neck.

One of Ever's hands appears on the back of his head, holding him to her.

The entire scene before me—sky, trees, people, every single fucking blade of grass—becomes red, a filter just dropped over my vision in an instant.

Get.

The fuck.

Off.

"Excuse me, miss, that's no longer allowed," I say as I approach the two.

They both ignore me, allowing me to pick up a bit of what the dude's saying. Something about pickles.

What the fuck is the deal with the pickles?

"They're in the car," Ever's telling him just as I rip her out of his embrace.

This time I do steady her, but I don't bother removing my arms after she's balanced, caging her in against me.

Dude eyes me harder than the brunette just did. "Who are you?"

Squirming, Ever digs her elbows into my ribs.

Through the sharp pain, I say, "Crue Brantley, Miss Munreaux's personal protection agent, as well as the only one here with clearance to touch her. Until we identify Mr. Munreaux's stalker, everyone is a suspect."

Ever stills, but spins in my hold, the top of her head skimming my chin. As usual, she's anything but calm as a whole-ass storm rages in her gaze.

"Nathen's not dangerous," she argues.

Him holding her so intimately felt pretty goddamn dangerous to me.

"Can't be too careful," I deadpan.

"Umm…that's gonna be a problem, Zero," Nathen says…I guess to Ever. Not sure why the fuck they keep calling her Zero though. The only thing zero about Ever Munreaux is my tolerance level for her bullshit.

Over Ever's head, I tell Nathen, "It's only a problem for those that lay a finger on my protectee without prior authorization."

My threat hovers around us, making every muscle in the small group tense. Or maybe it's just my muscles. I want to fight. I want to fight *him*.

"Right! Well!" her friend—Scoops?—says with a clap and a strained laugh. "Ever, we'll meet you over there."

"That's not true," Ever argues as soon as her friends are out of earshot, and I finally release her.

"The fuck it isn't."

"Since when?"

Since I saw a man embracing her and had the urge to gut him on the spot. Contrary to what Ever said, I'm not a murderer, and obviously, the best way to stop those urges is to stop the embraces. *All* embraces.

"Since my talk with your father this morning," I lie. Between our run this morning and Ever's school, I didn't have time to speak with Arthur. I probably could've during breakfast but no one talks during that. No one talks during dinner either. Every meal with Arthur so far has been silent and tense.

Eyes hard, Ever opens her mouth, then closes it.

Finally, she whispers, "There is no stalker."

"Then go tell your friends that. Let your clones in on that little secret, too. Oh, and every Littoral employee while you're at it." I didn't get around to talking to every Littoral employee yet, but just about.

Crossing her arms under her chest and pushing those tiny titties up, she says, "Nathen is my base. He has to touch me. Lots of people on the team have to touch me."

"During cheerleading…sure," I allow…barely.

Her arms drop by her sides, some of her fight leaving her. "You sound so stupid every time you say cheerleading. It's cheer. You can just say cheer."

"Your friends sound stupid every time they call you Zero. Your name's Ever. They can just call you Ever," I argue, earning myself a roll of those hard eyes.

When she retrieves the pickles from the backseat, I immediately take them from her, telling her, "You can carry the pie." The pie doesn't have a glass jar that can shatter and hurt her. Or me, because I could easily see her taking a swing at my head with it.

Several of Ever's teammates call out to her on our walk to the gazebo, each one using that nickname.

"Why do they call you Zero?"

"Because I've hit the most zeroes."

I replay the sentence in my head, concluding it's gotta be another language because what in the fuck.

"What the hell does hitting a zero mean?"

"Hitting a zero means getting zero deductions in a performance," she explains while setting down the pie I'm ninety-nine percent sure she won't be eating on a table with five other untouched desserts.

"So, it's a good thing? Hitting zeroes?"

She rearranges dishes so there's space for more food.

"A very good thing," someone else answers.

I wait for them to pass before telling Ever, "It doesn't sound good."

"Neither does banning your protectee from being touched," Ever counters.

"I'm your protector."

She stops to blink up at me.

"It's my job."

Her shoulders twitch with something, a scoff maybe, then, "Exactly," ghosts past her lips, barely moving them.

A head of brown hair breaks the connection as the girl from earlier adds her own dish to the table.

Those fuck-me eyes locked on mine again, she asks Ever, "Who's your friend?" She glances at my scar but only briefly.

"He's—"

"Crue," I tell her myself, making sure to shake hands with her since these people don't appear to care about social status. Students of the elite Littoral, too, they gotta have some kind of money, but Ever and her clones must have the most, a fact they're happy to shove in everyone's faces with their fresh-off-the-runway outfits and their uber-healthy green drinks.

"Nice to meet you, Crue. Are you a fellow redbreast?"

At the mention of breasts, my eyes fall to hers. Bigger than Ever's. Fuller, rounder, but not as natural. There's definitely some padding going on. Still interesting though, especially when they start bouncing.

I glance up to see her holding back laughter.

Shit. She caught me.

"Redbreast," she says again, then points above our heads at the banner, reminding me that the redbreast—known to some as Connecticut's state bird and to most as the robin—is the university's mascot.

"No, I'm—"

"Eighmey?" Ever's voice cuts me off. "Weren't the ass-eaters in charge of bringing lawn games?"

With Ever behind her, Eighmey's eyes widen at me conspiratorially.

I mouth "Ass-eater?" to her and she shakes her head, trying to keep in another laugh.

"I had Larkin bring them all in her truck since my car's too small," she tells Ever without facing her.

"I could help you," I offer while shooting a scan over my shoulder for a truck. If it buys me more time with this girl, then I'm all—

The pickle jar is torn from my grasp, causing me to whip my head back around. Ever Munreaux's unpleasant face stares back at me. Or more accurately, her *glowering* face.

"I also talked to my father this morning," she says, spewing what I know for a fucking fact is another lie, "and he said since attackers are less likely to try anything in a public setting, you can watch today's activity from afar."

I hold my tongue because that's exactly what I was hoping to do anyway. I only brought the pickles over as a safety precaution. And I was only talking to Eighmey…for a different safety reason. My balls feel like they're about to explode. I'm getting concerned.

Using those pickles, Ever gestures toward the parking lot, repeating, "From afar."

She's such an asshole. Strawberry rhubarb would look good smeared all over her perfect face.

A lot of things would look good smeared all over her perfect face. It's a very jizzable face.

"Make sure to load up on anything with garlic," I tell her. "You know, for your…" I glance down so she knows what I'm referring to. "…problem."

While we were waiting in line at the grocery store, I looked up yeast infection remedies that didn't require more insertion. Greek yogurt and garlic were foods that came up, along with several topical recommendations. Coconut oil was the only one that sounded like fun.

"*Pleasure* meeting you," I say to Eighmey, my voice bursting—better that than my balls—with innuendo. "See you around."

As I'm walking away, I hear Eighmey ask Ever, "Vampire problem?" and smirk to myself.

Not anymore. I'm the only garlic she needs for that particular problem. No one's going near that neck anytime soon.

CHAPTER 14

Crue

THREE HOURS OF SITTING IN MY BRONCO LATER, THE SUN IS sinking in the west, sending colors all across our East Coast skyline. My ass asleep, I get out and stretch, keeping a close eye on Ever. Her mouth hasn't stopped moving since I left her under the gazebo but none of it for chewing. The only thing I've seen go near that mouth is a water bottle.

For all her yapping, at least no one's touched her again. Well, she did do more of those stupid handshake things that go on and on and fucking on, but they were with girls, so I let them slide.

One of the few girls Ever didn't do a handshake with heads my way, her grin visible despite the darkening haze of dusk.

I return Eighmey's smile but don't move toward her, instead letting her come to me. And come she does… Up to me.

Jesus, I need to jerk it already. Now that my nights are freed up thanks to those sensors I attached to Ever's windows and door, I actually can.

Tonight.

If I don't, I'm worried I might do something stupid like offer to rub coconut oil all over Ever's cunt for the next two to three…years.

And that can't happen. No pussy's worth a million dollars, not even Ever Munreaux's sick one.

"Hi," Eighmey greets from a few feet away.

"Hello again." My voice comes out an unnatural deep timbre.

"There's lots of food left if you want to get yourself a plate."

"I'm good, thanks. It's probably been sitting out a little too long for me to risk it."

"You sound like Ever. She's scared of food poisoning, too."

That solves that mystery.

"Isn't everybody?"

"True."

We both laugh.

"Can I ask you something?"

Eighmey raises both brows. "That sounds ominous."

"It's not. I was just wondering about the pickles." I don't trust Ever to tell me the truth.

Those thick eyebrows go even higher. "The pickles? Nathen's pickles?"

"Is that who they're for?"

"Yeah. It's one of the rituals between Ever and Nathen."

At my confusion, she adds, "Cheer's really big on superstitions."

Okay. Sure. Most sports are. But that doesn't explain the bulk-sized jar of pickles or the affection he gave Ever regarding them.

"What's the ritual?" I ask before questioning if I really want to know.

"Nathen ate a pickle once before we performed and we ended up hitting zero, so now the law, like, basically dictates that he has to eat one every time before stunting."

"You guys aren't cheerlead—" I catch myself. "You guys aren't cheering today though, right?"

"Cheering? No. We don't have a performance today. But anytime bases and flyers get together, they stunt. They will *always* stunt."

That's...a lot of touching. And I'm not sure what constitutes as cheering or not to know what falls within the guidelines I laid out.

Maybe I can talk to Ever's coach and see about getting her a female base next year.

"I got another question for you."

Eighmey chuckles but tells me, "Shoot."

"Is the shirt a part of your superstitions, too?"

"This shirt?"

She points directly at her tits, but this time I force my eyes to stay on hers.

"Ever was wearing one just like it on Monday."

"Honestly…" Tilting her head, she appears deep in thought. "It's not exactly a superstition… Although, I'm sure some people consider it one." Her head wobbles. "Okay." She puts her hands out, palms down. "When you win at Nationals, it's tradition for your team to run into the ocean after. But it's bad luck to even touch the water before."

"Are you serious?"

"Yeah. Nobody's allowed to touch it unless you place first."

"Isn't the competition in Florida?"

She grimaces. "Mm-hm."

"So the shirt, saying 'I got wet' is…"

"Another tradition, yeah. Even though it's a funny way to kinda brag about, you know, 'getting wet,' it's technically a badge of honor because you can only buy the shirt if you go into the water, and you can only go into the water if you win. So it'd be bad luck to buy the shirt before. See? It can get a little complicated."

"Just a little bit," I joke, and we share another laugh.

I like talking to Eighmey. She's funny. And nice.

Her eyes do keep resting on my scar but she hasn't mentioned anything about it.

I turn my head the slightest bit to the left, giving her more of my right side, and catch a group of people moving in this direction, a few of them faster than the rest. Those go to their vehicles and turn on their headlights before rejoining the herd.

"What's going on?"

Half-turning herself, she says, "Get your popcorn ready. The stunting's about to start."

Bathed in light, one of the bodies suddenly doubles in height as a man lifts a girl up above his head. She holds one leg up by her head for a second or two before she releases it, then comes right back down the way she went up. Another guy does the same with a different girl, except she never gets stationary, instead just kinda wiggles before falling backward into the hands of two other guys with their arms up. Spotters, maybe.

In the middle of it all, a barefoot Ever's standing several feet in front of Nathen, her shoulders briefly popping up close to her ears before she does a back handspring, finishing right into Nathen's open hands. He tosses her up into the air and she's…airborne. She's motherfucking airborne.

"Holy shit, she's flying," I mutter on an involuntary step forward.

"Yeah, she does that. Top girls always fly the highest, the prettiest, and the most."

"What does that mean, top girl?" I ask Eighmey without looking away.

After Ever does another flip in the air, Nathen catches her feet, one in each hand, then transfers both to one palm, his wrist bent back at a ninety-degree angle. Jesus Christ, that looks like it hurts, not just the angle but him holding all of her weight in one hand.

"It means she's the best. Freshmen almost never make top girl, but Ever did." Eighmey's voice lowers. "It's not like her dad wouldn't have bought her the position anyway."

I understand why Eighmey said it—I've had similar thoughts numerous times since working for the Munreauxs—but it still irritates me that she did. Standing here, watching Ever glide through the air like a bird, landing perfectly on Nathen's hands, then posing without a single quiver in her legs, arms, or posture, there's no question Ever earned that spot on her own merit. Her nickname's Zero for a reason. She has zero flaws. At least as far as cheerleading goes.

Damn it.

As far as *cheer* goes.

"You should've seen her at the party… Was it last night? Ever did this insane—"

"Ever didn't go out last night," I say, hoping to God that I'm right. She didn't get past my sensors on the first night, did she?

"Oh, you're right. She was MIA last night. Okay, then it must've been the night before."

"She does this kind of stuff at parties?"

"As long as there's someone willing to put her in the air, yeah. She flies anywhere she can."

Nathen brings Ever down to the ground, then after a couple breaths where they both lift and drop their shoulders, Ever jumps at the same time Nathen uses his right hand to push her lower back upward, shoving her into a midair backflip before she lands both feet on his right palm.

What the fuck? This shit is cheer? It's way more physically demanding than I thought.

All the bases and flyers continue to perform different stunts, but my eyes are all for my protectee.

Nathen's hands grab Ever's hips a moment before he tosses her above his head, making me think about those mysterious bruises. *Is that where she's getting them?*

"You might want to close your mouth. We could be here a while and I don't think you want bugs for dinner," Eighmey says, reminding me she's still here…and that my jaw is, indeed, skimming the ground.

"Why aren't you out there with them?" I ask.

"I'm not a flyer. I'm a stumbler."

"What? Like you stumble around?"

She chuckles. "No, it's a tumbler and a stunter. When I'm not tumbling, I help the bases hold stunts."

"You can't tumble out here?"

"I can."

"Can you show me something?"

Everyone disappears as Eighmey steps in front of me. Leaning in, she says near my ear, "You have to take your eyes off her long enough to watch me."

"I can do that."

"What do you want to see?"

What looks better holding your tits up, my hands or your push-up bra.

"A flip?"

"A flip?" Her lips dance with suppressed laughter.

"Yeah…of some kind. I don't know that many. Sorry."

"That's okay. A flip coming right up."

When she moves back, I instantly seek out Ever real quick. She's in the air again, one leg in Nathen's hold, the other stretched up behind her, her foot held up above the back of her head with both hands. She's in a motherfucking skirt doing this shit, exposing her underwear to everyone out here. Not that anyone else seems to be looking at that exact spot but they could.

Eighmey calls my name.

Watching me with a big smile, she does a cartwheel, three back handsprings, then something that looks like a back handspring except her hands never touch the ground, instead staying up near her hips. A backflip? Damn.

As soon as she poses at the end, I clap.

Past her, Ever's now looking directly at me. Those headlights are beaming right at her, so I don't even think she can see me, but it *feels* like she can. Her gaze is heavy, very heavy.

Winded, Eighmey jogs back over to me.

I give her a double high five, but she doesn't let go of my hands so we have a quick, flirtatious handhold.

"That looked like more than just a flip."

"A little bit," she says, echoing my earlier words.

"It was amazing."

"Thanks."

This doesn't happen. I don't connect like this with other people. Only once and that was…

"Did you go to Hide and Keep?" I can't help but ask.

"Yeah. Why? Did you?"

"Kind of. I was—"

This time when my eyes scan for Ever, she's on the ground and on the move.

Oh shit. She's coming this way.

I pull my hands from Eighmey's.

"Showing off for a bodyguard, Eighmey? That's pretty low, even for an ass-eater."

"Personal protection agent," I correct. Now that I know the

difference between the two, I do take offense. A bodyguard is a step above a bouncer. I've been a bouncer. This isn't that.

"He's—"

"The help. He's not here for you or your basic somersaults. He's working."

There it is. Again. The reminder that no matter what title I use, what clothes I wear, Ever, and people like her, will only view me as "the help."

Why'd she go through the trouble of buying me these expensive clothes anyway? Was it just to butter me up that day? Or was it so in moments like this when she decides to publicly humiliate me, that I'd feel like an even bigger jackass outfitted in labels I could never afford on my own?

For the four hundredth time since coming face to face with Ever Munreaux, I think to myself, *Fuck. You.*

But because I am the help, and I can't afford the clothes currently covering my body, I stay silent. I *never* want to talk to this stuck-up bitch again.

"Somersaults? Please. You could never—"

Arms above her head, Ever does the exact same routine Eighmey just did, only differentiating herself by landing softer at the end. She's not as out of breath either.

When she's done, she meets my eyes but I drop mine between us. I don't even wanna look at her.

"Nathen?" she calls out. "Come throw Eighmey!"

Nathen lumbers over, rubbing his collarbone as he takes stock of Eighmey, then Ever.

"Without a mat?" he asks the latter.

"Yeah, without a mat."

"She's not a—"

"What? A flyer?"

Eighmey sighs. "You know I'm not, Ever. You proved your point, okay? I don't need to break my neck to prove mine."

"The only point you just proved…" Ever steps up to Eighmey, looking between her eyes. "…is that I can replace you, but you can't replace me. Remember that the next time you think about monopolizing my bodyguard's time."

I don't know Eighmey well enough to know if she'll try something dumb like attack Ever on my watch, so I slip between the two before I have to break up a cat fight. I like Eighmey but Ever's safety is my literal job.

Guiding Ever to the passenger side of my Bronco, I get her seated before I remember she's barefoot. I really don't want to talk to her right now…

But I have to.

"Where are your shoes?"

"I don't know. Why don't you go look for them yourself," she snaps like I'm the problem.

I shut the door on her and pull in the deepest breath my lungs can manage.

She's the problem. She's the fucking problem. There was no reason for her to show Eighmey up like that. There was no reason for any of her bullshit. She's the one who told me to watch her from afar. I watched her! From afar! It was only those last twenty seconds that I didn't. Is she that insecure that she can't stand to have the attention off her for twenty fucking seconds?

Yes. Yes, she is.

After a tight grin goodbye to Eighmey, I leave the park without looking for Ever's shoes. I'm sure her spoiled ass has a hundred other pairs.

CHAPTER 15

Crue

SUDDENLY UNCONCERNED WITH BEING SEEN IN BARE FEET, Ever tears from my Bronco before I'm even in park.

"Hey!" I bark at her. "Wait 'til I'm—"

She slams the door so hard, my wallet cries.

Bitch.

Edwin materializes as soon as I make it inside, asking if I'd like the chef to heat up my dinner.

"Yeah, that'd be great," I say while hiking up the stairs, Ever's pussy cream hidden behind my thigh. "Miss Munreaux and I will be right down." I have to make sure she actually made it to her room first.

"Miss Munreaux has chosen to dine in her room tonight."

I halt my ascent. "Mr. Munreaux okay'd that?"

"Mr. Munreaux is out for the evening and wishes not to be disturbed."

My phone pings with the notification for Ever's door. She's in there.

I don't have to endure her shitty-ass attitude through an entire meal.

"All right. I'll take hers to her—"

"She already took her food up with her."

"She did?" I don't have to see her for the rest of the night. "Well…" I head back down, fitting the crushed box into my pocket. "Then I guess I'll be in the dining room whenever Chef Ryan's ready."

After Ryan watches my first bite, he leaves me in the enclosed dining room to enjoy my seared scallops atop a bed of baby spinach drizzled with spiced pomegranate glaze in complete solitude. The massive room with pillars in each corner and paintings lining every wall feels even bigger without anyone else in it. And lonelier. Ever has to sit in here and eat her meals by herself whenever Arthur is out? For how social she is, I get the feeling she doesn't have any real friends. None that she brings around here anyway.

Probably because she's a narcissist with bad manners, no humor, and a leaky pussy.

Technically, I don't know if it leaks all the time. I'm just assuming that's why she's always after dick, any dick, because another thing she seems to lack is standards. She wants my dick and I'm "the help."

Does Ever want my dick? Just because she was wet for me, doesn't mean she necessarily wants to fuck me. She's certainly drawn my cock enough times to convince me she does.

Doesn't matter. Ever Munreaux's not getting anything of mine. Except my loath—

My phone vibrates in my pocket and I pull it out to see it's Ever's door again. Is she coming down here?

I immediately glance at the door and roll my shoulders, trying to appear…indifferent.

I don't care whether she eats with me or not. It's not like I want her to.

But I can't deny that her company would make this meal a little less boring.

Another notification lights up my screen. Her door. Again.

She went back in? Alone, right? Because she's not allowed to have guys over.

But if Arthur instructed Edwin not to disturb him, and a guy showed up, it's not like he could do anything about it.

He could tell me.

Would he tell me? Edwin was scared to catch Ever's wrath over some bats. I know firsthand how pissed she gets when I interfere in her sex life. Edwin wouldn't want anything to do with that.

I'm half out of my seat when I get another notification, this one for her window.

"Shit!"

Abandoning my food, I take off in a sprint, my phone vibrating the entire way upstairs. I wait until I reach the hallway to our rooms to quickly swipe through them. They alternate between door and window.

What the fuck is happening?

"Ever! What's going on in there?" I bang on her door with an open palm. "Open up!"

She doesn't respond, so I try the handle. When that doesn't budge, I press an ear to the door, my body practically flat against the ornate wood as I listen for any sounds from the other side.

Holding my breath, I pick up a thudding noise, except it's far away, almost like it's—

Boom!

That same sound smacks the door from inside, making my head jerk back. I'm quick to recover though, returning to my same listening spot.

Another faraway thud, followed by one against the door.

I take a step back to check my phone, watching the notifications come through at the same exact time as the thuds. Every four to five seconds, a new one appears.

I push my thumb and middle finger into the outer corners of my eyes, praying this shit doesn't lead to a headache.

"Are you bouncing a fucking ball to trigger the sensors?"

A thump against the door, this time much louder, is my answer.

So unbelievably fucking petty.

But since I'm feeling petty myself, I call out, "At least I know your hand's too busy to be drawing my dick again," earning an even harder throw at the door.

Ever won't just get my loathing for the next three years of my life. She'll get my full, undivided attention.

I took my eyes off her for twenty seconds, now I'll be paying for it the rest of the night.

At least we're not going for another run tonight. She seems to choose when we do those on a whim.

I trudge my ass downstairs to grab my plate. Bringing it back up with me, I sit on the floor between Ever's room and mine, my phone next to me with its screen facing up so I can study the pattern while I eat. Any inconsistencies and I'm breaking down her door.

Forty-five minutes later, the timing between her bounces begins to slow.

An hour and a half after that, she's struggling to toss the ball more than once every ten minutes.

She's getting tired.

Eventually, both her room and my phone go silent. The last notification coming from her door lets me know she didn't go out her window.

I stick around a while longer though, making sure she doesn't start back up again because she's petty and it'd be just like her to wait until I'm in bed to resume her bullshit.

My head against the wall, my eyelids are just starting to sink when the overhead light flicks on. All the hallways in the manor have motion-activated lights. With me being so still, it automatically turned off…I don't even know how long ago.

No more bats. Please no more bats. Those last ones took me forever to catch—and release one hundred percent unharmed because apparently Edwin's not the only one who didn't want to anger their caretaker.

Eyes open and already on the ceiling, I rotate my head around to find…

"Ryan?"

The chef is at the end of the hallway, half his body cloaked in shadows as he shuffles from foot to foot.

"Oh, hey." He steps into the middle of the hall. "Sorry. Didn't mean to scare you. I just, uh…"

"No, don't worry about it. I needed to get up anyway."

I push myself up to standing and try to shake some of the grogginess from my head.

"Was she keeping you up?"

"I'm sorry?" Frowning, he comes a little closer, his body angled sideways.

Is that how I look to people when I'm hiding my scar?

I point at Ever's door. "She was throwing a tantrum."

"Is that what that was?"

"Oh, yeah, that was her. She was..." I debate telling him about the sensors I installed. Living in the pool house for most of his time here, he probably doesn't know anything about Ever's nighttime escapades. He wouldn't understand. "She was pretty worked up. But I think she wore herself out, so hopefully we can all get some sleep now." I force a light chuckle. I'm talking about a nineteen-year-old like she's a toddler.

Ryan nods but lingers, his eyes shifting back and forth over my feet.

I go out of my way to avoid making eye contact with people, too.

It's interesting to see the same behavior from the opposite vantage point.

"Do you mind if I take..."

Take? Huh?

I follow his gaze. Oh. Right.

"Damn, man. Sorry about that." I bend down to retrieve my plate and utensils. "I was planning on returning these later."

I didn't realize chefs cared that much about the dishware their food is served on or else I would've tried harder. Maybe? Is it really that big of a deal to get them back right away?

Without making eye contact, Ryan takes the dirty dishes from me. He only speaks eloquently when he's describing his cuisine, otherwise he seems to struggle to find the right words, making conversation with him kinda painful.

Maybe that's why he's so self-conscious.

I suddenly feel a bit of camaraderie with the chef.

"And Miss Munreaux's?"

He pivots in her direction, but I'm quick to cut him off, putting my hands up between us in case I have to physically prevent him from getting too close to the door.

"Actually…I'd rather not risk setting her off all over again. You okay with her bringing hers down in the morning?"

"Yes. Oh, yes. That is…more than fine. I was only trying to do my part in keeping the manor tidy."

It's a little weird to consider that now, at this hour. I finished eating hours ago, and considering Ever eats like a bird, I'm sure she did, too.

Also, and I keep this to myself as well, Ever's room is not exactly tidy. It's not what I would consider dirty either, but there's stuff literally everywhere—different colored rocks, cards with symbols I've never seen, shit with moss on it, a couple dead butterflies in frames. Organized chaos is the best way to describe Ever's room.

"We all know how important Miss Munreaux's beauty rest is."

"Yeah," I agree. If only she felt that way, she wouldn't try sneaking out every chance she gets.

"I look forward to seeing you both in the morning."

Before he can leave, I say, "Miss Munreaux was wondering if you could add Greek yogurt to her diet? Maybe with her breakfasts? Just for like…" Shit. I can't remember how long the website said. "A week. Maybe."

"A week?"

"Yeah." That sounds good.

"It would be my honor."

"Thanks… Oh, and, um. Can you make sure it's plain Greek yogurt? No sugar." Because that makes things worse down there apparently.

"Shouldn't be a problem. Anything else?"

"Uh…" Should I? I probably shouldn't. But I am responsible for her, and I guess, in a way, her pussy's current state. So, then, I should. "Some coconut oil, too."

"In Miss Munreaux's diet as well?"

"No, that's…just for me. To have. On hand." I'll give it to her… so she can apply it herself. I'm not offering to do it for her.

Now, if she asked me to…

Would she ask me to?

"Oh."

The chef spins and walks briskly down the hall, his stance normal now with the front of his body leading the way.

Fuck. He absolutely thinks it's to jerk off with.

"Have a good night," I call to his back, but get nothing in return.

I side-eye Ever's door again, hoping we didn't wake her. Thankfully, after several minutes of silence, I finally get to retreat to my room. Without turning on the light, I kick off my shoes, strip down to my brand-new, fit-like-a-glove boxer briefs, then face-plant on my bed, forgetting all about my plan to fuck my hand, and pass out almost instantly.

CHAPTER 16

I EASE OPEN THE DOOR BETWEEN MY ROOM AND CRUE'S. It's after three, so he *should* be asleep. Already adjusted to the dark, my eyes seek him out, finding his still form on the bed. On his stomach, his face is angled this way, his eyes closed, those full lips slightly parted.

I grin as I gently close the door behind me. Built into the wall to connect the two rooms, the door hasn't been used in years. While my mother enjoyed a few of the more fun aspects of parenting, night-time feedings and diaper changes did not fall under "fun." My mother's disinterest in her newborn evident during those first few days in the hospital, my father moved my nanny into this room before I was even released. He had the disappearing door put in so Winnie could promptly see to my needs throughout the night without disturbing the rest of the manor. She was responsible for all of my care, but wasn't necessarily allowed to *care* for me, not like a mother would her own child. *Or a nanny raising a child basically alone for eighteen years.*

As soon as I entered elementary school, my father made Winnie close the door for good, banning both of us from using it again. I didn't understand his decision at the time. I was so young, and the manor was huge and dark and cold, everybody in it like a stranger, even my own parents. It's not like he wanted me to climb into *his* bed after a nightmare. Why did it matter to him if cuddling my nanny soothed me?

But now, after everything that's happened, I do understand. He didn't want any attachments made, no bonds formed, no love exchanged.

My father's a smart man. Extremely intelligent in how both motorcycles and businesses operate. But when it comes to humans, and what they require, he's clueless.

I already loved Winnie. A sudden lack of access to her when I was scared didn't stop that. He could've moved her out to the pool house and I still would've loved her. She was my main, and sometimes only, mother figure.

Time has no effect either because all these years later, I still yearn for someone to protect me.

Since meeting Crue Brantley, I want that someone to be him.

But he doesn't want to. He has to, just like Winnie had to. And when my father decides Crue's job is done, he'll be forced to abandon me, too.

Crue twists his head toward the door to the hallway, then rolls to his side, giving me his back. I don't move a single muscle until I hear his breathing return to that same steady cadence I walked in on, then I tiptoe over to the bed. With him in only a pair of boxer briefs, I can study Crue in his entirety, my hand moving in the air like I'm sketching him. Practice, for later. I had it all wrong—what I envisioned under his costume. I practically made him a pristine doll, an unrealistic version of the man I met five months ago. This man before me is no doll. He is muscled, scarred, tattooed, and…real. So real I can reach out and touch him.

My drawing hand slowly gravitates toward Crue's shoulder to do just that. An inch away from his skin, I trail a finger over the blade, to the space I dream about hiding behind. I would disappear into Crue Brantley if I could.

But I can't.

I withdraw my hand and twist to leave.

This is exactly why I didn't want him sleeping in this room. Now that I know I'm not meant to have any connections, I shouldn't want them either. Why bother when I know they'll just be broken anyway?

Pausing, I gaze down at Crue again.

I guess the same reason a caterpillar becomes a butterfly despite the short lifespan—persistence.

I wasn't as persistent at five. I was obedient. Timid. Never even considered breaking my father's rules.

I'm not the same girl I was then. I'm not the same girl I was six months ago.

I could disappear into Crue…like this. As long as I'm careful, no one will ever find out. My father's obviously forgotten about the hidden door connecting these rooms, otherwise he never would've allowed Crue to stay here.

Moving as slow as a sloth, I lie down on the mattress, draping my body alongside Crue's without physically touching him. On my left side as well, I stare at that patch of smooth skin between his shoulder blades, wishing I could rest my forehead there again, this time without the barriers. Instead, I inhale, submerging myself in his outdoorsy scent. Tears prick my eyes as I replay the same questions I've been asking myself since my father declared he was my new bodyguard. *Why? Why him?*

It's like I manifested him right off the pages of my sketchbooks. I put so much energy, so much focus on Crue, that the universe had no choice but to deliver him to my front door…just not in the manner I was hoping for. I never wanted Crue as my bodyguard. I only wanted him as mine.

I can't even blame moldavite for the twist that feels almost cosmic but crueler because I don't own any. Literally formed from a meteorite hitting Earth millions of years ago, moldavite is believed to be one of the most powerful gemstones in existence. It's supposed to accelerate transformation at a quantum leap-type speed, bringing you your desires in unexpected ways. The one time I held a piece, I got so nauseous I had to leave the crystal shop, and I've been too terrified to go near the tektite ever since.

No, this was my own doing. The last thought I had that night was *look for me*. Now that's Crue's main priority, to look for me.

And for the next month, that's exactly what he'll be expected to do, by my father, for a hefty price.

A couple hours later, I leave my room with butterflies in my stomach all aflutter. As per our new usual, Crue's waiting for me in the hallway. The sight of him gives the butterflies a shot of espresso, I swear. I was just lying next to him, my body almost against his, and he has no idea. Nobody does. Major Danger's back to being one of my coveted secrets.

I take a moment to scan my bodyguard from his shoes up, noting how delectable he looks in one of his new outfits consisting of a tight black t-shirt tucked into dark pants. Both items accentuate his muscles nicely. Unfortunately, the hat hiding half his face isn't accentuating anything.

He opens his mouth, not to say "I'm sorry for my behavior last night. I'll never do it again," but to order, "Grab your dirty dishes." Then, to add insult to injury, he tosses something at me before stalking right past, giving me another glimpse of his back as he leaves me.

I get ahold of myself to question, "What the hell is that?"

"Your cunt cream."

My what?

I eye the mangled box at my feet. For my "yeast infection."

Feeling my body flush with irritation, I send the overcaffeinated butterflies away in a swarm as I kick the box into my room, then grab the bowl and spoon from last night off my nightstand.

I can't believe I was ready to forgive him. Just because he was asleep and quiet and perfect?

But now he's awake and saying the wrong things and doing the wrong things and just…

Ugh!

Why is he mad? I'm the only one here with a valid reason for being mad. He's my bodyguard, not Eighmey's. Why was he even entertaining her?

I take it all back. I'm not forgiving anybody.

He can kiss my ass. And Eighmey? She can eat it like the bottom feeder she is.

"What's the hurry? Is Eighmey downstairs, waiting for you?" I sneer after locking my door.

Without warning, Crue spins around to face me, his arms out wide.

"It was two seconds!"

"What was? That infamous 'stamina' of yours?"

"Eighmey's flips."

Maybe it was. I didn't time her. All I could think about was how torturous it was to watch. For the last five months, I haven't been able to forget a single thing about Crue and all it took was "two seconds" for him to forget my entire existence.

"Your fit last night lasted longer," he accuses.

"Fit?" Scoffing a little too hard, my free hand goes to my hip as I cock it to one side. "I was practicing my reflexes. It's not my fault your sensors were in the way."

"Do you have any idea how immature you sound right now?"

Yes.

"We both know you were throwing a ball at the sensors to punish me for giving another girl attention."

Not just attention. Praise. Affection. Crue clapped for her. He high-fived her. He held her close to him. He probably showered her with compliments. And he did it all with a smile on his face, not because he was being paid to, but because he *wanted* to.

I have never, ever felt such white-hot jealousy as I did last night. Not at my competitions when all of my teammates' parents showed up and mine couldn't be bothered to. Not when everyone else got to have birthday parties with friends but the only people to ever attend mine were on my father's payroll. Not when I got asked to every school dance but was never allowed to even attend one. All of those things pale in comparison to seeing Crue admire Eighmey for those two fucking seconds.

"The part I can't figure out is why do you even care who 'the help'—"

"Excuse me. You are not 'the help.'" I stroll toward him, one foot in front of the other until I'm only a few feet away. "You are *my* help. *My* bodyguard. *Mine.*"

"You dress me up like one of you." Crue's upper lip hitches as he gives me a once-over. "But don't want me to act like it. If I even try, you're quick to remind everyone, including me, of my station. So… what? Am I just a prop?"

"Don't be ridiculous." With a disappointed shake of my head, I rasp, "You're *my* prop."

Those moss-green eyes darken but don't blink.

I tear the hat off his head and toss it back down the hall, causing him to more than blink as he snarls, "Fucking brat. Why do you keep doing that?"

"Hats make you look common."

"I am fucking common," he practically spits before jerking back, his gaze above my head.

"Are you sure I'm the one reminding you of your station?"

"Pretty fucking sure." His voice lacks any real heat, at least not toward me. He's upset with himself for that little revelation.

I tug my sleeve down past my wrist, realizing I forgot to put on a bracelet. I could go back and get one, but then Crue might follow me and pick up his hat. I don't want him wearing that hat anymore. I don't want him wearing anything that obstructs his face. His scar is nothing to be ashamed of. Let people stare. They're going to anyway. Humans will always look for flaws in other humans, no matter what lengths you go to hide them. The more you own your flaws, the less they can be weaponized against you.

"Then be common with your head held high. Munreauxs don't look at the ground." Whatever pulls his head out of the shadows and into the light.

Finally, he meets my eyes. "I'm not a Munreaux."

"You represent one, and there's nothing common about him."

Before he can even try to retrieve his hat, I go down to the kitchen where my father and Chef Ryan are too busy talking to notice our arrival. The sight of my father engaging the chef in conversation makes me lose my appetite. It's bad enough he lets him sleep in the house, now he's being friendly with him, too.

My stomach threatens to forcibly eject those butterflies from earlier.

Dropping my dishes on the silver wave marble counter with a loud *clang* brings their chat to a screeching halt. As usual, I skip the pleasantries and get right to the point, telling the chef, "We'll take our breakfast to go."

Chef Ryan rigidly twists to face me and gives a nod before scurrying to the other side of the island.

His eyes on the sea, my father says, "Join me for a moment, Never."

"Sincerest apologies, Father…" I start heading for the door on the opposite side of the kitchen. "But I have an appointment this morning."

"Sit. Down."

Backtracking, I lower myself into my seat. When Crue tries to do the same on Father's left though, he tells him, "Get the food and go wait outside. I want to have a private discussion with my daughter."

Crue follows instructions without delay.

"Leave us," my father demands, and the next sounds are from Ryan's foam shoes as he exits the kitchen as well.

The moment we're alone, he reaches over and pinches the side of my hip. I try to squirm away but he just presses his fingers together harder until I whimper.

"Tell me something," he says after releasing my skin. "When you're married, do you think your husband will enjoy you interrupting him?"

I put a shaky finger up to my chin, pretending to think about it before settling on a sarcastic yet honest, "Since I haven't met him yet, I have no idea what he'll enjoy."

Another pinch in the exact same spot makes my skin scream and my blood simmer—in agony, in anger, in desperation to get the hell out of here.

Satisfied when a lone tear rolls down my cheek, Father releases me.

Damn it. I didn't want to cry this early in the morning, especially not because of *him*.

"That was rhetorical. No man wants a wife who talks over him. Your mother knew her place and—"

"Knowing one's place and liking one's place are two different things. My mother may have known her place but—"

"Never," my father warns. Unfortunately for him, five months ago I decided I'd rather endure thousands of his pinches than bite my tongue one more time. He's better off making good on his promise to sew my lips shut because hurting me where nobody's going to see the evidence hasn't stopped me from talking back. I'm already compliant in his demands. If he wants me quiet as well, he's going to have to cut out my fucking tongue.

"She wasn't happy in it because happy people don't throw themselves off the back of a yacht in the middle of the night!"

His fists slam down onto the table, making both his utensils and my shoulders jump.

"You were young," he says way too calmly. "You don't remember that night accurately. Your mother had too much to drink aboard the *Burning Rudder*, slipped, and accidently fell into shark-infested waters."

"Shark-infested? That's their habitat."

He pins me with a glare for so long I think he's going to escalate to something worse than a pinch.

My body instinctively shrinks back in my chair.

"Regardless, it was a tragic accident," is all he says.

I wasn't too young. I know exactly what happened and it was no accident. My mother was miserable for as long as I can remember, nearly catatonic the year leading up to her death. If she really did slip off our yacht, she did so intentionally.

And honestly, I don't blame her.

"Too bad you didn't hire a bodyguard to watch *her* every move."

"Mmm," my father agrees as he sips from his coffee. "Which

reminds me… You've been going around, starting a rumor that I have a stalker to explain your executive protection agent."

"People are taking an interest in my new twenty-four-hour shadow." Some of them too much interest. "Would you prefer I tell them the truth about my bodyguard?"

We have ourselves another stare-off.

"Do you know what our annual revenue was last year?"

I slowly shake my head. What does that have to do with anything?

"Five billion one hundred thirty-six million."

"Congratulations?" Like, why is he telling me this right now?

"The year before that, our annual revenue was six billion nine hundred seventy-five million. And this year, we're on track to take an even bigger hit."

"Yikes," I deadpan. "Maybe we should make some cuts of our own. Reduce some costs around here. I can think of two salaries that can go right now."

"The chef and the executive protection agent are essential, and like I've said before, non-negotiable."

The pools in my eyes spill over.

Everything with him is non-negotiable. Maybe that's why my mother didn't interrupt him, because it wouldn't have made a damn bit of difference anyway.

"This next month will be the most important month in Munreaux Motorcycles' history. What you say, how you behave, could affect the future of thousands of lives, not just ours." Hinging forward like a robot, my father places his hand on my hip again, his thumb bent and ready for my rebellion. "Do you want to see our family's legacy run into the ground?"

Kind of.

When I don't reply quick enough for him, his fingers begin gripping the material of my skirt.

"No, Father," I rush out, more as a plea than an answer to his question, but he accepts it as one anyway, letting his hand fall away while straightening in his chair.

"Then act accordingly." He picks up his fork to pierce a roasted cherry tomato. "Close your legs, shut your mouth, and reconcile yourself for this next phase of your life."

"Phase?" I scoff, unable to stop myself. "You mean the rest of my *fucking* life?"

His fork clatters to his plate but I'm out of my seat and backed up several strides before he can grab hold of me.

"I'm going to be late," I mumble as I rush through the door Crue and I entered, wiping angrily at my cheeks.

"You're going the wrong way."

"I need to grab something."

CHAPTER 17

CRUE'S ALREADY IN HIS BRONCO BY THE TIME I MAKE IT OUT front, clearly disinclined to open the door for me, even after I make eye contact with him in his side mirror, quirking a perfectly sculpted eyebrow at him.

He does, however, look away like I'm not even here.

I wish I wasn't. I fucking wish.

My hip is on fire, my makeup is streaked, and my bodyguard is ignoring me. Again.

At least I know what will get his attention.

I poke my head back into the foyer and call for Edwin to have my car brought around, then I cross my arms and wait. Less than a minute later, my Lucid Air Sapphire appears in front of me.

One of the techs gets out and hovers by the driver's door.

"Here you are, Miss Munreaux. Would you like help getting inside?"

He's a younger one, I'd say around Crue's age, and only been here a couple months now, so we haven't had the chance to properly get to know one another.

"Sure," I say like I couldn't possibly get into my own vehicle myself.

Before I reach his open hand though, I hear my bodyguard bark, "What the fuck do you think you're doing?" giving me a shot of adrenaline straight to my bloodstream.

Lookie, lookie who we have here. Major Danger *finally* reporting for duty.

With a stare so hard it could curdle milk, he sends the tech back to the garage. That's better. Not quite Munreaux-like, but a vast improvement. All he had to do was lose the hat.

"Your car's ugly," I inform him when he turns that same look on me.

"Thanks to you."

"We're taking mine."

"Why haven't you said anything before now? You've been riding in it just fine."

"Because…" I scramble to think of something. "It didn't reek like cat food before."

Cat food? Why am I like this?

"That's probably your fault, too," Crue mutters, glancing at the manor, then me. "Did you take your medicine?"

With or without a yeast infection, my pussy doesn't smell like cat food.

"In front of my father?" Shaking my head, I walk around to the Sapphire's passenger side.

"What'd he want to talk to you about?"

"How cheap your car looks, and since nothing about the Munreauxs is cheap, I can't be seen in it anymore."

His eyebrows dip. "Is that *all* he wanted to talk to you about?"

Did he hear something?

"No. He said you were fired, effective immediately."

His expression flattens out as he comes over to stand so close that shot of adrenaline doubles, making my skin tingle.

"Then why are you waiting for me to get the passenger door of *your* car?"

He opens said door.

On an eye roll, I get in.

Whatever. I didn't actually expect him to fall for it.

Dusting my immaculate high-waisted pleated skirt, I tell him,

"Because you just sent away who I really wanted to ride…" I glance up at him before adding, "With."

Crue closes the door, muting his colorful curses.

Totes profesh, Major.

"Where's your meeting?" he asks after he's taken care of his car and jumped into the driver's seat of mine, handing me a jar with granola and fruit atop a white creamy substance.

"More mashed potatoes?"

"What?" Crue pauses his dramatic perusal of my dashboard to look at me. "No. That's yogurt."

"How do you know?"

"Because Ryan said it was in his description."

"I didn't hear him—"

"Plain Greek yogurt. He said it. You can go in and ask him if you want."

I'm not going back in there, especially not to talk to that person. But Crue's getting a little too defensive about this.

"Did you do something to it?"

"No. Jesus. Just eat your breakfast."

He rolls down the driveway.

"And tell me where we're going."

"Littoral. I'm meeting with the dean."

"Is everything okay?"

"Mm-hm."

After using the visor mirror to reblend my makeup, I take small hesitant bites of my breakfast. Plain Greek yogurt tastes awful on its own, so I'm not sure I'd be able to tell if anything was done to it.

At a stoplight, Crue picks up the black tourmaline I keep in one of the center cup holders, inspecting the polished tumblestone.

"Why is there a rock in your car?"

"It's not a rock. It's a crystal."

"Why is there a crystal in your car?"

"Same reason I have crystals everywhere, because they have powers."

"What kind of powers?"

"That one's black tourmaline and it's good for protection."

"What do you need protection from in your car?"

"Shouldn't you, of all people, know? You're the expert on vehicular catastrophes."

The thud the black tourmaline makes from Crue dropping it back into the cup holder sets my teeth on edge.

Neither of us speaks, both of us focused on the winding road ahead as Crue gets back up to speed, the bright yellows, whites, and pinks of spring making everything seem so much more hopeful than it actually is.

At Littoral, Crue helps me out of my car, which is a first, and hopefully not a last.

Releasing my hand, he immediately latches on to my wrist.

"You weren't wearing this earlier." He thumbs my brown-and-tan beaded bracelet.

"How do you know that?"

"I just do. They don't ruin your aesthetic?"

Probably. But I don't care.

"No, they don't."

"Your clones don't wear them."

"They don't believe in crystals."

"These are crystals, too?"

"Yes."

"What's this one's power?"

"Tiger's eye provides protection from other people's bad intentions."

"Whose bad intentions?"

"Everybody's."

His head bobs slowly.

"For someone that claims to hate having a personal protection agent, you sure seem obsessed with being protected."

"You've noticed I'm a woman…correct?"

I ignore the goose bumps his once-over creates.

"What does that have to do with—"

"I'm constantly at risk of getting mugged, raped, kidnapped—"

Crue proceeds to roll my bracelet off my wrist.

"Um… That's mine."

Except, he puts it in his pocket like it's not.

"What… No… Because…" I stammer before settling on, "I need that back." Like right now. Today is not the day.

He dodges my hand when I reach toward his pocket, saying, "You don't need it."

"Actually, I do." I don't care if other people believe in crystals or not, I do, and they give me some semblance of security. It's not a superstition either. This morning's interaction with my father proved that. I wasn't wearing it and now I have two new bruises.

"I'm more powerful than any superstition. None of those things will happen to you when I'm around."

I continue my advance.

"And when you're not?"

Unfortunately, Crue matches my every step forward with two of his own backward.

"When I'm not what?"

"Around!"

He gives his head a single shake. "You don't have to worry about that for a while."

"You're not always around," I argue because it's the only thing that makes me feel alive right now.

Crue suddenly comes to a stop to study me. "Do you feel unsafe when I'm not?"

I throw up my hands. "I'm a woman. I *always* feel unsafe." Hello. That's my whole point here.

Closing some of the distance between us, he says, "The only times I'm not with you are when you're in your classes, your conservatory, or…your room."

Silence grows around us like a field of cornstalks, taller and taller until all we can see is each other…and cornstalks. Just like at Hide and Keep. For a moment, I let myself pretend we're back there, just the two of us again.

A smile tugs at my lips.

Crue's focus falls to them quickly before yo-yoing back up to my eyes.

"Do you want me to change that?"

Yes, but not just in my sketches or during my dreams. In reality. And I don't just want you in my room. I want you in my bed. In my shower. I want you everywhere, Crue Brantley. I want you.

I drop my gaze to the ground, away from the cornstalks, away from the fantasy, and tell him, "No. Of course not."

"Are you sure? I will follow you into hell if you want me to."

My eyes fly back up to his. "You would?"

"I'm already paid to face one demon. What's a few more?"

"Are you saying I'm a demon?"

He doesn't even blink when he replies, "I'm saying the devil wept the day you were born."

Letting the insult slide, I consider that scenario for a moment. Only for a moment because it's so far-fetched, it's nearly impossible to imagine, even more so than Crue being mine in all the ways I want.

Twisting away from him, I say, "No. He didn't."

He huffs out a sound of disbelief as he catches up to me. "So you admit it? You know the devil personally?"

Not caring if he hears me or not, I mutter, "Yeah, I know him." And I know he was too busy tossing back whiskey and smoking cigars with his golf buddies to shed a tear over my birth.

The talk with the dean doesn't take long, and when I leave his office, Crue's holding two drinks from the café again. After handing me the matcha lemonade—keeping the tea for himself—we go outside to meet up with the clones.

I sit on one of the metal eels, half-listening to them as I watch Crue take sips. Without that hat on, I can see all of his face. Each time he fits his mouth to the strawless lid, his eyes close briefly, savoring the flavor as well as convincing me that the only thing better than having twenty ounces of my own chai latte, would be licking it off Crue's lips.

"What shade was it again, Ever?"

"Hmm?" I say, making myself stop ogling my bodyguard.

"The dress you had custom made last month for the gala… Was it ivory?"

Crue rotates his head in my direction until his eyes hit mine. He rarely looks directly at me when I'm with the clones. He despises them as much as I do. Except for Paris, who he said "looks good no matter what."

He told me I was uglier than a glory hole.

"No, diamond white," I tell Kinnedy.

Crue looks at Topher, then away, giving us his right side again.

I glance at Topher, too, finding him staring at my bodyguard like he's a bug he wants to squash with his loafer.

"Topher?" I say, gaining the attention of the second guy in the group. He wishes he was first but Bradford Hoffman being in the equation means he can never be. "Did you bleed when you got Botox in your asshole?"

It sounds like Crue chokes on his drink, but with my eyes glued to Topher, I can't be sure.

Topher's face turns beet red. "What the fuck, Ever? Why would you ask me that right now?"

"I was thinking of getting some before the gala but didn't want to risk bleeding on my dress." I shrug and point at Paris. "Paris said she bled when she got Botox in her forehead, so I just thought…"

Paris shrieks while Bradford guffaws.

"Oh my God. I knew your forehead looked more plastic than usual," Kinnedy tells Paris, initiating a whole conversation about who's had what done.

Crue now forgotten, I tune the clones back out to search glory holes on my phone.

I didn't know it's not technically a paid position, more of a volunteer thing. Huh. Or that the exchanges mostly go down in public restrooms.

I zoom in on the picture of a stall. While the holes themselves are not exactly ugly, the cock poking out—

"Ready, miss?"

"Goddess!" I clutch my phone to my chest and glare up at Crue, my face probably as red as Topher's just was. "Why aren't you standing over there?" I gesture with my other hand, hoping he'll turn his head long enough for me to clear the tab.

He doesn't. He just scowls at me and drones, "The clock chimed. You're gonna be late."

"If you attended college yourself, you'd know most professors don't care if you're a few minutes late."

The clones' snickers make guilt race through me, shoving the embarrassment out of its way.

"I'll be sure to ask Johanna if she's one of them when I meet up with her later," he says.

Anger, jealousy, pure fucking hatred replaces everything—my body hot from the abrupt invasion.

Then I remember my talk with the dean and I push off the eel with a secretive smirk.

If Crue thought what I did last night was a fit, he hasn't seen anything yet.

At the threshold of my first class, Crue smiles at my professor. Or I guess more accurately Crue *tries* to smile at her because Johanna Flemming's positively oblivious to his presence right now. And according to the dean's promise he made me, she'll continue to be oblivious to Crue Brantley should their paths happen to cross again—on or off campus. Best of luck to her trying to move on from that divorce she may or may not be going through. It won't be with my bodyguard.

My smile stretches wider as Crue redirects his gaze to me, the friendliness long gone. As a parting gift to him, as well as a reminder from our talk earlier, I tap on my sternum with my middle finger, and mouth, "Mine."

I spend the class drawing Crue's left-side profile on the back of the exam, spending extra time on the crescent scar starting just under the outer edge of his eyebrow, following the orbit to end in the space between his eye and cheek.

"Interesting choice," I hear above me but don't take my eyes off Crue's graphite one.

I didn't choose him. The universe sent him to me, not once but twice, and I'm going to hold on with both hands until the very last second.

"I'm more curious to see how you did on the front though," my professor adds.

"I'm not turning this in."

"I'll have no choice but to give you a zero."

"I should've drawn you." Sitting back, I suck air between my teeth, but still, I remain focused on my work.

"Why? So I won't fail you? That's not how this works—"

"No, so that the authorities would have an updated portrait of you."

"Why would the authorities—"

"To put in the paper." I finally glance at the woman standing above me. "In the event you go missing."

We stare at each other until I paste on a bright smile and shuffle my stuff into a pile, my exam turned right-side up.

"Have a nice weekend, Johanna. I hear it's supposed to be beautiful. Might even take the yacht out for some deep-sea fishing." I've never fished in my life, but if she utters another word to Crue, about Crue, or tries to fight me for his portrait, I won't hesitate to use her as bait in—as my father would say—shark-infested waters.

I leave my speechless professor and join Crue out in the hallway. He doesn't ask any questions and I don't offer any answers. We don't even speak to each other until we're back at my car and he opens the door.

"What's that?"

"This?" Reaching in, he grabs the teddy bear sitting on the passenger seat. "It's yours."

"No, it's not."

"Sure it is." He thrusts the stuffed animal at me, forcing me to take it.

I inspect the little black bear with his redbreast burnt-orange ribbon bowtie. I've seen these around before. He must've bought it on campus somewhere.

"You wanted a prop. Something you can dress up." Crue's tone is downright scathing but I don't let it affect me. He bought me a teddy bear. Nobody's ever bought me a teddy bear.

"Does he have a name?" I ask.

"What?"

"A name. Did he come with one?"

"No. It's… It's yours. You get to choose."

"Hm." I get in.

Crue bends down and I lift my foot for him automatically. One, then the other, he removes my shoes.

"How's your…"

Assuming he means day, I say, "Fine."

"No, your, uh…"

"Exam? Fine." Who cares? Look at this fluffball.

"No, your…vag."

I finally pull my attention away from the bear. Crue's staring back at me, no heat in his gaze, no disgust in his demeanor, he's just…awaiting my answer…like he's…concerned? "Oh…yeah." That. I guess that wouldn't make sense for him to ask about my day. Or schoolwork. Just my yeast imbalance. "Um…itchy and smelly." *According to Crue.*

"Is that why you want to get Botox? To numb it?"

I almost laugh.

"No?"

"That's why your friend gets Botox, right? To numb his…ass."

"Did he tell you that?"

"Fuck no. I looked it up."

Imagining the pictures he might've come across in his research, I almost lose it.

"Topher does that for anal, so he can take bigger dicks deeper." I'm sure some people get it there for medical reasons, but for Topher, it's purely elective.

Crue's hold on my ankle tightens, not painfully, just noticeably. "Is that why you're getting it?"

Now I laugh. I was never considering getting Botox, not for my fake yeast infection and not for sex.

"What do you think about Lyndon?"

My bodyguard double blinks.

"What's a lyndon?"

"A name. For him." I jiggle Lyndon.

He releases my ankle and says, "I don't like it," before closing the door on me and Not-Lyndon.

For the few seconds I'm alone, I bring the bear up to my nose. It smells like him.

My eyes close on tears I'd die of embarrassment if Crue saw.

Major Danger gave me a teddy bear.

Thank you, Universe. Thank you.

CHAPTER 18

Crue

"WHAT ABOUT MALIN?" EVER ASKS, GIVING MORE consideration to the bear than I thought she would. Honestly, I assumed she'd just throw it away.

Last night at dinner, sans Arthur again, she did this, too—give name suggestions, none of which I liked. The bear wasn't meant to be a gift. More of an exemplification. She wanted a prop. I gave her one. But for some reason, she's taken a real liking to the thing and now she's obsessed with naming it. I don't actually care what she names it, as long as it's not Crue. I'm not her fucking prop.

I'm not a prop, period.

Before I can give my verdict on the name, she says, "Mm, too close to Milan."

Another weird thing that happened when I gave Ever that bear is she stopped being *such* a raging bitch.

"You don't like Milan?"

She glances over at me. "You do?"

We're on the way to the Flower Fest and she's trying to do…something to her hair. It looks fine to me, but she hasn't stopped fucking with it since we got in the car. Lots of pulling and huffing and inspecting from all angles, followed by more pulling and huffing. What does she expect? She's using a five-by-two-inch mirror on a visor.

"I've never been there…or anywhere."

Ever's quiet for a minute, then returns her attention to the mirror, allowing me to breathe a little easier. Ever Munreaux is hands down the most beautiful girl I've ever seen, including airbrushed models on magazines. I've become immune to everyday Ever, but this is not everyday Ever. She's wearing a lot of makeup, more than she puts on for school, and she's…overwhelming. My lungs are overwhelmed by her right now. *I* am overwhelmed by her right now. If this isn't what breathtaking is, I don't know what is because she's literally interrupting my breathing pattern over here.

"You'd like Milan."

"I thought you said you didn't like it."

"I didn't say that. I just don't want to name my bear after it."

"Something bad happen there?"

She groans, I *think* more about her hair than the question because she drops her hands to her thighs in a defeated gesture before turning and telling me, "No. I just associate Milan with my father. There's a big convention there every year that Munreaux Motorcycles is always front and center at."

"Isn't being front and center your thing?"

Without answering she returns to yanking at her hair.

"What's the problem?" I ask after the seventeenth huff in thirty seconds.

"It's this piece. It keeps coming out."

A piece? The way she's been tugging at her head I thought it was the whole damn scalp that was the issue.

"No one's gonna notice a fucking piece of your hair when you've got…" I wave my right hand over at her vaguely. "Other stuff going on."

"Like my boobs, belly button, short skirt, pom-poms, clapping, and…what else was it?"

"Chants," I supply for her, even though it hurts my ego. "In my defense, I didn't know what cheer was." I don't think most people do.

Ever twists her head my way, and without taking my eyes off the road I can tell she's grinning.

My lungs struggle to perform their basic functions.

I shake my head at myself. I should've called it cheerleading just to get under her skin. We've gone too long without fighting. I don't like it.

I don't like *her*. She may be drop-dead gorgeous outside, but she's ugly as fuck inside. That's what I have to remember.

That and how to draw air. God. Damn.

"You think you know what cheer is?"

"After the other night, seeing you…and Eighmey, I think I have a pretty good idea."

She faces forward again.

Yep, that did it. The mere mention of Eighmey pissed her right the fuck off, just like I wanted it to. I prefer Ever angry. At least then I know what to expect. It's when she's nice that she slips past my guard.

She tries reaching in the backseat, but I block her arm with mine.

"Whoa, whoa, whoa. What are you doing?"

"Getting my hairspray."

"You can't spray that in here."

"I'll roll down the window."

Another attempt.

Another block.

She's pissed off and probably wants to slap me. I've been hit by her enough times to know she'll use anything as a weapon, even hairspray.

"Stop. I'm fucking driving," I tell her when she tries a third time with no luck.

"What's wrong? Scared you won't get away with vehicular manslaughter twice?"

I roll down her window, letting the wind have at her hair, and not just one piece, but *all* the pieces.

Fuck you.

Fuck you.

Fuck you.

"Are you shitting me?" she screeches, her head in her hands as she bends at the waist, her chest to her knees.

The second the window's back up, she bolts upright to examine the rat's nest that's now on her head.

My lungs pause their malfunctioning to release a laugh.

I take it back. People like Ever Munreaux do have embarrassing moments.

"You're fixing this," she announces once we're parked.

"I don't know how to do hair. I'll probably only make it worse."

She doesn't say a word, just continues staring at me expectantly, so I get her bag and climb out, muttering curses as I go. No more pranks. Everything I do to her bites me in the ass and I wind up having to take care of her afterward.

After opening her door, I have her sit on the Sapphire's hood.

She digs through her shit until she finds her earbuds and a green rock.

"What's that one?"

"Jade. For luck."

"I think I need that more than you," I tell her honestly.

This is going to be a disaster. I don't even style my own hair.

I don't have hair to style. I buzz it for that very reason.

With a smirk, Ever slips the heavy stone into my front pocket, making a noticeable bulge in my pants. From the jade, not from my cock.

Once again, she removes the hat from my head.

"Hey—"

"You have to be able to see what you're doing."

"I can see just fine with it."

She tucks my hat in her bag.

Whatever. What-fucking-ever. It's not like we're at a fucking festival or anything.

"Just…tell me what I need to do."

"First, take the bow out so you can see what you're doing."

I pull the bow off, causing a horrible hiss from Ever as she jerks away from me.

"What? I did what you said."

"Not like that. You have to be careful, Crue."

She spends so much time calling me Major, I forget how much I like her saying my real name.

"Sorry, miss."

I pick up a muttered, "Annoying," that I ignore. It's not my fault her instructions were vague.

She walks me through what pieces of hair to move and where to move them. My fingers are bigger than hers and not nearly as skilled—at doing hair—so some maneuvers take several tries. Only needing the front part of her hair pinned in some sort of bump, I pick the bow back up.

"All right, explain *exactly* what to do with this."

"Bend over."

My eyebrows crash into each other. What?

"Pull down your pants."

My pants?

"And shove it up your—"

"Ever."

Her laugh hits my ears, tickling them, but I'm already shaking my head, trying to clear it all away. *Little shit.*

She tells me how to attach the bow, this time accurately.

Her head gets a little wobbly when I'm straightening it, so I grip where her neck meets her shoulder to steady her and next thing I know I'm sinking into her from behind, my lips against her ear, groaning how good she feels as I bottom out in her hot, wet cunt.

My balls aching, I curl my fingers around her collarbone and massage the back of her neck with my thumb as I debate what to do.

If I push, I can watch myself withdraw from her, those globes on full display as I drive into her over and over again, every inch of me gliding along every inch of her. But if I pull, I can feel her toned back tense against my front as I pump into her with short thrusts that keep me buried to the hilt as flames creep up my spine.

Decisions, decisions.

A real groan makes its way out of my throat as my feet shuffle forward.

"Did the hairband break?"

I release Ever's neck like it caught fire and jump back.

"No. It's… I'm almost done."

I poke at her hair and jostle the bow until my hard-on's gone down enough not to show through my pants.

Okay, it was Ever's rock at first, but now…yeah, it's me, too.

Another step back to take it all in and…

Uh.

"Turn around. Let me see it from the front."

Standing, Ever spins to face me. I have to work hard not to meet her eyes. She might see it there—the need.

Her hair… It's…

The corners of my lips sink. I knew this was a bad idea.

"What did you do?"

"I don't know," I confess. I couldn't replicate what I just did if someone held a gun to my head. I thought I was doing a decent job… until I grabbed her from behind and fantasy overtook reality. It felt so real. Too real. The fact that it wasn't makes me feel at a loss. Like I'm mourning, *grieving* something I won't ever get. I want that to be real. Bad. I want to have Ever Munreaux, my protectee, not only stretched out around my cock but at my fucking mercy.

She examines herself in the passenger-side window before shooting me a flat expression, flatter than the bow drooping forward, threatening to cover her forehead.

"I warned you."

One at a time, she puts her earbuds in, and says, "I'll get someone else to fix it," then presses Play on her phone.

"Why did you ask me to then?"

Shaking her head, she points at her ear. Using that same hand, she motions at my dick.

"I need it!" she says ten decibels too loud, gaining attention—and scrutiny—from more than one passerby.

"Miss?" I say with my hands out, glancing around at the judgmental stares. "Now's not really the time…" Five minutes ago was, but right now, we've got a crowd of families observing us.

Ever's gaze narrows on my mouth.

"My jade! I need it for good luck!"

Disappointment washes over me at the realization jade isn't my dick's name, and I hand over the rock.

Lucky stone in hand, Ever takes off without me.

It's funny because normally, she obsesses over having a perfect appearance at all times, but here, she doesn't seem bothered at all walking around looking like she got launched out of a tornado.

"Do you need your bag?" I call out before remembering her earbuds are in.

Without turning around, she sticks a thumb up in answer.

If she heard that, she heard everything else I said, proving exactly why I can't let my guard down around her. Because she's always playing me.

I tug my hat back on, pulling the bill low.

Walking side by side through the festival, she says, "Silas?" and I shake my head, not even needing to clarify.

"Xerxes?"

Assuming that shit's rhetorical, I don't bother with a response. Xerxes is not a good teddy bear name.

We spot a bunch of orange-and-white uniforms under a giant canopy tent. The girl Ever calls Scoops is the first to notice us. Her face is covered by as much makeup as Ever's, making her unrecognizable but not enough to hide the horror in her eyes as they settle on Ever.

"Please tell me the other girl walked away worse off."

Ever chuckles. "You should know me better than that."

I think she's going to say "I'm too prim and proper and prissy to fight," but she ends with, "I wouldn't let her walk away at all," and I almost laugh, too. Ever can't fight. She can get a cheap shot in like no one I've ever met, but fight? Actually fight? She's more likely to annihilate her enemies with that mouth of hers than physically hurt them.

"It's my fault," I say. I don't know why.

Scoops swings her gaze to me, her eyebrows almost as high as the tent we're under. "Really?" She drags the word out into about five syllables more than necessary.

"I accidentally rolled down the window on the drive here."

Now Ever's giving me suspicious looks, too. I'm not telling the truth about the car ride. Ever brings out the worst in me. In the heat of the moment, my actions seem justified, but after the fact, that shit's embarrassing.

"Can you help her?" I ask her friend.

Scoops rolls her eyes and grins. "Like you even have to ask."

When she whisks Ever over to a corner, I follow, setting Ever's bag next to her chair.

"Gimme," her friend says, her hand out by Ever's face.

Ever takes out an earbud and gives it to her. Scoops pops it in her ear, then gets to work undoing all of my…work. God, I did a terrible job.

Crossing my arms, I stand almost elbow to elbow with her, watching everything she's doing. She gives me a quick side-eye but doesn't say anything. She does sing though, clueing me in on what they're listening to. "Fly" by Nicki Minaj and Rihanna.

"Major?"

"Yeah?"

I don't know when I started responding to that name.

"Can you get the tape out of my bag?"

"What do you need tape for?" I ask, leaning down to see what her friend just did to get the bow to stand up like that.

"To cover my tattoo."

Cover her *rib* tattoo? Or does she have another one that I haven't seen yet?

"What's wrong with your tattoo?"

"Nothing. It's just the rule. All tattoos have to be covered up and piercings have to be removed."

That's fucking stupid. Her tattoo's not even offensive.

"Uh, yeah. Hold on. I will when she's done."

"Who?"

She tries to twist her head, but Scoops keeps her straight.

"Um." I glance at Scoops. "What's your name?"

To me, she says, "Technically, Dakota, but everyone just calls me Kota." Then to Ever, "Your bodyguard's watching me like a hawk, making sure I don't assassinate you."

"That's not it," I'm quick to say. "I'm just learning."

This time Kota lets Ever turn her head my way. Two sets of black-outlined eyes blink at me.

"Are you interested in becoming a hairdresser?" Kota questions.

"No. I just wanna be able to do this…" Fingers spread, I wave my hand over Ever's hair. "By myself. If I have to."

Kota and Ever exchange their own side-eyes.

"Do you have any colleagues you can recommend? I think I'd like having a bodyguard."

"Personal protection agent."

Ever snorts. "Don't you have a stepbrother to protect you now?"

"What if he's the one I need protection from?"

"Do you?"

"Are you in danger, miss?" I ask Kota. I don't know of any other personal protection agents but I could call…Ronny, maybe. I'm not sure how great of terms we're on after that awkward sobriety test, but as a police officer, it's his job to serve and protect. At least that's what it said on the side of his cruiser.

"No. No. Khaos is just…" Kota sighs. "Vexing."

"Then you can imagine how much worse it'd be having a bodyguard. They give you zero privacy."

I scowl at the side of Ever's face as she returns to her previous position of facing the tent wall, cradling her green rock in both hands. Zero privacy? After our run together last night, I gave her two uninterrupted hours in the butterfly conservatory, then she spent the rest of the night in her room, also alone.

"Who needs privacy when you have a man that can do your hair?"

Kota elbows me, but I shake my head. I'm not Ever's man and I can't do hair.

While Kota said it jokingly, there's no humor in Ever's tone when she says, "I do."

I don't fucking get her. First, she went out of her way to try to make me quit. Then, she reprimanded Paris, embarrassed Eighmey, and did *something* to Johanna, because according to Ever Munreaux, I'm hers. Her bodyguard. Her prop. Hers. I'm not a bodyguard and I'm nobody's prop but…

But being hers…

It doesn't matter because now she's back to acting like she'd give anything to get rid of me.

Until someone else comes sniffing around my cock, then I'm sure she'll be pulling that "mine" shit all over again.

I don't care. As long as that money's hitting my bank account regularly, I don't give a fuck what she calls me. I'm already answering to Major.

"Can you show me how to do the bow again?" I ask Kota before pulling out my phone and setting it to Video.

I'm trying to record Kota repeating the same motions as before just slower, her palms lifted to show me under the bow, her fingers twisted up in its band, but Ever's hand rubbing at her throat keeps distracting me. She hasn't gotten any new hickeys since I put up the sensors in her room, and the old ones have already faded significantly. Soon she'll be a pristine canvas, nobody's mark on her whatsoever.

Not even mine.

CHAPTER 19

Once Kota's finished, I kneel down in front of Ever to cover her tattoo with black tape that's more noticeable than the ink itself, smoothing out the tape more times than necessary. The skin my fingers graze pebbles, making me wonder about the state of her nipples. Are they hard? Does she need them covered with tape, too? That's something I could do for her.

That's something I want to do for her. Very much. Except I'll just skip the tape and use my tongue.

I glance up, finding my protectee watching me closely.

Fuck. I have to get a grip, preferably of my cock later to release some of this goddamn buildup. I'm as horny as Ever all of a sudden.

"Got it?" she asks.

Not trusting my voice, all I can do is nod.

Kota snickers, but I don't look at her to investigate why.

Ever hands over her jade before she and Kota run out of the tent to join the rest of the team.

The tape and jade back in Ever's bag, I'm about to zip it up when I hear, "So…did you keep someone?"

I turn around to find Eighmey, a half-smile dancing on her red-stained lips. With hair longer than Ever's, it's all up in a ponytail, curls both on top of and around her head giving her an additional seven inches of height. Damn. These cheerleaders are something else.

Kinda makes me grateful wrestling matches don't get cheerleaders. I never would've been able to focus.

"No, we were interrupted." Not that I wouldn't have liked to keep my butterfly. It's just I was on the clock that night and didn't really have anywhere to take her. Which she didn't seem to mind… Until she disappeared.

"Mm. I know about that."

"Do you?" Was it her? She's short enough.

"Yeah. Ever…"

Oh, the interruption from the other night.

"She can be a real bitch," she adds.

I bite my teeth together so hard my temples ache. Ever is a bitch. I call her that in my head at least a dozen times a day. But that doesn't mean I enjoy hearing anyone else say it.

Unclenching my jaw, I ask, "How about you? Did you find anyone?"

She shrugs a shoulder. "Maybe."

Maybe? What the fuck am I supposed to do with that? If anything, that leaves me with more questions.

"Eighmey!" some girl yells as she jogs through the opening, keeping me from asking if Eighmey was dressed as a monarch butterfly. "Oh, sorry." She laughs when she sees us. "Did you bring hairspray?"

"I did but there wasn't much left. I used it all up."

"I think Ever still has some," I offer, then search through Ever's bag until I find some brand I've never even heard of.

I walk over to hand the can to the girl.

She thanks me and promises to return it when she's done.

"Keep it," I tell her. Ever can afford to buy another. Hundred.

Outside is a flurry of activity. There's a lot of running around, counting, nodding, different types of flips, ass-shaking, that girl now spraying another girl down with the hairspray, and—

"I don't want to *monopolize* any more of your time, but could I get your…"

Eighmey's voice fades away as Ever comes into focus. She's airborne again but not like the other night. She's fucking soaring through the air, high up above everyone's heads, her body spinning too many times to count before coming right back down into six arms instead of just Nathen's two hands.

What the fuck was that?

Next to me, Eighmey says, "That's a basket."

Did I ask that out loud?

"She's gonna get hurt."

The sound of bodies colliding when Ever landed was not natural. It sounded painful. It looked painful.

Eighmey latches on to my elbow, making me realize I was moving. For Ever.

"She'll be fine. Ever doesn't make mistakes."

"I don't…" I don't know why anyone would willingly do that. Someone hoisting you over their head momentarily is one thing. Being catapulted into the sky with no safety equipment whatsoever is another and it's insane.

"So…can I?"

"What?" I flick my gaze to Eighmey, her expression hopeful. "I'm…not on social media." I think that's what she asked. If I was on some kind of app.

"At all?"

"No," comes out as I watch Ever get propelled into the air a second time, my heart feeling like it's going with her. I don't take another breath until she's slamming back into those same arms.

"Text then?"

Tearing my arm from her hold, I rush over to Ever and pull her out from the three guys surrounding her.

Her laugh dies off when she sees my face. "What's wrong?"

"You can't do that again."

"Do what?"

I gesture above our heads.

"You said it was okay for cheer. This is cheer."

She thinks I'm talking about her being touched. It has nothing to do with that.

"I changed my mind."

She steps close, too close while she looks like *that*, and pleads, fucking *pleads*, "Don't take this from me," like it's the only thing she has.

"It's too dangerous," I plead right back like she's the only thing I have.

Her features soften as she realizes I'm a pussy-ass bitch with a fear of heights. It's not my heights I'm scared of though. It's hers.

"If you die, I don't get paid," I say with a gruff voice in an effort to recover some of my masculinity. Shit's slipping by the second.

"Nothing's going to go wrong during my last performance. I promise."

I scoff, my lips numb. "Until next season and then we gotta do this shit all over again."

Ever doesn't reply, only gives a single nod. I'm not trying to jinx her. I just…

Fuck. I have to get used to it somehow. Maybe I just won't watch the baskets. The stunts, I'm pretty sure I can handle. Even though I don't want another man's hands on her, as long as Nathen's got one of his on her at all times, I should be okay. Dude's strong. He got his pickles. I saw him gnawing on one in the tent earlier. It'll be all right. Ever's gonna land right where she's supposed to, no hiccups.

"How many times do you do baskets?"

"How'd you know what they're called?" She laughs again, not mockingly, almost like she's impressed.

"Eighmey told me."

The humor disappears as she looks past me, her eyes narrowing. I don't care about Eighmey though. I don't care if Ever's mad she was talking to me. I don't even care if she was my butterfly. I don't fucking care.

"Ever?"

Her azure gaze returns to mine.

"How many?"

"Four."

"Okay. All right." I adjust my hat. "Well, uh, if you see me covering my eyes, no you didn't."

She shakes her head, a much smaller smile appearing as she teases, "You watch scary movies through your fingers, too, Major?"

"Something like that." Nothing like that. I don't have a problem watching other people get torn to shreds, but Ever? I don't want to watch her so much as break a goddamn nail.

Maybe it's because I do think she's too prim and proper and prissy. Or maybe it's because I want that million dollars. I don't know what the exact reason is but I do know I've never felt like my heart was outside my body until I saw Ever up there. If I don't watch her doing baskets, hopefully it won't feel like that at all.

Practice resumes, everyone doing what looks like half-assed motions through something that resembles a routine, not a championship-winning routine in my opinion, but… What do I know? I just learned what a basket is. Kind of.

A few more run-throughs, then the team's filing onto the main stage. I find a spot off to the side of the front to stand and watch.

While the team's simultaneously hyping the crowd and getting into position, Ever says something to Kota, sending her friend over to relay the message to Eighmey. Arms down, smile bright, Eighmey books it to the opposite side of the stage, unconcealed confusion on her face when others shoot her questioning looks. They all bounce and wave, only earning a smattering of applause from the half-interested audience.

Talk about embarrassing.

I clap and whistle extra loud.

I don't know how Ever finds me so quickly but our eyes connect for the briefest of moments.

For the first time in eight years, all the other looks in my direction don't bother me. And surprisingly, neither do the whispers.

The music starts, the Perplexus remix of "Poison" by Rita Ora pouring from the speakers. The beat drops, sending the first staggered row into back handsprings toward the rear of the stage. Fifteen seconds later, a second row follows. A few seconds after that, another, until the whole stage is in motion—synchronized twists, jumps, and backflips—nothing like what they did during practice. With so many legs and arms and hair—so much fucking hair—it's hard to focus on any one individual. At the thirty-second mark, flyers take flight, then there're bodies everywhere—on the ground, in the air, everyone moving, everyone doing something different.

Any time I catch sight of Ever, I try my best to track her, not really giving a shit about anyone else up there, but it's too fast, too chaotic, and I keep losing her.

My feet inch forward as they set up in the formation for baskets. I know I said I wasn't gonna look but I literally can't take my eyes off the middle one, hoping to fucking God it's Ever's. That's where the top girl should be, right?

I rip my hat off to see better, not even thinking about my scar, only Ever. Where's Ever?

Someone moves and I catch her black hair being bounced around in the middle of three guys.

Boom, boom. Two baskets thrown—one on each side—then Ever's, and hers is so much higher than the others. Jesus fucking Christ, they launched her ass up there like a rocket going to space.

Boom, boom. The first two baskets land, leaving Ever up there by herself.

I swear the couple seconds she's twirling stretches out to minutes, hours...

Fuck, when is she coming back down?

Then suddenly, *boom,* and I can breathe again.

Barely.

One down. Three to go.

Some shuffling takes place, then Nathen's got Ever in a handstand over his head. They hold briefly before she flips into standing on his hands. Two other guys come over to help or spot, I'm not sure, and she starts switching from one leg to the other, posing in different ways. She's just as graceful as a ballerina, except instead of dancing across a floor, she's doing it on two motherfucking palms.

The fucking talent, the technique, the strength. Her legs haven't trembled once. She's a beast, a monster, an athlete, and I can admit I stand fucking corrected. Cheerleading's a sport. No way some slob looking to add an extracurricular to their transcript could just sign up and do this shit. This is hard work and dedication right here.

With one foot held up above her head, Ever releases it and falls into the splits. All three guys catch different parts of her body—one on each leg and one in the middle getting a handful of…pussy. The skirts the girls are wearing are basically belts, flipped up from being in constant motion, their orange briefs beneath on full display the whole time, so it's easy to see what is quite clearly a hand on my protectee's pussy.

They're already preparing for another basket, hands moving so fast I can no longer tell who's grabbing what.

Flyers go up all at once and they come right back down.

Two down. Two to go.

More stunts, more tumbling, more insane athleticism at an insane pace.

Standing on Nathen's shoulders, Ever runs her hands down over her hair, her torso, her hips, all while swaying her body to the rhythm of the song, then she points at the crowd to accentuate the lyrics, getting a fucking roar of applause from the now riveted audience. It's sexy. *Too* sexy.

One corner of my lips quirks. She's sexy. Too sexy. Even without Kota's help fixing her hair, she would've been. No matter if she's trying or not, she commands everybody's attention.

I blink and she's off Nathen's shoulders, on the floor in front of him, doing something… I can't see her because Eighmey's doing a bunch of flips across the stage.

Fucking move.

By the time I get eyes on Ever again, she's about to do another basket.

Airborne, ankle grab, spread eagle—Jesus fuck, I'll be dreaming about that later—then she's landing.

One left. That's it. One gravity-defying aerial trick.

Still in her trio's arms, they flip Ever from her stomach to her back. Her legs spread wide open, they fling her up to sitting on the shoulders of another girl who's standing on a guy's shoulders.

I press a fist to my mouth as my own stomach drops out my fucking ass. That's too high, too many people, too many ways this shit can go wrong.

Another person runs over to help keep the girl Ever's on steady. Ever sticks her arms up in a V, smiling as she scans the crowd, her passion for this evident.

Is that a tear in her eye? It might just be.

Leaning far forward, the other girl's head dips as her hands push up on Ever's feet, allowing Ever to do a front flip off her, landing into a mass of arms—

Oh shit! It happens so fast I'm not even sure *what* happens just that someone's down.

Someone's fucking down.

Ever.

I don't see her, just bodies. Lots and lots of bodies as they all falter in their routine and start to congregate toward whoever got hurt.

I'm hopping onto the stage before I even know I'm moving, shoving those same bodies out of my fucking way.

"Ever? Where's Ever?"

My eyes spot her midnight hair before her face. She's standing. Thank fuck she's standing.

"Are you okay?" I ask, going over to cradle her face.

Without answering, she stares up at me blankly.

"Are you okay?" I repeat.

Barely above a whisper, "No," leaves her lips.

"What—"

I don't know if she jerks back or someone bumps into her in the commotion, but she's out of my hold, my fingertips still tingling.

"Jesus, there's blood everywhere," someone says.

Blood? I search Ever, finding no blood whatsoever.

The huddle beside us parts enough to reveal a crying Eighmey on the ground, her hands up to her mouth as blood seeps between her fingers.

Holy shit. There is fucking blood everywhere.

"How'd it happen?" someone asks.

"Either my leg wasn't tucked tight enough, or she wasn't in the right position, I don't know, but my foot…"

I pull my gaze from Eighmey back over to Ever. She's already staring directly at me in that same dead-eyed way as she finishes, saying, "It clipped her."

This was her fault? She made a mistake? She promised she wouldn't. She fucking promised.

Everyone begins rushing off the stage. Before we can get separated, I grab Ever, tucking her into my side. Her body's rigid as hell, her heartbeat anything but. I can feel it pounding beneath my touch.

While everybody rushes to Eighmey's side in the tent, Ever breaks away from me to retrieve her bag. I grab it from her just before she can get the strap over her shoulder.

She walks out without a word to me or her team. Are they mad at her for fucking up? It was just an unlucky accident.

Wrestling is practiced as a team but it's very much an individual sport. You win or fail on your own. It's both good and bad in that way.

"How's your foot?" I ask as we weave our way through parked cars. She's not limping at all. Or wincing.

"Like you fucking care," she mutters.

"Actually I do." Did she forget who the fuck I am?

"Really?"

She rounds on me so fast I almost run into her.

I return her glare with my own. I don't know why we're glaring, but if she's got one directed at me, I got my own at the ready.

"You care?"

"Yeah." If she's in pain, I'm the one who's gotta carry her. If she's injured, I'm the one who's taking her ass to the doctor. If she's at the doctor, then I'm the one standing guard, making sure that motherfucker isn't doing anything sus like that gyno she told me about because obviously her dad's a fucking weirdo who puts too much thought into who can and can't be in his daughter's pussy. His ancient friend's allowed to "inspect" it, but Ever's not allowed to fuck around with guys her own age?

Make that shit make sense because I'm fucking struggling to.

It took everything in me not to go back into that house yesterday when I heard Arthur raise his voice at Ever. I don't know what he said but I know how he said it and that was enough to see red. I had to lock myself inside my car and grip the steering wheel to keep from going in and bashing my boss's head in. For Ever. Because everything I do now is to protect *her*.

"You care you made me ruin my last performance?"

"How the fuck did I make you ruin it? I was just watching from the—"

"Not then. Before. When you were getting a cheer lesson from Eighmey."

I replay the last thirty minutes. The look on Ever's face when she found out who told me what a basket was, her last-minute modification to the routine that changed Eighmey's position in it.

"What the fuck did you do?"

"You saw what I did. You and everyone else. You all saw what I did!" she screams in my face, her voice about as reckless as that last basket.

My glare melts into a puddle of disbelief.

"You did that shit on purpose? You kicked a girl, your own fucking teammate, in the face, on purpose?"

"I warned her."

"You warned her not to take up your bodyguard's time. Not—"

"Exactly. *My* bodyguard. *Mine*."

I take it back. She's not a bird. She's more of a…bat.

She is like a bat. Active at night, a little creepy, and territorial as all fuck.

"And as my bodyguard, if I tell you I don't want you so much as glancing at another female while you're on the job, then you better develop a *fucking* cataract the moment one enters your vision!"

Goddamn it, why is this such a turn-on? She kicked a girl's teeth in over me. That's gotta be the biggest red flag… So then why the hell am I over here acting like a raging bull in a ring, completely entranced by that shit, about to charge straight at it?

"Why does it matter who I look at?" Especially when she's the only one I'm focused on anyway.

She swallows as she pops up those slender shoulders.

"How many ways do I have to explain it? The name Munreaux holds a certain standard of quality. It'd be the same if one of our salesmen was caught ogling a lesser motorcycle every chance he got. Except my father would fire the salesman. You're getting off with a warning because for some reason my father refuses to fire you."

Her possessiveness isn't for me as in *me* just myself, but me as in her employee, her possession. Her prop. It could be anyone. Edwin even.

Would she get mad if her professor was sniffing around Edwin though?

"What'd you do to Johanna?"

Her eyes blaze but she says, "Nothing," like it is nothing, like she's not burning up over hearing me say that name.

"Your meeting with the dean… Johanna wasn't the reason for it?"

The fire grows.

"Oh, she was."

"Then—"

"I didn't *do* anything to her." She pauses and I swear to God I can hear her add "yet" in her mind. "I had an informative conversation with the dean about Professor Flemming's behavior possibly interfering with my safety, which is supposed to be *your* main concern… Right?"

It's not a question. It's rhetorical, but meaner, like a jab.

"Right. Your safety is my concern. My only concern. And I don't like the way those motherfuckers handle you."

Might as well clear the air on everything. I got some shit to get off my chest, too.

Her posture finally thaws a fraction.

"Which ones?"

Any one that's ever handled you.

"The stunter…guys." Are they all bases?

She spins around, her back to me, and says, "Lucky for you, the season just ended."

"Unlucky for me, your need to fly didn't."

"So what?" she snaps.

I grab her elbow. "So…if anyone's going to…throw you…"

What am I doing?

"…between now and next season…"

Am I doing this?

"…it's going to be me."

Why am I doing this? I don't know the first thing about this shit. I spent a good portion of my life getting people to the ground, not keeping them off it.

She faces me fully again. "You're shitting me."

"No. You want in the air, I'll put you there."

Because she's mine, too. Mine to protect. And guys leaving bruises on her and copping feels during stunts isn't safe. Not for her and sure as hell not for me. I will end a motherfucker and there won't be anything involuntary about it. No one, not even God himself, is going to hurt her on my watch.

Unless it's me because fuck, does she deserve it sometimes.

"You don't know how."

"You can teach me."

"No, I can't. You're… You're…" She waves a hand at me, a blush infusing her cheeks. "Out of shape."

I drop her bag and step toward her. "Try me."

"What? Now?"

"Right the fuck now."

"I…" She pauses. "I don't have time. I have to get ready for tonight."

"That's hours away and you're already ready."

"I'm performance ready. Not gala ready."

I wouldn't know the difference because I've never attended a gala, but Ever looks pretty damn perfect to me, especially with those pink cheeks. She wasn't even winded when she got off stage and she wasn't flushed, so why the hell's she blushing now?

"Try me," I repeat.

Her blue eyes flick back and forth between mine.

"It's too dangerous out here. We need some kind of mat under us for when you drop me."

"I won't drop you."

"Yes, you will."

I want to argue again but I don't actually know that I won't. I'll try my damnedest not to.

"You know of a gym we could use?"

"Yeah. Mine."

She's got a gym?

CHAPTER 20

Crue

"**W**HAT ELSE DOES THIS PLACE HAVE?" I ASK AS WE ENTER the large gym with mirrored walls and flooring that has a slight bounce to it. I didn't even know the manor had a gym, let alone where it was. In my defense, Ever hasn't gone down to the basement.

"Have you seen the theater room yet?"

I spin back around. "You got a fucking movie theater in your house?"

Ever rolls her eyes. "It's not *that* big. It only seats ten."

"Only." I scoff. "I see why you haven't been in many movie theaters."

"You remember that?"

"Yeah…" I thought it was sad actually, but obviously I was wrong. Munreaux Manor has everything anyone could ever dream of. Excluding school, Ever has no need to leave it.

She busies herself with the sound system, putting on "Jealousy" by FKA twigs and Rema.

Her natural blush is gone, as is her uniform—at least the skirt and top. She's in another pair of briefs, these ones black…along with a sports bra. Essentially, she's down to her underwear, while I'm not but wishing I was.

Jesus. It's hot in here all of a sudden.

Glaciers. Frozen lakes. Icicles. All cold shit.

A sneaker in her hand, Ever leads me out to the middle of the floor.

"Whose shoe is that?" I ask, eyeing the shoe skeptically. It looks like a guy's.

"Mine."

"You don't wear shoes like that."

She shrugs. "It's still mine."

I take the sneaker and give it a closer inspection. "Did you add these?" On both sides, around the black logo, are intricately drawn bees.

"Yes."

"They're really good."

Color fills her cheeks again.

Without acknowledging the compliment, she slips the shoe from my hold.

"All right. Let's start with the basics. As a base, you need to lift with your legs, almost like you're doing squats with your weight in your heels. Your core has to be tight, endurance on point. And never, ever take your eyes off the flyer."

Putting her fist in the shoe, she holds it up for me, sole-side up, the toe closest to me.

"Now, to grab the flyer—"

"Why do you keep saying 'the flyer'? Just say you. You're my flyer. You're who I'm doing this for and you're the only one I'm ever gonna do this for."

Ever pauses, her eyes locked on the shoe.

"To grab…me, you're going to use your palms to catch my feet, and you want to cover as much of each foot as possible."

She awkwardly demonstrates how to grab the shoe's sole for me to copy. I think I've nailed it until she starts moving my fingers all around, then she places her soft palm over my knuckles to show me how to grip the sides. The size difference is laughable…until she guides my pointer finger with hers, her fingertip brushing along the length of my long digit, then nothing's funny at all.

Fuck. Fuck. Fuck. My athletic shorts won't hide shit if I get hard right now.

Antarctica. Avalanche. Snowballs.

My balls. Hitting Ever's chin.

Jesus.

My grip on the shoe tightens so much I can feel Ever's fist inside it.

"Good. Keep your index finger level with the heel."

I nod stiffly.

Ever takes the shoe and tosses it aside before giving me her back, only a few inches in front of me.

I'm studying the back of her head, remembering how good it felt to have her neck in my grasp, when she turns that head over her shoulder, eyebrows raised.

Shit. Was she talking?

"Yeah," I say, no clue what I'm agreeing to.

"Then put your hands on me."

Uh…

Taking a wild guess, I clutch her sides. Instantly, her obliques constrict between my hands and her back arches away from me. Fuck, I could get used to that.

"You're not ticklish, are you?"

"No!" she snaps before moving my hands lower so they're just above her hips. "You're too high."

I drum all of my fingers, getting familiar with the grip.

Those mysterious marks aren't visible at the moment, hidden by her briefs, but I remember them being about where I'm holding, maybe a little lower. I only saw them that once.

Ever's hands circle my wrists.

"Okay, now lift but don't let go of me."

She gives a little bounce and together we get her in the air, my hands on her the whole time, my eyes tracking her ass to just over my head. It's just a quick pop up before her feet are back on the floor.

"Again."

We repeat that a few more times until she tells me to go higher while also tossing her up a little.

The first time, I can't do it. I add extra height easy enough, but I don't so much as loosen my grip on her.

"If you can't even catch me from a few inches, how are you going to catch me from several feet?"

"I'll catch you."

"But you—"

"I'll fucking catch you."

I'm not worried about the catch. It's the release that's got me uneasy.

But this is what she wants and I told her I'd be the one to do it with her. If it's either me or someone else…

It's me.

She shakes her head but gets in position for another try. This time I do let go, her feet going up near my face before she comes right back down into my hands again.

"Perfect. Just like that, except this time, try to catch me the way I showed you."

Already?

"What are you gonna be doing? Spinning and shit?" This escalated so fucking fast. As did my sweating.

Ever shoots me a look. "You're not ready for elite stunts. I'll stay straight. You just focus on getting your hands under my feet."

Next thing I know this bitch is jumping and I'm releasing her, then she's airborne, and—

I'm supposed to catch her by the bottoms of her fucking feet? How?

I miss. Obviously. I miss and have to rush to catch her under her armpits so she doesn't smack the floor.

This shit is not easy. This shit is not fun. I don't understand why anyone does it.

"Again," she says.

Second attempt, I get some tit in the catch but it's way too quick to enjoy.

Maybe that fucker on her team wasn't getting off on grabbing her puss but I still don't like that he grabbed her puss. I'm grabbing anything I can to save her from a sloppy throw. His stunt was much more controlled, not to mention rehearsed. He could've found somewhere better to grab her.

On the third, I do it. I catch her. Somehow, some-fucking-way I catch her. I have no idea if my hands are positioned correctly but Ever's soles are in my palms and I'm her goddamn base.

"Fuuuckk."

I blindly wander around, my feet shuffling to stay under me as I work my ass off to keep balance.

What makes it even harder is the fact that I'm now staring straight up at Ever's ass. And pussy. It's a direct line of sight right up there.

Every detail of Ever's soaked panties in the car has been burned into my memory—fourth-degree-level burned on there—yet I've been revisiting each one like I was told I have early onset dementia and that day's the only thing I'm terrified of forgetting. The way the fabric was darkened in that one spot, spreading bigger the more turned on she got. The smell of her arousal… Literally mouth-watering. Days later and my mouth is still hankering for a taste. One single fucking lick.

She's not wet now though. At least not enough to show through her briefs. If she was…

"Keep your elbows locked," she scolds, and I realize I was lowering her.

Probably—preferably—on to my face.

I press up, creating some distance.

"Don't lift any higher. Just stay right here."

"Why?" I grit out, inexperienced with this kind of strain on my wrists.

"Because we're starting with the basics. This is a simple toss hands."

Simple? My scoff comes out choked and makes my arms shake. Or maybe that's me actually shaking.

Shit. I'm shaking.

"How do you get down?"

"Okay. Push up—"

My wrists give out before she can finish her instructions, causing her to drop suddenly. I wrap my arms around her as quick as I can though, locking them around her thighs.

I'm panting and sweating and goddamn, this is so much harder than I thought it'd be. But this part…isn't so bad. Having Ever's ass in my face is exactly what I was imagining. Exactly what I was craving. Only without the material.

"I told you you'd drop me," she says with a wiggle of her hips that only makes me want to extend my jaw and take a giant bite.

I lied. I wouldn't stop at one lick or just her pussy. I'd eat every fucking crumb of Ever Munreaux, leaving *none* behind.

"And I told you…" I ease my hold, letting her slip through my arms, the back of her body sliding down the front of mine until my lips are on the crown of her head. "I'd catch you."

Blizzards. Icebergs. Sleet pelting my face to cool it the fuck down.

I practically shove her away, putting an arm's length between us.

Stepping even farther away, Ever tucks her hair behind her ears, saying, "If you had any sort of stamina, you wouldn't have had to."

This girl's always questioning my stamina.

I bring her ass right back, not against me but damn near close.

"Let's go again."

"That wasn't a challenge, Major. It was a fact. Even if your wrists were strong enough, I need to get ready."

"I don't give a fuck." About the gala or my wrists. "Let's keep going until I nail it."

"I have to—"

"All you gotta do is put on your dress. It'll take you two seconds. Come on, let's try again."

Spinning her around, my hands are already on her waist but she makes sure to twist to give me the stink-eye.

"You have no idea what it takes to be a woman."

"No, I don't." Thank fucking God. It sounds terrible. "Now shut up and let me throw your ass."

Her chuckle makes me smile.

But I wasn't kidding.

After a synchronized bend to our knees, I'm tossing her up again, catching her feet much easier this time. And because I know I'm staying like this, I focus on my grips, making sure all my fingers are where she taught me to put them.

"Good?" she asks after a few seconds.

"Yeah."

She talks me through a dismount which goes smooth now that my body isn't short-circuiting, then I immediately throw her into another one before she can even think about leaving.

On the fifth one, I tell her I'm ready to try something harder.

Hands on her hips, she eyes the clock on the wall.

"Come on. Teach me something else," I say, hoping I don't sound like I'm begging. When you're not failing miserably, it's kind of rewarding to pull off a stunt. And maybe even fun.

I think I'm having fun anyway. It's been a while.

Clearly, the bar's been lowered to subterranean levels.

"Okay, but if you don't hit first try, I can't keep working on it with you tonight. The glam team is probably already here, waiting for me in the salon."

"An actual salon?"

"Have you even toured the manor?"

"No. I only go where you do." I cock my head. "Minus the conservatory."

"Why don't you explore when I'm in there?"

"You didn't seem to like it last time I did that."

"That's because you rummaged through my room," she spits even though I did not rummage. I did some light reconnaissance. "I don't care about the rest of the house."

I only went in her room that one time out of desperation, otherwise I stick close to the conservatory. In case Ever pulls any of her bullshit.

Or in case...she needs me.

But since I'll never admit that to her, I say, "It's not gonna work."

"What?"

"You trying to shake me so you can sneak someone in there."

"In my atrium?" she questions like the possibility horrifies her.

"Oh, that's right. You don't share that either." She threatened bodily harm when I got too close to it. I thought it was just me but…I should've known. Vicious little bat.

"I don't share anything that belongs to me, Crue."

It could be her using my actual name or it could be her gaze drilling into mine, but either way, the message is clear—I'm included in that statement. I belong to her.

"They're just butterflies."

She flinches as if I slapped her, those sea-glass eyes falling from mine faster than her body did on our first stunt. The urge to apologize overwhelms me. I don't know why that hurt her, but obviously, it did.

It's probably the same when someone says Zeus is just a dog. He's a member of our family.

But I mean…butterflies… They are bugs. They can't invoke the same emotional bond a dog can.

Giving me her back again, she says, "We'll try a toss extension. It's the same concept as before, except you have to toss me a bit higher because you're going to extend your arms up to lift my feet above your head."

That's nothing compared to what I saw her and Nathen do earlier, but her feet have only come up as high as my shoulders so far, so it's a jump for me.

For once in my life, I'm questioning my stamina, too.

After shaking out my wrists, I get her above my head, my arms locked, then she tells me, "Do you want to pull lib?"

A quiver runs through my elbows. "Which lip?"

Even with her life literally in my hands, she snickers.

"It's lib with a b. I'll raise my left foot out of your left hand, then you'll immediately bring it over to help with my right foot."

Fuck. Fuck, fuck, fuck.

I instantly envision her body falling like a hand on a broken clock, from twelve o'clock to six in a single drop.

I'll do whatever it takes to keep that from happening.

"Ready?"

No. "Sure."

I release her left foot and she immediately brings it up in a knee-bend, her arms above her head in a wide V. Both my hands hold her right foot, my left one not feeling as secure as I'd like. I've got her, but it's not great. If her leg wasn't ramrod straight and her core probably hard as granite, I'm not sure I'd have her at all. Ever's an amazing cheerleader. It's too bad her temper got the better of her today. She would've had a perfect performance to end the season with. The fact she sabotaged that just so she could prove a point is…still hot. Maybe even hotter now that I know firsthand how incredible she is. She must've worked *hard* to compromise that basket.

"Back to two hands?" I ask.

"No, we'll dismount from here."

"My shit's too shaky here." My arms have literal fucking tremors.

"Then adjust until it's not."

"I don't know how," I grit, earning myself more laughter but no further guidance.

All right. Guess it's all on me.

Ever holds her position steady, allowing me to remove my left hand completely. The second I do, my right elbow buckles and I'm using that free hand to grab Ever's falling body. The human body is nothing like a clock's hand either. It's so much more unpredictable when a person drops.

I get my arm wrapped around her waist, but the momentum pulls me forward so abruptly, we both wind up falling. Just like in the woods, I twist our bodies as hard as I can so mine takes the brunt of the fall with Ever landing on top of me.

"Why'd you take your hand off?"

"Maybe…because…I don't…the fuck…I'm…doing," I pant out between heavy breaths, missing at least one word but not giving a single fuck. Ever's still on me, both our faces to the ceiling, which isn't helping my lungs, but I can't seem to let go just yet. That was close. Too close.

I don't want to do this shit ever again. I could go the rest of my life without trying another stunt. Easy. But I know the second Ever decides she wants to fly again, I'll be back at it without resistance. I'm gonna have to start watching tutorials or something if I want to get better though. That and hairstyling. Fuck, my hands are gonna be busy the next three years. My hands, my fingers…

Suddenly aware of my fingers splayed out across Ever's naked stomach, I curl them into her middle, holding her against me tighter. Her abs harden, making my cock do the same.

All at once, I roll her off me and sit up, hiding my semi between bent knees that I prop my elbows on for more coverage.

My voice gruff as all hell, I ask, "How long do you think it'll be until you're ready?"

Next to me, I catch Ever on all fours in my periphery. I refuse to turn my head in her direction. Not that I need to. Her in the compromising position has already been added to my overflowing vault of fantasies.

"I need to shower, then hair, makeup… Probably a few hours."

Now I do look at her. "Even with people helping you? I could do your hair faster than that."

She chuckles as she gets to her feet. "You don't know how to do hair."

"Yet."

"Tonight's not the time to experiment. My father will tolerate nothing less than absolute perfection when I walk in."

But she let me earlier. She didn't even seem to care that I did such a bad job and she was about to be on stage in front of hundreds of people. Was it really only because Arthur wasn't going to be one of them?

CHAPTER 21

I SHOWER WHILE EVER DOES, QUICKLY RUBBING ONE OUT, THEN I walk with her down to the salon, pretending I didn't just come imagining her naked body all lathered up, my hands running over the places hers probably were.

Surprisingly, the salon's on the main floor, behind a door that I've passed multiple times but never paid any attention to because it's always closed.

"I'm gonna be in here a while. Why don't you take a tour of the manor?"

I shake my head. "Not a chance."

"Major, there's nowhere for me to go. Nothing to do. No one to fuck."

She kinda snarls the last word like I've already accused her but that didn't even cross my mind. I'm in here to watch…and not *just* her.

"You're infuriating."

So are you.

While she gets situated in one of the two height-adjustable chairs, I take my place near the hairstylist.

The tall woman gives me an awkward double glance, so I start to introduce myself.

"I'm—"

"He's my bodyguard. He takes his job very literal, so be careful pulling on my hair. One wince from me and he'll shoot you in the head."

That gross exaggeration hangs in the air for a few moments where both the stylist and makeup artist give each other uncomfortable looks.

It's not until Ever laughs that the other two women do as well.

I shake my head at Ever in the mirror and she rolls her eyes, putting her feet on the vanity in front of her, her phone between her bent knees with a cheerleading video already playing. From the color of the uniforms, I can tell it isn't today's performance. Or even Littoral.

She's in a silk maroon robe with her initials embroidered in white on the chest. I assumed she was naked underneath but with her legs up, making the material bunch at her hips, I can see her underwear. Lacy white underwear. Simple, elegant, innocent. On anyone else, they'd look virginal. On Ever, they look like a bow I want to pull off with my teeth before doing the unholiest of acts to what's underneath. There'd be nothing virginal left of Ever when I finished with her.

I rip my eyes off the panties and focus on her head where the stylist is massaging some kind of product into the strands.

Damn. I missed something.

The makeup artist is busy sifting through her giant tackle box of beauty shit, so with a stern expression on my face and my hands behind my back, I mimic the same motions as the hairstylist, scrunching and unscrunching my fingers. I don't know what she put in Ever's hair but I can practice the application part.

"You look like you're constipated," Ever deadpans, and I shoot her a scowl. Her head is bowed toward her phone, but her eyes are on me through the mirror.

My hands freeze.

"I'm concentrating."

"I won't hurt her," the stylist promises with a sideways peek.

I give her a tight smile, not exactly wanting her to think I'll shoot her but also not wanting her to pull Ever's hair.

She timidly returns it, then glances at my scar.

I go to adjust my hat before remembering I didn't put one on after my shower. I didn't even put it back on after the festival. I forgot all about it honestly.

Ever snaps, "Go put something else on. You're not going looking like that."

I'm her fucking personal protection agent. I'm going regardless.

Both the makeup artist and hairstylist stop what they're doing to inspect my outfit. And my face.

Damn it.

I tell the brat as calmly as I can, "I'm not wearing this. Whenever you change, I will, too."

Ever's own scrutinizing stare now alternating between the two women, she says to me, "We're gonna be here a long time and I don't need you up my ass—"

"Three years to be exact," I say, cutting her off. "And I plan on being up your ass every fucking second of it, so get used to it."

Azure eyes drill into mine in the mirror again.

The stylist assures me, "It won't take me *that* long."

I return my attention to what's happening to Ever's hair but keep my hands still.

After a few minutes, Ever says, "Chloe, can you take a step to the right…"

Is she fucking serious right now? I can't even stand near another woman?

"…so my bodyguard can see your hands at all times?"

Thankfully, Chloe listens, giving me a better view of what she's doing.

If Ever knows why I'm really here, why does she have to waste time being such a bitch about it?

She probably can't help it. Bitches bitch.

I watch as Chloe dries Ever's hair, noting she uses a brush the whole time as well as downward strokes from roots to ends. I've never used a hair dryer before but I've caught glimpses of my mom using hers over the years. She didn't seem to have any technique whatsoever, just random, chaotic movements that blew her hair every which way, including into and all over her face. Not once do any strands touch Ever's face though, allowing the makeup artist to start on her part.

With everyone's focus finally off me, I repeat slow, measured rolls of my wrists behind my back until the hair's dry and we move on to the next process.

An hour and a half later, Ever's hair and makeup are just about done when I'm shooed from the room so she can get her dress on.

Only needing my suit, I hustle upstairs and put it on. I secure my fancier watch, too. Since I don't know how to tie a bowtie, I take that down with me, letting it hang loose around my neck. Ever did say she'd teach me how to tie one.

Except when I enter the salon, she's nowhere to be seen.

"Where is—"

"Oh, she's in the bathroom," Chloe explains, filling a rolling suitcase with all the stuff she brought even though she didn't really need anything. This salon is stocked. But her tools are her tools.

Speaking of…

Approaching her, I ask quietly, "Is there a way to practice on hair when you don't have any?"

She arches an eyebrow. "About how long?"

I gesture to where Ever's stops.

"Is that what you were doing the whole time?"

I nod and shrug.

"But why can't you just—"

My head's already shaking. "I don't… Because she's… We don't really…"

"Get along." This is said with zero doubt and earns another noncommittal gesture. It is what it is and it is evident. Ever and I don't like each other. For the most part. We've had our moments over the last couple days but they were just that—moments.

"I need to learn how to do her hair just…without…her."

Chloe chuckles. "You need a mannequin. I have one you could probably use."

I shoot a glance at the closed bathroom door. "Uh…"

"Not here. I'll have to cut some length off first, but I can drop it off while you guys are gone."

"All right, yeah. I'd appreciate that. Just tell me how much you want for it and—"

"It's nothing fancy. Trust me. It's just the one I used in beauty school. I don't even know why I still have it."

"But it'll work?"

"It'll work."

She gives me some recommendations for online tutorials to check out, then asks, "Do you need some help with your bowtie?"

Without waiting for an answer, the hairdresser comes at me, but I'm quick to step out of reach, saying, "No, that's okay."

The last thing I need is for Ever to come out and see another woman in my face.

"I was going to wait—"

The bathroom door opens.

"For…"

Ever comes out, causing me to forget what I was talking about. "Um…"

"Uh-huh. I see." Chloe chuckles again, and my eyes briefly flick to her, registering her amused expression before returning to Ever.

See? What does she see?

All I see is Ever.

I saw her hair. Some of the pieces in the front are pulled back and twisted to look like a braid or a crown—I'm not sure because Chloe didn't specify—while the rest of the midnight strands are in soft curls.

And I saw her makeup. A brown smoky eye—a term I did pick up on—with a touch of shimmer on the inner corners, and mink lashes—heard that one, too—that make her light eyes pop even more.

But I didn't see her dress. Ball gown? It's a ball gown. White and lacy as well, except nothing virginal like her panties. With a low plunging neckline and no straps, the top is a transparent corset with delicate flowers covering her tits and cascading all the way down the full-length, flowy skirt.

And I sure as hell didn't see the look in its entirety. Ever looks like a bride about to walk down the aisle to the luckiest man on earth.

Staring at me, she asks, "You need help?"

My lips part but nothing comes out, not even a puff of air. She's taken every single ounce of it because she's literally breathtaking. There's no other way to describe her. Earlier, when I said the same thing, that wasn't breathtaking. That was breath-disrupting. *This* is breathtaking.

"Say yes," I hear whispered beside me, and blink. Was I not blinking before? "Your bowtie. Say yes."

"Yes," I croak out.

Ever's lightly glossed lips quirk…

Until something nudges my arm. Then those lips turn into the most beautiful frown.

The woman next to me… I think she elbowed me. What's her name again? Who even is she? It doesn't matter. Not to me.

But definitely matters to my protectee, who looks like she's about to go on a rampage.

I start walking toward Ever, away from her next victim, fighting to keep her eyes the entire time.

Look at me, Ever Munreaux. All I see is you. All. I. See. Is. You.

If my own mother was in the room right now, I wouldn't know it. The most famous celebrity could walk in and I wouldn't even notice. An atomic bomb could detonate, and *still*, I doubt I'd be able to take my eyes off Ever. The moment she came out of that bathroom, everything and everyone ceased to exist.

All…

Except…

Her.

"I do," I rasp.

Something foreign infiltrates her eyes as they oscillate between mine. It looks kind of like uncertainty but Ever Munreaux's all arrogance, all the time.

"You do?"

I nod. "Yeah. I…" I lift the ends of the bowtie. "I need help with this."

The unidentifiable emotion disappears as she closes the distance between us.

My hands aching to reach out and grab her, I ball them into fists at my sides.

With her face less than a foot away from mine, I let my gaze roam every feature, memorizing each one. Forget her wet underwear. This is the memory I want to carry with me to the grave. Whoever gets to stand across from her, promising to love and protect her for as long as they both shall live, is in for the biggest challenge. Ever's a pain in the ass—as well as every other body part—but damn, going to bed next to her every night would make it all worth it.

While she's tying, a pop of color enters my vision. It's so jarring, I'm forced to scrape my eyes off her face to investigate.

It's a bracelet on her wrist, one of those beaded ones again, but purple this time. I don't need to know anything about fashion to know it clashes with her current attire.

"Another protection bracelet?"

I already told her she doesn't need that shit around me.

"No. Amethyst promotes peace."

"What's stressful about tonight? You worn out from the show?"

"Not that show, no," she says enigmatically.

"What other show was there?" I ask just as she finishes with my bowtie.

Instead of pulling away, she presses her hands to my chest, her fingertips drumming over my collarbones. Eyes on her hands, she says, "The one tonight. This is a very important night for my father, for Munreaux Motorcycles."

She must really need the bracelet if she's willing to jeopardize her dad's idea of perfection for it.

"How close do the rocks need to be to you to work?"

"My *crystals*? Preferably on my person, but the closer the better."

That's what I was hoping she'd say.

Trapping her forearm against my pec, I roll the bracelet off her wrist.

"No. Don't."

She removes her free hand, making me miss it instantly, but I keep hold of the other one, even as she tugs harder to free herself.

"Crue. Not this one."

"It ruins your aesthetic." I never thought I'd use those words unironically, but it's true, they do.

"I don't care."

"But your father might." And I can't have him raising his voice at Ever again.

I awkwardly fit my own hand through the bracelet, my fingers spread like a starfish to get it in place on my wrist single-handedly.

"They ruin your aesthetic, too."

"I don't have an aesthetic."

"Yes, you do. A dangerous one."

That makes me smile. "To who?"

"Everybody."

I have no idea what she means by that. Is it the scar? Does it make me look dangerous?

"Your rocks will be out of sight but still close," I tell her.

"You can't be that close to me the whole time."

"Yes, I can."

She stills and looks at me with a desperation I've never seen her wear as she whispers, "Promise?"

Finally giving in, I grab her just above the swell of her ass.

"I fucking swear."

I hear someone say, "The limo just pulled in," a second before two sets of hands are fussing over Ever's appearance.

Hairstylist. Makeup artist. People other than Ever…they do still exist.

I let go of Ever, but just barely, keeping less than a foot between us, until her shoes are brought out, then I drop to a knee, telling everybody, "I got those."

Without any straps to fasten, I help ease her feet into the high heels.

Finished, I look up at her, finding her gazing down at me through those mink lashes.

It's a good thing other people are in the room with us or I'd probably do something stupid like bring her forward, lift her skirt just enough for me to fit under, then dive. It'd be hours before I re-surfaced…if I did at all.

"Ready?" I ask, and she nods.

Getting to my feet has never physically pained me before, but right now, there's nowhere else I'd rather be than on my knees.

A million dollars, a million dollars, a million dollars. No one tastes better than a million dollars.

That'd be a hell of a lot easier to believe if my protectee didn't look like she might right now.

CHAPTER 22

I SIT RIGHT NEXT TO EVER IN THE BACK OF THE LIMO. NEITHER of us speaks to the other. She doesn't even look in my direction, choosing to stare out the window instead. But we both keep a hand on the thighs closest to each other. Once the vehicle's in motion, she reaches over to play with the beads of her bracelet. Each time she twists one, her fingertip grazes the underside of my wrist, the strokes on the thin skin creating goose bumps all over my body.

"Your dress is white," I say to distract myself.

"Perceptive."

"The dress your ordered a month ago was white."

Ever doesn't stop looking out the window but she does freeze her hand, her palm hovering centimeters over mine. If she were to lower it the slightest bit, we'd be holding hands.

"Maybe I ordered another white dress."

"Maybe there never was another dress."

It's a full minute before she resumes toying with the bracelet, repeating softly, "Perceptive."

So all that money did go toward my new wardrobe. She lied to…protect herself? Protect me?

"Carter."

"Who?" I give her a scathing look…until I realize she's talking about the teddy bear again.

"No."

"Grant?"

I shake my head.

"King."

"Nuh-uh."

"Arad?"

Forty minutes and at least fifteen more bear names later, we pull off the main road onto a long winding gravel one, passing several metal artistic structures along the way until we reach one that resembles a giant egg on its side. Judging by the lights inside, the egg is a house of some sort. Or at least a building.

The moment I'm out of the vehicle, the clones descend as if they'd been waiting for her in the goddamn bushes.

Paris gives me a friendly grin that I don't return as I help Ever out of the limo. Ever glances at her friend, then me.

I give her the barest shake of my head. Paris doesn't even register.

Fitting my hand to the small of her back, I guide Ever forward.

As we're approaching the futuristic house, Bradford in the lead, an artificial female voice says, "Welcome, Bradford Hoffman," then proceeds to greet each of Ever's friends by first and last name. The blinking doorbell cam comes into view, greeting, "Welcome, Ever Munreaux," and finally, "Welcome, guest," to me.

"Facial recognition," Topher says flatly. "We got that two years ago."

I guess I wasn't important enough to add to the list.

The front door floats open by itself.

That's not possible…and yet nobody appears on the other side of it.

What in the horror movie shitshow is this? Swear to fuck if fog rolls in right now…

I tug on Ever's elbow, getting in front of her and halting her advance to let the clones go in first. If they start dropping like flies, we're out.

"What is it?"

"Safety protocol," is all I say, watching as each clone crosses the threshold unharmed.

"It's a smart house, Major. No human assistance required." She sidesteps me with an equally unimpressed sigh like this is all *so* common. Maybe to her, but not to me. I've never seen a smart house. I didn't even know that was a thing.

Following Ever inside, we pause in a grand foyer, under a shimmering chandelier that's gotta be at least seven feet long. Interspersed between all the tuxes and gowns are several robotic servers with different selections of food and drinks on their trays. People grab from them without concern, like it's also normal.

And now I'm feeling like I'm in a different kind of horror movie, one where robots take over the world and humans let them because if we're too goddamn lazy to get the door, then we're definitely not fit to battle machines.

"My dearest daughter," Arthur croons, his eyes as sparkly as the light above us when he takes in his daughter's appearance from head to toe and back. Arms out wide, he gives her a half hug that doesn't even reach her back and a pair of cheek-to-cheek kisses that don't make contact either.

It's the happiest I've seen him around his successor and I have to wonder if it's the fakest, too.

Holding Ever by the shoulders, Arthur tells her, "You look just like your mother," with what might possibly be real emotion tinging his voice.

But all Ever does is give a tight smile, keeping her usual bitchiness to a minimum.

My boss doesn't even acknowledge me, only Ever's friends. After some small talk, the clones scatter into the sea of glamorous attire.

"Now." Arthur straightens his jacket lapels before holding one elbow out for Ever, and so quietly I'd miss it if I weren't standing so close, he whispers, "Showtime."

He leads her around, making introduction after introduction. Meanwhile, I remain three to four feet behind them, my head down, eyes on the floor but out to the side, surreptitiously on Ever so I can gauge her comfort level. As soon as I see her hands go behind her back, I shuffle closer, bumping into her with a mumbled apology as if the crowd caused our collision.

She instantly grabs hold of my wrist and I have to pretend to contemplate the plate of hors d'oeuvres rolling by. Luckily, they look good—mini lobster rolls on single pieces of bibb lettuce and half-dollar-sized crab cakes—because I don't know how I'd pull off being interested in caviar or steak tartar. Fucking yuck.

Since the robot waiter doesn't stop and Ever hasn't let go, I just pivot so we're back to back, my arm between us. I look fucking stupid but Ever's needs supersede my own and right now she needs her rocks.

The Munreauxs are talking to some gray-haired man named Penn Larson who hasn't shut up since he approached.

"Ah, Mallory, come meet Ever," I hear him say.

I'm just about to tune out when a male voice says, "My pleasure."

Suddenly, Ever's hand not only releases me, but pushes me away.

I turn to see a different guy kissing that same hand. Who the fuck is this? So far, all these wealthy fucks have kept it to just shaking Ever's hand or doing the fake double-cheek-kiss thing, but this motherfucker's really kissing her hand, his lips on her actual fucking skin.

"Mallory. Nice to finally meet," Ever greets with a dip to her head. "I've heard so much about you."

He's Mallory? I assumed Mallory was a chick.

"And I you." This is punctuated with *another* kiss to Ever's hand before he returns to his full height. "Although…gossip didn't do you nearly the justice it should've. You're positively resplendent." He follows that up with a head-to-toe scan, much like Arthur's, but with a hollowing of his cheeks as well.

He's practically fucking her with his eyes right in front of everyone and I, for one, don't like it. I hate it. In fact, I find myself wanting to rip his head off his body.

"I apologize if that was too forward," he says to Ever, but I'd prefer he say it to my fucking ass—that's how much I don't care to hear it.

But apparently, Ever doesn't feel the same because she tilts her head in a manner that even though I can't see her eyes, I *know* she's eye-fucking him right back as she purrs, "No, not at all."

Damn it, heads are about to roll.

"In fact, I was thinking the same thing about you."

She was? Ever is resplendent. That's a fact. An understated one, but a fact nonetheless. But this guy Mallory? He looks like every other asshole in attendance here tonight, only younger. His hair's darker than Ever's, sure. And he's tall, at least an inch or two taller than my 6'3". But his face is just as forgettably flawless as everybody else's, mine being the only exception. No matter how hard I try to blend in, I still catch the lingering looks on my cheek, the marred skin under my eye burning from the scrutiny.

Beside the pair, Penn and Arthur have gone awfully quiet, each of their eyebrows in varied states as they watch their offspring interact.

What? Are they hoping for some kind of connection between the two? Mallory's too old for Ever. Being younger than this crowd isn't difficult when everyone's in their sixties. He's still older than both me and Ever, probably in his early to mid-thirties. She needs someone younger, someone who can keep up with her.

But not too young, like those sluggish clones of hers.

Mallory holds out a hand to Ever. "Care to dance?"

Ever turns her head side to side, surveying their surroundings—their non-dance floor surroundings—giving me a glimpse of her lips. They're pulled high in a smile. She's happy. This guy is making her happy.

I don't know why that makes my intestines twist, but it does.

"Everyone will look at us," Ever responds in a shy tone. Is she flirting with him? Does she *like* him?

Doesn't mean *I* have to like him. If anything, I should like him even less. Her father hired me to keep fuckboys away from her. I don't care how old he is or how expensive his suit is, as far as I can tell, Mallory Larson could very well be a fuckboy.

"Everyone's already looking at you. Might as well give them something to talk about while they're at it."

That was so fucking cheesy. She better not go for—

Placing her hand in his, Ever lets Mallory pull her into an embrace, then their bodies begin swaying to the barely audible music.

She went for it. And I…can't be close to her. Shit. She needs her rocks.

Or she did before Mallory Larson showed up.

An arm wraps around my shoulder, and with his face so close to mine I can smell the seafood on his breath, Arthur Munreaux says, "What do you say? Time for a much-needed break?"

No.

"But Miss Mun—"

"She's fine. She's in good hands."

"The best," Penn Larson agrees.

Arthur's turning me away from the slow-dancing duo before I can come up with a halfway decent excuse for why I should stay and keep an eye on my protectee. "Because I want to" won't cut it. It's true though. I do want to. She might need my help. Penn Larson giving his son a glowing recommendation means absolutely fuck-all to me. Every parent talks up their kid. It doesn't mean shit. What if he says something that upsets her? What if he rubs his stiff cock on her? By Arthur's standards, Mallory's better than a frat bro. But in my opinion, it doesn't fucking matter who or what he's better than, he's still not good enough for Ever.

"Explore the grounds. See the art. Enjoy a moment of solitude."

"With all due respect, sir, I don't get paid to—"

"You get paid to do whatever the hell I tell you to do. Take a walk." Arthur shoves me in a way that isn't obvious to anyone but me, forcing my feet to move in the opposite direction than the rest of my body wants to go. Fuck.

I stride past sequins and cashmere, feathers and fur.

Fuck!

It's a job. It's just a fucking job.

So what if she's dancing with someone? They're in full view of Arthur, the man who writes my checks. It's his concern. She's his concern. Ever needs something, she can run to Daddy.

I deserve a break and I could use some fresh air away from all this stuffy-ass bullshit.

The open bifold back doors in sight, I swivel at the last second and head for the kitchen instead. Arthur hired me to protect his daughter's reputation. I chose to protect her body. But Ever needs me to protect the rest of her. That's exactly what I'm going to do... with or without my boss's permission.

CHAPTER 23

DON'T GO, DON'T GO, DON'T GO.

I watch past Mallory's arm as Crue disappears through a door, triggering a tremor that begins in my heart and works its way outward to my limbs. *No.* Where is he going? He said he'd stay close. He swore. Him being in an entirely different room isn't close at all.

"Most of the time, the fox survives."

Still searching the crowd in hopes Crue's face will magically appear, I don't bother with more than a "Mm" to my dance partner.

Mallory either doesn't notice or care, because he just continues on, mansplaining fox hunts to me despite my father partaking in the pointless expeditions every winter. A bunch of people on horseback, along with twenty hounds, and depending on the terrain they're going through, maybe even a whipper-in traveling in a vehicle, go on a wild goose chase, except there is no goose. They chase a fox…if they're lucky enough to pick up one's scent. Typically, guns aren't involved, so they literally follow a fox through the woods for "sport." It's just an excuse for men like my father to drink hard liquor at seven in the morning and feel the anticipation of murder without technically murdering anything—usually. Like Mallory said, *most* of the time the fox survives. Sometimes the dogs get a little too eager, sometimes the hunters do. Sometimes the fox just dies of natural causes because it's a wild creature living its life. The hunts my father goes on have scouts up ahead that keep the fox fed—essentially alive—along the way, ensuring the hunt is worthwhile because although chasing a heavily outnumbered, ten-pound fox through the woods is thrilling, chasing nothing through the woods is embarrassing. To him.

To me, it's all embarrassing. Of all the frivolous things we waste money on, fox hunting has to be the dumbest. And Mallory seems to be a huge advocate for fox hunts, so much so he's still talking about them two months after the season ended.

"…rode his horse right into a ravine and it took five of us to get them both out. I told my father we should've left him in there." His deep chuckle stretches several moments too long for a joke that didn't land.

At least I hope it was a joke. It wasn't the horse's fault its rider was an elitist dumbass.

"But I love it. I'm hoping to become Huntsman myself one day and lead my own hunt. The Huntsman has five buttons on his jacket…" Mallory stops dancing to point out five spots down his torso, his expression serious. "Everyone else only has four." Grabbing my hand again, he resumes our dance in a room full of people who are not dancing, completely unconcerned with that or the fact that I couldn't care less about anyone's buttons, let alone his. "I already have three American foxhounds I've been training myself. Unlike other breeds of hunting dogs, American foxhounds are great with kids so they're sound long-term investments."

I drop my eyes to the floor, wishing it'd fall away like a sinkhole. Not only is he already planning for a family, he's referring to dogs as investments. This is our first time meeting and these are the things he says to me?

Thankfully, the classical music stops, causing a hush to fall over the party. My father appears on the second-floor landing, tapping a tablet in his hold before returning it to a docking station on the wall beside him.

The house has never been lived in. World-renowned artist, Bardolph Villegas, was commissioned to make several sculptures for the property, including this one, making it an ideal location for private events.

As I turn to see Father better, Mallory wraps an arm around my back, trapping me against his side. That tremor kicks up, rattling my insides as if my skeleton is just floating in a hollow shell.

But if that were true, why does everything in there hurt so bad right now? Being hollow would be a dream compared to this.

Leaning down, Mallory nuzzles my ear.

I have to force myself to stay still and not jerk away from his touch. I don't know him for him to be so close.

"I'll have to thank your father for telling me you were a dancer."

I internally scoff. What did he get out of our dance other than the sound of his own voice?

My hand on his chest pushing to create some space between my ear and his hot mouth, I gaze up at him, and through a grin, reply, "I'm a cheerleader."

One of his eyes partly closes before he corrects it, his own smile growing. "That's over now though, right?"

The corners of my lips quiver with the added strain to keep them up. After a swallow, I nod.

Mallory gives my father his full attention while I, once again, give mine to the floor.

He's not that bad, I tell myself.

From what I've seen so far, he's not that great either. Would he stand for ninety minutes straight—without complaint—just to see how someone does my hair? Would he learn how to stunt just so I can fly? Would he insist on putting my shoes on me even when they're pumps and I'm perfectly capable of slipping them on myself?

Nobody compares to Crue Brantley. He's… Still missing. Where is he?

I send another glimpse around the room for him.

My father's voice invades my search.

"We're standing in a home of the future…"

And all Mallory can talk about is a tradition from the fifteenth century.

"The floor we've been standing on, walking over, dancing across…" He pauses and I look up to find him, as well as dozens of others, staring directly at me.

I nod at Mallory, silently blaming him for the impromptu dance, which triggers knowing laughter.

"All while generating electricity," my father finishes.

A surprised round of "oohs" and "aahs" rings out as people check under their feet, probably expecting to see sparks.

Father goes on to list other features of the smart home, from the presence detectors in each space to the AI companion robot.

"Growth takes courage and determination, both of which Munreaux Motorcycles was founded on…" He pauses for an enthusiastic round of applause, then lowers his voice ever so slightly. "And will continue to exude even in the darkest of times." Another pause, this one to allow solemn murmurs. A grin tugging at one side of his mouth, he says louder, "Which fortunately for us, are a thing of the past because like the movement-generated lights in this house, the future is looking bright. Very bright." Amidst the cheers, he holds up his glass and shouts, "To new horizons, may we race toward them the way we always have—fearlessly!"

Amidst the cheers, corks begin popping from the very few human servers, one of which delivers flutes of champagne to me and Mallory.

"To new horizons," he says to me.

"To new horizons." I clink his glass with mine.

Chatter, as well as movement, commences around us, and for some reason, a solo stationary figure pulls my eyes past our glasses over to…Crue. Across the room, my bodyguard's leaning against the wall, staring directly at me with a hand up to his mouth, his sleeve dropped a few inches to reveal my amethyst bracelet.

He didn't leave.

He didn't leave *me*.

Some of the weight eases on my mouth, allowing a real smile to take shape.

"Can I get a picture of you two?" a photographer asks.

"You can get several," Mallory replies before I can.

Lowering my glass, I lift my chin and press my tongue to the roof of my mouth, holding the pose.

Crue should look ridiculous with the purple beads against his all-black suit, but he doesn't. He looks sexy. Sexier than before. Sexier than ever.

I let myself imagine walking over there, the crowd parting like the sea as I stroll right up to him, taking him by the back of the neck and kissing him full on the mouth, no regard for the repercussions whatsoever.

After a series of shutters, Mallory says, "If we don't complete our toast, it won't happen," making me finally take my eyes off Crue.

It's stupid. He probably wouldn't even let me get close enough to kiss him.

And if he did, he might recognize me. I know I'd recognize him, even after kissing a lot of people since ours. I could pick Crue's lips out of a thousand others. A hundred thousand. A million. I would know his from a single lick. I've memorized every detail of our mouths coming together. It was brief yet left the biggest impression. *He* left the biggest impression.

The hand at my hip pats once, twice, three times, each one a little harder than the last, but I don't dare react. Not with Crue watching so intently.

When I glance up, Mallory's gazing down at me through lashes blacker than mine.

"I toasted with you."

"But you didn't drink."

"I didn't?" I got distracted and forgot all about the champagne. And Mallory.

"You didn't," he says with a deep chuckle. "Shall we remedy that?"

"We shall," I manage to get out with a straight face before taking the smallest sip in history.

My father appears, Mallory's father not a moment later, then the four of us get a picture together as well.

Despite the flashes nearly blinding me, I seek out Crue. Unfortunately, he's nowhere to be found.

Damn it. Where'd he go now?

"Would you care to accompany me outside?" Mallory asks me. I'm assuming anyway. I'm not paying him the least bit of attention, not while my bodyguard is missing. *Again.*

"Um, actually. I'm feeling a bit—"

Another thump to my hip that's a bit too hard to be coincidence.

"You wouldn't refuse me in my time of need, would you?"

Time of need? He seems needy, all right.

I glance at our fathers, the hope on their faces palpable. Could they be any more obvious?

I attempt to keep the sarcasm from my voice as I ask Mallory, "What exactly are you in need of?"

His thin lips spread.

Letting him lead me away, all I can think of is Crue.

Look for me.

"Someone needs to cut my mother off. She's already on her second rosé of the evening," Mallory says as soon as we're outside.

This is what he needed? To complain about his mother's drinking? Two rosés isn't bad at all. Our fathers are probably on their third or fourth whiskeys by now.

His hand glides down my back and settles on my ass, then he asks, "You don't drink rosé, do you?"

"Not really," I mutter with a half turn to try to get him off me.

I assumed there'd be people out here, too, but we're all alone.

Mallory pulls me closer, my cheek in his rough grasp.

"Where's yours, by the way?"

"My drink?" He's the one who took it out of my hands on our way out here.

"No, your mother."

He's heard so much about me but doesn't know my mother's dead?

"Martha's Vineyard," I say because that's where we were. Since her body was never recovered, maybe she's still there.

"I didn't realize anyone still went there. It's so overrun with commoners."

By anyone, he means people like us, the elites.

"They do." At least they did. A lot can change in five years. "My mother spent every summer there. We'd go visit her the last weekend of August before bringing her home."

"Your father has the right idea. Ship the missus off for the summer so he can have free run on the mainland."

It wasn't his decision. It was my mother's. She chose to be away from both of us, just like she chose death over life. And my father had free run anyway. They all do.

I tilt my head back. "Is that what you'd do?"

His dark gaze moves from my eyes to my lips. "That all depends."

I right my head, studying his red-and-white pocket square. "On what?"

He leans down and I hold my breath that he doesn't kiss me.

His lips on the shell of my ear, he whispers, "How satiated my woman can keep me."

Is this supposed to be a turn-on? Whispering sweet nothings about adultery into my ear? He's basically admitting to being a faultless cheater and I'm expected to swoon?

I'm more likely to vomit.

"Sounds like you have quite the appetite," I deadpan.

"Downright rapacious," he admits unabashedly, his hot breath trickling down the side of my neck as both his hands clasp my ass cheeks, trapping his hardening cock between us.

A gasp leaves my lips before I can stop it. Mallory is an attractive man. His family is both well-known and well-off. He fits into the same circles I do. I *should* want him.

Yet I don't. Not even a little bit. My entire world is full of endless circles. I crave something different, something unique.

Crue appears from the shadows, his steps slow but intentional as he approaches.

Now, *he* is unique.

Running my hands up Mallory's arms, I latch on to his biceps.

"We have that in common," I say without looking away from the only man that makes me feel gluttonous.

"Do we?"

"Mm-hm."

"Excuse me, miss? There's been a security breach. I'm gonna need you to come with me," Crue says from a few feet away.

Mallory's hold on me tightens, a move that does not go unnoticed by my bodyguard.

"What kind of security breach? This is an exclusive event in a smart house."

"So I've been told," Crue murmurs, his gaze locked on the hands currently squeezing my ass. "But that isn't my concern. She is, and she's in danger out here. I need to move her to a secure location."

Both men look at me, but I can't give in so easily. I could… But Crue left me alone after he promised he wouldn't. He has some groveling to do.

"I'm sure whatever—"

"Miss, if you'll come with me."

"It can't be—"

"Miss, please."

"As Mr. Larson pointed out, this is a—"

"Miss Munreaux." The deepening of Crue's tone silences me as does his hand on my elbow. "I need you…to follow me. *Now.*" His fingers curl around my arm, not painfully, just…desperately. Is something actually wrong?

I tear my eyes off his to give Mallory a shrug. "Sounds serious. I should probably do as he says."

"For once," my bodyguard mumbles.

"I'll call my limo and—"

Crue literally rips me out of Mallory's hold, putting his body between ours as he guides me in the direction of the house.

"Miss Munreaux's is already out front. After you, miss."

Crue doesn't wait for any sort of a response from me or Mallory, only shoves me toward the back door, through it, then down a hall that illuminates as we go, the lights triggered by our presence as opposed to motion like the ones Munreaux Manor has.

"Goddess, it's that bad?"

"Worse," comes from behind me in that same no-nonsense tone, making real fear enter my bloodstream. What the hell happened?

"Crue, what—"

I'm forced into a bathroom, the door slamming shut with just the two of us inside, me at one end, Crue at the other.

"What's wrong?"

"What's wrong? *What's wrong?* You were about to fuck that privileged prick."

Of course it's my fault. Of course! I didn't even want Mallory's hands on me, much less any other part of him, but no, it's always me. I'm always dick hunting. If dick is in the vicinity, I'll find it, chase it, and ride it. Hell, I don't even require a full team. I'm the one who deserves the five buttons. Me, the Huntswoman of the century!

Except I'm not. Not really. Hickeys are not proof of a fuck. It's proof of someone sucking on my neck. That's it. Some of them come from sex but not all of them. Even if they were, it's my body, my choice, my fucking life. I had six months to live it my way. Six measly months. Only five down and my father ruined that plan, too. He ruins everything.

"You know what? Fuck you!" I yell, expecting Crue to scream right back at me, wanting him to so I can forget this asphyxia for one fucking second. That's why I let guys suck on my neck so much—so I can focus on something other than the ever-present noose around my throat because it is *always* here, choking me, and I can't escape it. I won't. It will suffocate me.

It already is.

Ticktock.

My inhales become shallower and shallower, my lungs aching from the effort it's taking to pull in the slightest bit of air.

Breathe. Breathe!

I can't breathe.

Through the whooshing, I somehow hear a gritted, "Fine."

My chest about to cave in, I gasp out, "What?" What's fine? Certainly not me. I think I'm dying.

I kinda wish I was.

"You want off, I'll do it myself," Crue practically spits.

A hysterical sort of sound leaves me. Off? Does he mean…

Suddenly Crue's in motion until he's crowding me, my back against the wall as he plants his feet outside of mine, shortening himself by several inches.

He means off-off, as in orgasm. Is this the grovel?

I'm still not going to make it easy on him.

I shove at him, my limbs weak and numb and not making a difference. Nothing I do ever does.

Catching my hands easily, he looks between my eyes and says, "You want me to, don't you?"

Yes.

I make my head rotate side to side.

"That's not what it looked like the other day when your panties were drenched."

I choke out a garbled version of "Well," then rip my hands from his hold to rub at my throat to clear my airway. "They're not now."

Crue's gaze drops briefly before returning to mine. "No?"

"No," I lie.

"You still sick?"

All I can do is frown.

"Your pussy, it's not still… Have you been using your medicine? Eating your yogurt?"

"Yogurt?"

"I read it was good for your pussy."

That's why I've been eating it every morning?

"I'm…fine." I never even needed that cream. Or that disgusting plain yogurt.

"Then how 'bout I check to make sure?"

"If I still have a yeast infection?"

"If you're wet. For me."

"What if it's for *him?*" I point in a random direction, not even sure where Mallory is now. Not even caring.

Despite the fire in his eyes, Crue shrugs. "He'll never get the chance to enjoy it."

"Why not? A privileged prick like him wouldn't derail my future. That was your stipulation, right? As long as the dick—"

"As long as the dick…is mine. That's my new stipulation."

The guy from Hide and Keep, Major Danger, locked me in a bathroom with him and is telling me that not only can I fuck him, I can *only* fuck him.

I've dreamed about that exact scenario, but not this one. Not the one where he's being paid to be around me.

Another push to Crue's shoulder, this one much harder, only gives me a few inches of space, but he gives them to me, standing to his full height again.

We hold each other's eyes for what feels like hours but is probably only seconds.

"I need my hair done, you'll style it."

Crue gives a curt nod.

"I want to stunt, you'll be my base."

He crosses his arms. "Correct."

"I'm anxious, you'll wear my amethyst bracelet."

I reach for it, but he backs up.

"I have an itch, you'll scratch it."

Crue frowns as he unfolds his arms. "I thought you said you were using the medication."

"I meant sex! I need dick, you'll provide it."

"Exactly. I'm the—"

"You can't be my everything!"

His eyebrows crease a split second before he finally raises his voice, too, shouting, "Why the fuck not? You're mine!"

"Your…what?"

"You…" He half-twists like he's going to leave, but I want him to stay. I need him to. What am I to him?

"Hello?" I prompt.

Silence stretches so tight it almost snaps. Before it can, Crue spins back around, rushing out, "You're my protectee. My sole priority is to take care of you. *All* of you."

My scoff knocks around my chest, battering my already bruised heart. That's all I'll ever be to him.

"I don't need taken care of in that way."

His scoff sounds just as incredulous as mine did. "You need taken care of in every way."

"That's what our valet's for."

"Edwin doesn't do for you what I do."

"Ruin my life?"

"Make you so wet your thighs look like they're crying."

He tries coming closer but I stick out my arm, palm to his sternum, the thumps I feel beneath it identical to what's happening in my own chest.

"Stop." It's a warning but sounds like a plea. He's my father's employee. My bodyguard. My enemy.

I should hate him, everything he's doing, everything he will do…

And yet…

My fingers twist in the material of his shirt, pulling him the rest of the way to me because he's more than that. He's the object of my obsession, the catalyst for my transformation, the highlight of my existence.

Bending to my height again, Crue closes the distance between our faces, centimeters separating our lips.

"I'll make you feel so good you won't even consider looking for it elsewhere."

My lips suddenly dry, I lick them, my tongue grazing Crue's at the same time, the top one first, then the bottom. They're exactly like I remember—full and delicious.

His breathing accelerates, drying them all over again.

A whispered, "Prove it," from me sends crackles around their edges.

Crue's mouth descends so quick I have to whip my head to the side to avoid contact.

"Not that."

I see him flinch out of the corner of my eye and shut both.

"I can't kiss you?" Crue's voice carries the hurt I know is on his face, making me ache to cover my ears, too.

"That's not what you offered."

"Are you fucking…" he grits before my dress lifts, allowing air colder than Crue's voice to hit my thighs. "You're such a stuck-up bitch."

I know.

A hand dives into the front of my panties, causing a gasp from me and a curse from Crue. His tone several degrees warmer but still mocking, he says, "A stuck-up bitch that's soaked…for 'the help.'"

He's the one who said I'm *just* his protectee.

"Hold the commentary and get to work. You are on the clock after all."

CHAPTER 24

Crue

WHY DOES THIS PUSSY HAVE TO BELONG TO THIS PERSON? It's as hot as I imagine a demon's would be. Hotter actually, and not just temperature. I haven't even ventured inside yet. I'm still just massaging her lips. Lips that are so wet it's like a slip-n-slide for my fingers.

Fuck, she feels good. Better than I hoped.

I don't get it. Her pussy likes me enough to be *this* lubricated, but her eyes are closed tight, face turned away like she can't stomach the sight of me.

Good thing I don't need her stomach to make her come.

Selfishly, I would prefer to have her eyes. And her lips… After watching them spew insults at me all week, I'd love to test their ability to handle something else, something bigger, see how they look with something other than hatred dripping from them—cum or saliva, I don't care.

But this isn't about me. For once. All I ever fucking think about is myself. Always stuck in my own head, worrying about my own shit.

Ever gives me someone else to think about, to care about.

She wants silence? Fine by me. I only speak to her because I have to.

As long as she's not the silent one. She's still gonna talk, right? Tell me if she likes what I'm doing?

She better. Money only inflates my bank account, not my ego.

Ever's hips buck forward. "Are you going to fuck me already or not?"

"Mm. Not," I say just to piss her off.

And because she's pissing me off. She's always pissing me off.

Those azure eyes finally find mine. "Then why are you—"

"I said I'd get you off and I will."

"You also said your dick was mine but—"

"My dick is yours," I snap before I realize what I'm saying.

My dick's never been anyone's other than mine. Shit. This is happening and there's nothing I can do to stop it.

"All of me is. For the next three years."

The brows above her eyes inch closer together and her gaze drops.

Is that shame I see? Where was this humility when she was threatening her professor over me?

"Keep that in mind the next time you think about going to such great lengths marking your territory," I bite out, pissed all over again. Always angry, always—

"Maybe if you'd let me mark my territory by glazing your dick with my cum, I wouldn't have to."

Jesus fuck, that's what I'm talking about. From my tongue down to my cock, glaze me like a doughnut, Ever Munreaux.

On a growl, I thrust two fingers into Ever's demon cunt, skipping the one-finger prep job I'd usually do. She drives me fucking crazy, makes me feel different than I ever have before. She…

She makes me feel.

It's already happened—I'm hers—and I wouldn't stop it even if I could. After years of the same shit on repeat, I feel emotions again, too many and too much, but they're new, they're…something. In a long line of absolutely nothing, they're definitely something.

I grasp her chin with my left hand, my mouth aiming for hers, but she twists away with a gasped, "No."

Again?

She'll fuck the help but won't kiss the help.

I could turn her face back to mine so easily, barely any effort at all, but the fear of her biting my tongue off keeps me from doing it.

That and the fact I want her to want it. I want her to want anything I do to her. I'm offering myself up willingly, not because I'm being paid to—if anything, I *shouldn't* be doing this because I'm being paid—but because I can't see another man touch Ever the way Mallory did tonight. One look at him groping Ever's ass and I had to stop my-self from not only removing his hands from her body but his as well. I probably would've if he put up the smallest bit of fight. Thankfully he was a little bitch and let me pull Ever right out of his grasp.

Mallory Larson may have a lot going for him, but he doesn't have Ever Munreaux writhing on his fingers, dying to come. I do.

"Do you like that?" I ask, earning a nod but no eye contact.

Curling my fingers inside her pussy, not so much pumping, just playing, I step to the side of her and press up against the underside of her clit, my palm also massaging the outer portion for dual stimulation.

"Do you like *that?*"

Another nod, this one with some panting. It's not words but sounds work, too.

I guess.

I'd prefer words. I'd prefer to see how the devil's spawn kisses. And what her eyes do during an orgasm. Some girls' widen. Others' close tight. A select few have even watered.

"Look at me."

"No."

"Why?"

"It's awkward."

I don't know why girls think that. It's not true at all.

"More awkward than finger-fucking a girl that hates you?" Because this shit feels pretty damn awkward.

It's a few seconds before Ever says, "I wouldn't know. I've never fingered a girl that hates me."

"You've fingered a girl?"

"Only myself."

If my cock wasn't already hard as a rock, it would be now.

"Have you recently?"

She nods.

"Yeah? What were you thinking about when you did?"

Her swallow is so loud it triggers my own. "I..."

"Tell me," I practically plead.

"We're in your Bronco."

I knew it. I knew she didn't stop at just drawing me. She uses me as inspiration for getting herself off. I fucking knew it.

"What else?"

I increase pressure from both directions, adding a roll to my wrist like a wave coming in from the sea to knead the shore gently but thoroughly.

"Knees on the backseat, I'm leaning on the center console as I'm pounded into from behind."

Fuuuck.

My cock leaks, drooling over the vision Ever's creating in my head.

"I'm right on the edge. About to come. Oh, Goddess."

Ever's hand covers mine and she forces my fingers deeper into her. Even from this angle, I see her jaw drop.

No, damn it.

"Keep going," tears out of me.

"Then I… Then I…"

Come on. Come on.

"What? What happens?"

Ever's pussy gets about ten times wetter as her body shakes, the breath flowing from her open mouth sputtering. My bottom lip catches on her bare shoulder as I watch her come, my own breathing interrupted once again. No one steals my breath like Ever Munreaux.

My protectee suddenly stills and rotates her head toward mine.

I pull back to look in her eyes, studying them for any additional moisture. She didn't cry for me but her pussy sure the fuck did.

"Then I looked up and met your eyes through the windshield…"

Through the windshield? Wasn't I—

"Making me come all over some random's dick while you watched from outside your very own car."

Her lips split from laughter.

I rip my hand out of her panties and step several feet away.

"Fantasies aren't real for a reason. That shit'll never happen."

"It wasn't a fantasy, Major. It was a promise." The front of her dress is already back in place but she smooths it anyway, telling me, "Remember *that* next time you offer to fuck me without following through."

Feet frozen to the floor, all I can do is watch her breeze past me. What the fuck did she just say? She's threatening *me*?

I stick the two fingers I just had in Ever's pussy into my mouth and suck her juices clean off. Mm, mm, mm. Mouthwatering.

"See you in the limo."

Through a whole-face scowl, I drop my hand and spin to follow her.

She huffs but doesn't say anything as she leaves the bathroom, me hot on her heels because who the fuck does she think I am letting her walk through this party alone? And risk that motherfucker Mallory putting his hands on her again? I don't think so. He'll be eating dirt before getting a taste of what I just did.

Because I lied about her limo being ready, we have to wait out front for a few minutes, neither of us so much as acknowledging the other's presence. Once the limo pulls up, she scrambles into it, opting to sit as far away from me as she can possibly get.

Like I care. Like I fucking care. I only put her shoes on for her, and wore her bracelet for her, and finger-fucked her to climax. So what if I didn't fuck her? I do everything else for the ungrateful little brat.

"You're welcome," leaves my lips before I've even made the decision to say it aloud.

"Excuse me?" she snarls from her spot near the partition, making the next decision for me. Not only did I mean to say that shit, I'm doubling down.

Leaning forward, I look her right in the eyes, and repeat, "You're. Welcome."

"For giving me blue lips?"

"Blue *what*?"

"Lips! I'm all swollen from the amount of blood down there." She gestures wildly at her crotch. "And without a release—"

"You got a release. You got a fucking release!" I dust off my thighs as I sit back. "So just say thank you and—"

Something sails through the air so fast, it hits me in the forehead before I can react. By the time I realize what's happened, the object is in my lap.

Staring down at one of Ever's high heels, I grit out, "What the *shit* was that?"

A singsonged, "You're welcome," is the response I get.

I snap the heel off the shoe. Broken, like my patience.

Fuck her shoes. Fuck her. I'm done being nice.

Ever deadpans, "Those were vintage."

I toss both pieces on the floor between us. "Well, now they're trash."

She takes the other one off, but this time I'm watching and am able to knock it away before impact. This is exactly why her shoe privileges were revoked. She can't be trusted with anything that can be used as a weapon.

"I hate you," she seethes.

I shrug. "Not as much as I hate you, brat."

"I knew your wrists were weak but I didn't know your fingers were, too."

Oh, now she's going for the jugular.

"My fingers work fine. Your pussy's just—" I cut myself off, unable to lie. There was nothing wrong with her pussy. I'd slurp that cunt like soup.

"Just what?"

"I don't know, Ever. It's hard to think clearly while concussed."

"You are not concussed."

I don't respond and neither does she, so I pretend to look out the window, the weight of her gaze relentless.

Does she feel bad? Enough to nurse me back to health?

Quieter, she asks, "Are you?"

Hmm, no. But I'll give myself a concussion if it brings her back over here.

Looking at her again, I force another shrug. "Yeah."

Come on, Ever. Come take care of me.

She doesn't though. She just says, "Good," probably because she's incapable of caring for anyone other than herself.

"If I'm not outside your room in the morning, it's because I died in my sleep," I say, laying it on thicker than unstirred peanut butter.

"Maybe you should close your eyes now and see. That way the driver can take your body straight over to the morgue." She follows her cruel suggestion with a smug-ass smirk I'd kiss off her if she let me.

She may be evil but by God is she gorgeous, especially when she smiles. I don't even care that it's about my death, only that she's no longer ignoring me.

I roll my eyes at her…and myself. Banter shouldn't turn me on the way it does.

A vibration on my stomach jolts me awake, this time without the usual accompanying scent of honey. I crack an eye to see…my phone.

It's this manor, specifically this wing of it. Ever's scent is so strong, it fucking tortures me. Every morning, I wake up feeling as if she's right next to me, and I can't stop the disappointment whenever I discover she's not.

It's insane to even consider. She would never come to me willingly, not like that.

My phone's screen lights up, and I lift it off my stomach. Last thing I remember was returning a text to my mom, so I must've fallen asleep still holding it. Checking for her response, I find a notification for Ever's door instead. It's 2:57 a.m. Where's she going?

Nowhere without me.

I drag my ass out of bed, my eyes at half-mast and blurry because I'm fucking beat. I don't know how the hell Ever's awake right now. She did way more cheer shit than I did today.

Yesterday. Whatever.

A body much bigger than Ever's standing in the middle of the hallway puts all of my muscles on lock, prepped for fucking battle, until it spins to face me.

"Mr. Brantley? Is that you?" Chef Ryan whispers.

Who else would it be?

"Crue."

"Right. Yes. Mr. Crue Brantley."

My head shakes. I don't have the patience for this shit. Just get to the point already.

"What's up?"

"I apologize. I must've mixed up the doors."

He knocked on Ever's door thinking it was mine? Fuck. Hopefully Ever didn't hear it.

"Why? What's wrong?"

"There's a…" He jiggles his head. "I'm not sure how to describe it but it sounded like someone, a person, you know…perhaps, was trying to get in through my window. And I thought…"

"The house alarm wasn't tripped, was it?"

"Uh, no, I don't believe so."

"It's probably fine."

No offense to Ryan, his food's good and all, but I don't particularly care about someone going into his room. Only if they make it up to Ever's.

"That's a good point. I didn't think of that."

He hesitates, looking more spooked than awkward. For a second, I consider the possibility that Arthur lied and there really is an external threat against Ever. Could be. She is fucking irritating.

"I can check it out if it'd make you feel better," I half-suggest, half-sigh.

I wasn't hired to protect him, but if someone is trying to break into Munreaux Manor, better I know now than if they do get near Ever.

"Sure. Okay. Yes, I would like that. Appreciate you, uh, doing so. Thank you."

Jesus.

"Show me which room."

I take my phone with me, just in case Ryan did wake up Ever and she gets any ideas. She has more energy than my parents' golden retriever.

CHAPTER 25

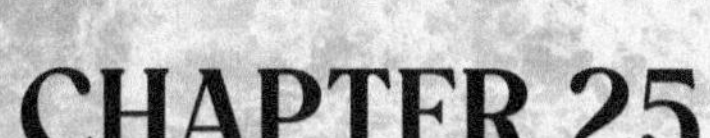

WHO THE HELL IS IN CRUE'S ROOM? HE PLEASURES ME, then sneaks someone in here immediately after?

She's short, shorter than me. And judging by her hair, which has some kind of knot at the top with strands sticking out all over, she just got fucked. Really fucked. The kind of fucked Crue was supposed to do to me but didn't because… I don't know why he refused to fuck me.

Maybe so he could come home—to my home—and fuck *her.*

Jealousy seizes me, overtaking every rational thought, even the ones reminding me to stay hidden, and I storm across Crue's room and grab her by that ugly hair to—

Ah! Her head! It's off her shoulders! Oh my fucking Goddess, I beheaded someone.

I wasn't even trying to. I just wanted to pull her hair a little. *A lot.* But I didn't grab her *that* hard, did I? Enough to rip her head off?

Oh shit. Oh shit. Oh shit. What do I do? I literally have someone's head in my hand.

Why am I still holding it?

I release the wiry-feeling hair, letting the head fall to the floor with a *thump.*

That's weird. I thought it'd sound squishier.

Gross.

Now what? Should I slip back out like nothing happened? What will Crue think when he wakes up and finds a decapitated body, as well as its detached head, in the middle of his floor?

Hopefully he takes it as a lesson. Don't sneak women into your room.

Not that I meant to remove her head from her body. Her body that was just—

Wait…her body. Where is it? There was only one thud. Shouldn't her headless body have fallen, too?

I glance around, straining my eyes in the dark. It was easier to decipher outlines of things from the wall. This close it's much harder to identify objects. Isn't this his desk though? Was she sitting on it?

Ever so slowly I pivot toward Crue's bed. No lump whatsoever, it's clear he's not even in it.

Okay, well, where is he? Every other night I've snuck in here he's been asleep in his bed.

But now he's missing and there's a head on his…

If she was on his desk, she would've been *much* shorter than I originally assumed. Too short to even have a torso…

That can't be right. That's…

What the hell am I talking about? It was just a head, already on the desk. I didn't decapitate anyone.

Did Crue? I can't really see him doing that, especially the leaving-the-head-on-his-desk-like-a-psychopath part.

But who else would've?

There's only three other people currently in the manor—my father, his valet, and the chef.

Fear overtakes my body, burning up the jealousy in an instant. Where is Crue?

The door to his room flies open, spraying the room in harsh light. My shirtless bodyguard stands at the threshold.

"Where have you been?" I demand.

"How'd you get in here?" He checks his phone.

I blindly thrust a hand toward the floor. "Who is this?"

Crue barely eyes what has to be a gruesome scene before saying matter-of-factly, "I don't know. I didn't name her yet."

That sounds like a psychopath to me. Damn it.

After a sigh, I ask, "Where's her body?" As long as he didn't fuck her, I'll help him get rid of the evidence. If he did fuck her, he's so on his own.

"She didn't come with one. At least not one that Chloe offered up."

Chloe? My hairstylist?

For the first time, I look down at the head, finding it doesn't belong to my hairstylist, or even a human. It belongs to a mannequin.

I didn't decapitate anybody. My bodyguard didn't decapitate anybody.

The biggest relief of all though? He didn't fuck anybody.

"Why did Chloe give that to you?"

Shaking his head, he closes the door behind him. "To learn how to do hair."

He's worth burying a body—or head—for. Unless…

"Do you two talk now?"

"Talk? We had one conversation and it ended the moment I…"

"The moment you what?"

"Told her to give it to Edwin because we wouldn't be home."

"So it was before the gala?"

"Yes. When you were in the bathroom, getting dressed."

That's what they had their heads together about when I came out?

Now that I think about it, I'm not sure Chloe's the best fit for me anymore.

"How'd you get in my room?"

"Your door doesn't have a lock."

With a wave of his illuminated phone, he says, "There's no history of you leaving yours."

Using that little bit of light, I busy myself retrieving the mannequin. "Maybe you missed it."

"I didn't."

"Must've malfunctioned then. I don't know what to tell you." Certainly not the truth.

The room goes pitch black.

"Why are you in here?"

"I was…" I set the head on the desk, heavily contemplating burying it still so Crue has to practice on my hair instead. "Just seeing if you'd died yet."

"You care? I'm touched."

I can tell he's holding his heart before he falls on his bed, face down…nothing like what a person with a concussion would do.

"Only about the smell. It'd be a terrible inconvenience to wake up to the odor of your rotting corpse."

Head turned to the side, he says, "Happy to disappoint. You can leave."

I stare at the door to the hall. I don't have the key to my room on me.

"But…" What's a good excuse? "You never answered my question. Where were you?"

"Why does it matter?"

"I could've needed you."

His head pops up. "Did you?"

Always.

"No."

He drops his head back down. "Ryan wanted me to check something for him."

Chef Ryan?

"Did you run into him in the kitchen or something?"

"Just because he works in the kitchen doesn't mean he lives in it." After a minute, he adds, "He was up here. Is that what woke you up?"

"When?"

"When he knocked on your door."

He was at my door? Fucking knocking on it?

He's getting brave. Too brave.

Instead of answering, I ask, "What'd he need?"

Even his chuckle is exhausted. "He was scared someone was trying to open his window."

"Were they?"

"Not that I saw. It was probably just a bug hitting the glass." After a pause, he says, "Or one of your bats."

"Yeah," I breathe while falling into the armchair.

"Are you just gonna watch me sleep?"

That's what I usually do. That's why I'm in here. That's why I have an alarm on my phone to wake me up at three a.m.

"No," I say with a touch too much attitude. "I just…was…wondering…" I don't have a reason for staying, at least not one I can tell Crue. But I don't have a way to get back in my room without that hidden door and I'm not taking my chances in any other part of the manor.

"Were you wanting to fuck or something?" he asks.

"You know me…super horny. All the time."

Appalled at how desperate I'm making myself look, my entire body cringes all the way down to my toes. I'll look more desperate if he finds out the truth though.

There's some shuffling around on his mattress and I can just make out him flipping to his back, his head lifted to see me.

"That's really why you came in here?"

The real reason I came in here is because lying with Crue while he's asleep is the only time I get him wholly, without judgement.

"Sure?"

More shuffling as he relaxes, then, "Draw me something. I think there's a pen in the desk."

"Is that another one of your stipulations for having sex with—"

"Just draw me something. We're not having sex tonight."

I remove my shoulders from my ears, letting them hang normally, but argue, "It's morning and I can't draw in the dark."

"Turn on the lamp."

"Won't that bother you?"

"There you go again."

I scowl. "What?"

"Caring about me."

If only he knew.

"Maybe I just don't want you to see the pillow coming when I cover your face with it."

Another deep, sleepy chuckle, this one pulling a smile from me.

"If you think I'm up your ass now, wait until I haunt you in the afterlife."

"What's your unfinished business?"

"My what?" comes out muffled.

"Only people with unfinished business become ghosts." I shrug even though he can't see it. "At least that's what the movies always say."

Crue doesn't respond for so long I assume he fell asleep, until finally, he says, "Everything."

I think about that for a while and about how true it feels for me, too. How do you leave life if you've never really lived one? I can see why some choose not to.

"What should I draw on?"

My only answer is heavy breathing, and when I turn on the lamp, Crue's eyes are shut, his face serene. In my afterlife, I hope I'll get the freedom I so desperately crave in this life. An eternity of watching Crue sleep wouldn't be enough, but I'd savor every minute of it just like I do now.

CHAPTER 26

Crue

THIS TIME I DO PICK UP THOSE FAMILIAR NOTES OF HONEY, the kind in a glass jar sitting on a table, with a walnut dipper sticking out of it as the sun streams through the window making it warm and pourable.

She's in here, with me.

Play it cool.

Fighting a hard-on, I slowly roll to my back, then stretch my arms out to the sides. People stretch every morning. It's not unusual.

The lower my arms go, the higher my cock rises, until—

Okay, where the fuck is she?

Only cool sheets beneath my arms, I open my eyes, instantly finding both sides of the bed empty. Trying to shake that disappointment away all over again, I stare at the ceiling, my hand rubbing my stomach. And cock. Just a little.

That was stupid. The fake-ass stretch. The anticipation. All of it. Ever Munreaux is not the type of girl to crawl into bed with a guy like me. She was only in here to terrorize me for some unknown reason.

She could still be in here.

Catapulting up to sitting, I scan the rest of my empty room. Over on the desk, right next to the mannequin head, are my sneakers, and since that's not where I left them, I know Ever's responsible. I go over and pick both up, turning them over. On the sides are doodles of birds, or maybe even bats, flying over the words PROPERTY OF EVER MUNREAUX.

My lips quirk. After I broke her shoes last night, she took it upon herself to replace them with a pair of mine. It's undoubtedly the cheapest outcome, so if she wants them, she can have them. They won't fit her but she can add them to the rest of her collection of shoes she doesn't wear.

They're much cleaner than they were, too, basically brand new even though I've had them for over three years now. I try to picture Ever going through the trouble of scrubbing my three-year-old kicks and grin ear to ear.

All at once, the smile withers up and dies. *What did she use?*

As soon as I enter my bathroom, I have my answer—my toothbrush. Its bristles now brown and mangled, it's completely useless to me.

She also left me a sticky note on the mirror with I BELONG TO EVER MUNREAUX written on it—an affirmation she'd probably love me to repeat each day because that bitch wasn't talking about the shoes. She was talking about their owner—me.

I shouldn't have fallen asleep. This is what happens when she's left to her own devices.

Speaking of devices…

I check my phone for when she left but find nothing. No notifications whatsoever. Just like when she showed up.

The sensor *is* faulty.

Goddamn it. It's always something in this job.

I'm banging on Ever's door, yelling her name, notifications lighting up my phone's screen like fireworks on the Fourth of July. What the hell? It's only faulty some of the time?

"What?" I hear from the other side and breathe a sigh of relief.

"Are you awake?" Stupid. Obviously, she is.

"Now I am. Why?"

"Nothing. Just, uh…seeing if we're gonna try more stunts today."

Shit. Fuck. Goddamn. That's not how I wanted to spend my Sunday. I wasn't going to stunt again unless she wanted to.

Why does my mouth suggest things without my brain in full agreement?

"Sure?"

"Um, okay. See you when you're, uh, you know, ready. Or not. You don't have to get ready…for me." I fucking frown. This morning just keeps getting worse. *I* just keep getting worse.

I'm half a step away from the door when she calls, "Crue?"

I lean back the other way, my ear near the wood. "Yeah?"

"You're welcome."

With a shake of my head, I return to my room without acknowledging that, especially not with a thank-you. At least when I said it, I actually gave her something—an orgasm. All she did was destroy something. Two somethings—my sneakers *and* my toothbrush. I didn't take a good enough look at the mannequin but it wouldn't surprise me if she did something to that, too. It's not hard to guess why the head was on the floor when I walked in last night. Like Ever's energy, her jealousy is inexhaustible.

I'd love to know why she was in my room at all. Or why she didn't seem to want to leave it. It wasn't to fuck. Unfortunately.

If she wants to sit in here and draw on my belongings, she can do it every night for all I care. Most of the stuff in this room was paid for using Arthur's money anyway. It's better than trying to track her ass down if she sneaks out.

Track her down… That's exactly what I'm gonna need to do now that the sensors in her room aren't working properly. But how can I get a tracker on her without her knowing it? Most devices are bigger than the size of a quarter. I can't hide something like that on Ever. She notices anything that could potentially ruin her aesthetic.

My gaze falls to my wrist, where her purple bracelet sits. She didn't ask for it back last night and I forgot to offer it.

That's not true. I didn't want to give it back. I still have the other one, too. Knowing her, she'll probably demand I return both soon. If only I could stick a tracker on them before I did.

What if I could? Most devices are too big, but that doesn't mean all are. Animal trackers aren't.

When we first got Zeus, my mom ordered a microchip for him without fully understanding how it worked—*under* his skin. She took one look at the syringe already loaded with the microchip and decided to go with a less invasive yet bulkier collar tracker instead. Even though I was younger at the time, I remember looking at the syringe, amazed how something as small as a grain of rice could not only track but also transmit that kind of information.

Hopping on my phone, I order a pack of twenty, springing for expedited shipping, then because those were the only sneakers I have, I look up the nearest shoe store and buy three pairs of the cheapest white ones they have, selecting the option to pick them up in-store. That should keep her busy until the trackers come in.

Now I just gotta make her think I hate what she did to my shoes. Ever's talented. Without the property claim on them, I'd wear those shoes with her art added no problem. But the more shit I give her about defacing my possessions, the more she'll want to keep doing it. If it weren't for her conservation efforts, I'd swear Ever's only objectives in life were to look amazing and piss me the fuck off.

"Haven't you been paying attention?"

Bags of shoes in hand, I lead Ever up the manor's front steps. I took her with me to pick them up, and while she's been eyeing the bags with obvious suspicion ever since, this is the first thing she's said to me.

"To what?" I mumble, acting like I'm barely paying *her* attention. I didn't know what time she was gonna come out of her room this morning, so I had to stand outside it for two hours. When she finally did emerge, she was smiling like the cat that ate the canary, thinking she's so cute for what she did to my shoes. I wasn't wearing them but I acted mad anyway. I've been scowling ever since just to keep up the ruse.

If she were my girlfriend and did that, it actually would be cute. I don't care. I'd wear that shit proudly.

But she's not my girlfriend and she's annoying.

"The Munreauxs aren't cheap."

"Okay," I say with even less emotion.

"We don't associate with cheap."

I want to say she associated with Mallory Larson but don't feel the need after making my feelings on the matter clear last night. Her association with him, and any man who isn't me, is over.

For three years.

It's weird to have a timeline on a… This isn't a relationship exactly. It's more situational. A situationship, I guess. Is that what the fuck this is? Not really. I'm her personal protection agent. She's my protectee. We hate each other, but we're fucking. We will be fucking. Eventually.

If we don't kill each other first.

Which is very possible if she doesn't spit out whatever the fuck she's trying to say.

"What are you talking about, miss?"

She growls and I almost forget to keep my frown in place.

"Your shoes!"

We both stop in the foyer to face each other.

"They're the cheap brands."

I look down at the top box.

"So what?"

"You can't wear them around me. Sorry. You have to return them. Immediately."

I lift my gaze to Ever's. Did she just apologize?

"I can't. I don't have any other pairs of sneakers to run in."

"Yes, you do. I saw—" She cuts herself off and squares her shoulders before continuing in a much calmer tone, "I'm sure that's not true."

Oh, there it is. That shame for engaging with the help. She was about to admit out loud to being in my room, snooping through my things, something a Munreaux should not be doing.

"How do you know?" I question with an arched eyebrow.

We hold each other's stare for a couple long minutes and I can see the moment defeat takes over her body, her shoulders drooping but her chin lifting.

"You don't need four pairs of sneakers."

"Three. My other pair is ruined, thanks to…"

Her sharp inhale has me giving in, too. God, I'm pitiful today. One fingerjob and I don't know how to act.

"Our last run. The mud got all over them, even inside." I doubt anyone's listening but just in case.

"You don't need three pairs—"

"I do."

"You—"

"Do," I finish for her, ending the argument once and for all.

"Be that as it may, the Munreauxs aren't cheap, so you will be returning them—"

"Like I've said many times now, I'm not a Munreaux. And until my first paycheck hits my bank account, these are all I can afford," I lie. I got that five-K bonus already, but that's my business.

Ever appears stunned as she asks, "You haven't been paid yet?"

I forget she has no idea how the real world works.

"It depends on the employer but typically paychecks are deposited every one or two weeks. Or if you're salary, monthly." Which for the first time in my life, I am. "Considering it's Sunday, I technically haven't even worked here a full week yet." It's crazy to think I only got hired on Monday. It feels like I've been at this a hell of a lot longer. At the end of three years, I'll be like every president coming off their term, looking like I served ten years longer than I actually did.

"Why didn't you say anything?"

"To who? You? So you can make fun of me some more about being poor?"

Ever's quiet for a moment, then says, "Well, I need to go shopping."

On to her this time, I just shake my head. "No." It's not worth watching her dad get upset with her again while she lies her way through an explanation for spending thousands of his dollars on me.

"You can't tell me no."

"No," I repeat before turning and heading up to our wing.

"Those shoes are ugly!" she calls out, the desperation in her voice giving her away. She thinks if I don't have any other sneakers, I'll have to wear the ones she decorated. It's not happening. I wouldn't give her the satisfaction of seeing those on my feet if they were the last shoes on earth. I'd go barefoot through the Lut Desert before letting her win.

"They'll match my other pair."

Another growl from her earns another smirk from me, this one I actually let free once I'm at the top of the stairs.

"I'll be in the gym."

"You better be," I mutter as I pick up the pace. If I had a tracker on her already, I wouldn't have to question that kind of statement. As it stands now, I can't trust anything out of her mouth.

In my closet, I quickly arrange the new shoes in a neat row, each pair on top of their boxes like an enticing display of in-season fruit at a farmer's market. Ever can act as high and mighty as she wants, but one look at these and she won't be able to resist. She doesn't want anyone to know she likes what she's not supposed to…

But I know.

CHAPTER 27

WITH CRUE OUT OF SIGHT, EDWIN FINALLY STEPS forward.

"Miss Munreaux, your father would like a word."

"I'm busy," I try halfheartedly.

"He insists."

Doesn't he always?

I follow the valet to my father's office.

My father's eyes don't move from mine as I sit in front of his desk. He doesn't speak right away either, choosing to swivel his head side to side, letting the unease build.

I try not to let it even though I am guilty of a lot of things, most of them enough to send my father into a rage. That's part of the reason why I do them.

"Explain to me what happened last night."

I figured it was only a matter of time before I'd be punished for that.

"I had a great time with Mallory. I feel I really got to know—"

"Why did you disappear so suddenly?"

"As I tried telling you last night, I didn't feel well, and—"

"The executive protection agent accompanied you home?"

"Per your mandate, he accompanies me every—"

"How did he know you weren't feeling well?"

Why does he keep asking me questions if he isn't even going to let me answer?

"I informed my bodygu—"

"How? I sent him on a break."

That is news to me considering he only left my side for…

That's why he disappeared. Father made him. He didn't willingly leave me at all.

"I texted him when it became clear I wouldn't be able to continue the—"

"Why did Mr. Larson seem to think it was a matter of security?"

"I felt that was a much more appropriate excuse—"

"You should've had Mr. Larson take you home then. Did he offer to?"

"I can't remember. I wasn't—"

"Feeling well? Yes, you've stated that al—"

"I wasn't interested in shitting myself in front of him," I snap, sick to death of not only being interrogated but also talked over. Even if everything I'm saying is false, I still deserve the chance to speak uninterrupted. "I'm sure even you can agree *that* would've made a terrible first impression, no?"

Silent now, he resumes the scrutiny meant to intimidate me.

I hold his eyes, wondering how they can be so different from mine. Not just in color but in the way they view the world.

"Every time I'm around you, I lament the fact I didn't make your mother abort you."

"Oh." I clutch my irreparably fissured heart. "Me, too, Father. Me, too."

"Finally, we agree on something. Maybe there's hope for us yet."

A scoff leaves me involuntarily. "I wouldn't count on it."

"I don't."

The deliberate hostility crumbles my resolve, forcing me to look away.

"Is that all?"

"No. Due to your disappearing act, Mr. Larson is requesting more time getting to know you."

Mallory had the chance to get to know me. He chose to talk about himself. And feel me up.

"So, we'll be hosting the Larsons for dinner."

"Here? At the manor?"

"Yes. To make things more *intimate*."

I exhale for so long it feels like my lungs have deflated entirely. "When?"

"Wednesday."

Hearing everything I need to, I push myself up from the chair and dash for the door, my insides in knots.

"And, Never?" my father calls to my back. "Wear red. It's his favorite color."

I leave the office on autopilot, somehow making it down to the gym, nothing registering along the way. If my father called off Crue for a few hours during last night's gala, he'll probably give my bodyguard the night off on Wednesday. I will be well and truly on my own, just like I always have been, just like I always will be.

Someone grabs my shoulder, making me jump.

"You ignoring me or something?" Crue asks.

"Always."

His frown gets to me. His presence gets to me. Why does he have to be stuck to me now but won't during Wednesday's "intimate" dinner? That's when I'll need him.

Will I need him?

I'll want him.

I always want him.

"Shouldn't you be used to it by now?" I mutter.

Without answering, he asks, "What did your dad want?"

How did he know I was talking to him? Did I pass him on the way down here? Did he follow me?

"To know why I left the gala early."

A hint of uncertainty crosses Crue's features. "What did you tell him?"

"That I had an upset stomach. So if he asks, you should say the same."

He steps closer. "You weren't actually sick, were you?"

I only shrug. There was nausea at some points.

"You should've said something."

"It doesn't matter. It never fucking matters," I blurt because I can't hold it in anymore.

"What doesn't?"

Me!

"Nothing. Let's just—"

Crue grabs my arm. "What doesn't matter?"

"My overall comfort."

"Comfort? You have a butler, a professional chef, and a personal protection agent, all at your disposal day and night."

The reminder of the chef slinking around outside my room last night tugs at the knot in my stomach. I would never ask for anything from Chef Ryan during the day, but especially not at night.

"You have a private movie theater, salon, and gym. You have a fucking butterfly conservatory. You have the most comfortable life imaginable. You—"

"Can you teach me how to wrestle?"

Crue appears bewildered momentarily. It seems out of nowhere for him, but it's been a long time coming for me. They can make back handsprings during fight sequences look good in movies all they want, but they're not realistic. I need to know how to defend myself properly.

"Why?"

"Why not?"

"I don't want to."

"I didn't want to teach you how to stunt but I did."

"Is everything tit for tat with you?"

"What are you talking about?"

"I ruin a pair of your shoes. You ruin a pair of mine."

"I didn't ruin them. If anything, I improved them."

His eyes widen. "I guess that's why they say art is subjective."

"What do you mean?"

"Your design…"

"Yeah. What about it?"

"What was it supposed to be?"

"Bats. A reminder of your first night in the manor."

"I thought they'd be better."

What?

"I'd like to see you draw something better."

"I'm just saying, they weren't as good as the stuff I saw in your sketchbook."

The sketchbook he was never supposed to see.

"I had better supplies, not to mention more time on the pieces in my sketchbook," I huff out, annoyed. Annoyed he's critiquing my art. Annoyed at my father. Annoyed I feel the need to protect myself in my own home. How is that living comfortably?

Crue lifts one shoulder. "If you say so."

I do say so. I'll prove it to him. Tonight.

"Whatever. Are you going to teach me how to wrestle or not?"

"I already told you. No."

"Do you have something better to do?" I ask, knowing full well his schedule is my schedule. And would you look at that? It's open today.

"I just thought you were gonna show me more stunts."

"We did stunts yesterday."

"Not all of them."

"Even I don't know all of them."

"You don't? The Queen of Cheer herself?"

I need praise like a fish needs water—no amount is too much—but flattery only works when it's genuine.

"Do you know every wrestling move?" I counter.

"Probably not *every* move."

"See."

"But I haven't wrestled in years. Shit changes all the time."

Is he scared to wrestle again? Is that what's holding him back?

"You're right. It was a terrible idea asking you."

His head dips in acceptance…of an apology I'm not giving.

"I'll get someone else to teach me."

When I try to swerve Crue, he catches me by my elbow and grits, "Over my dead. *Fucking.* Body."

I blink up at him and say sweetly, "That can be arranged."

He rolls his eyes as he drags me to the center of the mat. I have to capture my grin between my teeth.

"All right." He scrubs his hands down his face. "Get on your hands and knees."

The only thing on me that moves is my eyebrow rising ever so slowly.

"Why?"

"In wrestling, you either win with a pin or points. I'm gonna show you what a pin feels like."

"Wouldn't it make sense for me to pin you instead?"

He chuckles darkly. "If you can take me down."

The second I reach my arms toward him, he smacks them both away.

My skin stinging, I snarl, "You didn't even let me try."

"Yeah, I did. Your 'try' was slow as fuck. Go again."

I scan him for any weak spots, finding exactly zero. I mean, there is one. Every man assumes it's a strength, when really, it's a weakness. One tap and they're on their knees, crying like helpless babies.

As if reading my thoughts, Crue covers his dick and warns, "Don't even fucking think about it."

I throw my hands up. "Well, I don't know how else to pin you."

"The first part's called a takedown. And even if you did manage to take me down, you wouldn't know what to do with me."

"Ask all the guys I've had under me if I knew what to do with them."

A wildfire breaks out in my bodyguard's gaze.

"Tell me who they are and I'll go ask 'em right now."

"I…" Feeling the heat myself, I study a cuticle. "Can't remember. Too many to keep track of." More like I didn't bother trying.

"Then this should come naturally for you." Crue points one long finger at the mat. "All fours. Now."

And he wonders why I'm always wet around him.

"If I come naturally, why'd you make it look so difficult last night?"

"Jesus Christ, just get on your hands and knees before I change my mind."

With a sigh, I lower to my knees, then hands.

"Am I at least getting a spanking?" It takes great effort to keep the hope out of my voice.

"Keep it up, and you just fucking might."

Might is practically maybe, which everybody knows is technically no.

Why am I disappointed I'm *not* getting spanked?

Staring at the mat below me, I wait for Crue's instructions but nothing comes.

I glance over my shoulder to find him not even looking at me, his body half-turned.

"Crue?"

"What?"

What does he mean "what?" Aren't we in the middle of a lesson?

"What happens now?"

"Now I gotta pin you."

But he doesn't. He remains where he is.

"With telekinesis?"

"No, I...don't want to do this. I told you I didn't want to do this."

I should've kept it up and earned myself a spanking. At least I'd be getting something out of being in this position.

"That's it. I'm getting someone else to teach me."

Approaching from the side, Crue shoots to a knee, and in one smooth motion I'm rolled to my back, the ceiling suddenly above me, Crue's torso weighing down mine.

My chin on his lat, all I can do is gasp out the breath I had no idea got caught in my lungs.

"Nobody's dick touches you but mine," he says, sounding just as winded.

"Yours isn't even touching me."

"But anyone else pinning you would make sure theirs did."

I don't doubt that for a second. But also...

"And you won't?"

"I'll rub my cock all over every inch of you, Ever Munreaux…as soon as you can look me in the eyes while I do it."

The visual of Crue holding his rigid shaft, dragging the tip along my body, causing moans and goose bumps and shivers, plays out like a movie in front of my eyes.

It's impossible to get all of my swallow down on the first attempt. The second one isn't much better, so I leave my throat partially clogged to ask, "What makes this a pin?" I don't even know what happened really—it was so quick.

"You feel how both your shoulder blades are flat on the floor right now?"

"Yeah?" It's kinda hard to notice anything other than Crue. And what he just threatened.

"Then that's a pin."

"How long do they need to touch the floor for?"

"In high school, it's two seconds. College, it's one."

It's been a lot longer than two seconds, but I don't dare point that out and risk Crue getting up.

"It has to be done in this position?"

"What position?"

"Crucifix?" We definitely resemble a cross.

"This isn't a crucifix. That's something different. But no, you don't have to be perpendicular to your opponent. You just have to get their shoulder blades to touch the floor for one to two seconds."

"That's not very long at all."

"That's why there's constant movement in wrestling, not only to get your opponent's shoulders down but to keep yours up."

"How do you get out of this?"

"You don't. You're done. You already lost."

"But say only one of my shoulders was touching…"

I lift up one shoulder as high as I can manage with a man on me, only to have that man instantly readjust to pin me all over again.

"Hypothetically…what if I wasn't pinned yet? How would I get out of this?"

"From your back?"

"Yes."

"This is literally the worst spot to be in, especially if the person on top weighs more than you."

Exactly.

"But is there a way out?"

"If you work really fucking hard."

Unable to speak, I nod. I already figured that.

"You basically have to forget about getting your own pin for a second and focus all your energy on getting me off as quickly as possible."

When I turn my head to look toward his, my chin rubs along his shirt.

His face toward my legs, he says, "Getting me off *you*. I meant getting me off you as quickly as possible. You know what a bridge is, right?"

I roll my eyes and arch my butt and back up.

"No, hold on." Crue drives me right back down. "It's not the regular bridge. It's the wrestling bridge where your head, elbows, and feet are the only things on the ground. You're gonna do that *while* you turn away from me. Fast."

Just as my middle lifts a quarter inch off the floor, Crue says, "Shit. Hold on. I forgot something. It's been a while. You're gonna do three things simultaneously. During all that, you gotta scissor your right leg under your left leg."

"How do I scissor?"

"Sweep it underneath the other one to the other side."

I do as he says, feeling an immense relief as Crue rolls off me.

Unfortunately, it doesn't last long because his weight comes down on top of me all over again as he flattens me out on my stomach.

"Good girl," he rasps in my ear. He has my wrists captured above my head and his front is draped along my entire backside.

"How is this good? I just made myself more vulnerable!" I yell, my breath disturbing the strands of hair stuck to my lips.

"You're not more vulnerable. Trust me, you have a lot more options from this position."

"It doesn't feel like I have any options with all of your weight on me."

"This isn't all my weight. I'm only using one leg to hold you down right now."

He is?

"One? You're sure?"

"Positive. You couldn't handle all of me."

"Try me," I say just like he did yesterday.

Crue's voice is nearly unrecognizable when he says, "The second you promise to keep your eyes open and on me, I'll give you every inch."

Neither of us moves, both our breathing labored, his on the back of my neck, mine on the crook of his elbow.

It's not just him I do that with. I don't even think I keep my eyes open during any form of intimacy. Either they're shut or I'm looking around at stuff, wishing they were. It's weird that Crue's so obsessed with keeping eye contact.

Hot, but weird.

"How many inches are we talking?"

"Four?"

"*Four?*"

"Could be seven. Nine. I don't know. I've never fucking measured."

"Hmm." I rub my lips together, picturing the difference between four and nine inches. I think the norm is three to eight. Judging by what I felt at Hide and Keep, I'd guess eight or nine—hard. There's no way it's bigger than that because how could he honestly come up with four if it was? Ten inches or more is crazy. That's a golf club dangling between your legs. It's not even carry-on, it's checked baggage at that point. Having to stuff something that size into a pair of pants every day—even soft—you would know what you're working with.

"Hmm what?"

"Oh, no, nothing. That's just…a pretty big acorn."

"It's not a fucking acorn."

"Hey, no judgement. I'm just glad I solved the mystery."

"What mystery is that?"

"Why you're always so grumpy."

A burst of air pelts my neck and ear, causing a shiver.

"You're why I'm always so grumpy. You and your little fucking attitude and your little fucking outfits."

"You don't like my outfits?"

The weight on me shifts, easing a bit.

"I didn't say that."

I wait for him to elaborate but he doesn't.

Okay…

"So…is this another pin?"

"Are your shoulder blades touching the floor?"

"No?"

"They're not," he deadpans.

"I'm gonna get out of this?"

"Hopefully."

"You said I could."

"I said there are more ways to get out of this position…if you know how to execute them."

My eyebrows almost crash into each other.

"Teach me how to execute them then." Like, hello, that's why we're doing this.

"Since you asked so nicely…" He scoffs, and I shake my head using the extremely limited ability I do have. Even while we're literally at each other's throats we're at each other's throats.

"From here, you wanna get back up to base."

"Like before?"

"No, instead of making a tabletop, you're gonna keep your ass low, on your heels."

I yank my arms with no success at all. In fact, I'm pretty sure Crue's grip on them tightens.

"Why'd you do that?"

"To get to my base." Ob-vi-ous-ly.

"You'll gas out before you ever get there doing dumb shit like that. Just wait until I tell you what to do."

I make my sigh three times longer than it needs to be.

After mumbling something about my attitude, he says, "I want you to pull your knee up, sliding it along the floor out to your side."

"Now?"

"Yeah. Go ahead."

When I do, he rewards me with another "Good girl," this one making my pussy pulse now that freedom is on the horizon.

"You can either do the same thing with the other knee, or you can try to get up from here. Either way, you'll want to get your ass on your heels while walking your arms back until they're under you."

"Won't you still have my wrists though?"

"For now, yeah, but we'll work on reversing wrist control once you're off your belly."

Because Crue is leaning on the same side as my straight leg, I decide to raise up from here, using only my one bent knee.

Following his directions exactly, I slowly make my way up to the base he described. Crue's still plastered to my back, but I don't feel nearly as defenseless.

Unable to keep ahold of my wrist during the transition, Crue relocates his right hand to my stomach. His thumb gives it a tap I swear I feel on my clit.

"Okay, next, you're going to grab my right hand with yours and pull it away."

I flex my abs automatically, which he must take as a precursor because he growls out, "Not yet."

"I. Wasn't." With a swift jerk backward, I knock him with my shoulder, spurring more growling.

"Don't wear yourself out."

"I'm in better shape than you, remember?"

"You're also a hell of a lot lighter, making it easier to overpower you. You gotta be smarter, more patient, and twice as explosive."

I know I'm at a disadvantage. That's common knowledge among women. We are almost always at a disadvantage regardless of height or size or athletic competency. I don't need to be told that yet again. I need some skills that put me at less of a disadvantage.

"What do I do next?"

"At the same time you rip my right hand off you, you need to lift your left knee and left hand, breaking out of my hold to get up to your feet. You'll probably go slow because it's your first time, but usually it needs to be fast to catch your oppon—"

Using his directions, I break free of his hold as I stand, my movements definitely catching him off guard.

It worked. It worked! All Crue has me by is one wrist. That's it. I got up. I got out of it.

I did it.

I twist to face my bodyguard, finding him wearing an ear-to-ear grin.

"Was that explosive enough for you?"

CHAPTER 28

Ever

"**G**ood job," he says instead of the "good girl" he was handing out freely before.

"Now, how do I reverse wrist control?"

"You got a free hand. Use it to grab one of my wrists."

He immediately pulls his free hand out of my reach, so I grab the wrist of the hand holding mine.

"Why is this so important?"

"Wrist control is huge. It makes whoever has it feel in control, which gives a mental edge. It helps set up other moves, takedowns. It can prevent a takedown. Anything your opponent tries to do while you have their wrists, you'll be able to feel and react to quicker."

"I have one of your wrists, can I take you down?"

"From what I saw earlier, no."

"You didn't take me down either."

"Do you want me to?"

His skin on mine burns as he pulls me closer. He's been holding my wrist since he got me on my stomach, but it's more noticeable now that we're gazing at each other.

Is that why he insists on eye contact? Does it make it more personal?

All I can do is whisper out a "No. I want you…"

Crue's own voice comes out hushed with, "How?"

"On all fours. Now."

That smile returns, making him unfairly handsome. He's sweaty. He's an asshole. He's being paid to clam-jam me. And still, every bit of my body is attracted to every bit of his, especially those eight or nine inches I've had the pleasure of feeling pressed against me but haven't seen in person…yet.

My lips stretch apart so much so they hurt. I usually only smile this big during performances, except this is no performance. Not on my part anyway.

"Since you asked so nicely…"

Finally, he releases my wrist, but I decide to keep his a little longer.

"I 'asked' the same way you did."

"Tit for tat," he tsks.

I shrug and let go so he can get down on all fours.

Talking me through what he did to me, I weave an arm under Crue's armpit, then up and over his neck before rolling him on to his back, with me topping him perpendicularly.

"Congratulations, you just got a pin. You win," he tells me.

"Just like that?"

"Just like that. In a real match, it wouldn't be this easy. Your opponent would be countering your moves the entire time."

I sit back on my heels to look down at Crue. He brings his hands up under his head, his elbows out and raised a few inches off the mat.

"What if someone's between your legs?"

"What do you mean?"

"This is only one position, right? You can get pinned in other ways?"

"Yeah."

"Well, what if someone's trying to pin you and they're between your legs?"

"Between your legs how?"

Walking on my knees over to his bent legs, I spread them wide.

Crue automatically cups his package. "What are you doing?"

"Showing you what I mean."

He doesn't remove his hands, but I lower my top half between his thighs to demonstrate.

Pressing my palms on the floor next to his ribs, I hold myself suspended above him so none of me is technically touching any of him.

"Like this."

Guys have looked down at me from this position but I've never done it to them. I've been on top, but not between their legs like this. It feels more powerful somehow, maybe because the person on bottom is vulnerable. I couldn't imagine imposing my power on someone like this. To be between someone else's legs who doesn't want you there and still proceed to fulfill your own wishes, all for your own pleasure, that's despicable.

"Yeah… This doesn't really happen in wrestling," Crue drawls.

"In the history of wrestling, I'm sure there has been at least one time where someone ended up between another person's legs."

"If it did happen, the person on the bottom was fucked and probably lost."

"But what if…they hadn't lost yet? What if there was still time?"

"Time?"

"Like on the clock," I rush out, then look away. "Or whatever."

Maybe I am fucked.

I start to sit back until Crue's knees clamp on my sides, trapping me.

"Where are you going? We're not done."

"Why not? It's not like you even wanted to teach me how to wrestle anyway."

"You didn't want to teach me how to stunt but you did."

"Tit for tat," I accuse right back.

"You want to know how I'd get out of this?"

"Yes."

"You give me permission to wrestle you?"

Pressing forward, Crue's knees loosen to let me lean down until I'm only a few inches from his face. My eyes alternating between his… that are alternating between mine and my lips, I say, "I give you permission to do anything you *want* to me."

I'd take his begrudging handouts like a pigeon takes

crumbs—ravenously. But that doesn't make it right. Because he doesn't actually want me. He only fingered me out of his delusional sense of duty.

Crue lifts his head, almost capturing my lips, forcing me to jerk back.

"Except for that."

"God-fucking-damn it!" he roars before fisting the front of my shirt, pulling me back down.

I start to panic, my hands scrambling against the floor to keep him from closing the distance completely. Suddenly, one of them gets trapped against his ribs, then we're rolling, reversing positions.

One second, I'm hovering over him, the next, he's straddling my stomach, his definitely-bigger-than-four-inches cock digging into me because he's hard. Very hard. Is that what he was hiding under those hands?

"I want to kiss you."

He does? Like actually?

"Too bad," I make myself say. "I said no. Not. That."

"Tell me why?"

"Tell me what you did to get out of that first?"

"In that position, you gotta squirm, flop, anything to get out."

I snort out a laugh of disbelief. "Flop?"

"We literally call the person on bottom a fish. Then you straighten your legs, trap whatever hands you can against your sides, and roll until you're back in control. Now, why the fuck can't I kiss you? No one will ever know you kissed the help."

It has nothing to do with who you are, Crue, and everything to do with who I am!

"I didn't say you couldn't kiss me."

He's instantly lowering, and I have to whip my head to the side to finish, "I said you can't kiss my *mouth.*"

Does he want to kiss me like *that?*

"But only if you want to..."

Please want to.

"Only if I want to?" he questions against my cheek, his full lips dragging over my skin, turning that pulse in my pussy into an ache.

All I can do is pant, the sound loud and honestly kind of embarrassing. Why is this so hot? This is nothing special. For the last five months, I've had guy after guy stuck to my neck like suckerfish cleaning a tank. But something about Crue doing it feels different internally.

Crue kisses down the side of my throat, asking at my collarbone, "Does it feel like I want to?" Jamming one knee between mine, he spreads them apart to settle himself between my thighs, then rolls his hips into me, his solid cock grinding against my pussy.

Barely over my heavy breathing, I hear him say, "For you? The stuck-up, spoiled little brat that hates the mere sight of me?"

One hand gripping the back of his head to keep him in place, I wrap my legs around his back, hooking my ankles and bringing him in even harder.

"I thought we already established it's not the sight of you I hate, Major."

"You mean how your pussy cries for me?"

"Weeps," I correct with a hip roll of my own.

Crue groans into my neck.

"Because you want my cock to fill you up?"

For answer, I reach between our bodies, grazing the cock in question. My eyes close on a moan I feel reverberate down to my toes.

I cannot believe he said four inches.

Crue thrusts into my hand, but says, "You know what I need from you first."

"Condom?" I pretend to guess. "I don't have one on me but we can—"

"Your eyes. That's what I need from you. Just look at me and I'll fuck you like you've never been fucked before."

"But I..."

The back of my knuckles graze against my clit with each pump from Crue, bringing that wave of euphoria closer...

"I..."

And closer...

"I…"

And…

Both our movements frenzied intention, we work together to send the wave crashing over me, dowsing my entire body in a frothy warm haze.

"Jesus, that was…" Crue French-kisses my chest between praises about how hot that was, how good it felt even though only one of our shorts is soaking wet right now. *Mine.*

When I catch my breath, I finally finish my thought, telling him, "I have been fucked face to face. Maybe we could try another position, one I haven't been fucked in, so at least when I'm not looking at you, it's because I can't."

Crue's lower half halts all movement while his forehead drills into my jaw, almost painfully.

"How are you always so fucking infuriating?"

"It's a talent." An underrated one at that. You have to have zero shame, incredible restraint, and be able to calculate better than a mathematician.

"Are you on birth control?"

Eyes still shut, I nod.

"Can I nut in you?"

He insists on gazing into my eyes during sex but says things like "Can I nut in you?" One of those things is *nothing* like the other, and I just…

Men are so, so confusing.

"Is that what you want, Major?"

His lips come up to tease my ear, and at first his voice is a soft caress, a stroke straight to the flame that is my core. "I want you walking around in your fifteen-hundred-dollar outfits, the perfect image of Daddy's little princess…"

But then his tone hardens, a bite without the soothing kiss afterward as he spits, "Knowing the cum leaking out of your cunt is from your *destitute* personal protection agent."

See, I could leave it here and let him have the last word. He's obviously been holding on to this grudge since I called him that in my father's office. But I'm way too petty, horny, and yeah, infuriating to be the bigger person.

So I correct him with one…whispered…word. "Bodyguard."

It's both the wrong and right thing to say. Right because the growl he unleashes is feral and sends a thrill through me.

Wrong because before I know it, he's scooting back, forcing my ankles to unlock as my shaky legs fall away.

No, don't go.

Thankfully, he seems to stop with some part of his body still between my thighs.

Without my sight, I have no idea what's coming next, giving this an additional layer of exhilaration.

I feel eight fingers curl into my waistband, then he's dragging my shorts and underwear down.

He's staying.

It's silent for a while, and my cheeks heat imagining Crue looking me over.

"What are these from?"

Assuming he's talking about my underwear, I say, "My stylist, like everything else I wear."

"No. These bruises." His hands grasp the sides of my hips, making me jolt off the floor.

Crue catches my ass, keeping it suspended in the air.

Opening my eyes, I right my head to see Crue between my thighs, sitting on his heels as he watches me carefully.

I shake my head. "Nothing."

"There's too many to be nothing. How'd you get them?"

"You did stunts with me. You saw for yourself how physical they can be. Probably just from that. I've never really noticed them to be honest."

Crue's stare doesn't let up.

He doesn't believe me.

I shrug one shoulder as if I couldn't care less whether he does or not.

"Who did this to you?"

"I just told you they're from cheer."

"I cheered with you and I didn't leave these kinds of marks. So who did?"

"You did a few stunts. You didn't cheer with me. There's a lot more momentum in a routine."

"I don't like 'em."

"Don't look at them."

"I want to look at all of you." Finally, he lowers his gaze…while lifting my ass a few more inches. Twisting my hips to the side, he lays a kiss on each of the dozens of bruises there, then does the same to the other.

My nostrils flare from the effort it takes not to cry. *I should've kept my eyes closed.*

"Now…"

He fits my legs over his shoulders, raising my ass even higher, my own shoulder blades almost off the floor. When our eyes collide over my pussy, I immediately relocate mine to the ceiling.

So awkward.

"Do you want to see how good I can really kiss?"

"Personally, I'd rather feel it."

"When I get done, you're gonna be begging me to kiss you on the mouth."

"Dreams only come true if they're possible. Stay realistic."

"Begging," he repeats thickly, confidently.

That's all the warning I get before he kisses my clit, his whole mouth sucking the nub like it's the tip of an ice cream cone on a hot summer day.

A strangled moan leaves me as I lift my shirt off my stomach, then chest, the heat too much. While circling my nipples through my sports bra, I start rolling my hips to meet Crue's mouth, gliding my slippery pussy along his tongue and lips.

On a groan, he cradles my ass cheeks, making it easier for me to ride his face from this angle.

After every rotation up, his tongue dips between my walls with one long lick inside so he can suck my clit before I lower back down. The pace is good. It feels amazing. Crue is a phenomenal kisser.

But it's not enough to remove my gravity and send me into orbit.

I dig my heels into his back, grinding my pussy against his face even harder with each figure eight motion.

"It's right there. It's right there. It's right there," I chant, my voice a desperate squeal as I greedily chase my second orgasm.

All at once Crue's face disappears from my pussy and my lower half is lowered to the floor.

The next second, his breath feathers my chin.

"Beg me."

"What?"

"Fucking beg me."

"No." Shaking my head, I turn it away. "Never."

I hear a zipper, then Crue's fist is brushing my pussy lips.

He's gonna do it. He's gonna fuck me.

Goddess, yes.

Except this time when I reach between us, he jerks away.

"You'll get this when you look at me."

"Then what…"

"Fuuuck. Fuck, fuck, fuck."

Heat spreads up my stomach, and now I do open my eyes because how is this happening again?

Looking down, I spot Crue's hard cock caught in his still pumping fist, drops of cum dripping off the tip into the puddle on my stomach.

"You just… You didn't even…"

I get to my elbows and turn my angry eyes on him. I'm surprised to find his just as turbulent.

"Crue, what the hell?"

Staying in my face, he releases his dick and proceeds to sweep his cum down to the top of my pussy before pushing a big dollop of it inside me with his fingers.

I gasp at the intrusion, my bottom lip jutting out.

He switches his attention from it to my eyes, then looks down between us to watch himself pump his cum into me literally by hand.

"Crue." It's meant to come out outraged, except my hips are already lifting, wanting more. Wanting it all.

"I told you I was gonna ruin your fucking rich-girl aesthetic. At dinner, I'll be sitting across from you, smiling at the fact my cum's pooling in your designer panties."

He groans like he's in pain.

"But…" My head falls back between my shoulders. "Why…"

His mouth closes over my throat, sucking right where I swallow and making me lose my train of thought.

"Crue," I pant, my hips bucking faster and faster. "More."

"God, you're a fucking brat," he says, but adds a third finger, filling my pussy so good. "All you had to do was look at me and I would've pumped you with my cum correctly. Now look. I gotta do it this way."

Crue uses the rest of the cum to circle my clit with his palm.

"I'm gonna…"

My hips buck wildly, my rolls only making it halfway through completion.

"Show me how good you're gonna come on my cock next time we do this and you give me what I want."

My walls seize up around those fingers as a small scream tears from my throat.

"It's…" I fall to my back, my chest rapidly rising and falling as I return to earth. "That was…"

"Yeah? Imagine how much better it would've been if you'd listened like a good girl," Crue rasps, somehow sounding just as breathless.

I push at him. "Get off me." I'm still naked and wet and fucking mad. I should be mad. That was rude. Yes, he eventually finished me off but it's the principle of it. He stopped right at the best part. And he didn't even fuck me. Again.

"What's your problem? I just—"

"You. You're…" What was that word Kota used to describe her stepbrother? Vexing? No, vexing has an air of thrill to it. Nothing about Crue right now is thrilling. He was a second ago, more than thrilling, but now, he's purely… "Annoying."

"*Me? I'm* annoying?"

"All these stipulations." I start ticking my fingers. "I can't fuck anyone else. I can only fuck you. But I can only fuck you if I maintain eye contact the whole time like a fucking serial killer!" My voice hitches on the last three words. "You want me to kiss you. You want me to beg." Forgetting what number I'm on, I throw my hands up. "What's the matter with you? Who cares if I prefer to close my eyes?"

"I care! Having your head turned away and your eyes squeezed shut doesn't seem like you want it."

"You want to know what I want? I want to fuck whoever I choose to, not just who I'm told to!"

Shit. I shouldn't have said that.

The door is closed and nobody ever comes down here, but still, I shouldn't have said it, not even to Crue. Especially not to Crue.

"If I tell you I want something, that should be enough," I add much quieter.

"It's not. There's a difference between consent and enthusiastic consent. I prefer the latter."

"You're lucky you have any of my consent at all."

"Because I'm 'the help'?" he sneers as he tucks himself back in his pants and zips up.

"No, because I hate you. I hate everything you stand for."

"The feeling is mutual, little bat."

I think he meant to say brat, but… Whatever.

"Great," I say.

He shrugs. "Good."

"Good."

"I already said that."

"I'm leaving."

"Not until you're fully dressed."

I rip my shorts and underwear out of his hold. "I wasn't planning on it."

"Good."

"You said that already!" I snap, feeling the last shred of my control slip away, probably gone forever.

This is what he's made me.

"You're such a bitch, you know that?"

Yes, in fact, I do.

Ignoring Crue, I get dressed again.

As usual, my shadow tries following me.

"Don't follow me right now."

"I don't have a choice. It's my job."

"I'm going to the atrium."

"I'll wait outside for you."

"You can go get fucked." Not by anyone else, just…himself. He knows that, right?

"And waste my cum on someone more deserving? Nah."

"Joke's on you. I'm gonna douche it all out of me."

"Wait, what's a douche?"

I finally open the door, saying, "You," before walking out.

CHAPTER 29

Crue

EVER DOESN'T SPEAK TO ME THE REST OF THE DAY, BUT THE next morning, I check the new shoes in my closet, finding one pair tagged in graffiti-style wording that says EVER MUNREAUX WAS HERE.

I knew she wouldn't be able to resist.

With no notifications on my phone overnight though, I'm still worrying while waiting for her to come out of her room.

Thankfully, she does. And when she does, she's cuddling the bear I gave her.

I'll take that as a good sign.

"How about Art?" I suggest to break the ice.

Unfortunately, one withering look from Ever has everything freezing back up again, even the walls around us.

That's not a good sign.

We were finally getting somewhere…I thought.

I wanted to fuck her yesterday. Jesus Christ, did I want to. It's a miracle I lasted as long as I did. A couple of tugs on my cock and I was spilling seed like a farmer in the spring.

Which was hot. The whole thing was. The way she tasted. The way she didn't get shy. The way she took charge and moved for me so easily. The way she seemed to like my cum not only on her but also in her. Fuck.

I don't know why she has to be so stubborn. Why can't she look at me during sex? I never said it had to be the whole time. Just the beginning.

And some of the middle.

And preferably the end.

But not the *whole* time.

She's so fucking dramatic.

I was about to let it go anyway. If she would've kissed me, I would've dove into her deliciously wet cunt no problem. I would've fucking slathered my cock with her pussy juice.

But no. She said "Never." She'll *never* kiss me on the mouth. What kind of bullshit is that?

How am I supposed to feel about that?

I don't know how I feel about any of it.

I'm trying not to feel anything. It'd be stupid as shit to. Not only is this my job but it's short-term. Not short-term by my standards necessarily, but definitely by other people's.

I know I didn't feel great leaving things the way we did yesterday. She was in her butterfly conservatory for four hours before coming out to go for a run.

I don't feel great now either because even though she's right here, her mind couldn't be further away.

I gotta make it right with Ever. Or at least better. If I don't, she'll probably try to smother me in my sleep tonight.

"I think Art's a good name," I say. "Because you like to draw."

She doesn't respond in any way whatsoever.

Shit. What can I do?

What I always do to get her attention. Fight.

"Like how you drew on another pair of my shoes last night."

Nope. Nothing.

Oh. My bad. I forgot who I'm dealing with. A demon.

"Maybe Lucifer's more fitting since that's two pairs of my shoes you've ruined now."

Just before we reach the kitchen, my phone vibrates in my pocket.

Halting on the stairs, I pull it out and…

What? A video message?

One glance at Ever and I see her waiting in the stairwell, too. That's suspicious. Her phone isn't out though. So maybe not.

Then who…

Against my better judgment, I open it. Not a moment later, the screen gets taken up by a celebrity. Did someone send me a post from social media?

I'm about to close it out when the video starts playing automatically.

"Ayo, Crue, this is Julez. I got a message for you."

Julez? The rapper? Why the fuck would he have a message for me?

"Before all that though, I'm supposed to tell yinz to come see me this summer on my Family Julez Tour hitting whatever-the-fuck city is near you."

The rapper rolls his eyes while taking a hit from a blunt. It looks like he's in a recording studio, but with a lot more people in it than I would imagine is supposed to be in one.

"*The* Collette's gonna be opening for me, so don't miss it." The background, as well as everyone in it, disappears as Julez brings his phone in close to his face to say quieter, "Mark my words, she's gonna be my wife one day."

He cracks up, probably because he's high but also because… Collette is a popstar with a kid and a squeaky-clean image. Julez not only is a rapper but has a rap sheet as well. It's clearly a joke.

"Anyway, about this message. Ever wanted me to tell you…" Julez holds his phone out as far as his long arm can stretch, then says, "You're welcome."

The video ends, returning the staircase to silence.

Does she know him personally?

If that was a favor though, he wouldn't have plugged his tour.

"You paid him just to say that?" I ask, getting—no surprise—nothing in return.

See. This is why I'm always fucking grumpy. This shit right here.

Feeling as petty as my protectee, I delete the personalized video message, then go into the Recently Deleted folder and do the same there, too.

Never listening to that motherfucker's music again. It's too bad because I actually liked the song he did with Collette.

Ever and I descend the rest of the stairs without another word to each other.

You're welcome. That's what I should've said to her yesterday instead of all that "good" bullshit.

I didn't know what else to say. She got so angry so fast. She just…

I'm supposed to think like she does and guess what her next steps are so I can protect her before anything bad happens, and for the most part, I have been. It's the stuff that involves me where my brain seems to shut down and stop working altogether. I never know what she's gonna say or do to me.

I don't have experience with this—girls, sex. Well, sex repeatedly with the same person. That's a whole different ballgame than a one-night stand. One-night stands are such low pressure because you're never gonna see that person again. At least that's the hope.

Ever literally told me to get off her while her cum was still drying on my cheeks. If that happened during a one-night stand—which it *never* has—I'd never have to face that girl again. But I don't have a choice here. I don't just have to face Ever, I have to continue facing her every minute of every fucking day for the foreseeable future.

That was shitty. She owes me an apology for that. Will I get one though? From the carelessly malicious Ever Munreaux? Not likely. There are only two scenarios I can think of that happening. One, Ever tricks me again. Or two, hell freezes over. Shit might be frosty between us right now but Satan's spawn is still fuming. Her willing to pay a celebrity to deliver a smartass message for her proves that.

"Good morning, Miss Munreaux. Will you be eating your breakfast—"

"To go," Ever says shortly, cutting off Chef Ryan.

As usual, Arthur's already in here, eating at the table. Sometimes he acknowledges his daughter, but most times he doesn't. It seems he only does if he has a bone to pick with her. Luckily, he remains silent today, allowing us to be on our way in the span of a couple of minutes.

In Ever's car, she sets the teddy bear on her lap, giving me a view of the face that was tucked against her chest.

"What the fuck happened to him?" His face doesn't look anything like it did when I gave it to her.

Lifting the bear, Ever examines him like she hadn't noticed. How could she not? The face is concave at this point.

"Crue?"

The first word she says to me and it's my name. It could be worse.

"Yeah?"

"No, him." She jiggles the stuffed animal. "He's Crue."

It's worse.

"His name's not Crue."

"Yes, it is. I named him Crue 2.0 because he's better than you. He didn't mind one bit that I didn't maintain eye contact."

It takes me several minutes to figure out what that means.

"You fucked the bear's face in?"

"I guess it's a good thing you stopped when you did, or the same thing might've happened to yours." Meeting my eyes for the first time since we left the gym yesterday, she pops her eyebrows in challenge.

A challenge I would love to call her bluff on. *Fucking try it, little bat.* I'm not made of terry cloth and stuffing. My face, and every other part of me, can handle a violent ride. In fact, I welcome one.

I rip the bear from her grasp and toss it in the back without looking away from her. Fuck that no-named bear.

Ever only rolls her eyes, equally unimpressed and unbothered, before nibbling at her egg and sausage bite, no yogurt in sight.

No idea what to say next, I begin the drive to Littoral. Halfway there, I have to break the silence.

"I looked up douche, by the way."

Because the Sapphire's electric and hardly makes any noise, I hear her mutter, "When you looked in the mirror."

I choose to ignore that.

Bitch.

I knew douche was an insult toward guys, but I didn't know it was an actual tool…thing for girls.

"And douching isn't all that good for you. It messes with your levels."

"Levels? Levels of what?"

"Your bacteria."

Ever's quiet for a bit, then says, "Okay," like she's not sure why I'm telling her this but she's the one that threatened to use one.

"So…I hope you didn't actually douche."

"You spend a lot of time concerned about my vagina."

Way too much time. More now that I've felt it and tasted it. It's become a hobby of mine, thinking about that cunt.

"Someone has to. If you're fucking a teddy—"

"Oh my Goddess. Every girl humps a stuffed animal at least once in her life. It's like a part of growing up."

"You're nineteen."

"Well, I've never had one to try it on. I thought I'd see what all the hype was about."

"Because your other ones were too expensive to disfigure or…"

"I've just never had one before, period."

Now I feel bad for throwing the bear.

Kind of.

Not really. It should've been *me* she humped. It's the number one reason why I have a face.

Probably.

"And?"

"And what?"

"Did it live up to the hype?"

Ever shakes her head for several moments too long.

"Did you come?" I ask, more fascinated than I'd ever admit out loud.

"Well, yeah… I mean… If I rub my clit on anything long enough, I'm gonna come."

So she's a clit-climaxer. I figured she was but not all women are. It's good to know she hasn't been faking it with me.

It's really good to know.

I eye the bear through the rearview mirror, wondering how many times she came on him.

After I get Ever to class, I jog back out to the car and bury my nose in the bear's caved-in face to see if I can pick up on her scent. I don't know if she was wearing underwear or not, but I can't really smell her pussy. Sadly.

I look the animal over for anything that could pass as a smear of cum, finding none. The gleam in his now-lopsided eye appears gloating, or at least that's how it feels, sealing his fate.

I give him an arrogant smirk of my own…all the way to the closest trash can. Just as I'm about to let go though, Ever's face flashes in my mind. She was really happy when I gave her the bear. If she was telling the truth about never having a stuffed animal before, this would've been her first one.

"Fuck," I say as I walk his smug ass back to the car. After a half hour of trying to redistribute the stuffing back to his face, I sit him on the passenger seat again, exactly like I did the first time except with a face that isn't even close to perfect.

But mine isn't either and she did name the fucker after me, so…

Happy humping, Ever.

I flip Crue 2.0 off before shutting the door and hustling back to Ever's classroom.

CHAPTER 30

Crue

Two days later, I'm waiting to escort Ever to dinner when she emerges from her bedroom wearing another long gown, this one black with a slight shimmer to the material. Only held up by two thin straps, it hugs her body, showing off every curve.

She's stunning, but ridiculously overdressed for a meal in, and unfortunately, she's already wearing her shoes.

"What are you so dressed up for?" I ask in case I missed something.

There's nothing on her schedule for tonight, but we haven't talked much the last couple days, not since the conversation about the teddy bear. She lit up finding him waiting for her, just not enough to actually say anything about it. Not even a thank-you. If only she knew how badly I wanted to incinerate that stuffed motherfucker.

"A funeral," she says with zero emotion.

Jesus, someone should have told me that. Anyone. I had no idea.

"I'm really sorry," I rush out. I don't know who died or how close they were to her. "I need to get changed."

Ever looks past me to my room and nods. "Okay. I'll wait."

I can't keep the surprise out of my voice as I ask, "You will?"

This better not be another setup.

"You're accompanying me, aren't you?" Her tone lacks its usual bitterness when talking about our arrangement. Maybe she's finally coming around to her new reality.

My nod is slower. "Everywhere."

I return to my room and change into my black suit as quickly as possible. Out in the hall again, Ever's got her back against the wall, staring up at the ceiling.

Her gaze lowers to me, giving me her full attention for the first time in two days. She looks tired. Considering she's been sneaking into my room every night—without triggering her door alarm or waking me—and vandalizing my shoes, I can understand why.

"Do you have my tiger's eye bracelet?"

"I think so." I know so. The microchips came in yesterday, so while Ever was tending to her butterflies, I worked on attaching the trackers to the two bracelets I have of hers.

"Can you wear it for me?"

"You don't need—"

"Please…just get it."

She sounds tired, too. Has she been sneaking out of the house? I doubt it. She would've bragged about it.

Something else is going on with her.

"Is that the brown one?"

"Brown and tan, yeah."

After I've got her bracelet on my wrist, we walk down the hall side by side.

"Are you sick?" I ask.

"Terminally."

My feet, and heart, stop.

"Miss?"

She continues on, no longer concerned with waiting for me.

"Ever."

Finally, she stops.

I catch up to her, giving her a thorough once-over. "What is it?"

"I'm screwing with you, Major," she says in a tone that's not even remotely humorous.

I don't stop my scan of her, searching for anything that'd explain this behavior. She's practically lethargic.

"So you're not sick?"

Humor emerges, dancing across all her features, lighting each one up as it passes. Then without answering, she turns for the stairs to the foyer…where Arthur's standing.

The first thing he does when he sees us is bitch.

"Black? I told you to wear red."

"I thought this was more appropriate," Ever says in complete monotone, making me almost snort in agreement. Who the fuck wears red to a funeral?

"The Larsons are already coming up the driveway."

The Larsons? We're going to a funeral with them?

I can't be in the same vehicle with Mallory, especially not with Ever.

"Edwin, can you have someone bring Miss Munreaux's car around?" I ask the valet, only getting silence in return as he continues waiting patiently by the front door.

All right…

I look to Ever for some help since she has more pull around here than I do, but the floor seems to be much more interesting to her right now. Arthur's the only one who acknowledges the fact that I even spoke and it's to screw up his face.

Fuck it. I'll go get the Sapphire myself. Anything not to be cooped up with Mallory and Ever. *And Arthur.* I don't know Penn but it's safe to assume I probably wouldn't like him either.

"I'll be right back," I murmur to Ever.

Arthur steps in front of me, waggling a finger. "It's too late for you to leave now. You'll just have to stay in your room for the night." That finger points, and I look from it to the stairs, then back.

What?

"I'll have Edwin bring you up a plate later. You need to disappear before our dinner guests arrive."

Dinner guests? Ever said…

I glance at Ever, who's quietly studying me and Arthur now. So it was a setup?

"But Miss Munreaux wanted—"

Arthur chuffs out a laugh. "That's irrelevant."

How does he know? I didn't even finish what I was gonna say.

"Up you go. Out of sight until tomorrow."

Is this actually happening? I'm being dismissed for the *night*? The motherfucking night? While Mallory Larson is here? For fucking dinner? With Ever?

Obviously, Ever knew about this. She's dressed for it for fuck's sake. But why the fuck didn't I? I'm her personal protection agent. I'm supposed to do *everything* with her.

Why does it have to be for the whole night? Why can't I just eat somewhere else while these rich fucks rub elbows over their saffron-sprinkled, chili-oil-drizzled cuisine, then get back to my job once they're finished?

It is just dinner…right?

My boss turns away from me, heading for the door but not before he grabs hold of Ever's elbow to drag her along.

She's being taken away from me.

My hand aches with the urge to reach for Ever's.

Why is she being taken away from me?

Instead, I quickly pass the bracelet off to her behind Arthur's back.

She takes it, then singsongs, "Enjoy your alone time, Mr. Brantley," showing the first bit of animation in days. Of course it's at my expense. She's probably been counting down to this very moment.

This is why I can never put any sort of trust in her. She will always only care about herself.

Face hardened to granite, I force myself up the stairs. Once I reach the top, I can't help sending one last withering glare back.

Arthur's hand, no longer on Ever's elbow, is a fist at her side and something about it causes her to arch away from him.

Ever whips her head away from her father, giving me her side profile. Her face is strained and…glistening. She wipes at one cheek, causing a drop of something to fall to the floor below her.

Holy shit, she's crying. Ever's crying and I'm not with her to comfort her.

I grip the banister so hard my fingers burn. What did Arthur do to make her cry?

Her hip. The bruises there.

Motherfucker. The call's coming from inside the goddamn manor.

Unable to focus on the hair in my hands, I pick up my phone and refresh the app. Again. The damn dot on the map remains right where it is. Again.

It's been in the same spot for over an hour. What the fuck are they doing in there? I know Mallory's with Ever.

After a torturous ninety-seven minutes of watching that dot sit stationary, Ever must've finally left the dining room to go outside. From there, I switched to a live view by spying out my window, where I saw her and Mallory walk out together before disappearing into the hedge maze. At first, I was relieved. Anything to get her away from Arthur. But now, an hour fucking later of her dot sitting idle, I'm anything but relieved.

Back and forth, back and forth, from one side of my room to the other. I'm probably wearing out the hardwood floor, but I don't give a fuck. If Arthur didn't want this room trashed, he shouldn't have banished me to it. For the night. Without my protectee.

Should I go after her?

I could.

Assuming Arthur's entertaining Penn Larson and his wife somewhere in the manor, most likely overindulging on limited-edition liquor and imported cigars, my employer might not even notice if I were to take an evening stroll out front. I've been through that maze once already. I can find Ever in it again.

I will. I'll find her.

I'm going.

I've got one shoe on when Ever's door notification appears at the top of my phone screen.

If she's down in the maze, who the fuck's at her door?

I'm ripping my own open the next second, only to see someone just opening hers. I squint through the darkness. *Ever?* Her body's turned the opposite way and she's got the bottom of her dress bunched in a fist, but it's her.

It's her. Thank fuck, it's her. She's here.

And she's alone.

I draw my first full breath in…hours? Was I holding it the entire time? I couldn't say. I have no fucking idea what I did after I left Ever in that foyer with Arthur. From that moment to now, it's all a blur of trying to keep my mind busy and failing miserably.

I ask the first thing that pops into my head. "Why are the lights off?"

"They must be malfunctioning, too," Ever says with a shrug.

Leaning against my doorjamb, I cross my arms over my erratic heart. Between that and the single shoe, the pose isn't giving me the confidence boost I was hoping for.

"Have fun tonight?"

"Loads," she says, indifference weighing down her tone. "You?"

"Loads," I echo in the same manner. "Where's your bracelet?"

"My—" She pauses to examine her wrist. "Oh, it must've fallen off."

Her back to me, she hasn't looked at me, her head down as she lingers in her doorway. Her hair's messed up and she lost her bracelet. I wonder how those things happened?

Goddamn it. I should've gone after her sooner.

"Did you fuck him?"

"If I did, it would've been with my father's blessing."

"I gathered that," I drawl. It's painfully obvious Arthur Munreaux and Penn Larson are trying to set up their trust-fund babies for a possible love match. "So, did you?"

I hear her inhale, then exhale before saying, "No."

Even though I probably shouldn't, I believe her. Ever loves when she bests me, specifically when she gets to rub my face in it afterward.

"Is that all?"

She's withdrawn again, just like earlier. What's going on? *Is she sick?*

"Is everything okay?"

I drop my arms and the front. *Just talk to me already, Ever. Fuck.*

"Why wouldn't it be?"

For starters, you live with an abusive piece of shit. Second, you were subjected to a dinner with not only him but his crony and his crony's old-ass offspring.

Mallory's old. I said it.

"You're just—"

"Trying to go to bed but can't because my bodyguard would rather interrogate me? Yeah, tell me about it."

For all I know, this girl *is* nocturnal. I'm not sure when she actually sleeps. But right now, she's acting like sleep's all she cares about.

Meanwhile, she's all I care about.

She's not *all* I care about. I just…

It's been a rough week. I need her to be okay.

I need her to be okay where I can see her and talk to her and touch her.

Then maybe I'll be okay because right now I feel as far from okay as possible.

"Why are you in such a hurry all of a sudden? You spent all that time down in the maze—"

"How'd you know where I was?"

Shhhit.

"I saw movement out my window and thought the Larsons were leaving. But it was just you—and *him*—going in the maze." I keep the rest of my thoughts to myself. What did you two do in there? What did he do to you? What did you *want* him to do to you?

Just because they didn't fuck doesn't mean they didn't do something else.

"It's none of your business and I'm tired."

"You're my business. And you're never tired." She only pretends to be when she's up to something. It's not like I can depend on the shitty sensor I put on her door to notify me even if she was.

Or the bracelet tracker she already lost.

It should not be this hard keeping tabs on a five-foot-two cheerleader.

Without responding, Ever takes another step into her room, and I lurch forward, both arms out. They want her in them so bad.

I want her in them so bad.

"Wait."

For some reason, maybe because she can hear the desperation in my voice, she does.

"I don't… I want, uh, you…"

"I know it's shocking, Major, but I'm actually not in the mood."

"No, not for that. I, um… I wanted you to, uh…" Shit, shit, *shit*. What do I say? "I want you to draw something…" I'm out of sneakers. She already drew on all three new pairs. "On me."

"On *you?*"

"Yeah. I've been wanting to get a new tattoo." It's technically true. After the first tattoo, you always want more. It's an itch that'll never get fully scratched.

"I can sketch you some ideas tomorrow."

She takes another step, but so do I. "Ever?"

This time when she stops, she lifts her head slightly, enough to show some of her neck. Without the hallway lights on, I can't tell if she has any hickeys though.

Something's going on in this wing of the manor. Too many damn glitches.

"I haven't had my eyes on you in hours."

"Don't tell me you missed me. I spend more time away from you at school."

Despite her not looking at me, I shake my head and promise, "I won't." But I could. Easily. Because in school, or her conservatory, or even her bedroom, I know she's safe. Tonight, I didn't and it…fucked me up in ways I didn't even realize until I saw her at her door just now and the fist around my heart loosened. I was forbidden from protecting my protectee, my one fucking purpose these days. It didn't matter that the order came from my boss because every part of me still wanted to protect his daughter. A dot on a screen can't compare to making sure she's not only safe, but okay, in person. Ever's whereabouts mean nothing unless I'm right next to her.

"Can you just come to my room? Please? So I can sleep knowing you're safe?"

"What makes your room so safe? You hate me."

Except...I'm not so sure I do still hate Ever.

"Because I'd hate myself a lot more if anything happened to you." Something's already happening to her. Arthur is hurting her. He could've been doing it right in front of my face and I missed it.

I did that before and it cost a life. I'm not willing to risk Ever's.

When Ever speaks, her voice is tiny. "I need to change."

I shrink my own to say, "I have clothes." They're not designer and she'll swim in them, but they'll keep her warm. If they don't, I will.

I will anyway. If she lets me.

God, I hope she lets me.

"I need to wash my face."

"I have a sink."

"I need a minute."

"I have..." Nothing to counter that with. Damn. "You'll come over after?"

"Okay."

After watching her door close, I rip my one shoe off, then dash across my room to collect the other, tripping to hurry and drop them back in the closet without looking. For the first time in my life, a girl is staying the night with me. Not just any girl. Ever Munreaux.

She's gonna stay the whole night...right?

Hands on my hips, I take a look around. How do I ensure that beautiful creep stays the whole night?

CHAPTER 31

THE DOOR CLOSES WITH A CLICK THAT HAS MY SHOULDERS bunching to my ears, everything too much right now. Lights, sounds, I need it all gone.

I finally let go of my ruined dress, the front torn all the way up to my navel, my underwear shredded in several parts.

Turns out he didn't come at me from the side. Why would he? Mallory didn't give a shit about my shoulder blades, only what was between my legs.

Sucking in lungfuls of air, I go to my bathroom, recoiling when I see who's looking back at me in the mirror. Not who. What. Eyes lifeless, cheeks smeared in black, lips spattered with crimson, jaw rubbed raw, chest scratched—I am unrecognizable. Already.

I didn't want to be this, not now, not ever.

At least now it was preventable. It should've been. I have a full-time bodyguard.

Crue promised me he'd follow me into hell if I wanted him to. I was there! I wanted him! But where was he? Locked in his room?

His door doesn't even have a lock.

He should've disobeyed my father and insisted on staying with me. He should've shown up at the last second like they do in the movies. I practically challenged him to. He should've—

If he'd done *anything* more than what my father told him to, he'd be holding both a pink slip and a restraining order right now, barring me from ever seeing him again.

As heinous as tonight was, I'd do it all again for these next three weeks with Crue. I'd do it all again just to spend one more *day* with him.

Wiping the droplets of blood off my bottom lip with a shaky hand, I thank Goddess I don't feel any cuts underneath. It's all his.

Crue's wrestling pointers did help, but they weren't the only moves I needed to get away from Mallory. Wrestling is clean, this was not. Wrestling has rules, this had none. Crue let me move him, Mallory…did not.

Dress still on, I step under the showerhead and turn on the spray, the water soaking me from the crown of my head down. Beneath the veil of wet hair, I let a few tears free. A few turns into a dozen, and before I know it, I've lost count. I don't blame the salty droplets. I want away from here, too.

I want away from me.

I roll the dress down, the material stickier than Mallory's hands. My bra and underwear are next, the costly garments useless at my feet as I wash my body, my own hands foreign and unwelcome.

When I get out, I reassess my reflection. None of the physical signs are there anymore, yet they're all I see. My complexion clear once again, I look normal.

I feel anything but.

He had no right to do that to my body. He had no right to do this to my mind. It doesn't matter that he didn't complete the rape. His attempt changed me. Forever. No amount of showers will ever be able to rid me of tonight's memory.

I have no idea what to do or how I'm—

Crue knocks on our shared wall, not impatiently, just two soft taps to remind me of my promise.

I don't want to go over there.

But I don't want to be here, alone, replaying…everything. There's nothing I can do about what happened. There's nothing I can do about what's going to happen.

All I can do is hold on to the one thing I do want while I can. And for once, I don't have to in secret. He's going to let me.

Crue opens his door before I even reach it.

"The sensor worked that time, too."

"Weird," I say like I have no clue.

After ushering me inside, he props his phone on the nightstand, screen-side down.

"You decorated?" I point at his lamp. It's on, but there's a black shirt draped over the shade, making the room a deep sepia.

"No. I was, uh… I was trying to make it darker in here."

"Why?"

"I don't know." He puts a hand in his pocket. "Oh, before I forget." Pulling out my amethyst bracelet, he passes it over to me. "I noticed earlier I still had this one."

"Thanks."

I put it on, a calming energy immediately falling over me, then pull the sleeves of my crewneck over my palms, my fingers curling to keep them in place as I spin in a slow circle.

"You need anything?"

I almost ask him for something ridiculous just to see what he says. But the mannequin head catches my attention. Its hair is different than when I was in here early this morning. And beside it is a plate full of untouched food.

"Is that your dinner?"

The barest hint of acknowledgement echoes in the space between us.

"You weren't hungry?"

Crue has a hand on his head when I face him again, but he quickly drops it to say, "I guess not."

"You didn't realize you didn't eat?"

"No."

He doesn't seem to know what to do with his hands either as he lifts, then lowers them, his fingers clenching and unclenching. What's the matter with him?

"Are you sick?" I ask.

"Terminally."

That makes my lips pull to one side.

Quieter, he adds, "At least that's how it felt."

I nod, understanding…but not. I know how tonight felt for me. How did it feel for him? He sat in his room safe and unmolested. He even got his dinner hand-delivered to him where he could've enjoyed it without a leering audience.

What part of that made him feel like he was dying?

I start to turn back around when one of those hands shoots out, pointing.

"But I did practice." He goes over to the mannequin, showing me his work. "For you."

My eyes meet his. "Next special occasion, I know who to go to."

"I'm not there yet, but I could do your hair right now. If you want?"

I'm already shaking my head. "That's okay. I don't—"

"Nothing elaborate. I could just… I don't know. I could put it back for you…so it's not in your face while you work."

"I can manage a ponytail by myself, Major," I whisper.

"No, I know." He runs another hand over his nodding head. "I know you can. But, uh…" That hand falls and Crue lets me see the vulnerability I thought I heard in the hall. "I want to do it for you."

"Why?" comes out even quieter.

"So I have a reason to have my hands on you, too."

I cover up a sob by shaking my head and spinning in the opposite direction. "That's, um…" I clear my throat. "That's really pathetic."

"I know," Crue says much closer than he was a second ago, his breath teasing the side of my neck.

"I just came in here as a favor. I don't—"

I feel him run his fingers through my wet hair and moan. How could something feel so good after going through something so bad?

Against my ear, he says, "I've been stuck in this room all night, going fucking crazy imagining all the things someone else could be doing to you. I had to do a dummy's hair over and over and *over* again…" His fingers mold to my skull and pull my head back, triggering another moan, this one deeper. "…just to keep myself from climbing out the window and going after you." He takes a deep breath, nuzzling the skin below my ear, then finishes on a whisper, "It was torture, not seeing you. Be a good girl for me and let me do your hair so I can make sure you're here, you're real, you're okay. Please."

My knees quake, my legs like jelly.

Lips to the ceiling, I rasp, "Pathetic."

"Unquestionably." His mouth closes around that same skin, sucking gently while his tongue swirls. But then he closes the space between our bodies, bringing his erection against my back and I arch away from it, from him, bile rushing up my throat.

Crue spins me around.

"What's the matter?" Under drawn-tight eyebrows, his eyes search mine.

"Nothing." I focus on his neckline, wishing I could slip inside his shirt and curl up against his chest, letting Crue's heartbeats drown out every other noise in the world. "You said you wanted to do my hair, so…do it."

He rolls his eyes but chuckles. "I was getting there. I just got distracted. You have a very distracting neck."

"That's what all the boys tell me."

Crue's humor disappears.

"Don't be shy, miss. Drop those names."

"Maybe later." And by later, I mean never. Some of those names I'll be taking to my grave without ever uttering them aloud. Everyone jokes about beer goggles but hard alcohol goggles are where the truly bad decisions lie. "And don't call me miss. I hate it."

"Don't talk about other guys. I hate it."

We hold each other's gaze.

His jealousy is so funny because as hard as he tries, it'll never reach the same level as mine. I would never ask for his exes' names.

I'd simply go online and stalk every person in his life until I found them myself.

My bodyguard nods at the bed. "Sit."

"Do you have a hair tie?"

He brandishes his wrist, a black band around it. "Chloe left some with the head."

Now my eyes are rolling. I just leave out the laugh as I say, "Of course she did."

"Finally. *Finally*. My feisty little bat is back. All it took was mentioning your female hairstylist."

He said it wrong again.

"You know you're saying bat, right?"

"Yeah." He smiles unabashedly, but reading my confusion, he explains, "You're nocturnal, territorial, creepy, and—"

"I'm not creepy."

"Have you seen your room?"

"I like crystals and tarot cards. That doesn't make me creepy."

"It's not just those. It's the moss and candles and dead bugs—"

"They're butterflies I picked up off the atrium floor."

He studies me for a minute.

"Your room is dark and feels like a lair. It's creepy."

My eyes drift over to the lamp with the shirt on it.

Crue follows my gaze and shifts on his feet, coughing.

Is that why he put that shirt on there? To make his room darker? For me?

Maybe I am more like a bat than a butterfly. At least he called me "his."

After climbing on the mattress behind me, Crue starts separating my hair into sections…I assume to braid it but I don't have the heart to tell him it's too short. I do have the heart to tell him one thing though.

"Oh, and Chloe's not my hairstylist anymore."

Crue's hands freeze, then he pulls my hair back until I'm looking up at him. Up on his knees, he towers over me.

"Why not?"

"I fired her."

"Because…"

That chuckle finally comes through.

"Because she helped me?" he asks.

"No, don't be ridiculous."

He scowls but lets me lower my head again.

I wait until he resumes his task to add, "It was because she talked to you."

"Vicious little bat," is all he says.

His fingers are gentle and patient, the slow movements soothing. My scalp feels like it's being zapped by tiny, pleasurable shots of electricity, lighting up all of my nerve endings.

Just as I predicted, he does try braiding my hair, the first few times in a regular braid, then in a French braid with the help of a slew of video tutorials. None of his attempts result in anything resembling either style, so after what feels like hours, he ends up putting my hair into a low ponytail, his knuckles brushing the back of my neck giving those same bursts of tingles.

When he asks to see his work from the front, he tucks the hair that fell out behind my ears.

"Those almost never stay in a ponytail."

He shrugs. "Just another reason for me to keep touching you."

It's weird—this unspoken truce between us. I like it, too much, but it's weird. Who decided on it? And when? I can't pinpoint an exact moment where things shifted between us. Was it really when I came back from dinner? Obviously I was too tired to fight with him but what's his reason for being like this?

Dropping my eyes, I scoot back several inches, giving him more space on the bed.

"Where are you thinking of getting your tattoo?"

"A tattoo parlor."

"Yeah, obviously. But I meant on your body."

"Oh. Um." Brows pulled together, he looks down at himself, rotating his arms.

"You don't know?"

"Yeah. Of course I do. Right here." He holds out an arm…the one without any tattoos.

I survey all that blank canvas, asking slowly, "Where?"

He rubs his wrist. "How about right here?"

Is he asking me? Or is he not sure?

"It'll have to be something small and without a lot of detail."

He thinks for a minute, then pulls his fingers up his forearm to the space right below the crook of his elbow.

"Let's do here instead. Do you need a pen?"

I pull the permanent marker out of my sweatshirt's front pocket. "This will work better on skin. It'll wash off after—"

"I don't want it to wash off. I told you I'm getting it tattooed."

Okay. This has gone on long enough. I suspected the tattoo story was a ploy to get me over here, but now he's taking it too far.

"Crue."

"Yeah?"

"You don't even know where you're getting it, let alone what you're getting—"

"I know what I'm getting."

"You do?"

"A butterfly."

I fight to keep my expression neutral. "Why a butterfly?"

"I don't know." Crue's green eyes plummet to the comforter. "I've been wanting one for a while…"

I ache to ask exactly how long? Was it since November?

"And you're really good at drawing butterflies. I just thought… you know. You'd be the best person for the job."

"Any kind of butterfly in particular?"

He nods, all hesitancy gone as he says, "The orange-and-black one. Monarch?"

Not only is Major Danger getting my art tattooed on his body for all time, he's getting it *for* me…he just has no idea.

"Yeah. That's a monarch. Lie back."

Crue smirks but obeys, lying on his back, arm stretched out for me, palm-side up.

I move to straddle his wrist before thinking better of it. His hand would be *right there.* One flick and he'd be grabbing my pussy.

Instead, I sit between his arm and hip before leaning down to inspect the skin, feeling for any blemishes. Aside from a sprinkling of dark hair, it's all smooth.

"They're probably gonna have to shave some of this," I tell him, scraping my nails through the short hairs.

He hisses, then grits, "'Kay."

I glance up at his face, finding his gaze locked on mine. "How'd you get your other tattoos if you can't even handle my nails?"

"I can handle your nails."

"But you just—"

"That wasn't out of pain."

I try to keep my eyes on his…at first. After that, they make the trip south to Crue's pants or, more accurately, where his erection is straining to get out of them.

"Ignore that. It'll go down."

With a shake of my head, I redirect my focus to his arm again.

Ignore the impressive erection less than a foot away.

Ignore the impressive erection less than a foot away.

Ignore the impressive erection less than a foot away.

It's harder than it sounds. Literally.

Using my middle finger, I trace an outline of what I'm envisioning, measuring how big I can realistically make a butterfly.

I hear another hiss, followed by a muttered, "Maybe not," and smile to myself.

Ignore the impressive erection less than a foot away…that isn't going down anytime soon.

"If it's too much, I don't have to do this."

"It's not too much and you're the only one I want to do this."

My smile tries to double, but I bite my lips between my teeth and sit up. Resting his arm across my lap, I tuck his hand against my side. I'm just uncapping the marker when I feel his fingers playing with the back of my arm.

"You have to keep your arm still."

The arm in question goes limp on my thighs.

"Sorry."

A couple minutes after I start the wings, Crue mumbles with a thick voice, "I could fall asleep like this."

"So go to sleep."

"You won't try smothering me?"

"No promises."

We both chuckle and it feels good.

"Make sure you skip the pillow and just sit on my face."

I frown and look up at him. His eyes are closed but one of his eyebrows lifts the same time the corner of his lips do.

"You'd be okay with me sitting on your face? While you're asleep?"

"Okay with it? Shit, I drift off every night imagining it."

I shake my head. No, he doesn't.

Does he?

"Even after you saw what happened to Crue 2.0's face?"

He points at his facial scar with his free hand. "An airbag going two hundred miles an hour, hitting me with over two thousand pounds of force couldn't crush my face. You think I'm worried about you riding my tongue?"

"Riding your tongue? Aren't you supposed to be asleep in this scenario?"

He's smiling now. "I don't care if I'm in a coma, your pussy gets within an inch of my face, I'm chowing the fuck down."

Speechless, I return to my drawing.

Ignore that image.

Ignore that—

"So?" he questions with absolutely zero context whatsoever.

"So what?"

"Are you gonna do it?"

"I'm kinda busy right now, not to mention you're…" I stop to wave a hand at him even though his eyes are still closed. "Awake."

The fakest snore I've ever heard tickles my ears, making me laugh.

"You don't snore."

Crue stops the farce to chide, "See? All that sneaking in here while I was asleep, you could've been sitting on my face."

"I didn't know I had your permission before."

"Now that you do, will you?"

Probably not. Crue's the peace in a sea of chaos and lying next to him as he sleeps calmly gives me more than oral ever could.

Ignoring his question, I tease, "Is this what happens when you miss a meal?"

Crue's hand grasps my elbow, and without a hint of humor, he says, "Be my dinner."

Feeling his gaze now, I keep mine locked on my work. "I was joking."

"I'm not."

"You said tonight wasn't about that." Please don't make it about that. I can't…right now.

"Then stay the night and be my breakfast tomorrow."

"Relax your arm."

"Agree to stay the night."

"Crue—"

"Stay the night with me," he practically begs, gripping my arm tighter as he sits up.

"Why?"

"Because the safest place for you is in my arms."

I scoff. "Just because you don't want me in someone else's, doesn't make your arms the safest."

"They're the safest because I'd take on the world for you."

"Is my father paying you enough for that?"

"No, he's not… But I'd do it anyway."

Finally, I lift my eyes to search his. Our heads seem to have some sort of gravitational pull, tugging us closer together.

"Why are you being like this?"

"Like what?"

Attentive. Amazing. Perfect.

"Nice."

"Because the last person I failed to protect died. Tonight made me realize how much I don't want that to happen to you."

Genuine sincerity stares back at me.

"What happened tonight?" He didn't see anything, did he? He didn't *hear* anything…did he?

"My reason for getting up in the morning was ripped away from me and there was nothing I could do to get her back."

The pain in his features, raw and vivid, reveals what tonight was for him. It was torture. I still don't understand why.

"It's just a job, Major," floats through my lips like a puffy cloud on a summer day—aimlessly.

"No, little bat, you're not."

CHAPTER 32

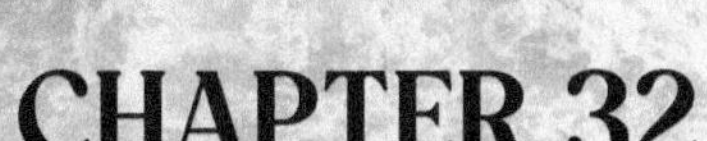

SEEING THE POSTERS OF CRUE'S BED, MY HEART JUMPS INTO my throat, making it nearly impossible to breathe. I fell asleep. I never fall asleep.

Shit. He's gonna find me here and know how creepy I really am.

How did I let myself fall asleep? I was tired after everything last night—

Last night…

I didn't sneak in here last night. Crue invited me into his room. He wanted me to stay the night. Begged me to.

I force my heart back down. I'm okay. He knows I'm here…this time.

Except now, he's the one at *my* back, his arm along my stomach, keeping me to him as he spoons me from behind.

"How long are you gonna make me wait?" I hear him ask in a thick voice.

Wait for what?

Pretending I'm still asleep, I stay silent.

Because I must've fallen asleep working on his butterfly, our bodies aren't perfectly lined up, so his growing erection presses into my back instead of my ass.

"I know you're awake. Your heart just started racing."

Damn heart.

I scrunch one eye. "What are you waiting for exactly?"

"Your pussy on my tongue."

"Oh, right."

"What do you mean 'oh, right'? Get your ass up here and sit on my face."

His hand grips the fabric at my stomach, awakening my own desire. I wasn't sure I'd feel that again so soon after Mallory's attempted assault.

I should've known better. I'll always want Crue.

"I just woke up."

"So?"

"So I have to go to the bathroom."

"Fine. Go."

"Mm, thanks," I mock before sitting up.

I make the mistake of looking at Crue over my shoulder. Hunger is bleeding out of him, threatening to consume me whole.

Goddess.

"You better hurry. I haven't eaten since lunch yesterday."

My pussy throbs the entire way to the bathroom, making it difficult to pee once I'm inside. I want him. I want him *bad*.

I take extra time at the sink, running my hand under cold water and wiping myself up.

When I come back out, Crue's sitting at the foot of the bed, arms behind him holding him up. Everything about him appears relaxed… except that massive tent in his sweatpants.

"Come here," he says with a jerk of his chin.

After watching my approach, he comes off his hands, running them down my arms, past my fingers, to the bottom of my sweatshirt.

"Can I?"

He asked.

He *asked*.

I swallow and nod.

Carefully, Crue pulls the sweatshirt up until it's over my head. Without a bra on, my top half is completely nude.

I don't know why but I suddenly feel self-conscious, and with my pinky nail hooked on my bottom canine, I blurt out, "I have, like, no boobs."

"You got enough," he rasps as he pulls my hand away from my mouth, biting the same nail I just did before sucking the tip.

I watch him through hooded lids, wondering how a gesture so small can make me feel so much.

After kissing my palm, he places it on the back of his neck.

"I'm going to kiss you everywhere you let me." His hands cup my jaw, and one thumb massages my lips. "Can I kiss you here?"

I give the barest headshake.

"Then I'm gonna kiss as close to this mouth as I can get."

Slowly leaning forward, he kisses that thumb. His lips never touch mine, yet my heart races all the same.

After he pulls back, he says quietly, "One day you will beg me to kiss you there. Until then…"

Lowering, he kisses both shoulders, both collarbones, then both boobs, quickly sucking on the second's peak.

A moan builds in my throat and I bring my other hand up to grasp his head, holding him to me.

He guides me backward by my hips enough for him to lower a knee to the floor in front of me, kissing his way down my stomach to my shorts' waistband.

Hooking his thumbs in the top, he drags them and my underwear down, his lips never leaving my skin as he kisses down one leg, ankle, and foot, before taking the same path up the other side.

Crue leans back to see my body in its entirety. Feet, knees, thighs, pussy, stomach, chest, then finally, my face.

Through dark lashes, his eyes don't even look human when they meet mine, the color almost glowing.

"Jesus Christ, Ever, you're gorgeous."

Goddess, I want him in me. Now.

"You should see what you look like." Because I've never seen anything hotter than Crue Brantley kneeling before me.

I let my knees go soft and start to lower myself, but Crue catches me.

"Hold on. Not yet."

Rearranging his legs so he's sitting, he brings me forward again until I'm in a standing straddle over his chest. He reclines a bit, then helps me step around each of his shoulders so I'm standing directly over his face.

Only a matter of inches between his nose and my pussy, he says, "Now you can do your thing."

"My *thing?*"

"Rub your clit on my tongue long enough for you to come all over it."

He asked, repeatedly. And now he's giving me all the control.

I'm in control.

He won't do anything I don't agree to.

He's not Mallory.

Biting my bottom lip, I prop my hands on the mattress, arch my back, then close those inches until my pussy meets Crue's parted mouth.

Automatically, he seizes my ass cheeks, hard enough for me to deepen my arch, my clit in perfect position for Crue to flatten his tongue against. Instead of rolling my hips, I choose to stay where I am, keeping the pressure as I grind up and down on Crue's tongue.

He's not Mallory. This is different. I want this. I want Crue.

Tension builds between my legs, mounting to impossible heights.

Yes. I want him. I want to do this with him. This is how it should always be. My choice. My say. I decide what happens to my body.

My breath grows heavier and heavier, as do my nearly non-existent boobs. It's right there. I'm just about to come. I can feel it... And then...

I don't?

But I want this. I'm turned on. I like Crue. A lot. And I want to come. Now.

Why won't it...

I twist my hips slightly left, rubbing my clit but I can't find that firework feeling again.

I try right. Come on, come on. Where is it?

No?

No. It recedes completely.

I slow my movements. It still feels good. Really good. But it doesn't grow bigger than a low sizzle, like a sparkler.

Maybe I did come but was too distracted thinking about coming to notice? Or did my overthinking stop the orgasm altogether?

Ugh.

I shudder and moan a convincing little, "Ah," before immediately hopping off.

"What was that?" Crue is quick to ask.

"That was great. Thanks," I say, realizing my mistake a moment too late. We don't say thanks to each other.

"Thanks?" he repeats, his eyebrows drawing closer together. He brings his knees up, resting his elbows on them as he watches me gather my clothes.

That shyness creeping back up from before, I make sure I'm bent with my ass away from Crue's face.

"Did you come?"

"Yeah."

"Why didn't it seem like it? And why are you being so fucking weird?"

"It's not weird to get dressed. I do it every day. Anyway, I should probably get back to my room before anyone sees me coming out of yours." I freeze with my shorts halfway up my legs. "Unless you want me walking around naked for anyone to see…"

"I want you to be straight with me. Did you come?"

Eye level with each other, his light eyes probe mine.

"I don't know," I admit, then continue putting my clothes on.

"How do you not know?"

"I was about to, and then just…didn't?"

"So you didn't come? You just said you didn't know. *After* you said you did."

"It's a confusing time for all of us."

The confusion on Crue's face seems to double, confirming my statement. It is.

"Why did you fake it?"

"Hello?" I shake my head and spread my hands out, but Crue just looks at me expectantly. Has he never considered the possibility that a woman faked an orgasm with him? "I didn't want to hurt your feelings."

He scoffs. "Since when do you care about those?"

"Since you just sat there and made me do all the work," I snap because bickering is our main form of communication. I'd rather argue with Crue than admit to everything going on inside me right now.

"I was doing what I thought you like."

I did like it. I really did. It's just… I don't know what's wrong with me. I lost it. And who knows if I'll be able to find it again. Maybe last night did more damage than I thought. I don't *know*.

I mumble, "Whatever," to myself, to Crue, to this whole situation, but Crue only takes it as a challenge.

"Let me try again."

When he grabs for me, I twist out of his reach.

"I have to get ready for school."

"I thought you said your professor doesn't mind you being late."

That was before I subtly threatened to end her life.

"My father does."

That gets him to stop. Because it is a job. I am his job. Regardless of what he said last night, I am.

Crue hops up. "You're right. Can't rush perfection."

My bodyguard's words don't sound sarcastic in any way, yet there's a blankness in his expression that keep them from feeling genuine.

"Aesthetic first, pleasure last." *If at all.*

"Right," he agrees with a nod I don't believe for a second.

"Right," I echo, eyes narrowed on him. Why is he being so compliant all of a sudden?

"I said that."

Without another word, I stomp past, knocking my arm into his. Why did I agree to stay the night with him? Technically I didn't agree, my body did. Annoying. My body is so annoying. First, passing out next to Crue, then, this…malfunction. An actual malfunction, too.

The sensor on my door hasn't malfunctioned once and neither did the lights. I turned them off last night in case Crue did something ridiculous like wait up for me, which he did because he's an overbearing asshole.

He's not an overbearing asshole at all. He's caring, and if I could've collapsed in his arms and told him everything, I would've.

At his door, I hesitate before turning back around. His hands are on his head again.

"Crue?"

"What?" he barks.

That's not very caring.

Returning his energy, I sass, "Are you going to walk me to my door or not?"

When he drops his hands, I see the butterfly I drew on his forearm, and a warmth spreads through my chest.

But then he says, "Sure. Just let me grab your collar and leash first," freezing it all to a solid.

I slam his door in my wake. With a sharp tongue like that, it's no wonder I didn't come on it.

The only thing Crue says to me between my bedroom door and the kitchen is a murmured, "Take your breakfast to go," which I was already planning to do for my own reasons but am now curious about his.

Before I can ask him, we're already entering the kitchen, my father seated in his usual spot. The sight of him has my feet growing ten times heavier. By now, he'll know last night didn't end well and he'll inevitably blame me.

Wordlessly, Crue maneuvers me to his left side, but again, I was already planning on going this way. Well, not on this side of the island—the chef's side. I only wanted to stick as close to the outside of it as possible. So as confidently as I can, I stroll between the island and the custom Diva de Provence range, surprising the chef as he minces chives. I've never ventured into his work area, but desperate times call for desperate measures. I'd rather face Ryan right now than my father.

"Good morning, Miss Munreaux. How can I serve you this morning?"

Sickening. He's beyond sickening.

"Miss," Crue tries to call me back.

What'd he expect? He's the one who put me on this path.

My father's voice makes everyone else's sound like children's. "Ah, Never, I've been waiting for you."

My eyes flit between Ryan's, Crue's, and the back of my father's head, all three men expecting…something out of me.

I look at Crue again, his nostrils flared as his jaw flexes. What is he so mad about? He's the one that basically called me a dog.

Is it because I'm standing next to Ryan? If I wasn't repulsed by the mere thought, I'd get even closer to the chef just to spite him.

"Apologies, Father, I'm on my way out to make up a test."

Crue frowns.

Keeping his gaze straight ahead, my father lifts his head. "Why do you need to make it up? Did you miss class?"

The same time Crue says, "No, she didn't," I start to explain.

"During the test, I was starting a different project for my professor, Mrs. Flemming." She still goes by Mrs. I'm not sure she was being honest when she told Crue she was getting divorced. "I'll be working on the project the rest of the term, so I'll be busy…a lot more."

Crue's frown deepens but he doesn't question me.

"Would you like me to make you something to take with?" Ryan asks, leaning toward me enough that I have to lean, too—away from him.

"I don't have much of an appetite this morning." Especially not now.

The chef returns to his regular posture before twisting to address Crue.

"What about you, Mr.—"

I rush to add, "Mr. Brantley was just telling me he doesn't either."

One hand on the counter, I turn a nice big smile on my body-guard. *Contradict me publicly, I dare you.*

"Are you sure? I can pack you both something for later," Ryan offers.

Crue's eyes drill into mine.

"That's not necessary. We don't want Miss Munreaux to be late."

"No, we certainly don't."

I peer over at Ryan, finding him watching me while he sprinkles the chives on my father's omelet, probably trying to figure out why I'm over here but not wanting to outright ask and draw attention to himself. He's smart like that.

I need to be, too. Why would I approach him? Nothing other than food, that's for damn sure.

"For tonight's dinner, I'd like a steak salad," I tell him.

Instead of saying, "It'd be my pleasure," he just says, "Pleasure," making me want to scream at the top of my lungs. I hate this manor and everyone in it.

I consider doing it.

"Ready, miss," Crue says more than asks.

My lower jaw shifts on its hinges. He knows I despise when he calls me that.

Forgoing any niceties, I skirt around Ryan. Both Crue and I ignore my father's call for my return to speak with him. I'll stab pencils in my eardrums before admitting to hearing that. If he wants to talk to me that bad, he can get up off his ass and come get me. I'm done making anything easy for him.

Inside my Sapphire, Crue breaks the silence. "If you're not gonna let me fill up on your cunt, you could at least let me eat real food."

Should've thought of that before he insinuated I was a dog that needs walked. I was trying to be considerate, letting him walk me to my door.

I was also, if I'm being completely honest, scared.

No one should be scared inside their own home, but that's just a fact of life for me, now, forever.

"You should've just grabbed something off the counter."

Also, my cunt is no longer on your menu, I almost add but don't because that's not what I want at all. I just need to figure out what's going on with me first. I've never not come when I could've. I've had bad sex where, of course, I didn't come, but the reason was obvious. This time it wasn't and that freaks me out.

"I was trying to get you out of there as quickly as possible."

"Why?"

He's quiet as he puts on his seat belt, but then mutters, "For your test."

I have a sneaking suspicion Crue knows there is no test. But if that's true, why else would he want me out of that kitchen?

CHAPTER 33

Crue

THAT EVENING EVER GOES FOR HER REGULAR SEAT, THE ONE to the right of her father's. Arthur always sits at the head of whatever table we're at, with Ever on his right and me directly across from her on his left. I've eaten enough meals with the motorcycle mogul to know he's right-handed.

I need to put myself between the two, but don't see a way to do it without raising suspicion. Fuck it. This is probably gonna start a fight but what's new?

"Why don't you sit next to me tonight?" I suggest to Ever, earning myself a nasty sneer I was expecting but still don't like to see directed at me.

"Why? So you don't have to look at me?"

She has no idea. None. I'm lucky enough that Ever Munreaux's the sun, but if she were the moon, I'd become nocturnal just to gaze at her every night.

"Not exactly," I say while prodding her back…all the way over to my side of the table.

Because she's still pissy about this morning, she sits two chairs away from mine. Since I don't know if Arthur's even gonna be okay with her sitting somewhere else, let alone that far down the table, I have no choice but to pull out the chair next to her and take a seat. If he makes her move, I'm moving, too. Arthur's not getting close enough to hurt Ever again, not on my watch.

The second my ass touches the cushion, Ever's shoving to her feet again.

I grab her elbow.

"I'm sorry, okay?"

She shakes me off, but doesn't move, hopefully waiting for me to expand on that. I don't really know what to say. Other than the truth.

"I fucked up. This morning was—"

"Oh, don't *even* try pulling the regret card right now."

"I'm not." The only thing I regret—

The only *things* I regret are not getting Ever to the finish line and how I acted after finding out I didn't.

"You think I regret…*that?*" I say vaguely since I'm not sure when Arthur will be barging in here.

"You acted like it."

"And you acted like a—"

"Dog?"

Although Ever *can* be a bitch, she's no dog. I shouldn't have made the collar and leash comment. That was out of line. But once again, she lied to me. All she fucking does is lie. She lied about those bruises on her hips. She lied about that test this morning.

I wanted her stripped down, at her most vulnerable with me, and I thought she was. She was completely bared to me, standing over my face, fucking my tongue, and still, motherfucking *still*, she put up a front. She could've told me. She could've said it wasn't doing it for her. I would've stopped. Instantly. I would've done anything she fucking wanted me to. All she had to do was be honest. But she can't. She'd rather keep up the tough exterior that she uses with everyone else.

I hate that she doesn't see me differently. I hate that I don't know how to be different. How the fuck am I supposed to break down her walls when I'm still scaling my own? I tried last night. I tried really fucking hard. I've never been good with girls. I've never *been* with girls, not like that.

Regardless, I know how I behaved was wrong. I'm not a total dumbfuck. Just irrational…when it comes to Ever Munreaux.

"You know you're not a dog, Ever. You could never be a dog." She doesn't budge, so I try a joke, saying, "Dogs don't even fly."

Not even that does the trick, her face hard as she glares at me.

The door swings open, cracking Ever's façade as she redirects her attention to whoever just came through it. Only after she sits down do I follow her lead, giving Edwin the floor.

"Mr. Munreaux sends his apologies that he won't be joining you two for dinner tonight."

"Thanks for the heads-up," I tell the valet.

Chef Ryan strolls in behind him with his hands full of our plates. He makes it a point to regard us as he sets each one down, questioning, "Was there something wrong with the previous seating arrangement?"

"Yeah, Mr. Brantley—"

"Miss Munreaux," I speak over Ever, practically booming, "had an issue with her food this afternoon when a piece of chicken got stuck in her throat."

That's a real thing. Apparently, people choke on chicken a crazy amount. My mom's hairdresser does. Once, when she went to the emergency room for it, the doctor called her a "chicken choker."

Both men's eyes widen, their jaws dropping.

"Momentarily," I add. "Thankfully, I was able to perform the Heimlich maneuver right away and dislodge it. She's been a little shaken up ever since though, so I thought it best to sit next to her in case it happens again."

"You're a hero," Edwin praises, his worn gaze on mine.

Used to the opposite sentiment being hurled at me, all I can do is give him a tight smile.

Ryan's eyes, however, are all for Ever as he looks her over. "Are you all right, miss?"

"Ahem." I clear my throat, readjusting in my chair. "She's fine."

The chef doesn't so much as blink, as if I didn't even speak.

"Would you like me to cut your steak into smaller bites for you?" he offers her, like I didn't think of that. If she was a real chicken choker, I would've.

"I can—"

"That is *so* sweet of you," Ever croons.

I cut my glare over to her. She can't possibly mean that. She didn't even say that when I did her hair for her.

So quick I almost miss it, she glances my way, then she's sitting up and propping her chin on her interlocked fingers, focusing on her chef again. *The* chef. Ryan's her dad's chef. He's nothing to her.

He better be nothing to her.

"But I don't think that'll be necessary. If you wouldn't mind cutting up Mr. Brantley's food though…" Her hand covering her mouth from my view, she mock-whispers, "He's not a very strong eater either."

Oh, hell fucking no. Did she just imply I can't eat pussy? I'm a *very* strong eater, in *every* regard. I was off my game this morning… or something. I don't know what went wrong. I let her lead. Lesson learned. Won't happen again—the letting-Ever-lead part. The other part…it will happen again. Soon.

Now, in fact.

"Maybe I should stay—"

"No, you can go," I tell Ryan, my eyes drilling into the side of Ever's face. I don't give a fuck this isn't my house. I don't give a fuck this isn't my staff. Ever is *my* protectee. I will see to her needs.

Every.

Last.

One.

Of.

Them.

"Um…" Ryan lingers, a hand out at our food—the food I no longer have any interest in, not because I'm a weak eater like Ever just claimed, but because I got my eye on something much, much more appealing. The second we're alone, Ever's getting devoured.

"Yes, well, before I go…" Ryan jumps into his descriptions, but I don't hear a word. I'm too busy counting down the seconds 'til he disappears from my periphery. *Get the fuck out of here, Ryan.* I'm about to gorge and I don't want an audience, especially not for the first bite. Oh, I'm fucking biting. I'm throwing everything I got into it this time. Ever won't be able to say shit about me not putting in enough effort after tonight.

I quickly take a single bite of the pork medallion and give a half-assed, "Mm."

Ever draws out her first bite, taking her sweet time.

On their way out, I tell Edwin and Ryan, "I'll bring our dishes out when we're finished." *No need to bother us again. Now fuck off.*

"That was curt," Ever scolds as soon as it's just us, but she has no room to talk. She's never been remotely pleasant to Chef Ryan… until today.

With one swipe of my arm, I slide everything in front of me to the spot to my right. My glass of ice water wobbles but I don't bother steadying it. If it falls, it falls.

"What are you—"

Ever's pulled on to my lap next, both of us hissing when she lands on my hard-on, and because I can't resist, I thrust up into her.

"Excuse you. I'm trying to eat."

"So am I."

I push the back of her head down, her face pressed to the table's smooth surface. Her ass lifts in the process, giving me a fantastic view of it after one flick of her skirt. She's wearing panties but they're stretched thin from the angle, making them almost translucent. Still working with little to no restraint, I bend down and bite one perfect globe.

"Crue," she whisper-shouts with a back arch I feel in my balls.

"Still think I'm not a strong eater?"

"I've been bitten harder by mosquitoes."

I half-scoff, half-laugh before tearing her underwear in the middle, exposing her ass crack and hole.

Palms on the table, Ever tries to push up, but one drag of my tongue up an ass cheek has her staying in place, stomach down, ass and head up, just the way I want my dinner—on display.

I'm dying to give her a rim job but worry about eating her pussy after. With all the research I've had to do on female anatomy lately, I've learned pussies are complicated. They're overly sensitive to some things but not others. They can take a pounding from a ten-inch cock no problem. But if a single strand of a different bacteria is introduced? Jesus Christ. Out of commission for days, sometimes weeks. After the instant potato fiasco, I can't fuck up Ever's levels again. As a newly converted cuntarian, I wouldn't survive weeks without a taste of hers.

I rip the hole in the fabric bigger until I see the pussy that occupied most, if not all, of my thoughts today. Goddamn, it's beautiful. She's beautiful. Every fucking bit of her.

I lick those wet lips, making them even wetter.

"My father—"

"Isn't here," I whisper, then run my tongue up her slit, coating the tip in her juices before swallowing them down with a moan.

Days. I wouldn't last days without this.

Ever attempts to stifle her own moan.

"But what if he walks in?"

I almost snort. Arthur Munreaux doesn't run late. He doesn't hurry from one thing to the next. And he sure as hell doesn't make it a point to catch up with his daughter.

"No one's coming in here," I tell her confidently, because that's the truth—nobody checks in on Ever to see how she's doing. If it weren't for me, she'd be alone in this house all the goddamn time.

Before I got here, she *was* alone in this house all the goddamn time.

We're kinda the same in that way. Except my loneliness was a choice. And I was never completely alone. Through everything, I've always had parents who love and interact with me. From what I've seen, Arthur rarely interacts with Ever, and he…doesn't love her. I don't think he does. He's never once acted like it, and if he's uttered the words, it wasn't around me.

That realization makes me understand Ever a little bit better. She's not unlovable. She's just unloved. She's not a bitch—

Well, she is. Ever Munreaux is definitely a bitch…but she has reason to be. Sometimes. She had no reason to insult my oral skills, especially not to another man.

Unless it's true… Was I really that terrible this morning?

It was the technique. It wasn't mine. I was trying to compete with a motherfucking teddy bear. I'm a red-blooded man with enough moving parts to please a woman in multiple ways, all at once, damn it.

Kicking my chair out behind me, I kneel on the floor. I don't dive right in though, instead hovering close to her entrance and just breathing, the cool air teasing Ever's thighs and causing goose bumps. I kiss each one, making my way in, but still not touching her center…yet.

Up, down, all around, I lick everywhere but Ever's hole.

All of a sudden, her slim hand appears under her, and I watch mesmerized as two of her fingers dip into her wetness before swirling over her clit.

I catch her wrist and suck those fingers clean.

I hear a frustrated, "Crue," and smile around the digits. I couldn't resist.

Returning her fingertips to her clit, I say, "Don't stop until I tell you to."

Her fingers immediately start circling the swollen nub.

I resume my teasing, loving the way she's shaking already. Tongue flat and wide, I rub against her bare pussy lips, prepping her, then I make it pointed and spear between her folds, fucking her so deep her nails nick my chin.

Pulling back out, I bend down lower and burrow between her fingers to suck her clit between my lips, rotating my tongue over it.

"Oh my Goddess."

Easing up so her fingers can continue, I shower her in compliments, my breath more liquid than air as it sprays her pussy lips.

"You're so beautiful. You're fucking perfect. I want you to come for me. Come on my face, my hand. Give me everything, everywhere. I want it. I want you."

I grab both ass cheeks and thrust my tongue inside her cunt, groaning at the feel, the taste, the warmth. Jesus fuck, I could live in Ever's pussy.

I help her pop her hips, fucking me as much as I'm fucking her.

Her movements grow irregular and small cries of pleasure escape her, telling me she's close.

She tries clenching her ass cheeks together, but I spread them apart, forcing her down on me harder. Some animalistic sound echoes through the dining room, then her walls squeeze my tongue, coating it in cum.

"Good girl," I say after a wet kiss to her quivering lips. No blue lips for her tonight. She came and she came hard.

And that was only the first.

Her fingers on her clit have slowed but are still moving.

Getting to my feet, I slip two of my own fingers into her soaked pussy, pumping in and out with a bit of an arc upward that runs my thumb up her crack.

Her ass bucks up again, driving me crazy. I want to bury myself in every part of her, including this ass.

"Crue, I'm making a mess," she complains, only mildly convincing.

I press a kiss to the back of her neck. Against the skin, I whisper, "You better."

On a moan, she lifts her head and for a second I think she'll turn it over her shoulder so I can kiss her, but she doesn't.

"Head down, ass up, Ever. I haven't gotten enough to eat yet." Not even close.

Almost instantly she drops her forehead to the table and sends her ass into the air for me.

I bite back a grin. This is how this morning should've gone. There's nothing fake about any of this.

I replace my fingers with my thumb, stimulating her G-spot with it while my drenched fingers join hers at her clit, then I lean down to flatten my tongue against her asshole.

"Oh, God—" Ever's words morph into incoherent noises.

Did she forget she told me to eat her ass the first day we met?

I didn't.

Several strokes like that, then I run a soft tongue up and down until she relaxes there a bit. After I switch to figure eights, she's loosened up enough for me to poke the puckered hole with the tip of my tongue.

"Fuck," she pants.

Exactly what I was thinking, little bat.

Slowly, I start to tongue-fuck her asshole, paying close attention to her body for any sign she wants me to stop. Her deep moan spurs me on, so I grab her thigh and knead the flesh roughly. In my pants, my hard cock leaks, making me wish I had a third hand to jerk myself off. I'd come all over Ever's ass, painting her in my cum, then I'd finger-fuck her ass with it, making sure I mark her in there, too.

I groan at the fantasy, setting off Ever's climax. She comes harder than before. Keeping my hand where it is, just slowing my movements like Ever did after her first O, I gently withdraw my tongue to nibble her ass cheeks on their descent.

I kiss and suck down to her thighs, praising her for coming, for trusting me.

"You can stop," I say as I pull my hand away from her cunt.

The hand beneath her goes limp but she doesn't try removing her arm, fully collapsed on her mahogany dining room table.

That's a sight I could get used to.

After I return her to her chair, I retrieve mine.

Settling into it again, I say, "I'd like to see your bear do that."

Surprisingly, Ever chuckles. "You're ridiculous."

I look over at her and take a mental picture of the sight. Slumped in her chair like her backbone is made of gelatin, her black hair is damp at the hairline, she has a red imprint on her forehead, and I swear to God her eyes have stars in them. One thing's wrong though. She's too far away.

One-handed, I drag her chair a few inches closer to mine.

"Yeah? You're delicious." I jerk a nod at her. "Eat your steak salad before I hand-feed it to you."

"I can feed myself," she says, laughter infusing her voice.

I know she can…but I'd still do it for her if she let me.

CHAPTER 34

AFTER LAST NIGHT'S "FEAST," CRUE HASN'T LET ME GET MORE than a foot away from him. At breakfast this morning, he practically kept me tucked against his side as we grabbed our food and left. My father didn't try talking to me again but he doesn't really need to. Anytime I'm in the manor, I can feel the anger rolling off him from several rooms away. I know he's pissed. It's sad he's not pissed for my sake. I think that'd be the normal fatherly reaction to his daughter almost being raped. Unfortunately, my father's not normal.

Everybody wants a billionaire father…until they realize he'll do anything to stay that way.

I'm coming out of my last class when I see Crue holding out another matcha lemonade for me. For some reason, he has one for himself, too. He's made his dislike for the clones' preferred drink known, so why would he subject himself to the torture of drinking one?

I snatch it out of his hand without a word.

We walk down the hall side by side, neither of us drinking from our cups.

Paris and Brad hesitate at the stairwell, giving me lingering looks.

"Your clones are watching," Crue points out. "Aren't you gonna take a sip for them?"

With an internal roll of my eyes, I fit the lid to my lips, pretending to drink the green liquid.

"That's it?"

I side-eye my bodyguard.

"You didn't notice anything different in it?"

"Did you poison it or something?"

"Then how would I get paid?"

A garbage can in my sight, I head right for it, but Crue's hand on my elbow stops me in my tracks.

"I'm joking. Just try it."

"I did. It tastes the same."

"Really? You're gonna pull that shit again?"

"What shit?"

"Faking it."

It's all I ever do! The words churn inside me like an unspoken tornado.

It takes immense restraint to keep them in, so much I don't dare move anything else, especially not my arm to lift the cup to my mouth.

Crue eyes the lemonade. "Take a drink, little bat."

If I am a bat, I'm the vampire bat. They seek out the same prey night after night based on its breathing pattern while it's sleeping. Both agile and lightweight, they can drink blood for up to thirty minutes without even waking up the source. I don't sneak into Crue's room at night to drink his blood, but I'm in there for longer than thirty minutes and I haven't woken him up yet.

"Did you come in it?"

"And rob you of getting to drink that straight from the source? No. Drink up."

"If you poison me, I'm so coming back to haunt you, too."

"As long as you're a succubus," he mutters, reminding me he gave me his consent to sit on his face while he's asleep.

Unable to respond with anything remotely appropriate for our current surroundings, I tap his cup with mine in cheers before swallowing a tiny—

Wait. This isn't matcha lemonade. It's not lemonade at all.

I study the side of the transparent cup. It looks like the same lemonade I get all the time—a milky green. But it tastes like a chai latte... Not just any chai latte but a chai latte with almond milk and three pumps of pumpkin brown sugar. That drink's tan though. How is that even possible?

"What is this?"

"Can't you tell? It's your drink. The one you actually like."

"But it…doesn't…look…" I take another pull, this one longer. It doesn't look like it, but it is it.

"I dyed it green."

I blink up at Crue, then his own green drink, some of it gone already.

"Did you do the same thing to yours?"

"No, mine's a matcha lemonade. I had to order at least one, you know, for appearance's sake. Aesthetic first—"

"Pleasure last," I finish.

"Not for you. Not anymore."

He ordered something he hates and is drinking it just so I don't have to. He chose my pleasure over his.

The smile that overtakes my face feels foreign it's so big, so genuine.

"Thank you."

After studying me for a minute, he asks, "Are you fucking with me right now?"

I try not to let his suspicion dim my mood. It is warranted after all. I haven't been very grateful to him. Or nice.

"No. I appreciate this. For real."

Despite his frown, I sip more tea.

Neither of us speaks as we regard one another, so I turn and resume walking. Crue keeps pace next to me every step of the way… until I'm suddenly yanked sideways through a doorway, the green liquid splashing up onto my face.

"What—"

"Everybody out," Crue tells whoever's inside, his voice bouncing off the walls because it's a bathroom. The girls' bathroom to be exact. "Security…purposes."

Keeping my focus on the floor as the three girls pass me, I slowly dab the drops from my lips and nose.

The second we're alone, I inform him, "That wasn't the least bit believable."

"I don't care." Unapologetic, my bodyguard sets his drink on the countertop before doubling back to lock the door.

Our closeness becomes palpable.

I lift the dyed drink between us. "I thought the point of this was to be able to enjoy it in public."

"The public's gotten enough of you today. It's my turn."

"You couldn't wait until we got home?"

"You're lucky I waited this long."

Stepping up close to me, he cups the back of my head and pulls.

When I start turning away, his other hand grabs my chin, stopping me. Hysteria fills me just before he pushes his thumb up to cover my lips again, kissing it instead.

His nose pressed to mine, he rasps, "Why didn't you come to my room last night?"

I did, you just didn't know it.

"I thought you got your fill at dinner." My body grows intolerably hot at the reminder. The same body that's been begging for more of Crue's touch since the moment he withdrew it.

"That's funny." His chuckle tickles my lips.

I lower my jaw and try to catch it in my mouth.

Crue slips his thumb in, goading my tongue into a playful dance.

Closing my lips around his second knuckle, I suck on his thumb as he slowly thrusts it in and out. I bite down.

Crue groans, then removes his thumb, allowing me to ask, "What's funny?"

That same hand travels down the front of my throat, making a quick stop to caress my breast before continuing on to the bottom of my pinafore dress.

"That you thought I'd ever get my fill of you."

A core-igniting need overtakes me. I *need* Crue inside me, and not just his tongue or his fingers.

Just as he begins lifting the fabric, I say, "No."

Other than pulling back to look at me, Crue doesn't dare move any other part of his body, as still as if he was petrified.

It's exactly how anyone should act upon hearing that word. The bare minimum really. Crue doing it only makes me want him more.

"Fuck me."

"Here? I was just gonna—"

"Here." I can't wait either. Last night, he reminded me I can enjoy intimacy and I don't have to overthink it. In fact, it's better if I don't.

Crue's moss-green eyes oscillate between my lips and eyes.

"Not until—"

"I can't kiss you."

Cocking his head to the side, he frowns. "*Can't?*"

Why did I have to phrase it like that?

"I'll do anything you want, except that." *Please don't make that be the determining factor again.*

"Promise you'll look at me then."

"I…"

I drop my gaze, my entire face following after, then I sidestep Crue and go over to stand in front of one of the sinks, placing my drink next to his.

Can I look at Crue? Most days I feel that's all I do. The days I don't, I wish I had. He's a Leonardo da Vinci painting amongst heavily edited selfies. He's *The Starry Night* in a world overrun by AI-generated images. He is a true original work of art—flawed, unparalleled, and utterly mesmerizing. Looking at him is a privilege I count myself lucky to have for the time being. If I could, I'd look at him until my vision stopped working.

"I promise," comes out quiet, yet feels like it echoes.

Crue comes up behind me, gripping my stomach and bringing me into him. Automatically, my hands rise to hold him to me, too, and a moan escapes me as I root my ass against his hard cock.

"You have no idea what you just started," he says near my ear.

I tilt my head, giving him better access.

"A secret affair with my bodyguard?"

Lips teasing the side of my neck, he corrects, "Personal protection agent."

Now it's my turn to chuckle. Chuckle *and* shiver because the smallest nibble has me shaking for more.

Someone knocks on the door, threatening to interrupt.

"Out of order!" Crue yells over his shoulder, refusing to let them.

Focusing on me again, he maintains eye contact as he scrapes his bared teeth over the thin skin at my throat, making me hiss. He doesn't close his lips and suck though, setting himself apart from every other guy I've been with. I both love and hate it. I like having my neck sucked on for a reason.

Although I don't feel the noose right now. All I feel is Crue.

Taking my hands from behind his head, he repositions them to frame the sink, then straightens to flip the back of my dress up, pulling my underwear down enough to uncover my ass.

My pussy clenches in anticipation.

It takes him a matter of seconds to undo his pants, shoving them and his nondescript boxer briefs to his knees.

I have to move my hips to the side to get a better view of the cock I've spent months imagining, drawing, wanting. The sketch my imagination conjured absolutely pales in comparison to the real thing. Crue's cock is long and thick and upright.

Our eyes meet and I can't help myself. It's just too good to pass up.

"Where did you learn how to measure? School for giants?"

I've caught glimpses before, but not in its full-mast entirety yet.

Shaking his head, Crue laughs a little, a bit of pink creeping across his cheeks. Is he embarrassed? Nervous?

"There's no way that's four inches, Crue."

His chuckle grows. "I told you I've never measured."

"You should've."

Another headshake, then, "I'll let your cunt do the measuring."

While one hand pumps his rigid cock, Crue uses the other at the base of my spine to push along each vertebra until I'm bent over the sink, my palms flat on the concrete countertop. This school is ancient, but the restrooms are not. They've been remodeled several times since Littoral first opened its ultra-exclusive doors. Housing crystal chandeliers between each vessel sink as well as touchless faucets, the university's bathrooms are the ultimate display of vintage and contemporary working together.

With a chin-jerk at the backlit mirror less than a couple inches from my face, he warns, "Eyes on me the whole time. Don't even think about closing them."

I'll try, I think, already questioning if I'll be able to keep that promise.

He kisses the side of my neck at the same time I feel his tip at my entrance, his finger and thumb wrapped around the head, dragging it through my slickness.

"Don't get all patient on me now, Crue. Fuck me already—"

He plunges his cock between my walls, earning groans from us both, but only making it about halfway in.

In all fairness, that's what I get for turning down foreplay. I'm wet enough, but I'm not nearly relaxed enough.

Crue grasps my hips and works himself deeper into me, withdrawing an inch, only to regain two or more, until eventually, he's bottomed out, his lower stomach mashed to my ass, his ball sack brushing my clit.

Fully sheathed, he pauses to look down between us.

Glancing back up at me, his smile nearly makes me come on the spot. It's that sexy.

"You okay?"

All I say is, "Mm-hm," even though I'm more than okay.

"I'm not too big? You're pretty tiny. I wasn't sure—"

"My body's good with the impossible, remember?" I reassure him. He has *no* reason to be insecure about his dick. Not with me. I'm obstinately obsessed with him. Whether his dick was two inches or two feet, I'd love it so long as it was mine.

And right now, it is. Finally.

Major Danger's cock is mine.

Now my smile matches his.

"Your pussy..." Sounding like he's out of breath, he rocks into me, hitting my cervix and making me gasp. "Your pussy feels like it was made specifically for me, hugging my cock so tight, so warm, so fucking good… Jesus Christ!"

There's another knock at the door and I shush Crue.

He groans. "I'm not pulling out one fucking inch. I don't give a fuck. You're gonna have to come on my cock just like this."

I don't want him to pull out either. Unless the custodian shows up with the keys, then he'll have to.

"Just keep doing that," I whisper breathily.

Our eyes holding each other's the entire time, he stays deliciously deep, rolling his hips into me rather than thrusting in and out.

"Show me how to touch your clit."

"You…don't know how?"

"I don't know how to touch *yours*. Show me what *you* like."

"We don't have a lot of time here."

"Fuck time. You're all that exists right now."

It's a travesty I'll never get to kiss Crue again, not just because he was good at it, but because there's never been another person I've wanted to kiss more. And there never will be.

I reach down to swirl my middle finger over my clit, pressing harder at the top than at the bottom.

Crue's hand covers mine, his middle finger draped along mine, feeling exactly what I'm doing. A few rotations, then he's nudging me out of the way to take over, using the same amount of pressure.

My jaw drops, the need for air more prudent than a moment ago. Why are we so out of breath? We're both in better shape than this. I give Crue a hard time, but he's been improving every time he runs with me.

"Shit, Ever. Do you have any idea how fucking beautiful you are right now? I could flood your cunt with cum just watching you like this." His other hand grabs a handful of my hair and twists my head so he can say against the shell of my ear, "Now show me how you kiss."

Despite the warm pleasure spreading up my body like ivy, those words have me freezing up like a block of ice. "I didn't agree—"

"Not me. Fuck!" He drops his head on another guttural groan.

I ease my muscles a fraction…only to tighten them all over again, earning the same reaction.

His gaze returns to mine. "Unless you want me to nut before you get the chance, you better relax your fucking cunt."

At no point does Crue pause the circles on my clit, so I want to believe him. I just don't understand.

"How else am I supposed to show you how I kiss if I—"

"The mirror," he grits.

I arch an eyebrow before *slowly* releasing my tight grip on his shaft.

"You want me to kiss a mirror?"

He immediately resumes his previous movements.

"Goddamn, that was close."

My brow remains sky-high. "Crue?"

"I want you to kiss me, but since you won't…for whatever fucking reason…I'll settle for watching you kiss my reflection."

Tentatively, I stretch my neck out toward the mirror, toward Crue's reflection. His fist at the back of my head guides me closer, until my lips are brushing the glass.

Crue's eyelids droop as he watches my pursed mouth press against the mirror.

"That's it. Good girl."

Seeing his reaction, *feeling* it in all the places we're touching, gives me the courage to take it further, to really kiss his reflection as if it's him. I sneak my tongue between my lips to lick at the cold, flat surface. It doesn't compare to kissing Crue. Nothing can. But when Crue starts kissing the side of my face, licking and sucking as if he's imagining my mouth, too, the pretense becomes a little more believable.

Holding the side of his head to mine, I make out with the mirror while Crue makes out with my jaw, both of us watching the other. It's a sight to behold, one we wouldn't get if we were kissing each other traditionally.

The warmth both deep inside me as well as just outside builds and builds and builds until I feel like I'm ablaze from head to toe. The tip of Crue's cock hits just the right spot on my cervix, lighting a very, very short fuse, triggering sparks to explode beneath his finger before waves of intense pleasure roll through me, not once but twice, one immediately after the other.

Forgetting we're technically in public, I unleash a moan so loud anyone walking by could hear.

Crue's hand in my hair tightens as his teeth sink into my jaw, keeping me locked in place while he weathers his own climax, releasing a groan practically identical to mine.

Both my forehead and nose mashed to the mirror, my rapid exhales fog it up. I'm so fucked if anyone comes in right now.

I'm so fucked anyway.

Finally, Crue's finger on my clit slows, not to a complete standstill, just a lazier pace, like maybe he doesn't even realize he's still doing it. The fact he hasn't pulled his dick out though makes me think it's intentional. It's not enough to make me come again, at least not yet, but it does keep a constant purr in the back of my throat.

Crue suddenly pulls his face away from mine, and still staring at each other, I see something dark enter his gaze.

"Fuck you, Ever Munreaux."

My body too fuzzy to react appropriately—with outrage and vitriol since he's saying this while he's *clearly* still inside me—I just drawl, "What'd I do now?"

The pressure on my sensitive peak disappears entirely before Crue brings his glossy middle finger up to his mouth, sucking my— our?—cum off. He groans again, and I swear I feel his buried cock twitch inside me.

"You ruined me."

He says it so matter-of-factly, I don't know if I should laugh or cry. Both urges overwhelm me simultaneously, and not just from the sensations still racking my body.

Instead of doing either, I make myself scoff, "You ruined me first."

Months ago, if we want to get technical.

CHAPTER 35

Ever

"YOU DON'T HAVE ANYTHING THE REST OF THE DAY, RIGHT?" Avoiding Crue's gaze in the mirror as I try to fix my makeup, I shake my head. Already dressed, all he had to do was wash his hands and he's set to stroll back out of the bathroom looking relatively the same as earlier. My appearance, unfortunately, takes a little more correction. Crue's teeth left an imprint on my jaw that no amount of makeup is covering up.

I finally shoot him a scowl, and he smirks.

"Do you know how many fucking hickeys you had on your neck when we met?" Before I can even open my mouth, he answers himself, saying, "Too many."

I roll my eyes. Like I could remember.

Like I want to.

"Hickeys can be covered up with a turtleneck. This…" I point at my jaw. "Can't."

"I'll keep that in mind next time."

A shiver races up my spine. Next time. One of these days—soon—there won't be a next time, but today, there is. And that makes me so…happy. I'm pretty sure the last time I was happy was at Hide and Keep.

Biting my bottom lip, I keep my growing smile to myself.

"So you're going with me then?"

"Where?"

"To get that tattoo."

"The butterfly?"

He nods.

Or course I'm going with him to watch my art get inked onto his body.

Not wanting him to see how excited that makes me, I blow out a long sigh and grab my chai latte before spinning around to face him, whining, "It's not like I can go anywhere else."

Crue broadcasts his smile openly. "You know I'm on to you now."

Oh. Shit.

"About what?" I ask with a steady voice despite the dizziness threatening to overtake me.

"When you're faking it."

The laugh that leaves my numb lips is as artificial as it gets, yet somehow Crue doesn't notice, proving him wrong. Thank Goddess.

"Would a scarf work?" he offers.

"For what?"

He points at my jaw.

I look my bodyguard over, asking skeptically, "Do you have one on you?"

"No, but you could use my shirt as one."

"And what? Let you walk around shirtless?"

"*Let* me? I'm—"

"Mine. More now than ever. Just because you turn into a marshmallow after sex doesn't mean I do. The only one that gets to ogle you is me."

Crue has the audacity to laugh.

"You're really fucking cute when you're possessive, you know that?"

"No," I answer honestly. It doesn't feel cute. It feels natural, like a knee-jerk reaction. Someone eye-fucks my bodyguard and I immediately want to cause harm to them in the worst possible way. Very simple. Very reasonable.

"Well, you are."

"I doubt Johanna Flemming shares that opinion."

The expression he pins me with is pure confusion. "Who?"

"My professor."

He shakes his head. "Nah. Doesn't ring a bell."

I catch the side of his lips curving upward as he turns for the door.

Good bodyguard. *Very* good bodyguard.

Holding the door open, he waves me through, saying, "After you, little bat."

Parked in front of the tattoo parlor, Crue doesn't rush out to get my door like he usually does. Instead, he's…checking all around us.

Curiosity getting the better of me, I do, too.

What is he looking for?

"Do me a favor," he says.

"What?"

"Lift up your skirt for me."

I return my attention to Crue, finding his already on me.

"Why?"

"Just do it."

Hem up to my chest, I lift my dress.

Arm draped along the dashboard, Crue leans over, his gaze locked on my thighs.

"Why aren't your panties soaked through?"

I release the fabric from my fingertips, cutting off his view and causing him to lift his eyes to mine instead.

"Why would they be?"

"I just filled you to the brim with my cum."

"I'm aware. I'm the one that had to put toilet paper in there to catch it."

His eyebrows nearly jump off his forehead. "In your pussy?"

"Ew, no. In my underwear."

"Is that what took you so long in the stall?"

The same stall I had to kick Crue out of when he tried following me in it.

"I wasn't gonna let it ruin my outfit."

"I wanted it to."

"Is that why you fucked me?" I sneer.

"No."

His face comes in close to mine. When he makes no move to cover my lips with his thumb, I inhale sharply. Luckily, he only presses a kiss to my chin, his top lip *just* below my bottom lip.

I don't dare release my breath.

"I fucked you because you begged me to." Another kiss, this one half a centimeter higher so our lips do graze. "And because I was dying to sink my cock into your sweet." Kiss. "Little." Kiss. "Cunt." Kiss.

Only after he sits back do I exhale.

"Little?"

"What? Isn't that a good thing? To be tight?"

"It's a normal thing. Vaginas aren't airplane hangars."

"I know that." He frowns, not so much like he's offended. More like he's confused.

"Do you? You didn't seem to know girls have to pee after sex."

"I...didn't. I'm not usually around..." He gestures vaguely. "After."

"What do you do, run out while you're still wearing a condom?"

His silence tells me everything...and nothing.

As uncomfortable as this next question's going to be, it's necessary. It's a little late considering the deed's already been done, but I'd rather find out now than not at all.

"You do use condoms, right?"

"Yes. Every time. Except today obviously. You?"

"Yeah. Same."

Neither of us willing to expand on our previous partners, we both find different spots in the car to focus on for a while.

Crue speaks first. "It was so much better without one."

I'm quick to agree. "Mm-hm." It was. But for me, the lack of protection was only one small part of what made it so great.

"I'm new to all of this."

"Sex?" I mock. Crue definitely wasn't a virgin.

"Females." He makes more random motions with his hands,

causing me to glance back over at him. "The only woman I've spent a lot of time around is my mom and she never told me about…you know…anything really. Not this kind of stuff. Not anything that'd help me help you." Those green eyes make their way over to my blue ones. "I'm trying to learn as fast as I can, but there's a lot."

I know he is. And he's probably never going to know everything. Sadly, I probably won't either. For all the ridicule females are constantly under, we're not studied medically as much as we could or should be. Knowledge is power after all and the more knowledge we have about ourselves and how to not only survive in the bodies we're in but also thrive, the more powerful we'd be.

What's the biggest threat to a patriarchal society? Empowered women.

"Do you mind explaining to me what was wrong with calling your cunt little?"

"It's not that it was *wrong*. I just have to question that descriptor coming from a man with seriously skewed depth perception. I mean, *four* inches is—"

Crue's laughter cuts me off before he exits my car. He's still smiling as he opens the passenger door, maybe even while he's putting my heels back on. I can't be sure as I'm too focused on watching his back muscles flex beneath his shirt. I do know he's not when he bites one of my thighs, promising to ruin my panties next time.

Next time.

Inside the tattoo parlor, the artist is still setting up his space, so Crue and I walk around, perusing the hundreds of sketches on the walls. All different styles. All different perspectives.

"You never told me why you're getting this tattoo," I say without taking my eyes off a snake wrapped around a sword.

"I've been wanting another one for a while."

"But why a butterfly?"

"Why not?"

We move to another wall.

"So there's no reason at all for that specific kind?"

"Does there need to be?"

My gaze plummets to the floor. No, there doesn't.

I hoped there was though. I hoped it was me, the girl in the cornstalks who left a big enough impression for him to want a reminder on his body for the rest of his life.

But that kiss—*our* kiss—from Crue's perspective could've meant something completely different than what it meant from mine.

It could've meant nothing to him. I could've meant nothing to him.

I probably did.

"Do you always have a reason for the stuff you draw?"

"Not always." I shake my head. "But usually."

The heat of Crue's stare blasts the side of my face and I brace myself for what I know is coming next.

"What's your reason for drawing me?"

Relocating my hands to behind my back, I twist my fingers together before saying, "I told you already."

"You told me bullshit. You don't spend *that* much time drawing someone you look down on."

"You do if you don't know anyone else worth capturing."

There's a pregnant pause where I replay my words no less than two hundred times. Capturing? I sound like a psychopath.

"On paper," I add in vain.

"What makes me worth drawing?"

I glance up at him.

"What doesn't?"

Even though I know it's coming, it still squeezes my heart to watch Crue tap one long finger to the scar under his eye.

I wait until my voice is clear to say, "You can place the same rose in front of a dozen artists and you'll get a dozen variations. The colors will be different, the size, everything. Some will include thorns. Some won't. Some will focus on every blemish because that's reality. Nothing's perfect. Some will only capture one or two because imperfections aren't nearly as ugly as we assume our own are. Someone in there won't even include a single flaw because all they see is a beautiful rose. The subject is the same, yet everybody's perspective on it is vastly different."

"You draw my scar. You see it."

"I do." I glance at the crescent scar before meeting the eyes above it. "But it's not all I see when I look at you." Because I do draw realistic, I do include it in my drawings, but that doesn't make Crue any less beautiful to me.

"What else do you see when you look at me?"

My answer is immediate yet honest. "A misplaced time traveler."

Crue frowns. "What makes you say that?"

"You don't belong where you are."

"Where do I belong?"

"I don't know. And I don't think you do either or you wouldn't be my bodyguard, stuck living the same day over and over again."

"What I was doing before being your *personal protection agent* was repeating the same day over and over. This gig's the most challenging I've ever had."

"Is that why you took it?"

"I took it because…" Now he's the one looking away. "Of the money. After three years, I should have a little over a million dollars stacked up."

A million dollars? He won't even make a tenth of that.

"What are you planning to do with it?"

"Promise not to laugh."

"Not if you say you're gonna spend it on a time machine."

He rolls his eyes before bringing them back to me. "No. Just regular travel. I want to go somewhere no one knows me."

I don't laugh, but I do tell him, "See? You don't belong here."

"Do you?"

"This is the birthplace of Munreaux Motorcycles. Of course I do."

"Do you *want* to be here though?"

Aside from the climate and the history, I don't know enough about Sea Haven to know if I like it, only that I don't like who I am here—who I have to be here.

"Anonymity isn't an option for me," I say instead.

"Especially not after you take over for your father."

I force my head to bob slowly.

"Why don't you want anyone to know who you are?"

"I just think it'd make it easier."

The tattoo artist beckons us over.

"Make what easier?" I ask on our walk to the back.

"Living."

My steps slow momentarily, causing me to have to hustle to catch up.

"What's hard about living here? For you?"

"The people. I can't go anywhere in Sea Haven without running into someone from high school. You saw what happens when I do."

The police officer. Sure, that was awkward, but not exactly flee-worthy.

As Crue listens to the artist's spiel about his process, I settle in next to the tattoo chair. This parlor isn't technically in Sea Haven. I assumed Crue drove this far out because he wanted the same artist that did his other tattoos, but there doesn't seem to be any familiarity between the two men whatsoever.

"So it's just the people from your high school you want to avoid?"

"Them…and anyone that recognizes my name and looks at me the same way you did when you found out."

"How did I look at you?"

He scoffs. "Like I was guilty."

"Well… I mean, you *were* drunk—"

"I wasn't though. I hadn't been drinking at all that night."

"Why did the news report that you were?"

"Because I said I was."

"Crue, why the hell would you lie about that?"

"I was covering for Yaz. She was the one drinking. She was the one…" He shakes his head. "Her dad was ex-military, a perfectionist, a real hard-ass. He had so many rules for her, the top one being not to date his wrestlers."

"She was your coach's daughter?"

Crue nods.

"And you were dating…"

"Looking back, I don't know if dating is the right word. We were—"

"I think I get it." I hold up a hand, stopping him before he can get too detailed.

"No, you don't. Nobody does because nobody ever asks. It's always just assumptions and accusations."

I could be saying those same words about my own life. I could be saying a lot of this about my own life.

I say to him what I wish someone would say to me. "So then tell me the truth."

"You don't want to know."

"Yes, I do."

He eyes the tattoo artist's bowed head. We wait until the tattoo gun turns on, then I scoot closer to Crue.

"Yasmin and I, we…considered ourselves together. I thought of her as my girlfriend, and she called me her boyfriend."

Each of those words hits me almost visibly, like I'm in one of those comic books with the onomatopoeia in the speech bubbles. *Wham! Bam! Pow!* But I fight not to show the pain. This is one of those rare instances where I actually did ask for it.

"We wanted to date but couldn't. Not really. Not like our friends could. We barely even talked outside of the few classes we had together."

"Because of her father?"

"Yeah. Wrestling was my life. I was on track to get a full ride to any college I chose. I didn't want to mess that up. She didn't want to defy him. She was…scared, I think."

I lose Crue for a few minutes while he mentally travels back in time.

He is a time traveler.

But is that why? So he can visit her?

"Crue?" I say, bringing him back to the present. To me.

"Anyway, yeah, we liked each other. We didn't even know each other, but we liked each other. You know?"

My eyes flutter closed on a half-nod. I fell for a man I never spoke a single word to.

"For homecoming, we both went with a big group of friends so her dad wouldn't suspect anything. And he didn't. It was perfect. We danced, we talked, we laughed, we got to hang out for once. It was the closest thing to a real date we'd ever gotten."

Pushing my raging jealousy aside, I try to picture a seventeen-year-old Crue being so carefree with his crush. I doubt it's something I'll ever get to witness myself. I don't think he knows how to be carefree anymore. I'm assuming because of what he's about to share.

"Things were going…well. So we decided to sneak away…just the two of us."

Just like that, the jealousy is back, trying to shove all rational thought out the window.

Crue studies me carefully.

I wave him on. Let's get this over with.

"The plan was to only be gone for a little while, twenty, thirty minutes at the most, before getting Yaz back to her friends so they could take her home. The second we got in my car though, she wanted to…" His eyebrows pick up what his voice just put down.

"Mm-hm." Got it. He's not a virgin. I knew that. I know that. We've both been with other people.

We'll both be with other people.

I don't exactly want to hear about either, but again, I asked for this.

"I never found out whose it was but someone in our group snuck alcohol into the dance and Yaz had been downing that instead of the water and punch I'd been drinking. I was trying to drive us somewhere private but she was fucking relentless. She was leaning over the center console, grabbing at my zipper, making it hard to even see the road. When we were hit by an actual drunk driver, my head was turned toward Yaz, trying to hold her off and…"

"Your scar."

"Yeah, from the airbag. That and the seat belt kept me in the car.

But Yaz wasn't even seated, let alone buckled, so she flew through the windshield. I was able to make it out to her before the cops got there and the only thing, the only fucking thing she cared about was her dad finding out about us."

"That's why you lied." He threw himself under the bus just like he did with me to Officer Ronny Veen.

He nods. "How else was I supposed to explain missing a fucking car headed directly at me?"

"Is that why you weren't charged with anything?"

"The cops knew I was sober. I blew a zero on the breathalyzer."

"How did it still end up on the news that you—"

"Because Yaz didn't want her dad to know the truth about why we were together. Me being drunk only explained why I was distracted, not why Yaz was in my car. She spun a story to her dad that made it sound like I tricked her into coming with me."

"She put it all on you?" As if I couldn't hate this girl any more. She put Crue in danger, then lied about it to save her reputation.

"Why didn't she just say she was sick and that you offered her a ride home? Other than you supposedly being under the influence, it wouldn't have been all that scandalous. You two knew each other through her father. It'd make sense for you to want to see your coach's pride and joy home safely."

"I couldn't tell you. Maybe because she was drunk. Maybe because she'd gone through a windshield. Either way, her brain obvious wasn't working at full capacity."

That doesn't excuse her painting Crue to be a predator though, especially when it sounds like it was nearly the opposite. I don't know if Crue sees it that way. He wanted Yasmin that night, but did he at that exact moment? If he told her no at any point, then she was the aggressor.

"You never got to ask her before…"

"No. Apparently, the worst of her injuries were internal, so… I never could've guessed that Yasmin being loaded into the back of that ambulance would be the last time I'd ever get to see her. Her dad was already there, by her side, so she… She ignored me. Wouldn't even look at me."

That's why it's such a big deal for him—me looking at him. Because she wouldn't. It also explains why he doesn't drink and why he's so adamant about consent. Wrongfully labeled as a drunk and a rapist, Crue goes out of his way to not be anything even close to either one.

"After that…" Crue's voice takes on a hard edge. "Her dad made it his mission to put all the blame on me. There was no evidence to back up Yaz's claims, not even that I'd been drinking. But I thought I was protecting her by staying quiet, by not refuting any of them. She didn't care to protect me back. Coach dropped me from the wrestling team while she was still alive and she didn't do anything to stop him. My life was over before hers was."

My stomach churns at the stark realization that my father and I are no better. At the end of this, I, too, will turn my back on Crue without a backward glance. I'll have to. And my father? My father could, and would, do even worse to Crue than some high school wrestling coach did.

"I'm really sorry," I whisper, unsure if he can even hear me over the buzz.

He shrugs the shoulder of the arm not being worked on, and when he speaks, his voice is softer, kinder. "If it turned out any other way, I doubt I'd be here with you now."

I almost choke in disbelief. Nothing about this predicament is a consolation prize, certainly not me. Or the money he's banking on but will never actually see.

I give Crue a halfhearted smile before looking down. The artist is on the bottom of the hindwings and abdomen, not too far into the design that should take hours to complete.

"Is there a restroom I can use?" I ask during one of the brief pauses.

The artist jerks his head toward the back of the shop. "Second door on the left."

"I'll come with."

Crue starts to lean forward, but I rush to tell him, "I don't need you to."

"I know," he shoots back, sounding slightly offended.

He notices the artist looking between us.

"I know. I just—"

"Is anybody else here?" I ask the artist.

"Nope. Just us. This is the last appointment of the day."

"See, Major? It's fine. I'll only take a minute."

The muscle in his jaw twitches. "Are you sure?"

"Yes." I smile brightly. Silly bodyguard, what's the worst that can happen? I fall in the toilet?

His eyebrows draw closer and closer as he lowers his voice for what's probably supposed to be only for me but the tattoo artist listening intently can clearly still hear. "You need anything?"

I don't know if he's referring to what we discussed in the car or if he's just asking in general, but since the only thing I could go for is a pantyliner, which I'm assuming Crue didn't magically acquire in the last hour, I shake my head, and tell him, "I'll be right back."

In the dimly lit hall, I breeze past both doors on the left, heading straight for the one with the EXIT sign above it. The cool air that greets me on the other side of it is a welcome relief.

Yasmin didn't care enough about Crue to help him but I do.

CHAPTER 36

MUSIC SO LOUD I CAN FEEL IT RATTLE MY BONES MASKS MY own heartbeat. It almost, *almost* drowns out that countdown, too…but not completely.

Ticktock. Ticktock.

The lips at my throat close, making me moan in approval.

That's what he's here for. To help me forget it. To help me forget… everything.

Unfortunately, it's harder than I thought it'd be. Much harder than it usually is. A few hours into this reprieve, I still can't get my brain to turn off.

Maybe because these lips pale in comparison to the ones I really want.

No. I'm not thinking about Crue. I'm done with that. Done with him.

Beads of sweat roll down my temples as I tilt my head back, resting it on the shoulder of the guy behind me and giving him better access. Like a pup nursing, he latches on vigorously, suckling the thin skin.

Our bodies sway together, his hard dick digging into my back as his hands roam my front.

I don't know him. He doesn't know me. Nobody here seems to. This is the closest I've come to feeling complete freedom since Hide and Keep.

I spread my arms out, then up, wishing I had my wings again, wishing I had wings, period. It's not enough to be airborne momentarily. I want to fly forever.

Across the club, I spot a black hat exactly like the one my—

I said I was done with him.

A scoff gets stuck in my elongated throat. Even I don't listen to myself.

But I will. Starting now.

I hereby emancipate Crue Brantley from my mind, my body, and my…

Heart.

It's not like he was in my heart *really*. I mean…

He was.

He is.

He shouldn't have been.

He was a stranger when I first tucked his memory in there. I didn't know anything about him. It was *stupid*. A *crush*, nothing more.

But he wasn't a stranger when I added to his chamber, stockpiling things like waking up to him holding my hand, watching him put my shoes on for me every time we exit a vehicle, seeing him flash me my bracelet from across the room, feeling him braid my hair, finding out he dyed my favorite drink so I can enjoy it.

Grabbing the hands on my stomach, I wrap them around me until the guy at my back is hugging me. That's what I really want—someone to hug me and tell me everything's going to be okay. I know it won't be, but that's what people in the movies always do and I've always wanted to experience it myself. It always looks so comforting.

Below heavy lids, I watch that familiar hat come closer.

That doesn't feel comforting.

I squeeze my eyes shut, telling myself it's not him. It can't be. Not only was he not wearing a hat when I left him but that was over three hours ago. If he followed me, which I stuck around to make sure he didn't, he would've found me already.

"That doesn't belong to you," I hear quite clearly despite being in a nightclub.

When I open my eyes, I find I was wrong again.

How many hats does he own and where is he storing them? I need to find his stash and burn it. I'm *sick* of seeing a hat on him.

The suction on my neck suddenly disappears, then the guy asks my bodyguard, "What doesn't?"

"Her. You have five seconds to remove every part of your fucking body from hers before I throw your ass in the Connecticut and let the tide take you out to sea."

"The Sound is an estuary," I correct Crue, unhelpfully if his expression is anything to go by.

He holds up his right hand, all five fingers spread wide, then starts counting out loud, "Five," before lowering his pinky first.

"I didn't think Ever Munreaux had a boyfriend," the guy I didn't give my name to murmurs near my ear, our bodies still moving, just at a slower pace. So much for anonymity.

"Four." Crue's ring finger bends.

Maybe he likes being watched. His cock certainly isn't shrinking away from the menacing figure before us.

"Three." Middle finger.

Without removing my gaze from Crue's, I say just as calmly, "I don't."

Crue lifts his eyebrows but lowers his index finger. "Two."

I don't. He's not my boyfriend. He could *never* be my boyfriend.

"One." His thumb now folded over the other fingers, Crue uses the fist to punch the guy plastered to my backside right in the face. Twice.

The high-pitched shout in my ear has me releasing the arms around me to duck in the opposite direction, but not before blood splatters the side of my face.

"Crue! Gross." I try wiping it off with a sweaty palm. Super gross. "This better not clog my pores."

Crue's in my face instantly, all patience gone, then he's dragging me by my elbow off the dance floor, obviously not concerned with skincare the way he should be.

As soon as we're clear of the crowd, I rip my arm out of his grip, almost taking a tumble to the floor. Something catches me though. I'm pretty sure it's this annoying bodyguard of mine.

"Don't you have a river to pollute?"

"I can't protect you if I'm in prison."

"You don't protect me."

"I just did."

"All you did was clam-jam me. Again."

"I've still got your pussy juice clinging to my balls and you're out here looking for your next fuck."

I raise a finger of my own between us. "Maybe if you peed after sex, too, you could've wiped that up."

He frowns and shakes his head. "It's hard for guys to piss right after."

Using his bare hands, he dabs at my face, removing the rest of the blood.

Is he still mad at me? It's hard to tell.

I lean into his touch before catching myself.

I should leave, run, as far as I can. But Crue's moss-green eyes have me rooted, my feet making themselves at home right here in the club.

"Because you're still hard?"

"Sometimes. Mostly it's because our shit's all clogged and pee sprays out everywhere." His hands demonstrate a fountain-sized spray range.

"I didn't know that. I'm new to…" Unable to recall the exact words used in our earlier conversation, I gesture at him and the other…guy… Where'd he go? There're too many people to see. I squint one eye, but no, that doesn't help either. Honestly, I don't think I could pick that guy out of a pair. He's…forgotten. Just like Crue was. Temporarily.

I *did* forget about him.

I'm almost positive I did.

"Males?" Crue scoffs. "No shit. You don't seem to have experience with anyone other than yourself."

I wave him away like a gnat but he doesn't take the hint. He never does.

It's him. He's the one refusing to let me forget him.

"Ugh!" I shove his chest, not even shifting him a single inch. "Why'd you have to look for me?" I didn't want him to…this time.

"Because it's what I do. I find you. I'll always fucking find you."

That's…sweet actually. I hate how much I like him.

"Okay but *how* did you find me?"

Turning his head to the side, he looks around us as he mutters, "Luck."

It must've been. I learned my lesson last time and now only use cash when I don't want to be rounded up like livestock.

"They serve minors here?" he asks.

"They served me."

"How much?"

Considering I'm still alive, not enough.

I put my hands at what I think is four inches apart. "About…" Then I pull them farther apart, hopefully to about eight inches. "Four inches' worth."

"You're an asshole."

"The feeling…is mutual." I do remember him saying those words.

A smile teases those full lips I love so much.

"Oh yeah? You think you're an asshole, too?"

I nod. Wholeheartedly I do.

"Why'd you even run away?"

"I didn't run. I strolled out the door."

"Why?"

"Asks the captor to his captive."

"I wasn't holding you hostage. I asked you if you wanted to go with me and you said—"

"I didn't have a choice!" I yell. "I never do!"

"What else don't you have a choice about?"

"You!" Now I'm the one scoffing. That face. How dare he be shocked by that. Has he met my father? "Do you really think this will end any differently than it did with Yasmin?"

"*What?* How are the two even remotely—"

"You think my father will let us be together?"

"I never considered asking him. It's not his call."

"Isn't it? Come on, Crue. You were literally hired to gatekeep my pussy."

"He's trying to protect your reputation."

I arch an eyebrow. "I'm sure that's exactly what Yasmin's father told himself, too."

That shock turns into something a little less clueless and a lot more sinister.

"So, what? You just want to stop what we're doing?"

"I guess," I lie. "We only fucked once."

"And it's all I've been able to think about since."

"Maybe try a crossword puzzle or something. It's not *that* serious."

He yanks the sleeve on his shirt up to reveal his new tattoo. "Serious enough to get you inked into my skin."

Under a transparent bandage, the ink is visible. The monarch butterfly wings are the ones I drew, but between them is the body of a bat I did not.

He knows.

I look up at him, the confession on my tongue. What comes out instead is an accusation. "You changed my design."

"If you would've stuck around, you could've changed it yourself." He gestures to his scar. "The butterfly is for the first person that treated me as something other than this." His finger moves to hover over the bat's body. "You're the second."

Does he know?

"So, the butterfly is…" I croak, my voice as raw as I feel. He was getting a tattoo for me while I was being an asshole.

"A mystery. I never got a name, number, not even a clear enough look at their face to be able to identify them again."

He's being careful not to disclose the butterfly's gender, probably so I won't get jealous.

He doesn't know.

"What if that person comes back into your life?"

"I belong to someone else now, don't I?"

"No." I force the word out with a headshake that feels more like a nod. "Because we're not together. We can't be. Just like you and Yasmin, our interactions are limited to a couple of rooms."

"I've already made you come in three." The three fingers he holds up are swollen and bloody. "I'm not that scared little teenager any-more. I don't have anything left to lose."

Yes, he does. He just doesn't know it yet.

"That doesn't change the fact that at the end of this, I will walk away…by his side, not yours."

"Do you want to be with me before that?"

I shake my head. "That doesn't matter."

"It does to me. What you want matters to me."

Tears prick my eyes, making my nose sting. Just because I've gone so long without love doesn't mean I didn't need it all along, didn't crave it with every fiber of my being.

Cacti are drought resistant, too, yet they still require water. They can survive without it, but they only thrive when they're consistently watered.

I don't know if Crue loves me but a lot of the things he does feel like what I imagine love to be, and like a cactus, I've been soaking it all up, conserving it for those future periods of drought.

Crue makes me want to grow. He makes me want to be a bet-ter human being, someone who considers others' needs, not just my own. That's why I ran away tonight.

"I'm just trying to protect you."

His eyes search mine. "From what?"

Me.

"Getting hurt."

He grasps my face and leans way down until our noses are only inches apart.

"If you're gonna ask me to stop anything, ask me to stop breath-ing because that's the only way I'll stop wanting you."

I've never related to a statement more.

"That'd hurt you more," I cry.

"You don't want to see me hurt because you care about me, too. Because you want to be with me."

More than anything.

Another confused shake of my head as I try to keep the truth in. "I can't."

"In private, in the rooms where it's just us, you can. You're a flyer. You always land on top, remember?"

"What about you? Where will you land?"

He shrugs. "No worse than where I started."

No better either.

But whether we're together or not, he still won't be getting that million dollars.

"Say you want this. Say you want me."

"You know I do," I practically whisper.

"What was that?"

"You know I do," I repeat slightly louder.

"I'm sorry?" He pretends like he can't hear me. "What do you want?"

Oh, whatever.

I turn to leave but Crue catches me with an arm around my waist, growling, "Get your ass back here."

He buries his face in my neck, smelling the skin there instead of kissing it. Somehow it turns me on even more than what that other guy was just doing.

"Tell me what I want to hear. What I *need* to hear. Speak it into existence, little bat."

Someone's been reading about manifestation.

I spin around to rip off that hat.

With a tilt of my head and a shrug of my shoulders, I admit, "You. I want you, Crue Brantley."

His hands on my face again, he pulls me up onto my tiptoes. The urgency in his touch matches the words pouring from his mouth. "If all I have with you is three years, promise not to spend another second of it out of my sight."

"I can't make that promise." Just like I can't give him three years. Three weeks is best-case scenario.

"Then promise you won't run away from me and into another man's arms."

That one I can make.

"I promise."

CHAPTER 37

Crue

I**T'S AFTER MIDNIGHT WHEN WE MAKE IT BACK TO THE MANOR.** Parking out on the street, I carry Ever on my back up the long driveway, listening to her tell me about the different species of bats roosting on the property. Her breath on my neck has my skin in a constant pebbled state and I'm counting down the seconds until I can return the favor.

"As long as they stay out of my room," I mutter.

"You must like bats at least a little bit, enough to get one tattooed on you."

"I like one bat. She's the exception."

Ever chuckles. "You like me, Major?"

"Sometimes," I answer honestly, making her laugh even harder.

I like her like this. Not the drunk part. The down-to-earth part. She doesn't give a fuck about her appearance right now. She's only on my back because I insisted on carrying her while she's barefoot. I could've put her shoes back on but…I didn't want to. After being separated from her for four hours while I got my tattoo finished, I want her as close to me as possible. Watching her dot on a screen can't compete with having my arms around her.

It's too bad she's not like this all the time. Her clones wouldn't know what to do if Ever started describing how bats use echolocation to hunt. It's probably why she's not like this around them. She does what everyone expects of her, no more, no less.

Although, she surprised the hell out of me back at the club. Ever Munreaux trying to protect me. Me. She still won't kiss me on the mouth but…

Why won't she kiss me? Is that for my protection, too?

Since I've been leaving my window unlocked this whole time for a quicker escape, we use that one to sneak back into the manor. As soon as we're both in my room, I grab Ever.

"You are sick, aren't you?"

"I may not get out much, but I do have some immunity."

"You won't kiss me. You said 'terminally' when I asked if you were sick before. You're scared how this is gonna end."

"I don't kiss anyone. I was joking. And I'm not scared. I have genuine reservations about starting a dead-end…" She waves a hand in a circle.

"Relationship." This situationship just got upgraded to a full-blown relationship. She can fight me on that. I'll be right fucking here. For three whole years.

That hand freezes in a stop motion but she doesn't dispute that label, only says, "Maybe I just don't like germs."

"You Frenched a public restroom mirror. That shit's gotta be dirtier than my mouth."

"I doubt that. The university's custodians are very diligent about keeping the campus spotless."

She's back to being a smartass.

"Stop fucking with me and be honest about why you won't kiss me."

Ever lifts her hand to my face. I lower myself automatically, shortening the distance for her. Her palm on my cheek, she says, "I'll kiss you…" And just when I think she's going to kiss me on the lips, she presses them to my chin in the same spot I kissed hers earlier before whispering, "Anywhere else."

She trails kisses down my Adam's apple, between my collarbones, then pushes me backward to sit on the windowsill.

Beneath raised eyebrows, I watch her get to her knees in front of me.

I thumb her bottom lip, rubbing the tip over the ridges of her teeth.

She bites my thumb, then sucks it, making my cock double in size…whatever size that may be. I should've never said four inches. I know it's not four inches when I'm hard. I can't even say it is when it's limp because it's never just one length. That motherfucker changes size all throughout the day. It'd be like measuring the temperature over a twenty-four-hour period. It's down, it's up, a storm rolls in and it goes into hiding. Who knows. Dicks are weird. Ever's pussy handles mine just fine, which is all that matters.

If this goes the way I think it is, we're about to find out if her mouth does, too.

"You can't distract me forever, little bat."

"I know." She starts undoing my pants, my cock already straining to get out. "We don't have forever."

No, we don't. Technically, no one does. It's up to each individual what they do with the limited time they have. This is the first choice I've made in years that feels right.

I tried hating Ever. I really fucking tried. It almost stuck…until she wasn't around to hate, then it turned into something else, something just as strong and overwhelming. I don't want to waste another minute denying what I feel for her, not even to myself. We only have three years together. I want to make every second count.

My cock free, Ever grips me just above my balls, making a groan tear from my throat. Jesus, this isn't gonna last long. I'm not gonna last long. Not with Ever smirking up at me like the beautiful little creep she is.

One look from this girl is all it took for me to be addicted.

"This is my first time."

"First time…"

"Giving head."

It is? I would've thought she was a pro by now. I mean, I'm glad she's not. My cock's gonna be the first one to be on her tongue.

Somehow that has my cock swelling even more.

"Kiss my cock until it spits at you."

"Okay… But I have to warn you, I spit back."

A chuckle rumbles around my chest. I bet she fucking does.

Her tongue flat against her chin, she licks up my cock before swirling it around my dick head.

"Look at me."

Ever obeys, keeping her eyes on mine as she swipes her tongue over the precum on my tip. She kisses the small hole that's soon to be a fucking geyser, coating her lips with the sticky fluid. She's never looked more ruined. Or beautiful. Goddamn.

I tangle my hands in her midnight hair to slowly guide her down my shaft, and oh, fuck, it fits. It fits *enough*. Her small fist has to work the portion her mouth doesn't reach, but the dual stimulation feels fucking amazing. She bobs up and down on my cock, slurping and stroking at the same time. It's not long until I feel tension gather in my balls.

"Just…like…that."

I groan and she moans and yep, I'm done. Honestly, I lasted longer than I thought I would.

"I'm gonna come," I warn her but she doesn't pop off like a first timer. She sucks every drop from me, draining my balls, then releases my cock to look up at me, her chin raised. Before she can even try spitting that shit at me, I cover her mouth with one hand and work my load down her throat with the other.

"Asshole," she says once I release her to tuck myself back in my pants.

"You want to give me a cum facial, you'll have to sit on my face again." She didn't do it properly last time. Or I didn't. I'm still a little lost about what happened that first time.

I'm still fucking embarrassed about what happened that first time. Damn it, I couldn't get her there.

"Did I do okay?"

"Better than okay."

Ever bites her bottom lip to hide her smile. I can't believe that was her first time sucking cock. She talked a big game the day we met. She called me a cum fountain.

At least now I know she's never been one.

"Let's get you cleaned up."

"There's no mess." Finally letting that smile loose, she motions at her face with a flourish, like someone on a game show presenting the grand prize.

It makes my lips mimic hers.

"No, but you still have another man on you."

I catch her little sigh as she gets up from the floor.

"I do not."

Apparently, I'm not making myself clear.

Leaning forward, I throw her over my shoulder, then stand, heading for my bathroom.

"We're gonna get a shower and I'm going to wash him off you."

"Can't I just change? He only touched my clothes."

I wish that were true but his mouth all over her fucking neck like a leech is seared into my brain. Since I can't unsee it, I'll have to settle for scrubbing his saliva off Ever's skin.

"No."

After I turn on the water, I set her down and spin her around to unzip the back of her dress, sliding the thick material down. Next, I pull her long-sleeve shirt over her head. She's only in her bra and panties for a minute thanks to my quick work, then bare before me, and I just can't help myself. I look. I look at every. Naked. Inch. I'd take three minutes with Ever Munreaux but my underserving ass somehow gets her for three years.

Ignoring the invisible timer above our heads, I kiss one shoulder, closing my eyes as I savor the moment.

Mine.

"I thought you were getting in, too?"

"I am," I tell her with a gruff tone.

She attempts to undress me but is way too short to even get my shirt past my chin, so holding back laughter, I help her out, pulling it off and adding it to the growing pile on the floor. I do my socks and shoes myself but let her take my pants down before kicking them the rest of the way off.

I carefully remove the bandage from my forearm. Thankfully, she's been wearing her purple bracelet ever since I gave it back to her. If not, I would've had to go after her right away. Being able to track her every move allowed me to sit back and finish the tat. It worked out because even though I'd been considering getting the bat, I wouldn't have had the courage to with her watching.

Ever's gaze sweeps down my front, her thoughts a complete mystery.

"What?" I ask when the suspense becomes unbearable.

"It's just… You…"

What about me? Does she like what she sees? Does she not?

Her azure eyes pierce mine. "I've been to the Met, the Louvre, the Tate, the Vatican."

I nod slowly like I know what those are. I've heard of one hosting a fashion show and one sounds kind of like a church…maybe. But the other two? Not a damn clue.

"I've seen a lot of art from all over the world. Rare pieces. Historic masterpieces. Entire collections too valuable to be viewed by the public. I've also made a lot of art. None of it, not one single piece, compares to…" She waves a hand down my body. "You."

Hearing shit like that might make me do something stupid, like fall in love with my protectee.

I grab her face between my palms and consider doing it—kissing her. So what if she does have something contagious? I'd risk it. I'd risk everything for her.

I already am. I was all talk earlier. I know there will be consequences if Arthur finds out about us, but fear alone isn't strong enough to stop a moving train and apparently neither am I because I can't stop this need to protect Ever, to be around Ever. I want her safe. I want her happy. But most of all, I want her to be both *with me.*

The only reason I don't say "fuck it" and seal my lips to hers is because she hasn't given me permission to.

"Are you still drunk?"

She tries shaking her head. "I think I'm high though."

I inspect her pupils. They appear normal.

"What did you take?"

"Nothing. I told you before I don't do drugs."

"Did he slip you something?" That motherfucker. I should've thrown him in the river.

Ever's eyes fall to my lips.

Kiss me, Ever. Kiss me until the world goes dark.

She doesn't. Instead, she whispers, "You drugged me."

"I didn't—"

"You're doing it right now."

Backing up into the shower before I tell Ever what she's doing to me, I pull her in with me, the warm spray hitting us both at the same time.

My forehead grazing hers, I glance down between us, my breath heavy from the exertion it takes to hold back.

Billows of steam rise from below as rivulets of water stream down our bodies.

"I don't know how to do this," I admit quietly. It's one thing to picture yourself in the shower with someone else—dozens of times— but it's a whole different thing to be in here, looking at body parts you've never washed before. Tits seem easy enough. But her pussy… How the fuck do I clean that?

"This was your idea."

"I know." I pull my attention off those parts. "But I'm learning, remember? I just need your help until I get the hang of it."

"How many showers are you planning on taking with me?"

"All of them."

She laughs and turns her head out of my grasp to grab the soap.

I snatch the bar from her hold to clean my knuckles.

"This isn't like your soap."

When I was in her bathroom, I checked out the products she uses. Too expensive for me to ever afford, I opened them to see what the big deal was. The scent is the big deal. Ever's body wash smells exactly like honeycomb, to the point I almost fucking licked it.

"Okay."

"And my shampoo isn't as nice as yours."

"Okay."

"You're not gonna smell like you."

"Will I smell like you?"

"What do I smell like?"

"The ocean."

I do? I never knew that. No one's ever said anything. It's probably from the proximity of my parents' house to the beach.

"And cedar."

That'd be my soap.

"Then yeah, you're probably gonna smell like me."

Her lips stretching wide make mine do the same. Miss prim and proper isn't repulsed by the idea of smelling like me—the help?

"Tell me where to start."

"Well, what do you want to wash?"

"Everything."

"It's just like washing yourself. Start at my neck and work your way down."

"Not your face?"

"Where's your face wash?"

"I don't have any."

Her eyes narrow. "What do you wash your face with?"

"This." I hold up the bar.

"Of course you do."

"You want me to go get your stuff?" I don't want to leave this shower right now…but I will if she asks.

Thankfully, she shakes her head. "It's fine."

She leans back, soaking her hair and face, making her mascara run down her cheeks. Those sea-glass eyes peek up at me hesitantly before she wipes under them. She washes her hair while I watch, noticing it's similar to how Chloe worked with her hair—roots to ends. All I have are roots basically, so this is new. This is…

I want to be doing this. I don't like having her this close, this vulnerable, and not be touching her the entire time.

Using one hand, I cup the back of her head to help her rinse. She instantly relaxes into my hold, trusting me in a way no one ever has.

Once the shampoo's out, I awkwardly lather up the other hand, then replace the bar on the built-in shelf to carefully spread the bubbles over Ever's face using my fingertips.

Hopefully the water is dowsing the sweat I feel accumulating all over my body. I do want to shower with Ever from now on. Not only shower with her but wash her, too. I like taking care of her. All of her. If I fuck up on my first time, she might not let me try again.

It's not like I can watch a tutorial on this kind of thing.

I wouldn't anyway. I want to know how to take care of my woman, not other women.

I guide her head back under the spray, quickly rinsing her face, then retrieve the soap to start on the rest of her. More area to cover, I keep the bar in my palm as I do small circular motions over her throat and chest, making sure to pay *extra* special attention to those small perky tits. Her chest begins rising rapidly under my touch, testing my restraint to its limits.

My own breathing jagged, I move down to her stomach, then hips.

I'm just above her clit when she rasps, "Drop the soap and just use your fingers."

Never have I listened quicker. The soap hits the shower floor the next instant, causing a series of thuds.

I go right for her pussy like I usually would but her own hand joins, her fingers between mine.

"Let me show you."

She guides my slightly soapy hand down her pussy, gently pushing my ring finger and index finger to slide along the outside of her folds, my middle finger gliding over her clit.

I groan from the feeling. She's so slick and so wet. I'm already getting hard again.

"*Don't*," Ever warns when I hover there. "The soap will sting."

I learned that much while reading about douches. All those damn sensitive levels.

"I wasn't gonna." But I was thinking about it.

I collect the soap, staying bent over to wash Ever's toned legs, then I stand and have her spin to do her back, too.

As I reach her ass crack though, she turns and says, "I can do the rest."

I wondered if she was gonna give me any trouble here. As disappointed as I am that she is—have I not proven how fucking devoted I am to her?—it also shows she's never let anyone else do this before.

I'm her first for something else.

"Turn around," is all I say.

"Crue…"

"I ate that ass, Ever. I can fucking wash it. Turn around."

I wait for her to give me her backside again, taking a moment to admire those plump globes on display.

"What are you doing?" she asks over her shoulder, water running off her lips.

God, I want to kiss them right now.

"You're a fan of masterpieces, aren't you? Let me admire this one."

Her lips spread before she faces forward.

After I've had my fill, I clean her ass like I do mine. She squirms at first but eventually stills, allowing me to move on to the backs of her legs and feet.

She better get used to it. Now that I know how to wash all of her, there's no fucking way I'm not doing it every chance I get.

Once she's rinsed and the water running off her is clear, I tell her, "Put your hands on the wall."

"You got everything."

I *washed* everything.

"Put your fucking hands…on the wall."

As I wash myself, I watch her prop her hands on the wall above her head one at a time.

I shelve the soap and say next to her ear, "Spread your legs."

She obeys with a moan.

She's clean, she's compliant, and she's all mine.

All rinsed, I start marking her. I kiss everywhere on Ever's body, from her shoulder blades down to her calves, even that ass she was just acting stingy about. Each time I pull away from one kiss, I say, "Mine," before immediately going into the next, so she knows who all this belongs to now. A lot of people have done things to this body— kissed it, fucked it, thrown it, abused it. Nobody's taken care of it.

Until me.

If taking care of Ever Munreaux's the last thing I do, I'll die happier than I've lived.

Ever's pedaling her feet out, like she can't stay still anymore, the move making her ass cheeks bounce.

"Turn around," I rasp.

She does so fast she's a whirl of motion, then she's trying to grip my neck, but I'm quick to catch her wrists, pinning them above her head as I back her up into the wall.

"Keep them there."

"Crue," she whines, a fucking mess. A beautiful fucking mess.

My beautiful fucking mess.

"Keep them there until I say."

I step back to do some more admiring.

"Farther," I tell her with a nudge to one of her feet.

Ever spreads her feet apart until she looks like a sexy-ass capital A.

Chest heaving, she whimpers, almost undoing me. Almost… because I'm only halfway finished marking her tight little body and nothing's gonna derail me.

Some of my kisses are short. Others linger. Some of them have tongue. Others have teeth.

When I reach her pussy, I sink to my knees to spread her lips, spearing my tongue inside and kissing there, too. *Mine. Mine. All fucking mine.*

I eat her out until she comes, her hands clutching my head, her nails digging into my scalp.

"You didn't listen," I say when I'm done.

Out of breath, she gasps, "Do I ever?"

"If you want me to keep tongue-fucking you like that, you better start."

All she does is smirk. She knows I still would. I'm a glutton for Ever. No amount of her is enough.

After turning off the water, I dry her off first, then myself before carrying her into my bedroom.

"Can I borrow some clothes?"

I swear she's just trying to rile me up now.

"Not right now."

"When?"

"In the morning. After we get up."

"What if I don't want to sleep in here?" Her grin says she more than wants to but I'll play along.

"Who said anything about sleeping?"

I toss her into the middle of the bed, making her giggle. With a shake of my head, I climb on after her, pinning her body down with mine.

"I ruined you," she states simply.

"Yeah."

"I inspired your tattoo."

I settle myself on top of her, rubbing my dick side to side along her wet center. "Yeah."

"You belong to me." Her legs wrap around me, her ankles inter-locking behind my back.

"Yeah," I say with the same certainty as the first two times.

"Make me belong to you."

"I thought I just did." I half-laugh, but she doesn't. She just stares up at me for a long time before slowly shaking her own head.

"What'd you have in mind, little bat?"

"Make love to me."

I've never made love to anyone. At least not intentionally. I don't even think I understand what making love is. Just slow sex? I can do that.

I have to admit though, slow sex is pretty tame compared to what I assumed she'd say.

"That's it? No blood exchange?" I ask her, just to be sure.

Biting her bottom lip to keep a laugh in, Ever lifts her hips, teasing my tip.

Slow. *Slow.* She wants slow. I have to go slow.

It's hard once I sink into that pussy though. All I want to do is jackhammer into her so hard I leave an imprint of my dick head on her cervix.

"As you wish," I tell her like I'm her personal genie, not her personal protection agent.

I slide into her until I'm fully buried, then drop my forehead to hers.

"Ahhh," she says more than sighs.

"Fuck. Your pussy feels so good hugging my cock. You take me so *fucking* well. You…" What am I supposed to say here? Lovey shit? I'm not good with lovey shit?

I guess I could go with the truth.

As I begin rocking in and out of her, I say, "I think about this all the time. I think about you all the time."

"What do you think about?"

"Touching you. Kissing you. Fucking you. Sharing a bed with you."

The smallest change happens. Ever's body kinda locks up, enough for me to notice. It's only momentary, then she's back to normal.

I lift my head to check her expression. She's dopey, but according to her that's the effect I have on her.

I still don't see how that's possible. Ever's the most beautiful woman I've laid eyes on. She's richer than anyone I've met. And in a few years, she'll be more powerful than I can fathom.

Meanwhile I'm just me—a scarred-up, broke-ass nobody. In three years, I'll still be a scarred-up nobody, just a lot less broke.

But I won't have Ever anymore.

My speed picks up slightly. I can't help it. Because we do have an end date, there will always be an urgency between us.

"I want you in here, with me, every night. I want to fall asleep looking at you and know that when I open my eyes, you're the first thing I'll see. You're my favorite thing to look at. You're fucking gorgeous. You're perfect. And I'm—"

Shit. What was that? What was I about to say?

"About to blow," I lie because I don't know how else to finish that sentence without making an already complex situation more complicated. "We need to change positions."

I roll us so she's on top, keeping her legs stretched out alongside mine instead of bent. I don't let her sit up either.

"Grind on me."

"It's kind of hard like this—"

Each hand on an ass cheek, I get my fingers all up in her crack before pulling those cheeks both apart and down, making her gasp.

"Goddess, Crue."

Simultaneously pulling her down onto my cock, I circle my hips, thrusting up at the top of each rotation. My cock's gonna be waterlogged after this 'cause that motherfucker's not getting any air like this.

Sweat's already gathering between our stomachs, making all kinds of strange sounds that must have Ever feeling self-conscious because she freezes again.

I keep moving from below, assuring her, "I don't care. Make me so messy—"

"You need another shower?" she jokes.

"Make me so messy I'm as covered in you as you are of me."

My possessive little bat's eyes flare. Fuck, her domination over me is something to revere. I can't explain it. She just…owns me.

"As you wish," she says, sounding more like a genie than I did. Instead of having her for three wishes, I only have her for three years though. As comforting as that should be, it's not. Wishes can be finagled. Time can't.

Her elbows by my head, Ever grasps the top of my head with one hand, then makes her own circular motions with her hips, throwing her pussy and my cock into a risky dance with each other.

Now I'm about to blow.

"Ever," I half-groan, half-warn. I've *never* felt anything this amazing.

Her movements make her lips brush my nose, her chin nudging mine. Each time it happens I kiss that chin, until eventually I'm straight making out with it. I kiss it while replaying the way she kissed that mirror, pretending it's my mouth just like I did then.

Ever's moans pick up speed and volume. This isn't as slow as she probably wanted, but I'm trying.

I want her. I need her.

So I tell her. "I want you. I need you."

"I want *you*. I need *you*," she echoes back, spurring me on.

Biting her chin to keep her in place, I put my feet flat on the mattress, then thrust up as hard as I can. Even completely bottomed out inside her pussy, it's not enough. It'll never be fucking enough. I want to put more of me in her. I want all of me in her. I want to fill every part of her with me.

I prod her asshole with a slippery finger, begging she trusts me enough to let me right in.

Finding the muscles around it lax, I push past the tight barrier. Fuck. Yes.

"I'm... I'm gonna... Imma..."

She throws her head back, forcing me to release her chin. I lick the column of her throat, tasting salt all along it.

"That's my good girl. Come for me. Come on—" My voice gives out as I surge into her, savagely rubbing my base against her cunt.

I continue finger-fucking her ass as she bucks on top of me, flames licking at my own taint. I'm going to *explode*.

"Ever?" I grit.

She doesn't respond more than a hum in her throat.

"You better fucking come soon and hard, all over my cock."

"I'm try... I'm about..."

"Tell me what I gotta do."

We're not doing a repeat of that faking-it shit. I will do whatever I have to to make her come.

"Look at me."

She rolls her head forward to gaze down at me, her eyes fucking dazed. Goddamn, I do get her high.

Cum gushes out of my cock, but I don't react and let her know it. She'll stop and that's not happening until she comes, too. My erection begins to soften but she doesn't need that to get off. She needs… something.

"Tell me what I gotta do."

"I need you here with me."

"I'm here. There's nowhere else I'd rather be."

"Always?"

I hold back for a second before nodding. "Yeah. Always." Whatever she needs to hear. Whatever she needs to believe.

She leans down, opening up her asshole to me even more and allowing me to get my second knuckle in.

"This is mine. That's mine. You're mine," I chant to her as I work different spots of her body all at once. "You're mine. You're. Mine."

Her pussy squeezes my semi as she convulses, making me wish I had the power to decide when to come. I'd come with her in this moment, then again in a few minutes after getting another orgasm out of her.

It's pretty fucking special to get to witness her climax though, knowing my cock—even at only half-mast—my finger, and my words make her feel *that* good, enough to soak us both.

I let her ride out the spasms, then the aftershocks, before lowering myself to the mattress. Almost instantly, she collapses on top of me, our heartbeats identically erratic. There's so much moisture between us, it feels like we're back in the shower.

I wanted a mess. I got a fucking mess.

And I couldn't be happier about it.

I kiss the top of her head.

"You're mine, Ever Munreaux."

So soft I wouldn't hear it if it wasn't dead silent in here, she whispers, "I know."

CHAPTER 38

Surveying Lit U's quad, I inhale some much-needed fresh air after a long weekend full of sex, drugs, and rock and roll.

Technically, there was no rock and roll. What even *is* rock and roll? Anyway, the sex was *with* a drug, the only one I've ever allowed into my system. Except he hasn't just affected my nervous system. He's impacted most of my body's eleven systems—reproductive, respiratory, cardiovascular, probably even my immune system considering how much fluid we've been exchanging.

Goddess, Crue Brantley is addictive. We spent more time wet this weekend than we did dry. I wouldn't be surprised if his tattoo doesn't heal properly. He probably should've gotten it done after…

After…

After.

It's that word and those kinds of thoughts that keep this little bubble of ours from being impenetrable.

My eyes automatically lift to the university's focal point, the giant hands on the clock *tick, tick, ticking* high above our heads.

That choking sensation returns.

I squeeze my throat, willing it away. Please. Not while Crue is beside me.

Crue is beside me…providing immeasurable comfort in our small, precarious bubble. In it, I can breathe.

I can breathe.

I. Can. Breathe.

Feeling my airway opening up, I slowly lower my hand.

I can't afford to think about what happens after. Instead, I need to focus on the here and now.

Right here, right now, I have to go to class.

Walk.

My feet begin the trek across the quad.

Like the carbon copies they are, the clones all look over at me at the same time, expectant. Desperate.

It's not me they're desperate for. It's my name. My connections. My status. My "aesthetic." They wouldn't know what to wear if it weren't for me. They wouldn't know how to *be* without me.

I deliberate for all of ten seconds before coming to the conclusion I wish I'd realized sooner—I don't have to be around them. Nobody's here to make me.

I have to attend my classes, that's it.

So I walk right past my clones, acting as if they don't even exist, *wishing* they didn't.

Don't they wish they could be themselves? Or are they as trapped in their own false reality as I am?

Paris scoffs while Bradford calls out, "Munreaux, we're over here!"

I know. I'm not blind. I'm exhausted. Not from my weekend with Crue. But of *them*. Of who I am *with* them.

I much prefer who I am with Crue, who I get to be, who he lets me be.

I peek at him over my shoulder.

Staring stoically ahead, he pretends like he doesn't notice.

He waits until I face forward again to murmur, "Change of routine this morning, miss?"

My body no longer needing directions, I huff and pick up the pace.

What's the worst that can happen?

The clones will complain to their parents.

Their parents will mention it to my father.

My father will punish me.

That's not new. He's already furious with me. Has been since that dinner with the Larsons. The only reason he hasn't followed through on the threat in his gaze every time he pins me with it is because he hasn't had the opportunity to. Crue's been glued to my side around the clock, even during dinners. He used to sit on the opposite side of the table from me, but lately he's insisted on sitting right next to me.

The thing about Arthur Munreaux though, numbers are his sole focus. As soon as my bodyguard's out of the picture, my father will collect his pound of flesh—and not just figuratively—for all the transgressions I know he's keeping count of.

Honestly, a couple pinches on top of the dozens already coming my way are worth missing the clones' inane chatter for a day. They go to the same school I do, one of the best in the country, and yet the only subjects they're ever interested in discussing are the superfluous goings-on of the elite.

Oh, and our outfits.

I wonder what they'd think if they saw what I was wearing all weekend? The fact that Crue's sweats were about seven sizes too big for me didn't stop me from wearing them between our numerous sex sessions. They were raggedy and faded, but they were soft and smelled like Crue and felt like having an extension of him on me. If I can pull it off, I fully intend on stealing a set just to keep after—

There I go again. Worrying ahead instead of enjoying the present. What good has that ever done anyone?

The present is all I have, all I might ever have.

Passing my first class of the day, I head for a room about four... or five...doors down. *Was it six?*

I walk past door after door, craning my neck to scan inside without breaking pace. I know one of these is empty. I just don't remember which one...

"What are you doing? Your class is back there."

Ah. Finally, one with the lights out.

"I have to grab something first."

"What?" Crue asks as he follows me into the empty lecture room.

Spinning around, I close the door and fist his shirt, shoving him into the wall beside it.

His lips spread into a grin as he takes hold of my hips, bringing me closer.

"Call me miss again and I'll put a yellow jacket nest in your room."

"Will you be in there, too?"

What? "In your room?"

He nods.

"Probably not, no. There will be thousands of pissed off yellow jackets…because I put a nest in it…*if* you call me miss again."

"Then I'm not in there either."

He's missing the point of the whole… Ugh.

"It's your room. You have to go in it," I find myself arguing.

"Not unless you go with me, in which case, I have nothing to worry about since bats eat bugs."

"I'm not a real bat."

My bodyguard shrugs like he's not completely convinced.

"Did you know too many stings from yellow jackets could cause anaphylaxis?"

"Did *you* know…" Crue leans down until our foreheads are almost touching. "…that whenever you speak, I like to picture your lips wrapped around my cock instead?"

"Whenever you speak, I like to picture these wrapped around your cock." I bare my teeth at him, making him shudder.

"Jesus Christ. You fucking creep."

That earns a bigger reaction than the threat of death by wasps?

I try to back up but he tightens his grip, keeping me in place.

"Why'd you ditch your friends?"

"They're not my friends."

"Why'd you ditch them?"

"I just…think it'd be too hard."

His eyebrows cave in. "What would?"

"Imagining having sex with my bodyguard the whole time they talked."

Those brows do not smooth back out one bit. I'm pretty sure they dip even lower.

"Is that what you usually do when you're with them?"

Now I'm the one shrugging. "Sometimes." All the time. Almost every time. The clones are so dull and my imagination is so not.

"Why would it be difficult to do that now?"

"Before I couldn't do anything about it. Now I can."

One corner of his lips rises. "Are you sore?"

I hold back a laugh. Of course I'm sore. We've had sex so many times in the past two days, I lost count.

"No," I lie because no amount of pain would keep me from letting Crue have his way with me. He could fuck me into oblivion.

In fact, I hope he does. That outcome's much more preferrable to what awaits me.

Don't think about it.

"What do you imagine?" Crue asks.

"Right now, getting to class on time."

"You have twelve minutes. Tell me what you imagine. Better yet…" Releasing my hips, he holds his hands up by his shoulders. "Show me."

I lower my gaze to the bulge in his pants and bite my bottom lip. I also reach over to blindly lock the door. Thankfully, there's no window on this one.

"Go over to the desk."

"Which one?"

Even though I feel like I shouldn't have to, I point at the professor's desk. Who hasn't fantasized about getting freaky on the teacher's desk?

Once he's next to it, I undo his belt, then pants, pulling them as well as his boxer briefs down until his massive cock is freed.

"Lie down."

"On the…" He looks pointedly at the vintage oak desk.

Praying it holds both our weight, I nod.

As he gets settled on top, he encourages, "Do whatever the fuck you want to me. Show me what fills that beautiful, twisted head of yours."

I lift his shirt up to his chest, putting his abs on display, then stroke his cock a couple times, making his hips buck off the desk.

"Fuck, Ever. That feels amazing."

My hand freezes at his base.

"Better than my pussy?"

He guides my hand with his up the shaft to his tip, smearing his precum over my palm. "Nothing's better than your pussy."

Keeping eye contact with him, I lick my palm.

"Straighten out one leg but keep the other bent."

While he's pushing his pants down farther to do that, I shimmy my panties down my thighs, calves, and ankles, then bring them up to my hand with a heel.

I don't bother saying this next command aloud, since I know he'll question it anyway. So I just stick my panties in Crue's mouth—wetness out of course.

"You're welcome," I say before he can even thank me, not that he can with a mouth full of underwear.

His eyes widen but I see his cheeks move as his tongue works the crotch part over, licking them clean, I'm sure.

Lifting my tweed miniskirt, I climb on the desk and swing a leg over to straddle Crue's waist…facing his feet, with my bare ass on display for him.

Crue's deep groan is so loud I have to check if he spit my panties out.

He didn't.

Hypnotized, he kneads my ass cheeks, spreading them with rough caresses.

A wave of emptiness overtakes me, and with my pussy begging to be filled, I arch into his palms, wanting any part of him in any part of me already.

One hand on that bent knee for stability, I use the other to hold his cock in place as I sink down, impaling myself on the rigid shaft.

We both let out guttural moans as I reach the bottom, my ass settled on his lower stomach. It feels like the first time…every time. I love Crue's cock. I could take it and take it and take it, never, ever growing tired of it.

Voices on the other side of the door sound so close yet feel so far as the world outside of us blurs.

I immediately begin rolling my hips, grinding my clit against his upper thigh and making the desk creak.

It's not quite the glide I was hoping for, so pushing his knee out a couple inches, I look down and spit. The puddle lands right above the space where his groin meets his thigh, then I mash his leg against my clit again, spreading the moisture around. The spit won't last long but neither will I, not like this.

My body shudders over Crue's from the increased sensation. It's crazy how the smallest bit of lube can make such a big difference. I think that was part of the problem the first time Crue tried eating me out. With his tongue out of his mouth like that, it was probably drying out. Friction is great. Lubricated friction is superior.

Five fingertips dig into my ass as Crue also grabs a handful of my hair, yanking my head back until my chin's high in the air, my breath flowing from my mouth in one long gust.

Goddess.

He mumbles something that sounds like his own command. Ride me, maybe. Or fuck me. Something short, sweet, and totally unnecessary.

My hips resume the previous motion, and I make sure to stick my ass out with each rotation before clenching my cheeks together to help grip Crue's cock with my pussy walls.

We get a nice rhythm going, and just as I predicted, an orgasm tears through me not long after, hardly any notice whatsoever before I'm stalling out on top of Crue, all my muscles locking up as pleasure electrifies every single nerve ending I have.

With a growl, Crue thrusts up once, his body stiff as a board under me, his cock like a fountain inside of me.

Crue goes lax shortly after.

"Jesus fucking Christ, that was sexy," I hear behind me and smile. I think I smile. My lips are numb, so it's kinda hard to tell.

He releases my hair, and when I glance back at him, my underwear's no longer in his mouth, but in his fist.

"I'm keeping these."

I face forward again to hide an eye roll. Like I was going to put them back on anyway. They're drenched.

I need Crue's assistance to dismount without hurting either of us. A glob of cum falls out of my pussy during the transition and lands on the desk. We both stare at it, neither of us rushing to clean up the mess.

"It's yours," I tell him.

"Not all of it."

"Your cum leaks. Mine clings. Check your balls."

He actually glances down like he hasn't already been made well aware of that fact.

While he's distracted, I grab the sleeve of his jacket to use, but he yanks his arm away and gives me a lip snarl I just shrug at.

"Well, I'm not wearing as many clothes as you, even less now that you've stolen my underwear."

Back on his feet, he lifts a small trash can up to the desk and aggressively swipes the cum into it before rubbing his palm along the inside of his jacket.

"What are you gonna do for panties?"

"Go without." It's not ideal considering I'll be leaking his cum for a while, further proving that mess was definitely his.

"You're in a skirt."

"So?" I ask while fluffing my hair in the back.

Coming up behind me, he bats my hands away to fix it himself. After practicing all weekend—on me, not the mannequin—he's improved greatly. He still can't get it into a braid but that hasn't stopped him from trying, or me letting him because I love his hands in my hair.

"Some motherfucker could see your pussy."

"They could." I smirk at the growl he unleashes. "But they won't. I have a lot of experience maneuvering in a skirt."

"You flashed me," he argues.

"That was intentional. You were flirting with my professor right in front of my face, remember?"

"The only thing I remember is the overwhelming urge to bend you over your desk and fuck your cunt in front of Littoral University's entire student body."

My smile grows. I guess I was wrong. Not *everyone* fantasizes about doing it on the teacher's desk.

Crue spins me around to face him, his expression serious.

"I don't want you going commando."

"Do you happen to have an extra pair on you?" I ask even though I know he doesn't.

I'm pretty sure he doesn't.

"Only mine. You can wear those."

"Those?"

For answer, he bends down, removing his shoes and pants, then boxer briefs.

"Crue," I scold. "This is going too far. I understand…" And secretly love. "…your desire to take care of me in certain areas, but sharing underwear?" I shake my head even though he's focused on pulling off his boxer briefs despite my solid argument here. "Next it'll be our toothbrushes."

Without looking up, he says, "Should've thought of that before making me use your thong as dental floss."

"I didn't?" I put my underwear in his mouth. What he did with it was his choice.

Crue tugs his pants back on—sans underwear.

I throw my hands up. "I'm not wearing them."

One arm around my waist, Crue drags me to him. "You will if you want to leave this room."

"They're too big," I say, one notch below pouting.

"They're the best we have at the moment."

"They'll ruin my aesthetic," I do pout, quite pathetically might I add. I don't want to wear them.

"Yeah, well, prison stripes will be ruining mine if anyone catches sight of my girl's pussy."

My already gelatinous legs threaten to give out entirely. Not only did he threaten murder, again, but he also used the words *my girl*.

If we didn't just have sex, I'd so fuck him right now.

I do have a twisted mind.

"Be a good girl and wear them."

I rip the boxer briefs out of his hand. "Fine. But we're *not* sharing toothbrushes."

With a chuckle, he takes them back, bending to a knee in front of me. "You'll put my dick in your mouth but not my toothbrush?"

"I'm not putting anything of yours in my mouth anymore," I grumble, earning another chuckle from him.

Over one stiletto at a time, he carefully gets the boxer briefs I picked out for him onto my legs, then pulls them up.

I glare at him the whole time, knowing he's probably going to hold me down and brush my teeth with his toothbrush now. And he'll like it because he's the real creep.

Just before my pussy's covered, Crue presses a firm kiss to my clit, whispering, "Until next time."

When he stands, he puts his thumb in its usual place on my lips, kisses it, then says, "That goes for you, too."

Every frigid molecule in my body thaws at once.

I know he's dying to kiss me, yet he never crosses that line.

After putting his own shoes on, he leads me toward the door, saying, "Let's find you a bathroom before the clock chimes."

Using both hands, I tug on his hand and wrist, making him stop and turn to me.

"What?"

From the top of his head to the bottom of his chin, my gaze touches every inch of his face, even that scar he spends so much time trying to hide.

"What's wrong?"

I shake my head. "Nothing. I just wanted to memorize you like this."

A single crooked eyebrow matches the uncertainty in his tone as he asks, "Like what?"

"Mine."

He smiles as those green eyes give my face the same appraisal I just gave his.

"You got plenty of time to memorize me like this."

No, I don't, I think as my throat threatens to shut.

CHAPTER 39

Buzzing prickles my subconscious, and I know without a shadow of a doubt Ever followed through on her threat of putting a wasp's nest in my room.

I flex the arm I fell asleep holding my tormentor with, surprisingly finding her still there.

Fuck. She's gonna get stung.

I instantly fling my body over hers.

Ever gives a sleepy chuckle but doesn't say anything as I tuck my elbows against her sides, trying to cover as much of her as possible.

Another buzz has me hunkering down, the side of my face pressed to Ever's. This is gonna hurt so fucking bad. She said you can die from yellow jacket stings but she didn't say how many. Guess I'm about to find out.

"What is that?"

"Bees," I grumble, anticipating the first of hundreds of stings.

Ever's head pops off the bed, nailing me right in my fucking temple.

I say, "Shit," at the same time she moans, "Ow."

My pain quickly recedes as I focus on hers.

"Are you okay?"

"Kind of." Her body wiggles beneath mine, coming out of its slumber. "Why are you on me?" She shoves me off.

Without thought, I attempt to scoop her under me again. "So the bees can't get you—"

"What? What bees?" she asks, holding me off. And pissing me off. I'm trying to save her.

"The ones you put—"

Hold on. She isn't scared of the bees. She doesn't even know about them.

I flop onto my back and look up at the ceiling. I don't see anything flying around up there.

"Crue? What bees?"

Now that I'm semi awake, that doesn't make any sense. Ever's diabolical but she's smart. She said it herself, she wouldn't stick around after putting a yellow jacket nest in my room.

"I thought there were yellow jackets…"

"Yellow jackets aren't bees. They're wasps."

That is absolutely not the point here. I don't think. Jesus, I'm out of it. I must've been out cold.

If it wasn't wasps though, what was that noise?

I shake my head, clearing it some more, then squint over at my nightstand, the light from my phone's screen barely visible from it being face down. It's probably my mom. She texts me every couple of days now. Just not this late usually.

Checking it, I frown when I see the notification. "What the fuck?"

"What is it?"

"Nothing," I tell her before setting my phone back down, face up this time. "Your door's piece-of-shit sensor's acting up again. Go back to sleep."

It hasn't malfunctioned since Ever started sleeping in my room, so I haven't had to keep an ear out for that sound.

I pull her back into my arms, exactly where she was, exactly where she belongs.

"Sorry I woke you," I whisper, pressing a kiss to her head.

"You were gonna sacrifice yourself for me, Major?"

If I wasn't so damn tired, I'd think she was surprised.

"I am your personal protection agent."

I bury my nose in Ever's honey-scented hair. We moved all her products over to my bathroom last week because even though she didn't mind smelling like me, I did. I like Ever to smell like Ever.

Our bodies meld into each other's again, but not ten seconds later, another notification comes through.

Ever lifts her head again while I give mine a shake.

"Just ignore it."

"What if it's somebody?"

I'm about to say that's highly unlikely until I remember Chef Ryan getting our doors mixed up that one time. Would he really do that again? If he was in a panic, maybe.

Pussy.

Sighing, I get up.

"Stay here."

Ever snuggles under the covers, probably missing my body heat already. Every night, we fuck hard, then we cuddle hard, our bodies never more than a couple centimeters apart unless one of us is using the bathroom.

"I'll be right back," I promise as I tug on a pair of sweatpants.

Out in the hall, the chef is standing at Ever's door again.

This fucking idiot.

When he hears me call out to him, he spins to face me but his hand placement gives me pause. It's not high at all, like one would expect a hand to be after knocking. It *looks* like he was touching the handle.

Something about his pants have me doing a double take as well. They're not his usual chef's pants, but I swear I've seen them before. I've only ever interacted with Ryan on duty, so I don't know how I would've.

Did I run into him outside of the manor somewhere?

"Mr. Brantley, my apologies. I didn't mean to wake you."

He didn't? Then why the fuck else would he be at my door in the middle of the night?

"What can I do for you?" I ask him without bothering to correct the name. I stopped after I realized it was a waste of my breath and that I don't really care what he, or anyone else, refers to me as. There's only one person under this roof I care about using my name and she moans it on the regular now.

Ryan glances at Ever's door. "Oh. I was hoping to give Miss Munreaux something."

So he got the right door, just not the right time. Now isn't exactly the hour for making social calls.

Actually, fuck that. No hour is right for him to pay Ever a visit. He already gets to see her at meals. If I had it my way, he wouldn't even get that with her.

"You didn't knock already, did you?" I ask, knowing full well he did.

His eyes widen as he bobs his head. "Um, yes, I do believe so. Yes, I did."

I groan like he's putting us both in danger from the notorious Ever Munreaux, the very one waiting for me to return to her and warm her little ass up.

"However," he says, all hopeful. "She doesn't seem to be in."

"She's in." *My bed.*

Ryan studies me.

I clear my throat and cross my arms over my bare chest, holding one bulging bicep to appear more intimidating.

"She's probably sleeping. It's late after all."

"Right. Yes. That does…uh…make sense." His gaze drops to the floor.

The pose worked.

I probably didn't even need to use it on him. Outside of the kitchen, Chef Ryan's the least threatening guy ever. There's something about him that keeps me from trusting him though.

"What'd you need to give her?"

"There was a dessert she asked for…"

I filter through all my memories from the last couple days, struggling to find one where Ever asked the chef for anything. She rarely acknowledges him at all, but I can't remember her saying a single word to Ryan recently.

"I wasn't aware Miss Munreaux liked dessert."

"Ah, well, there is this one."

"Which one?" She's my protectee. I need to know everything about her, including what I can give her to make her smile. Besides my dick, which she does still put in her mouth even after swearing it off.

"Clafoutis tart."

"What's that?"

"A French dish with pitted black cherries baked in a vanilla short-bread, served with a delightful sugarplum crème fraîche."

Rich people food. Why couldn't it be a chocolate chip cookie? Something I can get from the grocery store?

"I can take it for you and give it to her in the morning when I see her."

"Oh…" He half turns his body away from me like he's searching for something. "I don't have it on me…um…right now. I was just going to see if Miss Munreaux would be interested in one."

At whatever the fuck time it is? I don't even know what time it is but it doesn't take a genius to know it's not indulge o'clock.

"You can ask her about it tomorrow."

His head dips. "Of course. Yes. Good. Again, I apologize for waking you. There was no…harm."

No harm?

I watch the chef disappear down the hall. It's at the last second before he turns the corner, catching sight of his diamond-encrusted watch, that I remember where I saw him.

I have to work to close my door softly. When I finally spin to face my room, Ever's not where I left her. She's not even in bed. She's next to it, lingering by the headboard with a stricken expression on her face.

"What are you doing?" I demand.

"I don't know. I just…nothing." She sits on the mattress, one leg folded under her. "I thought I might have to hide."

Guilt is practically rolling off her, so I try the arm thing on her, too.

"Did you fuck Chef Ryan?"

She dramatically rolls her eyes in plain sight, clearly not as affected by the pose as Ryan was.

"Did you?" I repeat.

"Are you shitting me right now?"

I drop my arms. "I saw him."

"It would be worrisome if you didn't. He serves you meals every day, as well as lives in the same house as you."

"In the pool house."

She frowns. "When?"

"My first day here. I knew you weren't alone." I point at her. "I knew you were a—"

"Watch what you say to me, Crue."

"Or what? Huh? You gonna go back to your room and wait for the chef to sneak in again?"

Now she's standing again, except not on the floor but on the bed. "What the hell are you talking about?"

I hold up my phone. "I've already caught his ass trying to get in there twice."

His excuses were bullshit both times. I should've known. I should've fucking known.

Like she's in a daze, Ever crumples to the mattress, her gaze on the ruffled sheets.

"So it's my fault?"

I mean, yeah, it is.

Isn't it?

"Is it?" I ask.

Her head shakes but she doesn't say anything either way.

Which, unfortunately, isn't fucking unusual. She opens up to me now, but only so much. Despite us being nearly inseparable lately, she still hasn't confided in me about Arthur abusing her. Even when I've pointed out the absence of those mysterious bruises, she'll lie and say she was right, they must've been from cheer. Except we still do stunts together, almost every evening before our run, and I haven't made a single mark on her in those spots.

"Ever?" I sit in front of her. "Tell me."

When she speaks, her voice is distant. "Before you got here, Chef Ryan stayed in the guesthouse. You remember what it was like in there?"

I nod. I wasn't in it for long but it left an impression.

"You remember the glass over the pool?"

"Yeah." It's how I saw Ryan in the pool house.

"I used to see him up there, watching me. It was…" She wobbles her head. "Disgusting."

I don't like that word, not from Ever. I don't like how this story is turning. I'd rather Ever have fucked him willingly than…where I think this is going.

"I tried to ignore it, ignore *him*. But it was difficult because he would stand right over me sometimes."

"And just watch you swim?"

"That's not what it looked like he was doing."

"What? What did it look like he was doing?"

She finally lifts her eyes to meet mine. "Take a guess."

I'm shaking my head. "No. I've already jumped to enough incorrect conclusions. You tell me. What was he doing up there?"

"Jerking off."

"You saw his fucking dick out?"

"I didn't have to. It was obvious." She mimics a guy masturbating, and yeah, it's unmistakable.

He had a private viewing spot above the hottest girl in Sea Haven, in nothing but a bikini, and he sexually assaulted her by jerking off right in front of her.

Goddamn it. God-fucking-damn it!

"Why didn't you tell your dad?"

"I did."

"You did? And he didn't fire him?"

"Obviously not, Crue," she sneers, making me feel like an even bigger dumbass than I already do.

"What the fuck? Why?"

"Because 'Chef Koch is a world-renowned chef. His food is a

delicacy we should be so privileged to experience.' And 'if I didn't like the attention, I shouldn't seek it out.'"

Arthur knew he had a sick fuck on the property terrorizing his daughter and he didn't do anything about it. Not only did he put the blame on Ever, but he's been forcing her to sit in front of Ryan night after night, letting the piece of shit watch her eat.

"What'd you do?"

"That day you saw me in the pool was the first time I used it in months and I only did because I knew he wouldn't be up there. I didn't know he was in the pool house or else I wouldn't have gone in the pool at all."

I misread her response to my accusation that day. She wasn't scared of being caught. She was scared of being preyed on again.

I misread everything.

"That's all you did though? You just stopped swimming altogether?"

She filled my bed with rat traps, my room with bats, for less. Way fucking less.

Why didn't she retaliate against him? I would've.

I, Crue Brantley, a twenty-five-year-old man with more bulk and skill and experience on my side, would've. I'm not Ever and it's not fair to say what she should've done. I can't begin to imagine how she felt at that time.

"Yeah. You know…kind of like how you stopped living." She peeks at me.

"What? What are you talking about?"

"After what happened with Yasmin, you stopped living."

I shake my head. "That's not…" What I did? Yeah, kind of. But why I did it? No.

I don't think so.

"Yaz wasn't the reason I shut down and stopped trying in life. The world being against me was."

"Why did the world turn against you?"

"I told you already. Because they thought I was a predator."

"But you weren't."

"No. Far from it."

"Because you weren't the one pushing for sex."

"No. It was…" I catch myself at the very idea and scoff. "Yasmin wasn't a predator. She was my girlfriend."

"How many courtrooms do you think that kind of excuse has been used in? People rape their spouses all the time." Ever lowers her eyes before whispering, "Labels shouldn't give anyone free rein over someone else's body."

"As true as that is, I don't think Yaz…"

"Sexually assaulted you?"

I say, "Yeah," but I shake my head, this whole turn in conversation catching me off guard. We were talking about Ever, not me. I'm a guy. I can't—

"You were okay with what she was doing to you?"

My head shakes harder. "I don't… I didn't say that… I just…felt like I didn't have any control," I admit for the first time, even to myself.

Ever asks softly, "What else did you feel?"

"When Yaz was doing *that*…" I don't know what the fuck to call it. "I was extremely uncomfortable, bordering on freaking the fuck out. And not just because I was driving, which was not great either."

I was a new driver, on the road at night, distracted to the point I could barely see through the windshield. Not only was it not great, it was fucking terrifying.

"But also because I didn't want Yasmin touching me like that. No, okay? That's the truth. I didn't. Not while she was hammered. Even though I liked her a lot, I'd already decided not to have sex with her that night. It would've been my first time, and I assumed it was hers, too. I didn't want our first time to be while she wasn't in full control of herself. I didn't want any of our times together to be while she wasn't in full control of herself."

I was a horny seventeen-year-old boy. Of course I wanted to have sex with my girlfriend, but at some point. When it was right. Nothing felt right once we got in my car. I figured we'd go talk, let her sober up a bit away from the liquor someone had been giving her, maybe have our first kiss.

"Jesus, we hadn't even kissed yet when she went straight for my dick."

Ever's eyebrows draw closer together, but she remains quiet.

"And how did I react?" I shake my head at myself.

Not how I *think* I would today. Not how most people *think* someone should in that scenario.

"Probably the best you could at the time. You tried to deescalate the situation," Ever finally says.

I didn't deescalate shit. Obviously.

"By laughing it off," I answer my own question with a laugh just as humorless as the ones in the car that night. "I should've pulled over."

"You don't know what would've happened if you did."

"But I know what did happen when I didn't. I crashed into an oncoming car, killing one person and injuring myself as well as another."

"Crue." Ever reaches for my hand but I pull it away before she can take hold.

"I don't know why I laughed. It wasn't funny." It wasn't fucking funny. Not when Yasmin refused to stop grabbing my dick or even sit down after my forced laughter was broken up by my pleas for her to stop. Fuck. Why wouldn't she just sit down?

"Laughing is a defense mechanism. Your emotions were just trying to regulate themselves so you could continue driving and hopefully get out of a seriously stressful situation. Like I said, you don't know what would've happened if you pulled over."

"I wasn't even thinking about that though."

"Maybe not consciously. But your survival instincts kicked in and made you keep driving."

I've carried a lot of guilt over that night. I've carried a lot of guilt over my *decisions* that night. *Maybe I should've just given in to Yaz, then she wouldn't have been so frantic. Maybe I shouldn't have agreed to leave the dance with her at all. What did I think was going to happen?*

Sex did cross my mind, and had she not been drunk, I probably, honestly, would've been down. But she was drunk and I wasn't down. I thought I was going to spend some time with my girlfriend. That's it. That's what I thought was going to happen.

I never could've guessed she'd become…whatever she was before the crash. She'd been nothing but respectful until we were alone.

"But my reaction was—"

"Just that, a reaction. It was a response to an action. Yasmin's action. She was in the wrong. Her action was wrong. Her…"

"Sexual assault." Fuck.

"Yeah. It was wrong."

"That's something I've never considered. Never acknowledged. I think because it's hard to see yourself as an underdog."

"You're not an underdog, Crue. You're a victim."

"I don't fit the stereotypical description of a victim."

"Society wants everyone to believe victims have to look and behave one way, but that's not true. Guys, at any size, can be victims. Girls, in any state of dress, or undress, can be victims. Anyone, regardless of gender, or age, or what they look like, or sound like, or dress like, can be victims."

The same can be said for attackers. They don't fit one mold either. Mine was an introverted teenage girl. Ever's was a well-respected chef.

One of us spoke up. One of us didn't. Both of us were blamed anyway. Ever's father turned it around on her, just like Yasmin's father did to me.

"I don't want to be anybody's victim," I say. Someone victimized me, but that doesn't mean I have to continue being a victim, especially not *their* victim.

"Neither do I."

"Is that why you put the lock on your door?"

"I didn't have to worry about it before. He was never in the manor overnight. Until…"

"I showed up."

Between following orders from her abusive father to unintentionally giving Ryan direct access to her bedroom, no wonder she fucking hated me.

"It's not your fault," she says, trying to soothe me. Me. Like I'm the one who needs it.

"Are you fucking kidding me, Ever? Come here." Without giving her a chance to turn me down, I climb over to her, enveloping her in my arms. I hear a sniffle and it might as well be a seismic wave from my heart splitting wide open.

"Jesus, I'm sorry. I'm sorry I didn't see it sooner. I'm sorry I treated you like shit." Although, she did deserve *some* of my treatment. Even she can admit that. "I'm sorry I doubted you. I'm so fucking sorry."

Her arms wrap around me, her hands clasping behind my back.

"I'm sorry, too. I'm sorry your life was stolen from you."

Was it stolen from me? It felt like that at the time. But now that I realize I've been looking at things wrong all along, I'm not so sure that's what happened. I didn't fight as hard as I could. I didn't really fight at all. I was…in shock. From the moment Yaz and I left that dance, everything sped up. My life went from a dream to a nightmare in an instant and it just kept getting worse. I did the same thing I did when I was in the car. I froze. I let my survival instinct take the wheel and I've been in a constant loop of nothing ever since, never stopping but never going anywhere either.

"What if you told Arthur about Ryan trying to get into your room? What do you think he'd do?" Because that's exactly what that motherfucker's been trying to do. Thank fucking God I'm a paranoid prick and put those sensors in Ever's room. Even faulty, they've kept him from getting to her.

I've kept him from getting to her, but the sensor helped.

I'm so grateful it didn't fail the times he tried.

I squeeze Ever tighter in my arms, sorrier than I'll ever be able to vocalize.

She scoffs. "Nothing."

"What if I told him? And showed him proof?"

Pulling back, she looks at me seriously. "Don't."

"Why?"

"Because you're more likely to get fired than he is."

We can't have that. We definitely can't have that.

Shit. What else can we do? He cooks food for fuck's sake. Anybody can cook good food.

Anybody can cook bad food, too…

"Okay." I bring her back into my arms. "It'll be okay. I'll take care of it."

Even though I'm an absolute jackass for even thinking she'd fuck that loser, Ever relaxes against me.

"How?"

"Don't worry about it, little bat. It's my job to protect you and that's what I'm going to do."

It's easier for me to choose not to be a victim. My attacker's out of the picture, out of my life. But Ever's is still here, terrorizing her.

That's why I'm going to get rid of him.

"Don't get sent to prison."

"I won't," I promise. Only the hospital.

CHAPTER 40

OTHER THAN OUR NORMAL EXCHANGES DURING MEALS, I haven't addressed the chef all week. It's tough because every time I look at Ryan, I want to saw his hands off using a serrated knife. But I don't want him to suspect anything. So, knowing that Ever's safe in my bed each night that goes by with him under the same roof as her, I bide my time, waiting until some of the awkwardness from Monday night has passed. He hasn't brought up the fancy tart thing to Ever, and to push the incident further from our minds, I haven't either.

If he doesn't think there's anything unusual about the lady of the manor getting offered custom handmade dessert from a top-rated chef in the middle of the night, then neither do I.

No harm, right?

Friday morning, I'm chomping at the fucking bit to put my plan into action and get him out of the manor, so I let us sit for breakfast for once, and strike up a conversation with Arthur, asking if he ever takes out his yacht for fishing.

Ever's the first to answer me, saying, "No, only for murder."

"Never," her dad scolds sharply, making me clench my fork until my knuckles turn white. "Not around mixed company, please. They don't understand your dark humor."

When he glances up from his food, he frowns at finding his

daughter on my left instead of his right. He didn't even notice before now. Luckily, he doesn't question the new seating arrangement.

"I'm not joking. My mother—"

"Suffered a terrible accident while at sea. Yes, we know. Everybody in the Northeast knows. The fact she isn't sitting at this table right now is, admittedly, a tragedy. One we don't want people to get the wrong idea about by spreading false, damning narratives, do we?" Arthur gives her a pointed look that she just scoffs at.

To me, he says, "To answer your question, no. *Burning Rudder* isn't meant for that type of recreation. Should I get the itch to throw a pole up, I charter a fishing boat."

"I bet you get luckier out on a boat than from shore," I say even though I have no fucking clue what I'm talking about.

"I wouldn't know. I've never fished from shore."

Ever's father moves the stack of papers next to his plate around, signaling his disinterest in continuing this discussion.

"I'm the opposite." I don't miss the tightening of Arthur's lips. I just ignore it. "I've only fished from the shore."

"Father says that's a poor man's hobby."

I twist to look at Ever. I can see the apology in her eyes, but she doesn't voice it.

Arthur doesn't bother denying it.

"Yeah, the craziest thing I caught was a barracuda," I say, then turn my attention back to Arthur. "Ever try it?"

"Barracuda? No. I can't say I have."

"It's been years since I've had it, but we threw it in a batch of ceviche." I smack my lips that makes everybody wince. *Poor man behavior.*

"Sounds interesting."

"It's delicious."

"Tell the chef to make you some."

Without anyone even addressing him, the nosey chef shuffles closer to the table, asking, "Mr. Brantley, is that something you'd like me to add to tonight's menu?"

"Hm." I pretend to think about it before asking Arthur, "Wouldn't you like to try some, too?"

Arthur frowns like he can't believe I'm still talking to him, then waves me off with an unenthusiastic, "Sure."

"Edwin?" I call, and not a moment later, the valet appears.

"Yes, sir?"

"Chef Ryan's gonna make some ceviche tonight. Want in on it?"

Edwin looks at Arthur, who gives a single nod without even glancing up from his report.

"I look forward to it."

"Awesome." I clap my hands once before turning to Ever.

I'm opening my mouth to ask her when Ryan beats me to it.

"Miss Munreaux, how about you? Will you finally allow me the honor of delighting your taste buds with something new and unexpected?"

To keep from telling him to never, ever speak to her again, especially like *that*, I ask Ryan, "What about your taste buds? Are you gonna try it, too?"

"I always test my dishes before service to ensure they exceed expectations."

"What's ceviche?" Ever questions.

"You've never had it before?" I ask like I don't already know she despises anything with citrus. I had to get creative in my research.

"I don't know. You're not saying what it is."

Just as Ryan jumps into what I'm sure will be a long-winded, overly complicated description, I tell her, "It's got citrus in it. A lot. That's what 'cooks' the fish."

"Then no. Obviously not."

Obviously. That's exactly why I chose it.

Breakfast returns to the mostly silent affair it normally is. It's not until we're on our way to Littoral that Ever says, "Sorry about that in there. I didn't mean to offend you. It was supposed to be aimed toward my father."

"It's okay." I am a poor man. So what? I didn't grow up on a yacht but I can still make the future owner of one come eight times in one night. And hopefully, when she's older and richer and on that yacht, she'll remember those nights with the kind of smile on her face that whatever dickwad she's with will have to ask her about, but she won't answer because it'd make him jealous as fuck knowing he's never been able to get her to come that many times.

Instead of feeling smug about that, a wave of melancholy washes over me, threatening to drag me to the deepest pit of hell. Ever won't be with me. We know that. But who will she end up with? Definitely someone rich. Richer than me. Hopefully someone that treats her better than…

Nah. No one will ever treat her better than me. I don't give a fuck how much money he has. Dude isn't cherishing her like I do.

I reach over to grab a handful of her thigh and squeeze, almost to the point of pain. Fuck. I don't want to let her go.

Thankfully, I don't have to for a few more years.

When that time comes, if I have to break my own hands just to let her go, I will.

I will.

I probably, hopefully will.

I'll have to.

Won't I?

"I didn't know you fish."

"I don't."

"But then why did you—"

"Do me a favor," I cut Ever off before I have to lie to her. I'd hate to do that at this point, after all we've been through. "Don't eat the ceviche tonight."

"I wasn't planning on it."

"Even if your father or Ryan insists you try it, don't. Throw a fit, do whatever you have to do, but don't touch the ceviche."

Ever doesn't speak for a minute, watching me closely while I keep my eyes trained on the road.

"Crue?"

I shake my head. "Don't. Don't ask me."

If I tell her the truth, she'll try to talk me out of it. I'm not backing out. I've waited multiple days for this. It's finally happening. That motherfucker is getting the ax.

"I don't want you to do anything that puts you in danger."

"I'm Ever Munreaux's bodyguard. I'm always in danger." I beam at her but she doesn't reciprocate the gesture.

With a sniffle, she corrects, "Personal protection agent," for the first time, nearly making me give in, too.

I can't though. Ryan needs to go.

I walk Ever to her first class, right by her clones with Ever ignoring them entirely, just like she's done every other day since we started fucking. As soon as the door closes, I run to the fish market and pick out the three biggest barracudas they have, all over seven pounds each, and from the Caribbean. Barracudas, especially the bigger ones, are more likely to carry the ciguatera toxin, which is poisonous to humans, even if it's cooked. Since there's no way to tell if a fish is infected with the toxin, I leave them sitting in the car during the rest of Ever's classes…just to be sure there's *something* wrong with them.

I can't give the spoiled, and hopefully poisonous, fish to Ryan straight out, or else I could just as easily be blamed, so I wait until about twenty minutes before dinnertime to awkwardly ask Ryan for that coconut oil I had him buy me. Then, while he's in the pantry, looking for that, I sneak a bag of my own cubed barracuda in with the prepared ceviche.

I study the bowl. I can smell it, the bad fish. The lime juice is strong enough to cover it, but I'm looking for it. I know that shit's turned. I also know it might kill me. It might kill all of us.

I shouldn't have asked Edwin to try it. He's the only innocent one. Ryan, I hope suffers. Arthur, too. Me? If dying's what it takes to free Ever from these demented fucks, I'll do it. I'll do it happily.

With a red face, Ryan returns with the coconut oil, his reluctance to hand it over obvious.

I take it from him with a mumbled, "Thanks," playing up the embarrassed act. Was he this embarrassed when he stood over my girl, yanking on his cock where she could see? Probably fucking not because he has his own act, too.

"Look familiar?" He gestures to the ceviche.

"Looks fancier. Yours has way more fish than ours did."

Ryan smiles proudly, happy to take full credit for the fishier-than-it-was-a-second-ago fish salsa.

He's such a douche, and not the kind that goes in pussies. Those actually serve a purpose sometimes.

"The Munreauxs wouldn't have it any other way," is all he says.

I think Ever would have it literally any other way. She doesn't act half as spoiled around me as she used to. She's pretty unpretentious when it's just us. She'll have the occasional slipup of not understanding how the real world works, but even then, she lets me educate her without getting all high and mighty.

She's like two different people—the one she is with me and the one she is with everybody else.

Maybe that's how everyone in love is though.

Not that Ever's in love with me. More so that's how I see her.

Except I don't love her…

Even if I wanted to, I couldn't because…

Love isn't…

And I'm only…

So I can't actually…

But somehow…

I do.

Fuck. I do. I love her. I fell for that five-foot-nothing, peppy-as-shit, pain-in-my-ass, creepy little cheerleader, and damn, was that a bad idea. I *knew* that. I *know* that. And yet, I still did it. I can't even pinpoint when. It just *happened*. One moment I hated her. *I tried to fucking hate her.* The next minute, it's like I couldn't function without her in my sight, knowing with absolute certainty that she was okay. Not even just okay. That she was taken care of. Happy. Spoiled. Because she's not as spoiled as everyone thinks, not with the stuff that matters anyway. Ever's drowning in designer clothing, but what puts a real smile on her face? Wearing my clothes that are so old they don't even have tags anymore. No clue what brand they are, how much they cost, or where I bought them from, but they make Ever happy, truly happy.

I make Ever happy, truly happy.

Once we enter my room, it's like stepping into another world, one where we both get to be who we really are. An abditory. Ever taught me what that is, as well as what the Louvre is—an art museum in Paris—because I sure as shit didn't know the first time she said it. An abditory is a place to hide or keep valuable goods, like art. That's where I fell in love with her—our own abditory—and that's where I'll stay in love with her…until I'm forced out of it.

Away from that room, and this manor, back in the regular world, it'll be easier to remember why I didn't like her to begin with. When she was the elaborately feral Ever Munreaux who threatened to put my dick in a chastity belt and had my Bronco painted with pink flames, it was almost easy to dislike her.

Almost.

I was still intrigued. I was attracted. I was spellbound. I *never* stood a chance against that nicely dressed weirdo with her fortune-telling cards, and her magical rocks, and her altars, and her… spirit. That's what it comes down to. Otherworldly or not, with or without enchantments, Ever's spirit is unmatched. She captivated me from the first second I came face to face with her.

I may not have liked her right off the bat, but I wanted her in my life. A life I didn't even want to be in but knew she needed to be in. And she did. She's been essential. A spark.

She helped me see what I'd been blinding myself to. She's shown me I'm capable of more than just dark and destruction.

If I die tonight, it'll be for her and it'll be worth it.

I'm ready.

"See you at dinner," I promise Ryan.

CHAPTER 41

THE DINING ROOM IS UNRECOGNIZABLE TONIGHT. IT'S STILL the same opulent room, but the people in it are different. They're bustling. Everybody's interacting, even Father. He never converses with Ryan or Edwin so jovially, but both men stayed at his insistence, serving themselves plates of ceviche. They're not delusional enough to sit with us and eat the whole thing. Most likely they'll scamper back into the kitchen for that, but for now, they're in here talking and laughing with each other, as well as Crue, in between bites of tortilla chips.

My bodyguard's not this conversational with anyone usually, at least not in the manor. If I was surprised by him this morning, I'm downright shocked right now. His teeth are showing, he's smiling so big. I've only seen him like that toward me.

But now every time he looks my way, it dims the briefest amount. No one else would be able to notice it, but I do and I hate it. What did he do to the ceviche? He's not going to eat it, is he? He hasn't yet. I've been watching him more than the others. I don't care about the others. I don't care about anyone else in this room, in this house, in this state, just Crue. I can't let anything happen to him. Not before…

Not until our time together is up. It's already limited enough.

My stomach pangs with worry, *not* hunger. I can't even think about eating right now. Not when I have to keep such a close eye on Crue.

I wish I never told him about Ryan. It's not worth it. Ryan's not worth it. I don't even care what he did, not anymore. I'd swim in front of him a hundred more times if it meant Crue wasn't in danger.

Why is he in danger? What did he do?

Crue puts a fish-covered chip up to his mouth.

Instinctively, I throw a hand out. "No!"

Everyone pauses to blink at me.

"Don't eat it all. I changed my mind. I'd like to try some, too."

Crue's eyes widen at me and he shakes his head minutely.

I tilt mine back at him.

Ryan rushes to my other side, spooning ceviche next to my chicken breast.

"Miss Munreaux, I'm honored to—"

Crue pushes to his feet, towering over me. And Ryan. He's tall and the chef is not.

"You hate citrus."

"So?" I counter while staring at the chopped fish, onion, and cilantro, wishing it didn't smell *so* much like lime juice.

"So why even bother? You know you're gonna hate it."

Yeah.

"Probably spit it right back out."

It'll be a struggle to keep it in for sure.

"My daughter has better manners than that, don't you, Never?" my father asks rhetorically.

"Won't it go to your hips though?"

Crue's reaching now. I eat fish. I just don't eat fish prepared in citrus baths.

It's bad, whatever he did. But if he's willing to put himself in danger, then so am I. Either both of us eat it, or neither of us do.

I glance up at him. "Cheer season's over."

Again, he shakes his head, his eyes a pendulum between mine as he begs silently with them.

I use mine to beg even harder. *Don't do this—whatever this is. Let them eat it alone. Let them puke and writhe in pain until their insides are desiccated. I don't give a shit. Please, please, don't eat it.*

I lift a forkful of ceviche.

Or I will, too.

Several moments pass, neither of us blinking, until finally, Crue scoffs and tosses his chip on his plate, pieces of barracuda tumbling off it.

I lower my fork instantly.

"I guess I should've expected this. You have been eating everything in sight lately."

Every man in the room gives my appearance offensive inspections except Edwin, who excuses himself a few steps backward in effort to blend in with the wall.

Newsflash: it doesn't work.

My stare turns deadly. He's resorting to weight-shaming me? That's a very low blow.

"Is this true?" my father questions.

"So what if it is?" I counter. Unless we're counting my recent intake of cum, I haven't changed my eating habits whatsoever. But I will not be shamed either way.

"Take it away," he instructs someone.

I tear my gaze from Crue's in time to watch Ryan remove my entire plate.

"I didn't eat!" I shout, my anger bubbling over.

"Apparently, you have. It's for your own good. I will not have my daughter turn into a pig before she's even wed."

Crue's frown is obvious even out of the corner of my eye.

This is his doing. He said that knowing my father would overreact. He should've known I would as well.

Standing quickly enough to knock my chair over, I swing an arm at Crue's plate, smacking it off the table. It lands on the floor with a clatter.

Neither of us it is.

"Never!" Father booms. "What do you think you're—"

"How's that for manners, Father?" With a smile in place, I curtsy, then spin on my heel and leave the dining room a whole lot quieter than it was when I entered.

Hours later, I'm waiting for Crue's knock on my door, letting me know it's clear to come out and follow him into his for the night, but it never comes. By eleven o'clock, I break down and text him, but don't get an immediate reply. Twelve o'clock, I still haven't received any response. Half past one, my phone is silent but I am not. I'm trying not to hyperventilate but it's not working.

Did he eat the ceviche after all?

I text him again.

When he still hasn't responded fifteen minutes later, I eye the door between our bedrooms. I haven't had to use it the last couple weeks. I get to sleep next to Crue with his permission now. Technically, it's at his insistence. He hates me sleeping alone almost as much as I do.

He could've fallen asleep, I guess.

But the timing is just too coincidental.

He wasn't actually mad at me, was he? I did him a favor. I would never let him put himself in danger for me. He knows that…right?

I'm going over there. Hopefully, he is just asleep.

I slide the door in the wall open, instantly discovering he's not. He's up…somewhere. His comforter is thrown back like he had to rush from bed, so he might've been asleep at one point.

The toilet flushes in his bathroom.

Hustling inside his room, I close the door behind me, then dart away from it as I wait for Crue to emerge from his bathroom.

Except he doesn't.

I venture closer to the en suite, hearing retching once I'm a few feet away.

Groaning, I close the distance and press my forehead to the door before whispering, "You did eat it."

He still could've texted me back and let me know. I would've come over regardless.

Would he have let me?

Obviously not or I would've been here already.

I wouldn't want him to witness me with food poisoning either.

Not like he'd listen. He's done plenty of things I didn't want him to do, like wash my *entire* body. Every. Single. Inch. Including. Crevices.

The toilet flushes again, followed my more retching.

Tears blur my vision and I crumple to my knees, my palm on the door.

"I'm sorry," I mouth, completely helpless.

I hate this. I *hate* this.

I hate Ryan. I hope he's in worse shape. I hope they're all in worse shape. Maybe not Edwin, but…I can't really afford to give him any real thought. Not when all of mine are currently preoccupied with the man on the other side of this door.

Damn you, Crue Brantley, why did you eat the ceviche? He had an excuse not to. His plate was on the *floor*. He could've stormed after me. He normally never lets me out of sight. Why did he stick around this one time and get another serving?

He risked himself. He…sacrificed himself, for me. Again. He did the same thing when he thought his room was full of enraged yellow jackets.

And all I can do is sit here, crying. A lot of help I am. A lot of help he let me be by keeping me out.

I still got in though and I don't have to be useless.

I search up food poisoning on my phone and how to treat it, not finding as much as I was hoping for.

"Ugh," I growl as I get to my feet, wiping angrily at my eyes so I can see what I'm reading.

Unfortunately, there still isn't much to go on.

It's good that he's puking it up. It would've been better if he puked sooner, like three hours ago.

Has he been puking that long?

I fight the urge to fall back into a heap on the floor. Crue would be strong for me. He would watch a damn how-to video for me. He would do whatever he needed to in order to ensure I was taken care of.

Even consume bad fish.

Leaving out his bedroom door—that randomly has a chair wedged under the knob—I run to the kitchen and grab a box of garbage bags, multiple waters, a bottle of pain reliever, and the activated charcoal I added to my list after seeing a viral post about brushing your teeth with it but never actually tried it. In my sprint back, I hear multiple pipes working at the same time and let a smile loose. He got them.

After placing the water and pain reliever on his nightstand, I empty Crue's laundry basket, then fit the garbage bag over it before setting it next to his bed. I read that was better than a bowl. Much smaller of a splash zone.

Ew.

Now I have to figure out how to get the activated charcoal in him. If it were me, he would hold me down, stick it in my mouth, then cover my mouth until I swallowed it. He's a lot bigger than I am though. He could flick me off like a flea.

Even when he's sick and weak?

I don't really want to find out. He's already going through enough.

I bring my phone up and search the best ways to take activated charcoal, thankfully finding a much simpler solution—mixing it in water. It does say not to take any other medications for a couple hours after consumption, so while I pour in a healthy dose, I hide the bottle of pain reliever in Crue's top drawer, that way it's not even a possibility.

I think fluids are about all he's going to be able to handle for a while anyway.

Returning to his bathroom, I don't hear anything save for groaning, so I put my ear against the door.

"Crue? Can I come in?"

More groans are my answer…that I choose to interpret as a yes.

Inside, I find Crue sprawled out on the floor. His forehead's sweaty and his complexion is greener than his eyes. My bodyguard is fucking green!

I instantly drop beside him, my eyes already leaking.

"I need you to drink this."

He weakly pushes away the bottle in my hand, but I don't care.

He's always pushy. Always making me compromise. He can do as I say this one time.

Not giving him a choice, I lift his head with a hand and bring the bottle to his mouth, pouring a trickle between his lips until they part enough for the water to get in.

He sputters, spraying black water everywhere, even at me.

My face wet with tears and spit, I press it to his, our noses touching as I say, "I need you to swallow it, okay? It's supposed to help."

"No," he moans with a sharp head turn that almost pulls him out of my palm. "Can't."

"Yes, you can." I readjust my hold on him, propping his head in the crook of my elbow. "You have to."

"Uh-uh."

"Damn you, Crue. You can't tell me 'no.'"

"Go away." He twists his head again but doesn't get anywhere this time.

I tighten my hold on him anyway, and sob, "I can't."

Why is he pushing me away? I'm trying to help.

His eyelids practically vibrate over his eyes as his body spasms.

Oh my Goddess.

"Kiss me."

"Poison."

"I know. I know." That's why he needs this activated charcoal in him. We're probably past the point of absorption if it's hit his stomach already, but it should help with elimination. "But you said if I begged and I'm begging. Kiss me, Crue."

There's no one else I'd rather poison me.

I pour a bunch of the black water in my own mouth, then fit my lips to his. It takes a few seconds for his lips to move even the slightest bit, but as soon as they do, I pry them open with mine before gently streaming the water into his mouth, pausing just long enough for him to swallow.

"Good boy," I croon before waterfalling more in my mouth and repeating the process until I've gotten a quarter of the bottle in him.

Letting him rest for a moment, I look over at the toilet where he's going to be headed next. It's dirty and stinks and makes me want to die because I've never cleaned anything in my life and vomit has to be the worst-smelling thing on the planet, especially someone else's, but there's no one else here and so I have to clean it for him. Ugh. I have to.

Do I have to?

Crue would do it for me.

Get over yourself, Ever.

"Okay." I steel my spine.

After I get Crue situated on his side, I hurry up and wipe the toilet down, my nose plugged the whole time, my eyes only at, like, half-mast. Talk about splash zone. The toilet's smaller than some of our bowls.

I hear heaving before a splash and let my eyelids flutter to a close. He's still lying on the floor. He couldn't even sit up to make it to the toilet.

When I gather enough courage to peek over at Crue, there's a chunky black puddle by his face.

Now I want to die.

CHAPTER 42

Crue

"O-F-F-E-N-S-E."

I crack my eyes at Ever's voice, wondering how the fuck I ended up at a football game and why—

I'm in the bathroom?

I've never seen it from this angle but it looks like my bathroom.

Am I on the fucking floor?

"Throw that ball."

And Ever's behind me?

"Uh…"

Ever's…chant? Is she chanting a cheer right now? Whatever she's saying ends as she starts shushing me, an elongated garbage can shoved in my face.

"Shh. Shh. It's okay. You're okay."

She pets my head.

What the fuck?

I push the garbage away and try to sit up, my back cold the moment I do. I half-turn to see Ever sitting with her legs spread in a wide V, one on each side of me, with her back pressed to the wall.

"Oh." She drops her arms and tilts her head at me. "You're up."

I groan at the churning in my stomach.

"Kind of," she mutters before pulling me back into her embrace. I go with her because she's warm and soft and makes the queasiness subside significantly.

Fully relaxed against her front again, I hear her ask softly, "How do you feel?"

"Like shit."

"Yeah. That happens when you purposely give yourself food poisoning."

Last night comes back to me in bits and pieces. I ate the spoiled ceviche. Everybody did. Except Ever. If I hadn't gotten her out of there in time, she'd be in her own bathroom.

Why is she in mine?

"What are you doing in here?" I croak.

"You were so weak you couldn't hold yourself over the toilet. I was scared you were gonna choke on your own puke, so…"

"So what?" I look down at our bodies. She has one arm over my chest, holding me to her. "You held me upright?"

"Yeah," she says with a shrug like I'm not almost a hundred pounds heavier than her.

"All night?"

"Yeah."

"How?"

"By reciting all the cheers I've ever learned."

"You didn't have to do that."

"I only did what you would've."

"I don't know any cheers," I say after a minute. She's right. I would've taken care of her, but I like to do that kind of shit. Ever barely knows how to take care of herself, let alone another person. What'd she do? Watch a fucking tutorial?

I glance at the garbage next to us. It seems to be just a bag but stretched over something.

She just might've.

"I wouldn't be too sure. You may have picked up some subliminally."

"What's that?" I point at the garbage bag thing.

"Your laundry basket. Less splashage, easy cleanup, and it helps with the smell."

Splashage. Cleanup. Smell.

I groan again. Jesus Christ. I've been puking my guts up in front of Ever Munreaux, the girl that has a maid clean her bedroom and bathroom for her. She doesn't even take out her own garbage. She leaves it out in the hall for Edwin.

"You need to leave," I grumble as I try to sit up, this time much slower because fuck, my body hurts. I don't know if it's from the food poisoning or sitting on a bathroom floor…or both.

Ever just giggles. "No, I don't."

"You weren't supposed to see any of this."

"Okay…but I did."

"How? I put a chair in front of my door."

At her silence, I glance back at her. Her lips are pursed and her eyes are downcast, then as if she can sense me studying her, her gaze lifts to mine. Her entire expression changes in a blink.

"I know. I'm the one that got past it."

I squint at her. "How?"

"What does it matter? I'm in here now. I've been in here for hours, taking care of you—"

"You weren't supposed to. I didn't want you to take care of me." For fuck's sake. I could've shit myself. That's something you can *never* come back from.

"Too bad. I did. And I'm going to continue taking care of you, so get used to it. I'm not going anywhere."

She immediately gets up and goes to the shower. Which has a bunch of tied garbage bags in it that are full of…stuff. Black stuff?

Did I fucking shit myself?

But I'm still in the clothes I was in last night, so…

"Ever?"

She stops to regard me.

"What the *fuck* is in those bags?"

I brace for the worst possible answer.

"Your vomit."

"Why is it black?"

Her gaze falls again, and with a voice holding only curiosity, no judgment, she asks, "You don't remember?"

"Remember *what?* Me puking in my own laundry basket?"

She perks right up, grabbing several bags at once. "Yep. Probably just something you ate."

"I didn't eat anything black."

Passing me, she shrugs. "Maybe the ceviche was so bad it turned black. I don't know."

The mere mention of ceviche has me gagging.

"Aim for the laundry basket," she calls over her shoulder, disappearing from the bathroom and leaving me to expel my stomach in private.

Nothing comes up, thankfully, but I kick the door closed anyway to get a moment alone and wrap my head around what happened. Ever Munreaux saw me at my worst and took care of me through it. She sat up with me all night—literally—holding me upright, so that I didn't choke and die.

The door opens sooner than I was hoping, then Ever appears above me.

"You were really out of it last night, huh?"

"I guess." I don't remember anything about…anything. There was cramping, an insane accumulation of saliva, then what felt like a never-ending purge.

Although, now that I'm trying, there is a moment playing at the edge of my mind. But it doesn't make any sense. My head hanging in the laundry basket, I heard Ever mutter, "How is the charcoal supposed to help if he can't keep it down?"

Obviously, that didn't happen because I've never consumed charcoal, especially not recently. If I had, that'd explain the black.

"Where'd you put those bags?"

"Out in the hall."

"For Edwin?"

She gives me a "duh" sort of look.

"How's he doing?"

"I don't know. I don't care. You've been my only concern."

"You haven't heard from anyone else?"

That earns me a different look, one that says I should know better. I should. I do. Nobody talks to Ever in this house.

"Why did you eat it?" she asks me.

"It was the only way."

"Only way to what?"

"Get Ryan fired. If I didn't get sick, too, it would've been suspicious."

"You could've died."

"It would've been worth it."

"For who?"

"You."

Her head rotates side to side, her eyes glassy.

"You should've told me."

"You would've tried to stop me." She did try. Fucking threw my plate on the floor. Brat.

"Because it wouldn't have been worth it. My freedom already has too high of a price."

I frown up at her. "What does that mean?"

"It means don't put yourself in danger for me ever again."

"It's my—"

"Don't fucking say it's your job again. We both know that's bullshit, Crue."

We stare at each other.

"It's my choice. I'd choose your life over mine, every time, without hesitation."

Voice raised with a crack in it as well, she replies, "Well, I'd choose yours!"

"Is that what you thought you were doing last night, trying to eat that shit?"

"Yes, actually. If you can poison yourself, so can I."

That doesn't even make sense. It defeats the entire purpose. And no, she fucking can't. She doesn't get to make that kind of choice.

"You sound so stupid right now," I tell her.

"You look so stupid right now."

"I feel stupid right now."

"Good. Don't do things without telling me again."

"Not that." I fully stand by everything I did last night. I would do it again and again and a-fucking-gain for her. "I meant lying here."

"Oh." She loses some of her steam as she takes in my pathetic position. "Can you walk?"

"How far?"

"To your bed."

I tap my chest with all ten fingertips, hating the feeling of being powerless but not these revelations. I knew Ever was possessive. I didn't know she was protective, too. And selfless? Gotta be honest, I never saw that one coming. She's going to make a hell of a mom one day.

Before I can stop myself, I'm imagining Ever cradling a baby, our baby, her motherly instincts sharpened to a fine point. She'll be loving all right, fiercely so.

I shake my head to clear the fantasy, and tell her as seriously as I can, "You'll have to carry me."

Ever widens her eyes while her face lights up from a grin, making her the prettiest thing in the world. Fuck any mountain range, river view, beachscape. A smiling Ever Munreaux is more postcard-worthy than any of those.

Stupid fucking girl. I love her with every ounce of my being. She better not ever put herself in danger again. I couldn't live with myself.

"I can't," she admits.

"What do you mean? You got past my barricade." Supposedly.

She rolls her eyes before stretching those dainty hands out to me. "That was a chair. You're twice my size."

I take her hands and pretend to let her pull me up. I'm not going to my bed though. Strangely, I'm not even that tired. Probably because I had a cheerleader for a pillow.

"What are you doing?" that same cheerleader asks when I turn on the shower.

"I gotta get the stench off me." Hopefully it'll wash away some of this humiliation, too. "I'll only be a minute."

Ever sheds her clothes in record time, absolutely fucking naked in seconds, exactly the way I like her.

But no, I'm gross. I can smell myself and I reek. I know Ever thinks so, too. How can she not? She's not used to unpleasantries and I'm currently unpleasant as fuck.

"That wasn't an invitation, little bat."

She scoffs. "I have an open invitation when it comes to showering with you."

"Not this time. Come on." I point at the door. "You gotta get out."

All she does is cross her arms over her chest, like that makes her more intimidating. If anything, it makes her more enticing. Her small swells are all pushed up, ready to be devoured.

I cross my arms, too, since that's *my* move. I'm more threatening of the two of us. What I say goes.

What I say sometimes goes.

What I say should go more than it actually does. I fold way too easy for Ever.

But I'm not folding on this. I'm showering alone. End of story.

"What if you fall?" she asks.

I almost fucking snort.

"We know your ass won't be picking me up. You just said so yourself."

"No." Smiling, she strides right past me, into the shower and under the spray. Hair wet, tits pointy, pussy distracting, she says, "But I'll stay on the floor with you until you can pick yourself up."

Thank fuck the water's running, otherwise she'd be able to hear the sound of me folding all over again.

I remove my clothes just as quickly as she did, then I'm in the shower with her, turning her around so I can wash her hair because even when I'm at my worst, I'll still put Ever's needs before my own.

"You don't belong on the floor." I have the strangest urge to call her butterfly. I have no idea why. Probably because she's being so sweet, unlike her bat-like tendencies. I just ignore it to add, "Your soul's in the sky."

She doesn't reply right away, but when she does, it's quiet yet serious.

"I belong wherever you are."

I don't bother with a response because we both know that's not true.

It's not until later that day that we leave the confines of my bedroom, coming across an apparition of Arthur Munreaux in the kitchen with a glass of cloudy liquid up to his mouth and what could pass as duffle bags under his eyes. He is the embodiment of ill.

"The virus got everybody then?" he says when we enter.

"Virus? Is that what this is?" I ask, playing along before I can start hinting at the real culprit.

"I feel fine," Ever brags.

"Keep your distance if you want it to stay that way."

She leans away from us, but asks, "Where's the chef? I'm starving."

"I don't even want to look at food right now," I say with a forced groan. I'm not exactly hungry but I wouldn't turn down a meal either. Which is weird because last time I had food poisoning, I lost several pounds from not being able to eat for days.

"The chef's unable to perform his duties right now, so we're on our own. It's a good thing none of us are hungry."

"I'm hungry," Ever repeats, getting zero acknowledgement from Arthur as he sips from his drink. "Probably because I didn't eat anything last night," she adds before shooting me a nasty side-eye.

I'd rather her miss one meal than wind up like the rest of us. Jesus, the manor even feels contaminated. The air around us is stagnant as fuck.

"Be grateful you didn't eat the cevi—" My body rebukes the word before I can even finish saying it.

Arthur's gag tells me his does, too.

"The ceviche?" Ever supplies with a gleam in her eyes as they lock on her trembling father.

"Yeah, that. It was disgusting coming back up."

"The ceviche was?"

Arthur has to cover his mouth to hold back another heave.

She's doing it on purpose now.

I flash Ever a quick secretive grin.

I don't have quite the same reaction anymore, but I doubt I'll ever be able to utter ceviche out loud again. I know for damn sure I'll never eat it again.

"How did it taste going down? Since I didn't get to try it."

"It was…" I consider how to answer that. It wasn't great. There was a distinct flavor to it that wasn't normal. But I want Arthur to come to that conclusion on his own. "It wasn't what I expected. Very different than the other times I've had it."

"Different how?" Ever asks.

"I don't know. Just…not as good as I remembered it."

"No, you're right," Arthur chimes in. "There was something off about it."

"Off? Uh-oh."

Now I'm shaking my head at Ever. She's acting a little too pleased about all this. She might as well be drumming her fingers together in front of her face, an evil smirk tugging at her lips.

"It's never a good idea to eat fish that tastes off."

"No, it's not," Arthur agrees, getting a little bit closer to where I want him.

"I'm surprised the chef didn't notice it," I say. "Didn't he say he always tests his dishes beforehand?"

Arthur frowns, deep in thought, but doesn't answer.

"Wait… What if it's not a virus?" Ever asks with more compassion than she had a moment ago. "What if it's…"

"Food poisoning?" her father supplies.

"Could be," I say, nodding. "That would explain why Miss Munreaux didn't get it." I almost throw her another grin. *You're welcome.*

She's on the move, going over to the refrigerator and grabbing a bowl out. Before she can even peel the plastic wrap back, I plug my nose.

"Oh my Goddess." Ever practically gags herself, but thrusts it toward her dad for his inspection.

One sniff and Arthur's expression turns murderous. "Goddamn it! Get it away from me!"

Forgetting all about my own survival, I quickly get between the two. I keep myself between Arthur and Ever at all times whenever they're in the same room together, never giving Arthur the opportunity to get within arm's reach of his daughter.

Ever tosses the bowl in the sink, uncovered, with a bratty, "It's not my job."

Even breathing through my mouth, I can sense how bad the ceviche stinks as I guide Ever away from Arthur. And the sink. Miles wouldn't make a difference at this point. It needs to be on another continent.

"Jesus, that's rancid."

"It never should've been served. Any cook with half a brain would know that."

Ever and I remain quiet, letting Arthur stew. Fortunately, it doesn't last long, then he's storming out, saying, "That error of judgement just cost a man his job."

We fucking did it.

I mostly did it. I got rid of that motherfucker.

My joy is cut severely short when I hear him call back, "That bowl better be gone the next time I enter the kitchen!"

Ever's lips stretch wide while I roll my eyes, knowing she's not gonna clean it up.

"Just the bowl?" she asks innocently.

She's so devious.

I love it. As long as it's not directed at me, I love it.

I turn back around to take care of the radioactive fish soup, except Ever surprises me by stepping in front of me, telling me, "I got it."

"You? You're gonna throw it out?" I hang back to watch this. "Do you even know where the garbage cans are?"

"Do you?" she's quick to shoot back.

All I can do is stand here, chewing on my own fucking hypocrisy. Edwin may take out my garbage as well. And the maid? She's a very insistent woman. So, she's been cleaning my room and bathroom, too.

"Looks like someone's acclimating to this lap of luxury nicely."

If we were in our abditory, I'd tell Ever her lap is the only one I'm acclimating to, and yeah, it's luxurious.

CHAPTER 43

"I THINK WE SHOULD SLEEP IN SEPARATE ROOMS TONIGHT," I tell Ever at her door.

"Why?"

"Because you need some sleep and I still don't feel very good. I don't want to keep you up again if I get sick." I haven't puked all day. Since Ever and I showered and my humanity was restored, I've actually felt fairly decent. I even got some food in me for dinner. A dinner I cooked for us since nobody else was around. I don't know if Arthur's waiting until Ryan leaves his room to fire him, or if he already kicked the chef out, but we didn't see him once today.

Edwin must've ventured out at least once because the bags Ever set outside my door this morning were gone by the time we left it earlier.

Ever's eyebrows nearly collide, but she says, "Okay."

"Goodnight," I say before heading to my own room and doing the same thing I did last night, shoving the desk chair under the doorknob at a 45-degree angle.

Ever should stay in her bed and get the sleep she missed out on last night. After staying up with me, she spent the day with me in my room, wide awake, so she's gotta be tired.

She won't though. She's going to sneak in here later. I know it. I know her. And when she does, she's going to find herself blocked once again. Since she refuses to tell me how she got past the chair I put in place specifically to keep her out, I want to see it for myself…assuming she can do it a second time. I'll let her in either way, but it should be interesting to watch her in action. She's so fucking tiny, she probably only needs a small crack to slip through. Just like a goddamn bat.

I settle into the armchair by the window and wait for the stirrings of my favorite nocturnal creature.

I don't expect hours to go by but go by they do. Slowly. Agonizingly. Three, then four, then five. Is she going to come? Or not?

It's somewhere around three o'clock in the morning and I'm just about to lift myself up when something moves in my periphery. My gaze locked on the door, I'm not expecting my motherfucking wall to open up…yet that's *exactly* what it does. Holy shit.

Not only is it opening, but there's a fucking figure coming through it. Every muscle in my body freezes. Is that a ghost? Ever warned me the manor was haunted but I didn't heed it whatsoever. She talked a lot of shit back then. Also, I didn't think ghosts were scary at the time. Probably because I'd never had one come right up to me and—

It's not coming up to me at all. It's not even paying me any attention. It's…going to my bed?

After closing the portal it just came through, the petite ghost leans over my bed. Is it looking for me? Does it do this every night?

Oh, shit. Is it looking for Ever? What if it's her mom's ghost? She doesn't come in here when we're fucking…right? That'd be weird. That'd be really—

The ghost glances toward the bathroom, revealing the face of my favorite nocturnal creature.

God, what a creep.

And me, for liking it.

At least now I know why the sensor on her door wasn't going off. She's been using some sort of secret wall-door between our rooms to get in and out of here undetected. That's how she got in here last night, too. She couldn't tell me how she got past the chair, because she didn't.

While she's still staring at the bathroom, I stand from the chair, causing her to let out a gasp.

"Goddess, Crue, what are you doing over there?"

"Are you scared, little bat?" I ask as I approach her.

She spins to face me, propping her ass on the bed.

"No."

Liar. I can practically hear her heart thundering inside her chest.

"How often do you use that?" I nod at the wall I obviously didn't inspect close enough but will first thing in the morning along with all the other walls in this room because what kind of rich-people shit is that.

Unashamed, she shrugs. "Not as much now." Now that I walk her into my room every night, keeping her in here for my own self-ish reasons.

"How many times did you use it before?"

"Just a couple…I think. To do your shoes."

"For my shoes?" I push into her personal space.

"Yep."

"You never came in here to do anything else?"

She gives it a second to think over before asking, "Like what?"

I scoff. She's playing dumb. How cute.

"Me."

Now she makes a sound in her throat. "You're the one that suggested I sit on your face while you were asleep."

That gives me pause.

"Did you?"

"No. You really think I would take advantage of someone like that?"

"Not even after I gave you permission?"

"You said you'd notice and wake up, so you tell me, did I?"

I don't think she did. And for some reason, that's disappointing. I can't think of a better aroma to wake up to than Ever's delicious cunt, begging to be devoured.

Taking off my clothes, I climb in bed and lie down where I usually do, face up.

"What are you doing?"

The snore I release isn't quite as obnoxious as the first time I pulled this stunt.

"I'm not doing it," she says, making me smile internally.

Yes, she is. She fucking better.

"You're not even asleep. You *just* laid down."

My snores increase as does the blood flow to my cock.

Ever must notice because she groans.

I stroke myself just to fuck with her.

"I'm going back to my room."

I instantly roll over and catch her hand with mine, yanking her onto the mattress with me before she can go anywhere.

She comes easily, giggling.

I lead her all the way over until she's straddling me, gazing down at me like a sexy queen of the night.

"Have pity on me, Ever. I'm sick."

"No, you're not. You're doing better than everyone else in this house."

"Why is that?" I can't help but ask. It is kinda strange how quickly I got over the food poisoning.

"You had a good nurse," she says with a shrug.

That's true.

"Let me thank you for your service."

"Crue. You need rest."

"I need sustenance."

"Then I'll go get you some—"

I tighten my grip on her hips, keeping her on my stomach.

"Sit on my face."

"That's not the kind of sustenance you need."

Probably not. But it's the only kind I want.

"It's exactly what I need," I argue. "You're exactly what I need."

The pad of her thumb covers my lips, then she bends down and kisses over it...as well as the corners of my lips.

I strain up into it, praying she removes the thumb. Something about the move, her being above me maybe, gives me déjà vu, which is impossible because she's never done this before. I'm always the one that "kisses" her like this.

Ever sits up again but the feeling remains. *Did she kiss me last night? I hope not. That would've been disgusting for her.*

She wouldn't have. There'd be no reason.

"How's your stomach?" she asks on her shuffle up my torso, her shirt already raised to expose her tits.

"Fine."

I help get that shirt off, throwing it off to the side.

"What about—"

"Ever… What's your middle name?"

"Chanel."

"Ever Chanel Munreaux, sit on my face."

"I'm still wearing underwear."

Not for long.

I tear the pair from the middle out until the seams rip, then I toss those, too.

"Hold on, hold on, hold on," I tell her and shut my eyes.

When nothing happens, I crack one open. Ever's suspended above my chin, just staring down at me.

"Sit."

She huffs. "You're so ridiculous. I thought you were about to be sick."

"I am sick…" Both eyes closed again, I tug on her hips, mumbling, "Of waiting," just before her pussy makes the briefest contact with my lips.

Hmm… Ever's light but not that light.

"I said 'sit.'"

"You have to be able to breathe."

"I'll be able to breathe," I lie. Eating pussy is a breathing exercise in any position. It hasn't killed me yet.

"This is my first time just sitting…like this. It's awkward."

I'm another one of her firsts.

"It's not awkward."

"Yes, it is. I'm just supposed to sit here and somehow not suffocate you?"

"You know how you grind on my dick? Do that to my tongue." I stick it out for her.

She grumbles but lines up with my tongue before lowering herself onto it.

There we fucking go.

I latch on to her hips with both hands, holding her to me like I would a cob of corn, then I chow the fuck down, licking and sucking and slurping, never once thinking about my air supply. Who needs air when you can inhale good pussy?

Ever rides my face, not exactly how she does my dick, but my tongue's a lot shorter than my dick. I can curve it though, which drives her wild.

She's moaning and her movements are getting sloppier, then out of nowhere, she jolts upright like a rocket, leaving my face soaked and my cock hard as brick.

Not this shit again.

I growl. "Ever—"

"I didn't come yet."

I know. I know what my girl's body feels like when she does.

"So what the fu—"

"But I'm about to, and I want to try out another position."

She scrambles off me, earning more growls from me...until she swings her right leg back over my head, straddling me again while facing the opposite direction.

"This way."

If she wanted me to lick her asshole again, all she had to do was say so.

Bending forward, Ever leans all way down to my cock, taking it in her hand and—

Shit! At the feel of her suctioning my tip, my hips buck off the mattress.

"Sixty-nine?"

Mouth full of dick, she hums, "Mm-hm."

Fuck yeah. Let's go.

With Ever's ass above me spread wide, I grip her ass cheeks like handlebars, maneuvering her clit to my mouth so I can pay it special attention.

The combination of her mouth and fist on my cock feels so good, the pressure building and building and building.

I flip us and bury my face in her pussy, triggering deep moans from Ever that vibrate my cock and balls. Still managing to roll her hips, she comes. And I mean she fucking *comes*. Unable to stop myself, I thrust my hips, fucking Ever's mouth with short, hard twitches until I explode, too.

Remembering she also needs to breathe, I pull out almost instantly, a few ropes of my jizz dousing Ever's face.

"Shit. Sorry about that." Not really. I knew she'd look sexy coated in cum.

"It's okay," she pants, waving me off. Then she does something even sexier. Using her middle finger, she pushes my cum between her lips and sucks her digit clean.

If she'd let me, I'd kiss the fuck out of her right now.

Since I know she won't, I settle for cuddling instead.

"So that was new for you, too, sixty-nine?" I ask as we lie side by side, her head on my shoulder.

"Yeah."

"You're not as experienced as you pretend to be, huh?"

She shrugs. "I like having my neck sucked on."

I grit my teeth. A simple yes or no would've sufficed. Unless it's their address, I don't want details about anyone else before me.

"Sometimes that leads to more, sometimes it doesn't. You made assumptions about me, just like my father does, based on the hickeys on my neck. I didn't correct them."

That's not entirely true. She talked like she fucked all the time. She acted like she fucked all the time.

"Why doesn't your dad ever let you go out and do things?"

Ever's quiet for a while before she says, "Same reason he keeps certain motorcycles in the garage."

"Because there's only one of you?" I guess, not completely understanding the comparison. It can't be for safety, otherwise Arthur would've never let his daughter cheer. In just my short glimpse of it, I've seen for myself Ever wasn't exaggerating at all about how dangerous the sport can be.

I admit it. Cheer's a sport. One I find myself enjoying the hell out of the more Ever and I practice together.

"To retain value."

The confusion doesn't clear whatsoever, only intensifies. Ever's a human fucking being. Not a collector's item.

"What age did you start sneaking out?"

"I didn't use to. I was too scared. I only started at the end of last year."

"Why? What changed?"

"Everything."

CHAPTER 44

THE NEXT DAY WHEN WE GO DOWN FOR BREAKFAST, THERE'S a new chef in the kitchen to greet us. Frederick's both older and shorter than Ryan, and has the disposition of an antique teacup.

I like him.

One look at Ever and I can tell she does, too.

After welcoming him to the Munreaux team, I inquire about his living arrangements.

"Mr. Munreaux is graciously allowing me to stay in the guesthouse."

"That's good," I say distractedly, already brainstorming what measures I can take to provide Ever private swimming time. Just because his appearance doesn't scream pervert doesn't mean he's not one. Ryan's had me fooled.

Speaking of…

Since Arthur's not in here, I ask Frederick, "What happened to your predecessor?"

He glances at my scar but I don't so much as flinch. I'm not wearing a hat, and for some reason, I don't feel the need to go get one. I don't even touch my eyebrow. I just focus on Frederick, waiting to hear what he has to say.

"Mr. Koch was just in here packing up some of his things. I believe he's still out front if you'd like to bid him farewell."

That's exactly what I'd like to do.

"Did he…" I go over and check several drawers until I find something that'll work. "He did. He forgot this." I hold up the mallet. "It was a present and he forgot it."

"Oh no," Ever says with zero emotion.

"I'll be right back," I tell her before jogging out front. Still recovering, Arthur and Edwin aren't around, so I don't worry about being discreet when I call out the pervert's name.

He's sitting in the driver's side of a car that costs more than my parents' house, the door still open. When he twists in his seat to address me, one of his hands grips the steering wheel. His right hand, the one he used to jerk himself off to Ever.

Propping my arm on the roof of his car, I lean down, invading his personal space to an uncomfortable level for both of us. Ryan only looks a hair better than Arthur did yesterday.

"Ah, Mr. Brantley. Please, please accept my sincerest apologies regarding the—"

His words turn into screams as I bring the mallet down on his knuckles. Once. Twice. Thrice. I raise it for a fourth, but Ryan whips his hand off the steering wheel.

"Fuck you and fuck your apologies, you rapey fuck." I tap the mallet three times against his forehead, causing him to writhe and beg. "You come anywhere near Ever again and I'll use this to bash your fucking brains in." One more tap, then I stand. "We clear?"

He doesn't answer fast enough, so I smack his cheek with the mallet, much harder than I did his forehead but nothing compared to what I did to his knuckles.

"Are we clear?"

Cradling his hand to his chest, Ryan nods, his face drenched in tears and snot.

"Good. Get the fuck out of here before I change my mind and brain you right now." I could. Thinking about what he might've done to Ever had he made it into her room has me bloodthirsty, and if he doesn't disappear from my sight soon, I will. People already see me as a monster.

I make myself slam the car door shut and step back to watch Ryan drive away, hoping his car's a manual. I didn't even think to check.

I didn't care.

Honestly, he's lucky to be driving away at all.

"So you do know where the trash goes?"

Hearing Ever, I turn back to the manor, finding her at the bottom of the stairs, leaning against one of the motorcycle statues, her arms crossed as she stares at me with mild curiosity.

I'm her monster. I'll do anything for her, including maim any motherfucker that wrongs her…even her father. If it comes to that.

"I figured it out." A little later than I would've liked but I'm just glad Ever did confide in me.

"If you're still in need of some sustenance…" She grins. "…Chef Frederick said breakfast will be ready soon."

"I could eat," I say without specifying what.

Later, when Ever goes out to check on her butterflies, she leaves the conservatory door open after stepping through it.

"I'll be out here," I promise when she glances back at me.

Even though I'm no longer worried about her running off, I still prefer to stick close to her.

"You don't want to come in?"

I regard the building, then her. "Do you want me to?"

For answer, she pushes the door open wider, silently inviting me in.

Inside, I'm immediately met with another door. In the tiny space, Ever explains the need to check for stowaways before leaving, then we go through the second door and it's like being transported to a whole new world.

"Whoa," I breathe as my head falls back to take in everything above us. The air in here is warm and humid, nothing like Connecticut right now. It's also brilliantly green. Green everywhere. Like a tropical rainforest without any predators. Butterflies of all colors and patterns flutter overhead, through trees of all heights, some as tall as the glass ceiling.

There's not a lot of sound in here. A small tinkling from running water maybe. Otherwise, it's like dozens of tiny book pages fluttering.

Ever's watching me closely.

"What do you think?"

"It's magical." There's no other way to describe it in here. It's amazing.

Grinning, she nods before scanning her conservatory like she's trying to see it all from my perspective.

"You never let anyone else in here?"

"Only Edwin when I'm away."

"So why am I here?"

"I need you."

"What do you need me for?" I don't know shit about butterflies.

Her eyes come back to mine.

"You're my security blanket. I only feel safe when I'm around you."

That warms me more than the rays of sunlight piercing the transparent roof.

"You are safe around me," I promise her. "Even from your dad."

"My father?" Her scoff is clearly forced, but it's her hands going behind her back that give her away.

Crowding her, I reach around and grab her hands back there, letting her fidget with mine instead. With the other hand, I rub the side of her hip.

"He was the one making those bruises."

Ever looks down between our bodies, keeping her eyes downcast for longer than necessary.

I release her hip to lift her chin.

Looking in her eyes, I swear to her, "And as long as I'm around, you don't have to worry about him hurting you again."

"He's not—"

"No more lies, butter—"

Ever's eyebrows jolt.

Fuck. I did it again. She's not the butterfly. She couldn't be. She said it herself she didn't go to Hide and Keep.

She also said she started sneaking out at the end of last year. Hide and Keep was at the end of last year. My butterfly disappeared after a helicopter appeared. Arthur denied having a helicopter when it was brought up, but he's a liar. Most of what he's told me about Ever has been false. Even if he doesn't have a helicopter now, that doesn't mean he didn't have one before. He has a helipad in his front yard. Why the fuck would anyone have a helipad in their front yard if they've never owned a helicopter?

"No more lies, bat," I say to try to cover up my mistake.

She drapes her arms on my shoulders, playing with the back of my neck to calm herself.

"I don't want to think about him and what happens when you're not around."

I don't either. It makes me irrationally angry when I do.

"Just be here with me for now. Be my security blanket."

"I'm your everything."

She cracks the kind of smile I would love to feel against my own.

Tearing my eyes off it, I ask, "What can I help with in here?"

Ever leads me around, letting me help with some of her tasks. While we work, she teaches me about the butterfly life cycle, pointing out any chrysalides she spots.

If this is another world, Ever's another girl in it. She's intelligent, patient, enthusiastic, and happy. So damn happy. Maybe even happier than when we're in my room.

That is until we come across a dead butterfly, then Ever's entire demeanor changes as she stops to pick it up.

"White peacock," she mutters as she cradles it gently in her palms. I'm not sure if that's its name or the kind though. It's white with light brown markings that somewhat resemble a peacock's, so it's probably the kind.

"I'm sorry," I tell Ever quietly, to which she shakes her head.

"It's natural. Everything dies at some point."

"It doesn't make it any less sad."

Ever doesn't respond as she studies the dead butterfly.

"Did your dad really kill your mom?" I ask.

"Depends on how you look at it."

"How do *you* look at it?"

"I look at it…" She peeks at me very briefly before continuing, "As my mother killed herself. Mostly. But my father's partly to blame, as am I."

"Why the hell would you think you're to blame?"

"My mother escaped to Martha's Vineyard every summer, like clockwork, and at the end of every August, my father and I would go meet with her, stay in our house there for a weekend, maybe take the yacht out, before bringing her back to Connecticut with us. As much as I'd like to think those trips were to escape my father, I know they were to escape me, too. We weren't close. We didn't talk about normal mother-daughter stuff. We didn't really talk at all. We played from time to time, but that was it."

"Played?"

"She was depressed. Severely. I'm assuming anyway, because no one ever told me what the issue was. But during the rare times when she wasn't…down, I guess…she was pretty emotionally immature. She never wanted to do anything she deemed hard."

"Having a kid is hard."

"She had me, but she didn't raise me. My nanny raised me. My mother only played with me when the mood struck."

That's really fucking weird. Children aren't toys.

"What would you play?"

"I don't know. Kid stuff. Imaginary stuff. We would play hide-and-seek in the maze out front for hours."

"Yeah?"

She nods, a small grin moving her lips. "As long as I was 'it,' she would play for hours. She would say 'look for me,' then go hide."

As nice a memory as that may be, there are some glaring issues with it. Ever's mom was troubled. Nothing that she's shared so far sounds normal. I know some wealthy people "summer" other places, but leaving their own kids behind to do it? I've never heard of that shit before. Also, what adult never takes a turn being "it"?

"It doesn't sound like you're to blame for her death at all. It sounds like she was incredibly selfish."

Her face loses some of its shine.

"She had an incredible daughter that she had absolutely nothing to do with except when it benefitted her. That's not a parent, Ever, that's a narcissist." The same could be said about Arthur. Actually, I'll say it—Arthur's not a parent. He's a narcissist. "If Alette Munreaux really did kill herself, that was about her, too. Not you."

"She didn't stay for me though."

"Doesn't make it any more your fault than that butterfly's death does." I nod at her hands.

"Doesn't make it any less sad either," she repeats my words.

"No, it doesn't." Coming to terms with the fact that Yasmin's death wasn't my fault hasn't made the loss any less sad for me, or in general. Loss is tragic, no matter what the circumstances are.

While Ever disposes of the butterfly, I take a seat on the bench by the pond. Feeling eyes on me, I look down to find one of the orange fishes staring up at me, its mouth in an expectant O at the surface. We hold a bit of a staring contest until a white butterfly with orange wing tips enters my vision. It lands on my thigh, so I try not to make any sudden movements.

I've never had a butterfly on me. It's kinda cool. They look so small and fragile yet fly out in the open, leaving themselves open to a number of dangers, then will land in precarious places like a grown man.

Reminds me of my flyer.

I watch as she returns.

"I think your fish is hungry," I tell her.

Ever mutters something about it always being hungry, then flits around, checking on things, before disappearing into a small back room. A minute later, she's back with a tub of what appear to be pellets.

As soon as she approaches the pond, *all* the fish swarm to her, their mouths open and waiting.

She tosses some of the pellets in, chuckling when the fish splash in their fight to get food.

Holding out the bucket to me, she offers to let me feed them, but I shake my head, more invested in watching her.

"Great orange tip," she says, nodding at the butterfly on my leg and setting the bucket by her feet.

Even though she didn't have the greatest examples of caretakers, Ever still became one herself. Her bats, her fish, her butterflies—Ever cares for them all, deeply. But only when she's out of the public eye.

In the public eye, she's nothing like this. It's like all those designer clothes are her costumes to support her role.

Costumes…

My butterfly's costume at Hide and Keep was elaborate. She even had contacts in. And a mask. The makeup and wig looked like professionals applied them.

None of that is unusual for Hide and Keep. Some people go all out. And plenty of them want to keep their identities hidden.

But my butterfly went the extra mile to ensure she couldn't be identified. She didn't even speak.

Who would want to do that?

Who would *need* to do that?

A girl who can't be herself around her own friends? A girl so known, she can't go anywhere without being recognized? A girl disobeying her powerful father's orders by sneaking out?

My butterfly was short and petite.

So is my little bat.

My butterfly was daring but in an inexperienced way.

So is my little bat.

My butterfly kissed me.

My little bat…won't. And she doesn't have a real excuse why she won't either, at least not one she's willing to share with me.

Did Ever technically say she didn't go to Hide and Keep? Or did she just use evasion as a way not to answer?

"Do you have any monarchs in here?" I ask despite spotting several already.

Ever's gaze shoots to my tattoo, so I twist my arm to give her a better view. She immediately looks away though.

"Probably," she says noncommittally, suddenly silent on the subject when all she's done since we stepped foot in here is talk about butterflies. All of them except for monarchs.

Now why is that?

"Tell me something about monarchs."

"Um…" She keeps her focus locked on the feeding frenzy. "They're beautiful."

"That's an understatement," I say without taking my eyes off her. "What else?"

"They're interesting."

Another understatement.

"What's so interesting about them?"

"Uh, let's see. Eastern monarchs do this insane migration every year to reproduce. It spans from Mexico all the way up to the Canadian border. After hibernating all winter on trees in certain Mexican forests, they wake up in the spring and mate before heading north to reproduce. Then in the fall, their great-grandchildren, with no one to guide them, no map to use, nothing to go off of besides some sort of inherited internal GPS, return to the same forests to hibernate."

"How come their great-grandparents don't go back with them?"

"Their great-grandparents aren't alive by then. During the trip, monarchs only live between two and six weeks, so the entire migration cycle usually takes about four generations to complete. The monarchs that hibernate over the winter can live up to nine months, but once they lay those first eggs in the spring, they die shortly after."

"Shit. I had no idea."

"Doesn't surprise me. Most people don't." Ever shakes her head.

During the motion, I catch a glimpse of orange and black on the back of her head and it's like I'm seeing her for the first time all over again. Not Ever Munreaux. My butterfly.

"What's something else most people don't know about monarchs?" I ask.

The great orange tip takes flight when I stand up.

"They can mate up to sixteen hours."

"Sixteen *hours?*"

Ever jolts at my voice, at my proximity. She tries to play it off by smiling but it doesn't reach her eyes.

"You can grab a handful," she says, talking about the fish food.

Instead of doing that, I grab her face, careful of the monarch on her hair, and turn her to me. Both my thumbs on her cheeks, I run my eyes over her face, searching for the similarities now that I know what I'm looking for.

It's all so fucking clear. Her reaction when she first saw me in her father's office. Her many drawings of me. Her refusal to kiss me. It's the only identifier I got from her that night.

I hinge one thumb over to cover her mouth like I always do. I don't kiss her though. I massage her lips with the pad.

Another memory loses its haze, sharpening in stark clarity without a filter of delirium over it.

"I'm begging. Kiss me, Crue."

Hide and Keep wasn't the only time our lips have met. Ever used her mouth to feed charcoal into mine when I was sick. That's why my vomit was black. That's why I felt better faster. She used it to counteract the poison.

Then she hid it from me, so I wouldn't try to kiss her again when I was healthy and discover who she really is.

I return my thumb to her cheek and lean in until our mouths are only inches apart. Ever's jaw clenches in my hold and my name climbs its way through her teeth.

"Yes, butterfly?" The nickname comes out naturally, because it's her. It's always been her.

"What? That's..." A million and one emotions flash across her face. "Why would you call me that?"

"It was you. The butterfly at Hide and Keep."

Another butterfly stops for a rest on one of my knuckles, its wings black with yellow stripes.

"I don't know what you're talking about. I wouldn't be caught dead at something as desperate as Hide and Keep."

Not dead but she was caught. I caught her. And I have every intention of keeping her…after I figure out how.

"Then kiss me."

"Why?"

"Kiss me, Ever. Prove to me you're not my butterfly."

"Crue. I'm not… I can't…"

"What's the big deal? You kissed me the other night."

That gets her to drop at least some of the act.

Her eyes also drop…to my shoulder.

She scoffs quietly. "Blue morpho. Of course one comes to you."

I side-eye the blue butterfly on my shoulder before quickly returning my attention to an even more beautiful butterfly. The *most* beautiful butterfly.

"You remember the charcoal?" she asks.

"I remember you. Your lips on mine."

"It wasn't like that. I was just doing what I could to help."

"I know." I pull her closer and lower my voice. "But I want it to be like that. I want your lips on mine again." I want her lips on mine forever. "Not just in sickness, but also in health, and everything in between."

"Crue…"

"Why didn't you tell me, butterfly?"

At first, I think she's gonna keep up the ruse, but then she says, "Because I'm different…than that. I'm…not…"

"I know exactly who you are."

"Really? Because I don't even think I do."

"You can be soft and sweet or intense and cruel. Your shine is unmistakable, yet you prefer the dark. You're fearless and graceful, like a butterfly. You're intelligent and selfless, like a bat." Ever's been telling me some wild facts about bats, like how deeply they feel emotions, even grief and joy, as well as how altruistic they can be. "You're multifaceted, Ever Munreaux. You're also mine. My butterfly *and* my little bat."

A single tear escapes the corner of her eye, rolling down onto the tip of my thumb.

"I'm sorry. I just wanted you to have the memory of how I was that night without who I usually am ruining it."

Her head in my palms, I keep her from lowering it to search those watery eyes.

"Ever, you're better than you think. You're better than everyone thinks. You're better than an anonymous kiss in the dark. Ruin the fucking memory…" I draw her even closer. "Just like you ruined me."

She's the one that closes the final inch, crushing my lips with hers.

I'm the one who deepens it though, sneaking my tongue inside like she sneaks into my room—unapologetically.

While she tastes exactly like I remember, her skill isn't the same at all. She wasn't a bad kisser at Hide and Keep, just lacked experience. She's definitely improved since that night. She's no longer hesitant or self-conscious. She knows what she's doing now, along with what she wants.

I'm so fucking glad it's me.

Relocating my hands to just under her ass, I pick her up off her feet. She wraps her legs around my waist and leans back, sending the butterflies on us flying. We both look up to watch them join all the others. It's a kaleidoscope of color and activity above us and around us.

My gaze falls to Ever so I can watch her instead. At no point in my life could I have guessed I'd be here, in a private butterfly conservatory, holding Munreaux Motorcycles' heiress, deeply, *deeply* in love with her. Ever worked so hard to make me hate her. But falling for her was effortless. I was already face-first at her Louboutin-covered feet before I even realized I'd fallen.

"You're magical," I rasp, pulling her attention back to me.

She grips the back of my neck and meets my stare with an equally intense one of her own. Does she love me?

Only one way to find out.

"And I think I'm in love with you."

Her laugh tinkles like the lightest bell chime, then she's saying, "You think? I *know* I'm in love with you."

She pulls me or I pull her, I don't know, but suddenly we're kissing again and it's magical, too.

As long as I live, nothing will ever top this moment. I want to live it over and over and over again.

"What are you doing for the next sixteen hours?" I ask the second we break for air.

With a smile like the Grand Canyon and eyes so bright they're practically sparkling, she says, "You."

CHAPTER 45

"**A**RE WE EVER GOING TO GET TO SEE YOU AGAIN?" CRUE'S mother, Phoebe, asks, her voice coming through my car's speakers.

Crue shakes his head. "It's only been one month, Mom."

I love listening to their conversations. They're never long but they're always a surprise. Phoebe really does care about her son. She checks up on him all throughout the week.

"It feels like it's been forever."

Even without seeing her, I can sense her misery. To her, it does feel like forever. She genuinely misses her son.

A knife twists in my gut. My mother spent entire summers away from me and not once did she call to check on me, and certainly not to complain about the time apart. She didn't care and she never missed me. My father, I understand, but me? Why didn't she miss me? I was just a child. I wasn't bad. I didn't talk back. I played any game she wanted to, whenever she wanted to, for however long she wanted to. I would've done anything to make her love me. Or even just like me.

Crue takes a right into my neighborhood using only one hand. I love when he drives one-handed. I'm going to miss watching him drive. I'm going to miss watching him.

"Maybe this weekend I can stop by the house to pick up some more stuff," Crue offers while shooting me a questioning look.

He's so hopeful. So ignorant.

I make myself nod, then drop my gaze. Crue will be returning to his childhood home this weekend…whether he wants to or not.

Focusing on the amethyst bracelet on my wrist, my other hand finds my throat, my thumb and middle finger gripping the sides as my palm massages the center.

I don't know how I'm supposed to live without him. He hasn't even left yet and I'm already having difficulty breathing.

This entire last week of classes, I've had a lump in my throat that no amount of water's been able to get down. If I didn't have a body-guard adamantly opposed to truancy, I would've skipped them all. I'm one hundred percent confident I would've passed them regardless—not like it'd affect anything even if I didn't—but with each class finished, that lump seemed to increase in size, and now that my classes are over, it's nearly clogging my airway.

I'd rather the noose than this feeling. This is from the inside. This is me. I'm doing it. My body is killing me.

I can't fucking breathe.

If this is a glimpse of what life without Crue will be like, I don't want it.

Unfortunately, I never get what I want, only what I don't.

Except for when I'm with Crue, then I get pretty much whatever I want.

I have to tell him.

I don't know what to tell him.

"Ooh, that would be lovely," Phoebe croons. "Dad was just saying how nice this weekend's supposed to be. Maybe we can have a beach day."

"We're not gonna be there that long."

"We? Your…protectee…has to come, too?"

Squeezing my thigh, Crue chuckles. "We do everything together."

I envision it happening, all of it—meeting Crue's parents, letting him give me a tour of his home, us all going to the beach together… like a family.

I tear my attention from the purple beads to regard Crue again.

"What if we went today?"

Today might be all we have left.

"Today?" he mouths, then says, "It's your last day."

"Last day of what?" his mother questions.

"Classes. My *protectee*..." He rolls his eyes for my benefit. "...finished her first year of college today."

Last year of college, technically, but I can't tell him that. What *can* I tell him? We're running out of time and I still don't know.

There's a long pause before Phoebe says, "I bet it'll be nice to have the summer off from enduring that every day."

"It's fine," Crue says way too quickly. "I'll, um, call you later, okay?"

"Okay." His mother sighs. "I love you. Be safe."

"Love you, too."

Another twist of the knife. They say it to each other so easily. No hesitation, no calculation. Just real emotion, real connection, real love.

"Why can't we go over there today?"

"I just figured you'd want to celebrate."

"What? Like with a party? My father would never—"

He scoffs. "I know. I know he wouldn't. It's just... It's a big accomplishment. Not everybody makes it to college."

Crue didn't.

I hadn't considered how difficult it's been for him having to go to Littoral every day.

"You could still go, you know. Considering the human brain isn't fully developed until twenty-five, it'd probably be more beneficial for you to attend college now that yours is."

"The schools around here..." Instead of finishing that thought, Crue just shakes his head.

"You don't have to stay in Sea Haven. You can go to any college in the country."

It's a while before Crue responds.

"I'll think about it...in three years...when I can afford to."

Now I'm the quiet one.

"So, about tonight..."

"What kind of celebration did you have in mind, Major?"

I don't want to go anywhere outside of this cocoon Crue and I have built for ourselves.

Ryan's finally gone, my father's been too busy getting caught up from his unexpected sick leave to even be around at mealtimes, Crue is…everything. When I'm not in class, we've either been running or swimming or stunting, or in the atrium, his bed, or shower. He's become my partner, my best friend, my lover, my everything.

"We can have Frederick make a clafoutis tart and eat it while watching a movie," Crue suggests as we pull up the winding driveway to Munreaux Manor.

A clafoutis tart?

"How did you—"

"Ryan told me. It's the only good thing he did."

That and leave.

"In your room or the theater?"

"'The theater,'" he mocks, but I can't laugh because the manor comes into view and with it, Edwin. He's standing out front, waiting.

Why is he waiting?

At the sight of my father's valet, Crue instantly removes his hand from my thigh, returning it to his own with a muttered, "What does Eddy want?"

Ticktock.

I contemplate grabbing that hand and telling Crue everything, to hell with the consequences, but I *can't*. It won't make any difference anyway.

The whole time he's putting my heels on, I study Edwin. His eyes do not touch on us once, yet I know with absolute certainty that he's out here for us. For me.

"I need to go to the atrium," I announce loudly as soon as I'm out of the car, Crue beside me.

Without missing a beat, Edwin steps forward. "Miss Munreaux, if you could follow me, please. Your father would like a word."

"I need to check on my butterflies," I repeat with a tremble in my voice.

"I can do that for you."

"No. I—"

"Your father insists." With that, Edwin spins, leaving me no choice but to follow.

"I'll come with," Crue assures me, but Edwin hears.

Over his shoulder, he says, "That won't be necessary. Mr. Munreaux does not require your assistance in this matter."

My heart starts racing. What matter? It's only Friday. I was hoping I had another day. I was counting on having another day. I need another day. I…want another day.

Ticktock. Ticktock.

Damn it. I'm not going to get another day. I should've known. I should've prepared for this. I was too blinded by all the good, I didn't want to plan for the bad. I purposely shoved it away, out of my mind, so I could be fully present with Crue and just enjoy my time with him. I knew it was fleeting. I knew the end was coming.

But like Crue said, it doesn't make it any less sad.

I muster up a soft smile for him, but not empty promises. I don't know if it'll be okay. I don't know if this will be over quickly. I don't know if I'll ever see him again.

I don't know anything…except that I love Crue more than drawing, more than butterflies, more than the feeling I get when I'm airborne because he makes me feel free and loved and needed all the time, not just momentarily.

That's exactly what this was though—momentary. Now comes the plunge back to earth, back to reality.

Entering my father's study, all he says is, "Close the door on your way out," to Edwin.

"What did you want to see me about, Father?" I ask as demurely as I can.

"We'll be leaving for Nantucket tonight."

"Why?"

"There are things you need to do. Tasks you must complete. Decisions you must make. It'd look bad if you weren't. For you, for everyone. You need to be there."

"What can I do to change your mind?" I ask him.

His eyes glued to his computer screen, he releases a hearty laugh, one I haven't heard before, more of a guffaw.

"You have a lot to learn when it comes to negotiations, my dear."

"I'm not your dear."

"No, but you are my greatest disappointment."

"Then why—"

"Because this is all you're good for."

I can't stop that knife from earlier plunging all the way in, catching more than one vital organ. I'm not killing me. He is. He's responsible for my mother's death and he'll be responsible for mine.

"I'll give you anything. I'll do anything. I just… Give me one more night." Screw negotiations. I'm desperate. "Please, Father."

"One more night to do what? Run away? Fill your belly with some bastard child I'll be forced to cut out of you myself? I wasn't born yesterday, Never. We'll depart as soon as it's dark enough. End of conversation."

A tornado of white-hot rage swirls inside me faster and faster, building bigger and bigger, until there's nowhere else for it to go but out.

"Why? Why can't you let me have this one thing? I ask you for nothing! Nothing! Grant me this *one* fucking wish and I'll do whatever you want for the rest of my Goddess-forsaken life!"

Finally, he looks directly at me. "What has you so emotional?"

"You mean other than you commandeering my entire future?"

"Commandeering? I have no need to commandeer that which I already own. From the moment you were born with the last name Munreaux, your future's belonged to me. No, this little outburst of yours is something different. Something deeper."

He's right. I am too emotional. I'm usually the opposite around him.

I immediately attempt to rein in the twister churning all around outside of me, stuffing it back inside, under the perfectly put-together outfit and flawless makeup. I even raise my chin for good measure.

"What do you expect? My life as I know it is over and you're not even giving me enough time to mourn it properly."

"You've had nineteen years to mourn it."

"That's not true. I only became aware of your plan last year."

"Now you see, that's what makes you my greatest disappointment. You should've been prepared all along for your servitude to Munreaux Motorcycles."

"That's why? I thought it was because I let the entire O-line of Littoral's football team run a train on me."

Surging to his feet, he slaps me across the face, making my head whip to the right, my brain feeling like it's between the prongs of a tuning fork after it's been struck. My head is vibrating.

At least my lie worked. Now he's the emotional one.

Vision blurred and ears ringing, I slowly turn back to face my flushed father, his finger already thrust at me as he fumes, "You will learn to hold your tongue or you'll find yourself without one!"

Since the idea of bleeding out from a severed tongue sounds a thousand times better than going to that island this weekend, I snark right back, "But won't my new—"

Crack!

The violent sound has me bracing for the second slap but nothing comes.

I glance over my shoulder to see the door open, almost at an unnatural angle—half hanging off its hinges maybe. Crue's lowering his foot to the floor just before he storms into my father's study, his face red as well.

Wiping the tears off my cheeks, I face forward again to hide the left side of my face from my bodyguard.

"Mr. Brantley!" Edwin calls after him, hot on his heels. "I apologize, Mr. Munreaux. I tried to stop him."

Father puts up a hand to silence his valet.

"I hate to interrupt," Crue says, zero pleasantry in his tone whatsoever. "But Ever has an appointment she can't be late for."

"Ever?"

Crue tries to correct his mistake too late by saying, "Miss Munreaux."

When he latches on to my forearm and pulls, I lean the opposite way.

Stop, stop, stop, stop, stop. Please just fucking stop. I don't care what my father says to me. I don't care what my father does to me. I only care about what he can, and will, do to Crue if he finds out we're together.

"Yes… Miss Munreaux…" my father parrots, his narrowed gaze alternating between me, my bodyguard, and his hold on me.

Shit. He already knows. Or at the very least, suspects.

I rip my arm from Crue's with a disgusted scoff.

He tries for me again, so I take a step away from him, out of reach.

"Enough to kick my door down?"

"It's important," is all Crue offers for explanation. No apology, nothing.

Father studies us for another minute before saying, "Whatever appointment my daughter has, cancel it. Never's busy this weekend."

"What's going on this weekend?" Crue asks.

"That no longer concerns you."

Here it comes. The snip severing all ties between me and Crue.

I grip the edge of the desk for support and hold my breath, wishing that lump in my throat would expand right this second to keep me from having to say what needs to be said next. This is going to hurt and not just me.

"As Miss Munreaux's personal protection agent, all her whereabouts are my concern."

"Not anymore, they're not."

"Sir? I was hired to get her through school. She's not done—"

"Oh, yes, she is. Today marks the last day of her college career."

I can *feel* the weight of Crue's stare on the right side of my face.

"But…she still has three years left."

"Three years? Munreaux Motorcycles doesn't have that kind of time. We need this now."

A shake of my head causes me to lose consciousness briefly. How hard did he hit me?

"You actually thought it was for three years?" I taunt with laughter I can't seem to control. Or hear.

Crue steps forward, into my right eye's periphery, but I don't let myself move a single muscle to see him better. If I do, he might see *me* better.

"You knew it wasn't?"

That I can hear just fine. The betrayal.

"Never didn't tell you?" my father asks Crue.

"Of course I didn't," I'm quick to answer. "I wouldn't tell this renta-cop wannabe if his ass was on fire."

Even with one fuzzy eye, I can see the pain slash across Crue's face, leaving behind a deeper cut than that airbag ever could.

Ripping his attention off me, Crue tells my father, "She's nowhere near ready to run your company yet."

It won't make a difference. Nothing will. His decision's been made for months. Years. Since my birth, apparently.

I am like veal, raised only for the slaughter.

Father pretends to mull that over before ordering Edwin, "See that Mr. Brantley signs the necessary paperwork before vacating the premises."

He's fired. We're over. This is the only goodbye we'll ever get. And if I want there to be as little damage as possible to Crue, I have to make this believable.

"I told you I'd send you back to where you belong," I singsong as if I wanted this. As if I couldn't be happier about this.

Crue crowds me from the side to sneer, "It's funny, *Never*…"

I fight not to wince at the name. I fight not to react at all, but it's like I can feel every cell in my body calling to his. My body *burns* to lean into his.

Lowering his voice, he finishes near my ear, "I thought that's where you belonged, too."

I do belong with you, I long to say, to shout, to etch onto my skin and heart and bones for all of eternity because it's true. I've always felt like an outsider in my own circle, in my own house, in my own life.

In Crue's arms is the only place I feel like I'm where I'm supposed to be, where I feel like I'm home.

Father's gaze drilling into mine, I reply to Crue without looking at him, "The reeking shack? Please. I've driven by salt marshes that smelled better than your little hovel by the sea."

My father makes a terrible sound in his throat. "That's why we live up here, away from the odor."

Although he could easily be referring to the coastal wetlands that stink like rotten eggs, I know Arthur Munreaux better than that. He's talking about the people. The lower class. Crue.

My Crue.

Nose stinging, I wave a hand under it.

"Edwin, can you take out the trash already? I've been counting down the days to be rid of his stink."

"Right this way, Mr. Brantley."

Crue doesn't budge.

"Let the door hit you on your way out," I tell him, adding a dismissive flutter of my shaky fingers. *Go.*

"You're intolerable," he grits, the emotion still evident in his tone.

I know. I know! I'm sorry. I'm so, so sorry.

"And you're trespassing. Leave."

I feel the air pouring from his nostrils.

Don't do it. Don't say anything damning. Please. I'm fucking begging.

"You're not gonna see me off?"

He's begging now, too. But I can't give in. I can't. I warned him. We were never going to last.

The final nail in the coffin, I close my eyes.

Just go.

Finally, Crue's body heat recedes, then I hear him stalk away.

Opening my eyes, I spin around in time to just make out his back disappearing through the doorway that has shards of wood sticking out of it.

Look for me. Look for me!

"Better luck guarding the cornstalks!" I yell after him, equally hoping he comes back and that he doesn't.

Just the two of us once again, my father says, "For a moment there, I was worried you were sullying yourself with the help."

"I do have some standards, Father."

"Like the O-line of the football team?"

"Football team of an Ivy."

"Fair point. Now…let's go over expectations for this weekend… as well as after."

Rotating my head over my shoulder, I skim the list filling the screen on the wall, my stomach roiling at the adjectives jumping out at me. None of them describe me. Or even a human. They're more fitting for a robot. A submissive, emotionless robot.

I'm not a robot though. I'm a flyer. That's exactly what I'm going to do.

Except this time, there won't be anybody to catch me.

CHAPTER 46

Crue

WHAT...

What just happened?

I can't stop my hands from shaking, the tremors making their way up my arms as I stare down at the bed. The bed Ever and I have been sharing for weeks but will never get to again.

Never?

Never.

That's what I called her in there. In there... What was that in there? With my ears trained on Arthur's office, the moment I heard his voice rise, I lost it. I fucking lost it. I knew going in there like that would put my job at risk, I just didn't care. All I cared about was getting to Ever—*protecting* Ever.

And now I can't even do that. I can't protect Ever from anyone, or anything.

I grind my jaw until I taste dust. I can't protect Ever.

I hear a knock accompanied with a "Mr. Brantley, would you like some assistance?"

Edwin's out there, waiting for me to pack my belongings. But all I can do is replay Ever's words. Her actions. Her animosity toward me. Over and over again.

It was like we were right back at the beginning again. What she said... How she behaved... It couldn't have been true, could it? Did

Ever actually mean any of that shit? Or was she just acting for Arthur's sake?

That's the sad part—I can't even tell. I can't fucking tell and now…

Now it doesn't matter. I'm fired. I'm done. I'm leaving. Forever.

Fuck!

I stuff some clothes in my duffle bag.

Why didn't Ever warn me? She knew. Supposedly.

Did she know?

"I'm not graduating, Crue Brantley. You might as well walk away now."

She did. She fucking knew. And she didn't say a word.

"I told you. I'm. Not. Graduating."

She said some words, but not all of them. Not enough of them. How was I supposed to know what that meant? Ever was dramatic as fuck when I first got here. She said and did anything to try to get rid of me.

I thought that was behind us though. I thought she loved me. I thought…a lot of things. I thought we had time. More than a few weeks.

All she had to do was correct one of the hundreds of times I talked about spending the next three years here. But she didn't. She stayed silent, letting me believe we had more time together than we did.

Why would she do that? She loves me. She said she loves me.

But…she's a liar. I've known that.

What else has she been keeping from me?

I eye the door between our rooms. I've only been in hers twice. Once on my own, which she did not appreciate, then again after I found out about the secret door. She didn't seem to appreciate that time either, even though we were on much better terms—in love. Allegedly. Always having her in my room was enough, so I didn't push her on it. I should've. Obviously, she's hiding something in there.

I tell Edwin, "No, I got it," then I'm opening the door to Ever's room the next instant, entering the dark space. Under her bed, I find the same sketchbooks as last time, only fuller now. I get hung up flipping through the latest additions. They're all of me, some of them while I'm asleep. She drew me when I was asleep? I had no idea.

The way she sees me, it's nothing like how she just spoke to me. Or about me. She called me trash. Told Edwin to throw me away.

Edwin. Shit. I need to hurry.

I search Ever's closet again. It looks similar to last time…except for the mysterious black lump in the corner. Lifting it up, I examine the material, recognizing it as the dress she wore to dinner that night the Larsons came over. Or it was that dress. Now it's just a mess of ruined fabric. Ripped all the way up the front, it'd show her pussy if she tried wearing it again.

I frown.

How'd that happen?

I think back to that night. I didn't see the front of her dress after dinner. It was so dark because of the faulty lights, I barely saw any of the dress.

The lights… The same ones that haven't given out since. I assumed because Edwin fixed them, but now I'm questioning that, too. I'm questioning everything.

Did Ever turn the lights off so I wouldn't see? She's a very talented liar. I've believed her for less.

Ever didn't seem like herself that night. That's the only thing I know for a fact. But was that because she'd just gotten fucked, willingly? Or because that motherfucker…

I can't even think it. I can't even *think* what Mallory Larson might've done to make Ever's dress look like this. It's in tatters.

Was it wanted or not?

I squeeze the material, releasing an odor like mildew. Ever does like moss and other nature stuff, but her clothes are always pristine. So why not this dress? What happened to it?

And why is it stuffed in the back of her closet? There's a dry-cleaning truck here every few days. She could've had it cleaned, possibly even repaired by now if she wanted.

I'll probably never know for sure. How would I? Even if I did get to see Ever again, which to be honest is the biggest stretch of all time after that cold-hearted castoff downstairs, I can't believe anything she says. I can't. I thought I could. I tried.

Fuck. I did. I believed her when she said she loved me. And that was after she admitted to keeping her identity from me.

She kept so much from me. So fucking much. Why? *Why?* What the fuck did she have to gain from constantly hiding shit from me?

Was it all a game? Was I just a goddamn game to her?

That's how it seems. That's how it feels, like I got played by a spoiled little rich girl with nothing better to do, no one else to…play with. Damn. I did get played. She's just like her mom. Emotionally immature. Narcissistic. Dead. To me at least.

I'm fucking done.

"Maybe it's a blessing in disguise," my mom offers.

Sitting next to her on the couch, my dad bobs his head. "The Munreauxs…have a reputation."

I fucking snort. I know. I was the one hired to protect it.

"So do I," I say, making the living room go silent. They know it's true. They're the ones who suffered right along with me, getting judgmental stares, callous comments, even death threats. They got so bad following Yasmin's passing, my parents had to get an alarm installed on the house. They've been paying for standing by me ever since.

After several minutes, my mom sighs. "You'll bounce back, honey. You always do."

Exactly. I've been bouncing from one assignment to another, never stopping to appreciate…anything. Not even my support system.

"Thanks, Mom," I tell her seriously. "You, too, Dad. I don't know what I would've done without you guys."

"Probably something rash and irreversible," my dad says, referencing the darkest time of my life—my senior year. I'd lost everything, or what I felt was everything, and I just wanted it to end. I even told my parents I was considering ending it myself, ending…myself. If it wasn't for their unconditional love and support, I would've.

"Probably," I confirm quietly, my thoughts, as usual, going back to Ever. She has no support system whatsoever, nothing to keep her from doing anything rash and irreversible. She had me though. I kept her safe.

Now she doesn't have me and I have no purpose. Again.

"I'm gonna go to bed."

Zeus's head lifts to watch me pop up from my spot on the floor.

"Stay here, buddy," I tell him. I need some alone time. I'm severely deficient in alone time.

"It's not even seven o'clock yet," my mom complains.

"I'm exhausted," I say, surprised to find I actually mean it.

I feel my parents' stares, as well as our dog's, all the way down the hall.

As soon as I flop on my bed, my phone chimes, and I have to flip to my back so I can pull it out of my pocket.

Ever's door.

Damn it. I forgot to turn those off.

My thumb's hovering over the settings when another notification comes through, this one for her window.

So she went straight through her room to her window and is probably leaving out it right now…

That's great. Fine. Let her sneak out. Like Arthur said, his daughter is no longer my concern.

I toss my phone to the end of my bed, out of reach.

Unfortunately, the move doesn't keep my mind from returning to Ever and where she might be going. A party? Now that I'm not there to keep her company, to entertain her, she's forced to seek amusement elsewhere.

Probably. That's probably where she's going. That's where she went before I moved in.

Parting my knees, I stare at the device down by my feet.

As long as she's still wearing that purple bracelet, I could find out exactly where she's going.

I slam my knees shut, cutting off my view.

That's the luxury of being unemployed. I don't *have* to worry about that kind of stuff anymore. I'm not being paid to care about Ever Munreaux's whereabouts, so I don't. I do not fucking care. She can go out right this minute and get fucked seven different ways, all of them new and different and new and—

Fuck!

I catapult my top half off the mattress, my elbows on my knees, my hands in fists on top of my ankles as I try to keep myself from grabbing my phone and checking her location. It's better not to know. It's better not to care. Which I don't. I don't fucking care about her.

Except…

What if that's not where she's going? What if she's coming…here? For me. She knows where I live. She could show up at my front door and apologize, tell me she didn't mean anything she said. And I'd…

What? Accept that?

No. She doesn't deserve my forgiveness that easily.

But if she did show up, I'd be willing to at least hear her out.

Is she willing to come clean?

I guess I'll have to see when she gets here. *If* she gets here.

I press my palms into my hairline hoping it'll push Ever Munreaux from my head.

She's not coming. She's the one that doesn't care. If she did, she would've said *something,* given me *some* kind of heads-up, *anything.* She didn't. She wouldn't even *look* at me.

We were fine until we pulled up—

When we pulled up…

When we pulled up, Ever stopped meeting my eyes the moment Edwin intercepted her. And she didn't seem like she even wanted to go with the valet. It's not surprising considering who he was taking her to—her abuser.

I snatch my phone up. I shouldn't have left her there.

Immediately opening the tracker app, I go right for Ever's location. She's still on the property. I'm worrying for nothing. She's probably just out for a run, burning off some of the frustration that comes with dealing with Arthur Munreaux.

Except her dot isn't moving. It's stationary as all fuck, even after I refresh the app several times. It *looks* like she's at the cliff, just sitting there, contemplating, possibly doing something…rash and irreversible.

Shit!

I scramble off my bed and burst out into the hall while trying to get one shoe on at a time, bouncing off the walls like a goddamn ping-pong ball.

"Where are you going?" my mom calls after me, but I'm already out the front door and remote-starting my Bronco.

The dot looks like it's at the edge of the cliff but what if Ever's not? What if she's already at the bottom?

CHAPTER 47

FUCK, FUCK, FUCK, FUCK, FUCK.

Only a slight hesitation, then I'm up on the curb, plowing into the Munreauxs' forest. I'm not parking on the street. It'll take too long to run through the woods and I need to get to Ever now.

I don't know what she's thinking, if she is at all, but she can't go over that edge. I stopped her once. I'll stop her again.

Please let me get to her in time to stop her, I send up to whoever, or whatever, might be listening. *Just keep her feet on the ground until I get there.*

Eventually, the trees become too tightly packed for me to fit between, forcing me to have to park halfway to the cliff. Leaving my car running, I throw the door open and take off, my legs pumping faster and harder than any of my runs with Ever. All those sprints trying to catch up to her were preparing me for this moment. I have to make it to her in time. I can't live in a world that doesn't have Ever Munreaux in it. I would rather spend the rest of my life hating her than one moment mourning her. I fucking reject that possibility.

Up ahead, I see a figure, and somehow dig deeper, making my legs go even faster. I explode out of the tree line with a frantic "Ever! Stop!"

Standing *way* too close to the edge, Ever startles, nearly giving me a heart attack. A few more inches and she'll tumble right over.

"What are you doing here, Crue?" Her voice is full of tears. And if I could see her face, I'm sure I'd find her eyes are, too.

Out of breath, I suck in two huge lungfuls of air before gasping, "You. I'm here for you."

She looks over her right shoulder at me, confirming my suspicion. She's been crying.

"Ever."

I start for her, but she lifts a palm my way.

"Don't. Don't come near me or I'll jump."

"All right." I put my hands up where she can see them, hopefully so she won't notice my feet that haven't stopped moving toward her and won't because my fucking ass she's jumping off that cliff.

"I mean it, Crue. Don't get any closer."

I freeze.

"Come to me then."

She shakes her head. "I can't do that, Major."

"Yes, you can. You're Ever Munreaux. You can do anything you set your mind to."

Her laugh is like nails on a chalkboard, there's nothing pleasant about it. "You have *no* idea who I am."

"I know you're my flyer and the only flying you do is above my head."

Rotating back toward the sea, she says, "Not anymore."

I shuffle a few feet in her direction, my voice taking on a hardness I haven't had to use with her in a while. "Get away from the edge, Ever."

"I won't."

"Get away from the fucking edge, Ever! You are my fucking flyer, my fucking—"

"Nothing! I'm your nothing! I was your protectee, your *obligation*, but now, I'm not. Now I'm *nothing*…to you." She takes a step closer to the edge.

Panic propelling me forward, I shout, "I wish that was true!"

Ever glances at me over her shoulder again, and this close, I can make out every feature on that half of her face, as well as how broken they all are. What the hell happened to this girl? To *my* girl? Black streaks of mascara cover her cheek all the way to her jawline where inky drops quiver, ready to fall.

"But it's not. I have never, ever wanted to hate someone more and I have never, ever loved anyone more."

"Pathetic."

"Unquestionably," I once again agree, this time with an embarrassing voice crack because I've never felt fear like this. If she doesn't back up from that goddamn edge…

"I broke your heart. I saw it," she says.

"Yeah."

"And you're still here."

"Yeah."

"Why?"

"You're my first thought every morning, the last thought every night, and you're sure as hell every thought in between. I assumed that'd stop as soon as the paychecks did, but it hasn't. Not at all. You're still here." I point to my head. "And here." My hand falls to my heart and I thump my chest with it in time with my erratic heartbeat.

She shakes her head, as if to clear it.

"You need to go. You're not even supposed to be here."

"I'm not," I admit. I signed a contract saying I wouldn't step foot within a hundred yards of the Munreaux property. Arthur can sue me for every penny I have. I'll gladly hand over all five million five hundred thousand of them if it means I can save his daughter.

"But I can't leave without you," I also admit. I did that once, one fucking time, and look what happened. The love of my life's about to jump off a motherfucking cliff.

"You don't understand. I can't. I *can't.*"

I throw my arms out wide. "Make me! Make me understand! I'm right here, goddamn it. Just tell me! I'm fucking begging you to!"

With a finger blindly jabbed behind her at the manor, she says, "He wants me to be something I'm not. Something I'd rather die than be!" Her head is shaking uncontrollably now, her body still too close to the edge.

She's going over. I can see it. I can *feel* it. She truly believes this is her only way out.

Gripping my head, I unleash a guttural growl. "Fine! Fuck! You spoiled, brat-ass, always-get-your-way, can't-ever-fucking-listen, biggest pain in my ass…" I rip my hands away, grateful I don't have long hair or it'd be coming with. "Fine! Okay? You win. Let's do it."

"Do what?"

"You wanna jump, Ever? I'll be right fucking behind you."

"Don't be stupid, Crue. You won't survive."

"If you go over that cliff…" I point at it, my hand trembling. "I won't need to. You are *my* flyer, *my* butterfly, *my* bat, my *everything*! And I'll be god-fucking-damned if I'm gonna spend a second on this planet without you!"

The fear doesn't stand a chance against the anger fighting for dominance. I'm fucking livid. I finally find the girl of my dreams and she wants to die. Die! Without me. Who the fuck does she think she is doing *anything* without me? From the highest peaks in the sky, to the deepest pits in the sea, where she goes, I go. I'm her man, her protector, her everything, even in death.

Fuck Arthur Munreaux and fuck his bullshit contract.

I've lied on a legal document before and I'm still standing.

Not for long.

I shake out one foot, then do the same thing with the other one.

Jesus Christ, this is gonna hurt so fucking bad. Hopefully it's over quickly.

Ever's gaze on the ground below me, she asks, "You're wearing the shoes?"

The ones she wrote "PROPERTY OF EVER MUNREAUX" on.

"Yeah."

Those water-logged eyes lift to mine. "You still belong to me?"

Like that's even a question.

"Always."

A new wave of tears floods her face. "But I hurt you. I treated you worse than Yasmin did."

"See! You don't fucking listen, little bat. I'm ridiculously, sickeningly, *pathetically* in love with you. You can carve my heart out and you're still gonna find your name engraved on it." Not Yasmin's. God.

What I felt for Yaz was a drop of rain compared to the ocean of love I feel for Ever.

She whimpers. "I'm not going back in that house."

She's negotiating. Negotiating is good. Negotiating means we're not plummeting to our deaths.

At least not yet.

"You don't have to. We'll go to mine."

"Your parents—"

"Are much more welcoming than yours. They're gonna love you."

Come on, Ever. You're worth love. Let me prove it.

"I want to but..." She returns her attention to the water, her black hair whipping around her face from the wind as she cries, "I can't."

I soften my tone to plead, "Come home with me, butterfly. Let me take care of you."

"I can't. I can't. I can't." A hand to her collarbone, she folds in half, chanting, "I can't," but it's not as coherent now. It's almost as if she's choking or something.

Shooting over to her, I wrap both arms around her from behind. "What? You can't what? Ever, talk to me."

"Breathe. I can't—" She coughs, clawing at her throat.

What the fuck? Is she having an allergic reaction?

I quickly drag her several feet backward and sit on the ground with her on my lap, the dark abyss out in front of us. Taking her hand in mine, I pull it off her throat. She immediately tears it away, scraping her chest instead.

She can't breathe... She's having chest pain... Anxiety? Panic attack?

I turn her around in my lap so she's facing me. The left side of her face is dark, darker than shadows cast by the impending night, like something happened to it. Like *someone* happened to it. Goddamn it. Goddamn it!

Ignoring what my intuition is screaming at me to take immediate action on, I focus on the emergency at hand.

"Look at me, Ever." As soon as her eyes lift to mine, I say, "Breathe. In through your nose, out through your mouth."

I follow my own instructions, showing her exactly what to do. She tries her best, but I can tell it's difficult.

"Keep going. In through your nose, out through your mouth."

The panic in her eyes refuses to ebb.

I replace her hand with mine and rub circles over her chest, keeping the pressure hard but still gentler than hers.

Her heart feels like what a hummingbird's wings look like when it's flying. So fast it's a blur of activity.

Shit. Could she die from this? That's how it feels for me and I'm not even experiencing it. I'm only observing.

"Fucking breathe, butterfly," I beg. "Just like this. In… Out… In… Out…" My own breathwork becomes jagged and shallow as I talk her through it. "In… Out…"

Her breathing starts to slow but her heartbeat doesn't.

On a growl, I tell her, "Don't you dare die on me or I swear to God I'll kill you myself."

Beneath my hand, her chest shakes with a bout of laughter. It doesn't reach her eyes though. Those are stubbornly wild and unsure.

It's her mind. I gotta get it off this…attack. She's being internally attacked by something.

"What's your favorite thing to draw?" I ask her.

"You."

I shake away the smile trying to take shape. Now is not the time for ego.

"What do you like about drawing me?"

"Everything."

Okay. Let's try again.

"What's your favorite memory?"

"Hide and Keep."

"What did you like about it?"

"Everything."

For fuck's sake.

"You gotta give me more than that. What did you like most about it?"

"Your back."

"My back? What about my back did you like?"

"I pressed my face to it and everything fell away. It was like you were my personal security blanket, blocking me from anything bad in the world."

The more she speaks, the slower her heart rate becomes.

"That's it. Good girl," I praise.

"I had never felt so safe before. You make me feel safe." She sobs.

"You are safe with me," I promise. "You're mine to take care of, mine to spoil, mine to keep safe. I won't let anything happen to you. I love you. I love you so much I need you to breathe. I need you alive. I need *you*."

All at once her body sags against mine.

I pepper her wet face with kisses, noting how swollen that left cheek is…and still choosing to ignore it.

"What was that?" I ask her.

"A long time coming."

"It's over now. We're fine. We're good." My heart's still racing, but as long as hers is under control, I can manage.

"Crue, I can't—"

"Hey." I carefully cradle her face between my hands. "You're okay. I got you. There's nothing else that matters right now. Nothing." Not even what is quite clearly a handprint on my girl's cheek.

Grabbing the sides of my face with just as much intensity, Ever presses her lips to mine, melting into me, and I take that as a good sign, the *best* sign. Ever Munreaux's alive and she's coming home with me. Everything else can wait.

CHAPTER 48

BEING BACK IN CRUE'S NEIGHBORHOOD FEELS MORE LIKE coming home than when I return to the manor. It's cozy here. Cramped, but cozy. There's a palpable community, full of different dynamics, styles, personalities. At the manor, it's just us. It's bleak and impersonal.

I'm never going back there.

That's why I opened the ceiling windows in the atrium before I left, to give us all a chance to fly away.

I never could've anticipated being caught by Crue yet again.

"How did you know where I was?" I ask him.

"I just…" He shrugs. "…know you."

He knows me better than most people, but he doesn't know all of me.

"You knew I'd be out there at that exact moment?"

"I saw you went out your window."

The sensor he installed. I forgot all about that.

One-handed, he pulls over to park along the front yard of his parents' house.

"And I got worried after…everything…"

Everything. Me. I unpinned a grenade right in his face and didn't even have the decency to look him in the eyes before releasing the spoon.

"I'm sorry. I'm sorry for what I said to you, how I treated you.

I thought my father was suspicious of us and I was trying to throw him off. For your sake. You don't know him like I do. He can be relentless toward those he feels wronged by."

His eyes fall to my left cheek and I pull his signature move—smoothing out my eyebrow.

Crue pulls my hand down, kisses it, then thumbs my cheek.

"Is that why he did that?"

"He slapped me because I mouthed off."

Crue takes a heavy breath, his chest expanding and contracting considerably before he says, "He's going to pay for that."

"He's got the money."

"Not financially." His green eyes lift to mine. "Me falling for you isn't wronging your father."

"It is from his standpoint."

"Because of how much I make?"

"That…among other things."

He scoffs, already aware my father's a top-tier snob.

"You didn't know he was gonna fire me?"

"I knew he would be letting you go soon," I say carefully.

"Why didn't you tell me the job wasn't for three years?"

"I tried." I told him what I could.

"Not hard enough."

"I'm sorry," is all I can offer.

Crue dips his head in a slow nod.

"I was blindsided and I panicked," I confess. "I thought we had another day together."

"Is that why you were on the cliff?"

Somewhat.

"I was on the cliff because…" How do I tell him without telling him? "The path that's mapped out for me is not the one I'd choose for myself." My eyes fill with tears I didn't know my body could conjure after crying for what feels like hours. "It's not the one I'd choose for my worst enemy."

"Is running Munreaux Motorcycles really that bad?"

"It is if your soul is in the sky," I half-joke, salty tears spraying off my lips when I laugh.

"Your soul's in the sky, butterfly, but your body's not." His hand at my face slides down to my chest, my heart, the one he tamed into total submission. "Your heart's not. And they won't be as long as I'm here to keep you grounded."

"How are you going to do that?"

He nods toward the house. "Well, first, I'm going to take you inside, to my room where we'll fall asleep in each other's arms, mostly because we want to but also because we have to. My bed is much smaller than you're used to. Hope that's okay."

"It's more than okay." I would snuggle with Crue whether we were on a container ship or a two-by-four.

"All right. Let's start there."

After he gets the car door for me, we approach the dimly lit house, my body filling with warmth.

Before Crue opens the front door, he pauses to say, "You might want to plug your nose."

"Your house doesn't stink, Major. Not like salt marshes or like dog. It smells nice."

"You're sure?"

"I'm sure. I was just being a bitch."

Silently, Crue bobs his head, then opens the door and waves me through first. Nobody's around while he gives me a quiet tour of the quaint house. There's no formal dining room, no office, no theater, no gym, and yet, there's still so much to explore. The walls and shelves are full of photos and knickknacks, all of them providing a visual history of Crue and his parents.

"Where's your dog?" I ask in a hushed voice.

"Zeus? He's probably sleeping in my parents' room."

"They don't mind?" My parents didn't allow pets, but if they did, they would never let that slide.

"They don't really have a say. He sleeps where he wants, sometimes even in my room."

"You don't care?"

"I don't know if you've noticed but I'm a pushover for those I love."

That makes me smile. "I noticed."

"Good. I've been making it pretty obvious."

Somehow, my smile widens.

"Come on."

We get ourselves some water before Crue leads me to his bedroom. It's not at all what I was expecting. It is small. But it's also bare. Aside from a bed, a dresser, and a nightstand, there's nothing else in here. No décor, no personality whatsoever. Nothing like the rest of the house, it could pass as a cell.

Was that his intent?

"It's not that dark, I know."

"It's not really anything," I mutter before eyeing him to suggest, "You could put a shirt over the lamp."

"Oh, yeah. Shit."

He proceeds to take the shirt he's wearing off, only stopping when he hears me laugh.

"I knew it." Every time I'd go to his room, there'd be another one of his shirts on the lamp. I figured that was why, but he never confirmed it until this moment.

"Just trying to make my little bat feel more at home," he says with a shy grin. "Want me to see if I can scrounge up some moss for you?"

"No." I roll my eyes. "Stick out your arms."

Shirt still in one hand, Crue spreads his arms out wide. "Like this?"

I step up to his front and they close around me instantly.

"This feels like home."

Crue hugs me tighter, blanketing me in love and security.

"My security blanket," I say with a sigh.

"Your everything."

With my eyes closed to keep the tears from falling, I breathe him in. "My everything."

After a while, we undress and climb into Crue's bed, our bodies coming together like magnets under the covers, our faces inches apart as we gaze into each other's eyes.

"Why did you go through so much trouble to get rid of me in the beginning?"

I raise my gaze to the ceiling. Even in the dark I can see every tiny island of texture on it. All of our walls and ceilings are smooth. No blemishes, no imperfections. It sets a tone, a standard, one that's expected to be upheld by the manor's inhabitants at all times.

Crue shakes me. "Ever?"

I could tell him it was just something I did to all the guards my father tried putting on me and it'd be true. But it wouldn't be the whole truth, not in his case.

"Because I wanted to keep you but knew I'd never get to."

"I'm yours to keep. No one else's. Never anyone else's."

But am I Crue's to keep? According to my father, I'm not. My last name makes me his alone. My father isn't the type to let go of his assets. If I thought there was a chance he would, I would've tried running away a long time ago.

I wouldn't have gotten very far, which is most likely more to blame for my lack of escape attempts than anything else. But I didn't have the same kind of motivation before. I didn't have anywhere to go or anyone to go to.

Maybe now that I have both, I can give this a real effort.

"Is that why you called me Never?" I tease. I know why he did that—to hurt me as much as I was hurting him.

"That was a mistake. I shouldn't have called you that."

"It was genius. It made the whole thing more believable."

"I still regret saying it."

We kiss, our lips seeking the forgiveness for all their sins.

"Crue?" I ask during a breather.

"Yeah?"

"Is that Crue 2.0?" I point over my shoulder at the closet I could've sworn I saw the bear sitting on the floor of earlier.

Crue's head jolts off the bed. "Is it? I don't, uh, know. I don't think it..." He drops his head, admitting, "Yeah, it is. I took that fucker on my way out."

"You were in my room?"

He nods.

"Why?"

"I wanted to see if I could find anything else you were hiding from me."

"And?"

"And... What's with the dress at the bottom of your closet?"

Oh shit. I was supposed to throw that away. I just...got busy. Crue and I have been practically inseparable since that night.

"Must've fallen off its hanger," I say shortly.

"It was dirty. And ripped."

I don't reply. I don't think I even breathe.

"Who tore it? You or him?"

"Him," comes out so quiet my own ears barely pick it up.

"Was it wanted?"

After a moment, I give my head a single shake.

He runs his hand through my hair, tucking it behind my ear.

"He's going to pay for that."

And just like I did when we were talking about my father, I say, "He's got the money."

"Why didn't you tell me that night?"

"What would you've done? Something to get you fired?"

His silence is telling.

"That's why I didn't tell you."

"What happened?"

"The usual. He just...wouldn't take 'no' for an answer."

"That shouldn't be the usual," he says, probably referring to his own experience as well.

"It shouldn't," I agree.

"How far did he get?"

"Not as far as he wanted."

"Did he hurt you or not?"

"He hurt me, but using the moves you taught me, he wasn't able to rape me."

"Is that why you wanted me to teach you them?"

I nod. "The word 'no' is a powerful man's top allergen, and Mallory is—"

"A nobody. I had to look him and his dad up. They own some kind of hydrogen plant. That's it."

I wait for him to expand on that but he doesn't. At all.

"Umm, well, power isn't earned. It's assumed. If Mallory believes he's powerful, then he is."

"You have a rich daddy. You have an aversion to the word 'no.'"

"I don't like when *you* tell me 'no,'" I argue.

"Are you powerful?"

"That's…" I shake my head. "No, that's different."

"How?"

"I'm a woman." Duh.

"But same logic applies. If you believe you're powerful, then you are."

"I have no powers."

"You fly."

I can only scoff.

"Okay, fine. What do you call what you've done to me?"

"Bribery?"

Crue's sudden burst of laughter triggers my own.

"You never gave me any money," he says.

"Only because I don't have any of my own."

"You can make it."

"How? I don't have a lot of skills."

"Then you focus on the skills you do have. Like, uh… You can teach art. Or coach cheerleading."

"Cheer," I correct automatically.

"You can coach cheer."

I think about that for a moment, trying to visualize me coaching my own team. I taught Crue pretty well.

"Have you ever considered coaching wrestling?" He wasn't a bad teacher either.

"No."

"Why not? You'd be good at it."

"Nobody around here wants me coaching their kids."

"Nobody around here knows who you really are," I argue with twice as much passion as before.

"They know the name and the headlines."

Yeah. That's all people know of me, too.

We lie in silence for a long time, Crue's hands on my hair and shoulder, mine on his abs and chest.

"How much did my father pay you?"

"Ever."

"What? It's not like I didn't know he was paying you. I was literally your job."

"Not like that."

"I know. I know. But how much?"

"Fifty thousand…plus another five as a bonus for making it past the first day with you."

I can't help it, I chuckle.

"You fucking terror," Crue says, zero condemnation in his tone, only admiration.

"Is fifty-five thousand a lot?" Obviously, it's not for my father, but for Crue, it might be.

"More than I earned all of last year."

Wow. Crue was really undermining himself before working at Munreaux Manor.

"So then you're doing it? Leaving Sea Haven?"

"That was the plan when I thought I'd have a million dollars."

"But fifty-five thousand is still enough, isn't it? You can move somewhere with that much. Right?" I don't know how much living expenses cost. I don't know how much anything costs. Technically, I don't even know how much my daily matcha lemonades cost because I purposely overtipped on every order.

"That money could be used on something more important."

"What's more important than your dream?"

"My dad's back has been bugging him for years. His insurance doesn't cover the kind of surgery he needs and he's in pain every day."

"How much is the surgery?"

"Around fifty-K."

"Can you move with five thousand?"

"If I was smart with it and lived frugally until I got a job…I guess."

"But you're not going to?"

He blinks long and hard. "I have to stick around to help while he's recovering."

"What was your plan for that when you thought you'd still be living at the manor?"

"Pay for help."

"What about after he's recovered? Will you move then?"

When he doesn't respond, I have my answer. He was relying on that million dollars. And now, he's stuck in Sea Haven, in this cell, probably forever.

Unless I can help. I don't have a million dollars, but I have access to money. Less after Hide and Keep. But I've been spending money frivolously for years. Now I have something I want to invest in—Crue's future…as well as my own. If he thinks there's enough, and wants me to go with him, then I will. I'll follow him for once. And we'll create our own future. Together.

CHAPTER 49

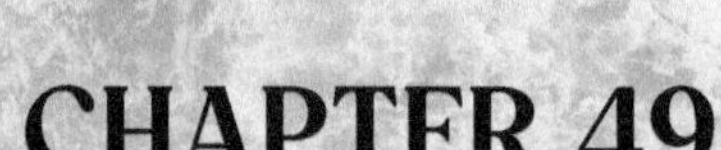

U NABLE TO PROCESS.

"What the hell?" I mutter, looking at the ATM screen in complete horror. I've never seen this message in my life. Did I enter the pin wrong?

"Daddy cut your cards," Crue says with a yawn, his hands in the front of his hoodie.

"No. He wouldn't do that." It hasn't even been twelve hours since I left.

I repeat the whole process of sticking my debit card in and punching in the pin number nice and slow so there's no mistakes.

I wind up getting the same message: UNABLE TO PROCESS.

I try my other cards, none of them working.

Pulling out my phone, I dial my father's financial advisor. Unlike last time I did this, the line rings and rings before eventually going to voicemail.

I hang up without leaving a message.

He cut me off? No matter how mad I've made my father, he's never gone to *this* extreme before, only limited the amount, as well as accounts, I have access to.

How am I supposed to do…anything?

"How am I supposed to eat?"

"That's why you dragged me out of bed? I could've made you breakfast at the house."

"You can cook?" He made us dinner once but it was just chicken breasts. And he overcooked them.

"Not everyone grew up with a chef, Ever."

"I'm aware." The heat on my face spreads down my neck as I think of a lie. "I just…wanted to take you out to breakfast…as a thank-you for saving my life—"

"I prefer gratuity in the form of sexual favors."

I stare at Crue.

He stares back at me.

Neither of us blinks.

"From who?"

He breaks first to roll his eyes. "Oh my God. I was joking…kind of. But I meant from you. Only you."

I'm in the middle of a breakdown right now and he's making jokes.

I continue as if he didn't interrupt me, saying, "I wanted to buy myself some new clothes, too." At least that part is true. The only clothes I have are the ones on my body.

"You can wear anything of mine."

"Not for interviews and stuff." No one's going to want to hire me in my schoolgirl outfit. At least no one I want to work for.

"You gotta fill out some applications before you go on interviews."

He must think I'm such an idiot. I *feel* like such an idiot. Why did I think my father would continue to support me financially?

Because that's the only way he's ever supported me.

"Well, how am I supposed to do that looking like this?" I ask Crue. "I don't even have makeup on." Thankfully, no bruise ever fully formed from yesterday's slap, and the swelling has already gone down, but that side could still use some coverage.

"You don't need makeup to fill out forms online. You don't need makeup, period. You're naturally beautiful."

He thinks I'm a beautiful idiot. A naturally beautiful idiot.

"Crue," I say when he turns away, heading to his Bronco as if my life didn't just implode before his eyes.

He stops to glance back at me. "What?"

"I think…" I shuffle from one stiletto to the other. "I'm poor."

Crue plugs his nose, and in a nasally voice, says, "I thought I smelled something."

I deserve that. And so much worse. I've been terrible, even when I was playing up my role as the Munreaux princess. I took things too far. Said things I had no business saying. I didn't understand anything about anyone. I never even bothered putting myself in anyone else's shoes to try.

I was a top-tier snob, just like my father.

"What am I supposed to do?" I ask both him and the universe because I don't have the first clue. If nothing else, I always knew I could rely on having money.

Luckily, Crue drops his hand but doesn't turn and run from me while he has the chance. I'm too defeated to run right now.

"Come home with me and let me feed you. We'll figure out a game plan after. It's only Saturday. We have the weekend to come up with something."

"Can we shower, too?"

His lips spread into a cheesy grin. "To wash the stench of poor off you?"

"Actually, I have a couple bucks around here somewhere." I pretend to check my pockets even though this skirt doesn't have any, then brandish my lovely middle finger for Crue, holding it up on my way past him to the Bronco's passenger side.

With my ex-bodyguard too busy chuckling, I open my own door for once.

All noise stops as he comes over to immediately close it before I can even get in.

Bending so he's right in my face, he says, "I don't care how much money you do or don't have, I get the door for you."

Major Danger's come a long way.

We have ourselves another tense stare-off until I say, "I love you, Major."

"I love you, too, little bat," he counters with the same no-nonsense tone, then opens the door and jerks his head to the side. "Now get your broke ass in the car."

After Crue makes us egg-white omelets—that are only slightly runny in the middle—we migrate over to the living room sofa, using his laptop to search for job listings in the area with immediate availability.

"How about this one?" Crue asks, rotating the laptop in my direction.

"Retail associate?"

"Selling clothes. You love clothes."

Do I? I know a lot about clothes, but I don't know if I love them. I'm not passionate about them, that's for sure. I've had to pretend to be, for the clones, and for…everybody. But I haven't felt like doing that for a while. I don't think I ever want to do it again.

"What happened to the cheer coach idea?"

"I looked into it a little bit. You need experience for that."

"I cheered all my life."

"Coaching experience. Plus, it helps to have some kind of degree."

Well, shit. Every plan from last night has already bombed and it's only ten o'clock in the morning.

"Retail associate, it is," I say with a sigh, taking the laptop from him.

Literally after the first question of Name, I freeze up. What address do I put? I've only ever had one, but the manor's no longer my home.

I can't put Crue's. I was only invited to stay here for the night, not move in permanently.

I don't have a home.

After sitting with that fact for a moment, I scan the rest of the form.

This job wants to know my experience, too. I don't have that. I don't have personal references either. I don't have any of this. I don't even have a car.

Even if by some miracle someone takes pity on me and hires me, how am I supposed to get there?

I check the store's location. Too far away to walk to.

I squint my suddenly swimming eyes at the screen, but it doesn't help make it any clearer.

"All I know is my name and social security number," I admit.

"You can just put that..."

I type in the nine numbers.

"...and I'll help you with the rest."

He's going to put down his address and he's going to offer to drive me to work and I'm going to become another excuse keeping him from living out his dream.

Just as the first tear falls, I announce, "I have to go to the bathroom," then shove the laptop at Crue before rushing to the back of the house.

What we've been living isn't reality. We can't just stay cooped up in a single room all day, every day. This is the real world now and I have to be an active part of it. I can't rely on other people anymore. I don't want to. I want to work. I want to support myself, not be a burden, especially not to Crue. Or his family.

But how? I'm broke. I'm homeless. I'm jobless. I'm friendless. I'm...

My father's words echo in my head.

"Because this is all you're good for."

"...this is all you're good for."

"...all you're good for."

I'm worthless. I have nothing going for me. I've spent the majority of my life focused on cheer, a sport that once it ends, it just ends. There are no professional careers in cheer like there are in football or basketball or tennis. Even the cheerleaders that perform at other professional sports games are not considered real cheerleaders, not like the kind of cheerleader I am. Those are more like dance teams made up of models.

Crowdleaders is what we call them and they tend to be more

along the lines of what people think of when they envision cheer-leaders. Crue did.

Crue. I don't know what to do. He likes taking care of me but I can't ask him to give up his dreams to do it. I need somewhere to live, something to drive. I need clothes, food, water. I need an entire fucking life. Unfortunately, I never learned how to have one of my own and now I don't have the first clue where to begin.

Money. That's the beginning, middle, and end. You can't do *any-thing* without money.

My car's worth a lot. The keys are always hanging up in the ga-rage…somewhere. I never paid close attention but I'm sure I could find them if I looked hard enough. Then if I sell that, I should have enough money for an apartment. Maybe even a cheaper car to get around in.

That's where I'll start.

"Can you drive me to the manor?" I ask Crue back out in the living room.

He doesn't even look up from his laptop to tell me, "No."

I'm almost at the front door before Crue notices and jumps up from the couch, putting himself in my path.

"Where are you going?"

"Munreaux Manor."

"Your dad—"

"I'm not going there for *him*."

"Why do you want to go there?"

"For my car."

"Arthur cut your credit cards. You think he's just gonna let you take a two-hundred-and-fifty-thousand-dollar car?"

Two hundred and fifty thousand dollars? That might be enough money for Crue to move.

"I wasn't going to ask him for it."

"You're gonna steal it?"

The doubt in his voice is insulting.

"I stole yours, didn't I?"

"No, not really. The keys were in it."

At the time, he sure acted like I stole it though. He was enraged I did.

"The keys might be in mine, too." They won't be.

I attempt to sidestep him, but he puts a hand up in front of me.

"I can't let you. Your father put his hands on you and—"

"I won't go near him."

"Ever. You had a fucking…fit…thing…last night at the thought of going back there." His expression softens. "Butterfly, don't go anywhere near that house. I don't want you to go through that again."

That. My panic attack. I don't want to experience that again either but it didn't seem like I had much control on whether or not it happened in the first place. It just did, and thankfully, Crue helped me out of it. If it does again, I know what to do. Think about Crue.

"But I need—"

"If it means that much to you, *I'll* go get you your car."

"How is that any better? You can't get within a hundred yards of the manor!" I shout, my hands airborne and turbulent.

He shrugs. He *shrugs.*

"I'm less than a hundred yards away from you right now."

"I was listed on there, too?"

"Your last name's Munreaux, isn't it? I'm not supposed to go near anything with the Munreaux label on it."

"You shouldn't have come last night. You put yourself in jeopardy."

"You put me in jeopardy the moment you approached that cliff."

"Maybe if you weren't a stalker—"

"Says the creep who used to sneak into my room to watch me sleep."

I scoff. "I didn't watch you sleep." *For long.*

"What did you do?"

"I just…" I gesture at him. "…would lie behind you and get my face as close as I could to the space between your shoulders without actually touching you."

"Because that's where you felt safest?" he asks, referring to what I told him last night.

"Yes."

"That's where you still feel safest?"

"Yes."

"Then stay here. Let me keep you safe."

"I won't even see my father. I'll be in and out."

"Even if that were true, theft is a crime, too. If you're willing to go to jail, so am I."

My ex-bodyguard is truly infuriating. First the cliff, now this.

He's constantly putting others before himself. It's his saving grace and his biggest detriment. That's why he hasn't left Sea Haven yet.

I never thought I'd agree with my father on anything, ever, but…

Crossing my arms over my chest, I say, "You can't steal what you already own."

Crue's laughter shocks the hell out of me.

"What's so funny?"

"I saw the registration for the Sapphire. You don't own it."

"Yes, I do. My father bought it for me."

"He bought it for you to drive, but legally, it's not yours. Your name is only on the insurance."

I spin to hide the newest onslaught of tears. How can one person cry so much in a twenty-four-hour period?

"So I really only have this one outfit?" I muse to myself.

Crue wraps his arms around me, saying into my neck, "And me."

But at what cost? I'll have Crue…and his future. We'll both be stuck here. Forever. And one day, those headlines everyone knows us for will become our epitaphs.

CHAPTER 50

Our bodies naturally start to sway together. God, I love this girl. I don't care what I have to do. She's not going anywhere near that manor again.

"It doesn't bother you?" Ever asks.

"What?"

"That I don't have…what I used to."

My body comes to a stop and I spin her around. She tries to hide her face from me but I catch the blotchiness. Was she crying again?

Even from afar, Arthur Munreaux continues to hurt his daughter.

"Does it bother me that you're not rich anymore?"

With a peek up at me, she nods.

"Fuck no. I never gave a shit about your money, Ever." I grab that mottled face and press my forehead to hers. "With or without money, I love *you*."

I hear the front door open behind me, then my mom and dad's voices. The moment they notice us, they cut off almost instantly.

If only their thoughts could be silenced, too.

"Mom. Dad." I turn around, smile already in place to set the tone for this new, and hopefully not too awkward, encounter. "I'd like you to meet Ever, my girlfriend."

Fucking surprise.

Ever pivots my way, looking at me quizzically.

"Girlfriend? I'm your girlfriend?"

It's a surprise to her, too?

"You are until I put a ring on your finger."

Her azure eyes widen.

How did she not know that? No, we never had "the talk," but I didn't think we needed to. Not after everything we've been through. She helped me ingest charcoal via allofeeding to counteract poison, and I saved her from throwing herself off a cliff. We're each other's lifelines.

Since lifeline isn't a widely accepted term, girlfriend will have to do.

Until I propose and make her my fiancée.

That only sounds mildly better though. Better to make her my wife as soon as possible.

"Well…" my mom says. "That's different."

I double-blink at her.

So much for this not being awkward.

"Different…but good," she tries to reassure. "It's nice to meet you, Ever. I'm Phoebe. And this is Reid."

They both take turns shaking Ever's hand, but my dad doesn't release hers right away, holding on to it as he questions, "Ever? As in…"

"Munreaux."

I step forward and pull Ever's wrist back, ending the handshake.

Both my parents alternate their gazes between me, my girlfriend, and the hand I just took out of my own father's grasp.

I don't explain myself or apologize. Blood relation or not, he shouldn't have held on to my girl's hand for so long.

Finally, my dad clears his throat, and says, "Beautiful, uh, motorcycles…I hear."

I almost fucking groan. Jesus.

"Yeah. Um, thanks. Although, I don't have anything to do with that." She laughs.

Imagining Ever designing motorcycles is pretty funny. In all the drawings I've seen of hers, not one of them was a motorcycle. She's a nature girl. Not an engine, cogs, and motor oil girl. What the hell was Arthur thinking trying to make her head of Munreaux Motorcycles?

Maybe he's dying and doesn't have any other choice.

One can hope.

"You would've if your dad had his way," I mutter to her before announcing, "Ever's staying with us for a while."

"No?" she says in that way of hers that sounds more like a question than it should. "I'm not."

I swing a frown her way. "Where else are you gonna go?"

She side-eyes my parents and lowers her voice for no real reason other than shame, obviously, because she says, "I don't know. I'll figure it out."

"I'll save you the trouble. You're staying here."

"But—"

I cut her off with our usual, "You're welcome," before she can get another word out. Over my dead body is she staying somewhere else.

Her foot stomp makes me chuckle, mainly because her foot is so small it doesn't make any noise whatsoever.

I press a kiss to the top of her head. Such a cute little creep.

"You're welcome to stay as long as you want, Ever," my mom says with a soft smile before squeezing past us to go to the kitchen. "We were planning on having a beach day. Would you two care to join us?"

"A day at the beach sounds nice." The job search can wait. I've never had difficulty finding myself a new job. And Ever…could use some fun right now. A little sun wouldn't hurt either. We've been spending way too much time indoors. The tan she got from Florida last month is long gone, replaced with an almost sickly pallor to her skin.

"The beach? We can go there?" Ever asks me.

"Yeah. It's right down the road," I say, a little confused. "It's not private or anything, if that's what you're worried about."

"It's not that. I just…" She shakes her head. "I've never been to the beach here."

I turn to follow my dad, and Ever shadows me.

"You have a beachfront house."

"We have a bay view house. We live too high up to go to the beach."

"But…Sea Haven is a coastal town. There are beaches everywhere."

"None that I've been to. My father said the beaches here were—" She glances toward my parents. "Uh…you know."

Oh. Right. Arthur's belief that it reeks down here.

He's not exactly wrong.

"Yeah, the beaches here can stink sometimes." It's not all the time. Most of the time though.

You get used to it.

We have.

We've tried. Some days are easier to ignore it than others. It depends on a lot of factors, like the heat and wind. Today's breezy, so it shouldn't be too bad.

"That's the Sound for you," my mom says. "A lot of sewage gets discharged into it unfortunately."

"The salt marshes and decaying seaweed don't help either," my dad adds.

"Just don't dig at all and you should be fine. That's where a lot of it settles," I tell her.

"So, no burying you in the sand?"

Ever finally smiles, and even though my first reaction is to give her whatever she wants, I'm not being buried in that fucking sand.

"No, sorry."

She tilts her head to show her dislike for the word, but I can't fold on this one. I haven't been buried in the sand since I was a kid. I'm an adult now. An adult who knows better. That sand is not only gross but full of—

"Ooh, you should let her bury you. After the crabs latch on, we'll pull you up and collect them so we can have a feast tonight."

—crabs. We have so many crabs here, you can't even walk barefoot on the sand without getting pinched. We usually catch them using raw chicken on string, but apparently my mother thinks I'd make better bait. I'd definitely be bigger bait. I'm just not convinced I'd be better.

And I'm not willing to find out.

"Not happening," I tell everybody, earning boos from both parents…and eventually Ever after they prompt her to join in.

Keeping the smile from my face so they can't see how much I'm enjoying this, I fold my arms over my chest and watch the three of them gang up on me.

That didn't take long for her to fit in. Not long at all.

"Did you bring your swimsuit, Ever?" my mom asks her after they finish their heckling routine.

"Um, no. I didn't bring…" She eyes me. "Anything."

Relocating condiments from the fridge to the counter, my mom nods. "It was one of those nights, huh?"

"Unfortunately."

"That's okay. It's still early in the season that it might not be hot enough to swim. And you don't need one to kayak."

All the ingredients for grinders in front of her, my mom grabs a plate and utensils.

"Oh…good."

"You've never kayaked, have you?" I ask Ever, going over to start opening everything.

"No. But I did stand-up paddleboard in the Maldives once."

My mom raises her eyebrows at me.

I shrug. My girlfriend's not like us.

Suddenly, Ever appears on my other side, completing the assembly line.

I can't keep the doubt from my voice when I ask her, "You know how to make a grinder?"

"I will in a minute."

She's not like us…yet. Soon she'll be a Brantley in every way, including legally.

"Here. I got it, Dad."

I rush over to take the kayaks from my dad's hold.

He puts both hands up. "All right, all right. You want to show off for your girlfriend. I get it. I used to be young and strong, too."

When he tries to lift the cooler, he winces.

"Dad—"

"Oh, I can take that," Ever says. Before my dad can even argue, she's strutting away with it in her possession.

Jesus, I love her.

The four of us, each weighed down with provisions, venture down the street, toward the water. The tide's already going out, so there's a ton of beach for us to set up camp on for the next several hours. We pass by canopies, blankets, chairs, coolers, playpens, a half-buried basketball hoop… Okay, that's a first.

Beside me, Ever's taking everything in with round eyes. She's wearing an old tee of mine, along with a pair of my basketball shorts that despite the waist being rolled down at least three times, are still too big on her. With a pair of my mom's size-eight sandals on her size-six-and-a-half feet, she's making loud *thwacks* with every step she takes, kicking up sand all over both of us.

If her clones saw her right now, they'd choke on their overpriced seaweed water.

"What do you think?" I ask her.

"It smells like you."

"So…it stinks?"

We both chuckle.

"No, the saltwater smells like you."

"Yeah, I figured that's where it was coming from." I've never lived anywhere else, so the saltwater's probably in my pores at this point.

"It's beautiful from down here. Less intimidating."

I nod and face forward. From this angle, you can see the sun reflecting off the water's surface, making it glitter. At the manor, I noticed there was no real glitter. Too high up, I guess.

"I don't know how to explain it. It's fresh. Renewing. I feel…new."

"You look it," I sorta joke. She looks happier like this than when she's in her usual attire.

Ever groans. "I can't imagine what I look like."

"Nothing like a Munreaux."

"Maybe that's a good thing."

"It's a very good thing." At least to me. "So your team never had any team-bonding exercises or anything on the beach?"

"Not while I've been on it."

"And you never went to any bonfires down here?" Connecticut residents, or Nutmeggers as most prefer, call almost all parties bonfires, whether there's a bonfire or not.

"Nope. None."

It's hard to believe that in nineteen years of living here, she's never been to a Sea Haven beach. Even if our house wasn't steps from the shore, my family would've taken advantage of living this close to the Sound.

The people that live up on the cliffs have multimillion-dollar views of a bay they won't go near. It's just like art. They only want it for the bragging rights.

Well, not Ever. She genuinely likes art.

"Phoebe!" someone calls out, causing all four Brantley heads to snap to the right. Technically, three plus a Munreaux's, but I'm trying out Ever's manifesting shit by thinking of her as my wife already.

"Oh, hey, Carol! Long time no see," my mom greets a woman who looks vaguely familiar. I think she lives a couple streets over from us, but I haven't seen her for a few years. The moment her eyes land on me, it becomes obvious why that is.

While her lips continue moving, her voice doesn't make it to us. It's not hard to guess why considering the person sitting next to her almost breaks their neck to gawk at us. At me.

Before I can tear my eyes away, I make out the words "be in jail."

Dropping the cooler, Ever stops in her tracks, which means I'm not the only one.

"Excuse me? What was that? We couldn't quite hear you."

Spinning around, I tell her, "Come on. It's not worth it." It never is.

"Yes, you are," she argues before returning her attention to Carol. "Say it again?"

"It wasn't for you, dear."

"That nose clearly wasn't for you either, but you're still trying to make it work, aren't you?" Ever quips.

Carol gasps and cups the nose in question.

Several passersby tune into the altercation. Some of their stares linger on me a bit too long to pass as curious. Fuck.

That familiar urge to hide returning in an instant, I yank my hat lower. I got too fucking comfortable the last couple weeks.

"Ever," I grit. "Let's go."

She surveys our audience.

I know she thinks she's helping by standing up for me. But she's only making it worse by drawing more attention. Carol isn't the only one with that opinion. At least she had the decency to voice it low enough to where I couldn't hear it. Most people don't.

"You shouldn't judge people you don't know anything about," she tells…everybody.

Picking up the cooler again, she comes to stand by my side, one hand on her hip.

"You deal with that all the time?"

I resume walking before muttering, "Not if we go out far enough."

Ever grows quiet after that. In fact, everybody does. Nobody speaks until we find a spot away from everybody to drop our stuff.

"Why don't you and Ever take the kayaks out first?" my mom suggests after we get everything set up.

I agree without hesitation. Any opportunity to get farther away from those people, I'm taking.

While I'm putting the kayaks in the water, I hear Ever yelp behind me.

"Ow!"

Up to her knees in the water, she's hopping around on one foot. I'm next to her in an instant.

"What happened?"

"I think something bit me."

Oh, fuck. My mind starts racing, thinking about all the creatures that could've bit her. It could've even been a jellyfish sting.

I lift her up, one hand behind her back, one under her knees.

Her feet out of the water, I see they're bare. There aren't any sandals floating around us, so…

"You took your shoes off?"

She nods miserably, tears barely held back, before snuggling me closer. "I thought I had to for kayaking."

"Aw, sorry, butterfly. That's on me. I should've warned you." I was so focused on getting away from here, I forgot Ever's new to…here. "There're crabs all over, under the water, under the sand, and if you step on one, or even just near one, they'll pinch you."

"That was a *pinch?*"

The pinch itself probably wasn't as awful as the shock of it. I've seen grown men brought to tears over an unexpected crab pinch.

I carry her to get her sandals, then we paddle out. As a fast learner, she has no problem keeping up with me, staying relatively close on my flank. Aside from my first few instructions on how to hold the paddle, the ride is silent. We pass house after house with only a few feet between them, giving them a condominium-like appearance. Nothing like Ever's neighborhood with multiple acres between each mansion.

"Do you like the water?" she asks randomly.

I glance around at it, then shrug. "I guess."

"You could work with it."

I nod before it turns into a shake. "I have no idea what that means."

"You could get a job working with water."

"Like a marine biologist?"

"There are a lot of roles in conservation work, not just biologists."

"You want me to be a conservationist like you?"

"You already are. All of your jobs have been protecting something, right? Buildings, people… You could protect sea life."

I hadn't thought of it like that before. What I was technically doing—conservation of sorts—never really registered. I was choosing jobs based on the ability to disappear from everyone's radar. Night guard of office buildings and storage facilities, the ones with entire shifts where I didn't encounter a single soul, were my favorites. I didn't like taking bouncer-type jobs, mostly because of the amount of people I was forced to interact with, but I still did it when needed. At least at Hide and Keep I could somewhat conceal my identity.

"I don't know the first thing about getting into that kind of work," I confess.

"I'm sure you could figure it out. You're good at finding answers to things you don't know."

That is what the internet's for. Or what it started out as. Now it's… I don't even know. It seems like people go out of their way to stay ignorant these days.

"It probably requires a degree—"

"You don't need a college education to make a difference in the world."

I consider that for a moment.

"What about you? Will you continue your conservation work?"

Ever doesn't answer for so long I have to check on her over my shoulder. The paddle across her lap, she's just staring at me.

I stop paddling, too.

"Too soon?" I know how hard it must've been for her to leave all those butterflies behind.

"No, it's okay." Nothing about her says it's okay.

"You did all you can."

"Did I?"

"You gave them a way out. It's up to them to use it."

"Would you?"

"Would I what?"

"If you were given a way out, would you use it?"

"A way out of…" She's not talking about…this, right? Us?

"Sea Haven."

Thank God.

I try to imagine what a way out of Sea Haven might look like. A job offer with a relocation package. A sudden windfall of cash.

One's much more realistic than the other…if I were looking for jobs elsewhere, which I'm not right now and probably won't until things have settled.

"Eventually," I say.

"Like when? After your father's surgery?"

I wobble my head from side to side, not committing to any one answer, and resume paddling.

Not a moment later, Ever appears beside me. "You're lying."

"I didn't even say anything."

"You wouldn't use it."

"I said eventually. Just not right this minute while we've got a lot going on."

"We?"

I hook my paddle onto Ever's kayak and pull us to a stop.

"Yeah, we. I know you heard me earlier but I'll repeat it as many times as it takes for it to sink in. You're my girlfriend. You live with me now. We live together, meaning we're in this…" I gesture all around us. "Everything, together. And since fairy godmothers don't exist, we have to find our own way out of Sea Haven. With both of us working, we should be able to pool our resources together, and in a few years, we'll look at making it happen."

"Years? But…you're miserable here."

"You know when I'm *not* miserable? When I'm with you."

"That's not always true. I was with you earlier when that woman—"

"I don't know then. Maybe you're my security blanket, too, because you make everything more bearable. That woman?" I scoff. "I already forgot her." I did the second I heard Ever in distress. It doesn't matter that she's no longer my protectee. Her safety will always take precedence in my mind.

Ever doesn't look convinced, so I cup the back of her head and bring her face as close to mine without tipping either of our kayaks.

Looking between those azure eyes, I say, "How can I think about anything else when all I'm ever thinking about is you?"

I expect a chuckle, or a kiss, or some kind of reciprocation. What I get is an entire-face frown, from her hairline to her dimpled chin.

"It's your fault. You ruined me."

It takes a few seconds, but finally, the muscles in her face relax. "What kind of conservationist does that make me?"

I laugh, then press a quick kiss to her lips. "I'm not in need of saving, little bat."

Taking the hat off my head, I expect her to launch it away from us. Instead, she puts it on hers before paddling ahead of me. While I'm full-on grinning, I swear she's got another frown. I just don't know why.

CHAPTER 51

AFTER SPENDING THE DAY AT THE BEACH, WE BEGIN THE trek back to the Brantleys' home.

Passing by a couple of kids with a bucket and some shovels, I'm hit in the face with invisible rotten eggs. I'm practically choking on the stench, my gag reflex fully engaged, when I hear Crue say, "Told ya. The sand holds on to it."

I've experienced the occasional sulfur onslaught while driving near salt marshes before, with the windows up to cut some of the potency, but there's no barrier out here. This is a full-on invasion of my senses.

"How can they stand it?" I gesture to the kids happily building a sandcastle, oblivious to the odor cloud they've unleashed with their plastic shovels.

"They're kids. They probably don't care."

"A lot of people around here don't even notice," says Phoebe.

"How? How can someone not notice rotten eggs?"

"They just grow accustomed to it. Like people who live near railroads," Crue's father says with a shrug.

"Isn't there a railroad nearby? I heard one last night."

"Is there?" he asks suddenly, searching around and making me chuckle. Grinning, he says, "I must've grown accustomed to it."

Crue got his sense of humor from him and his caring nature from Phoebe.

"A couple more nights and you won't hear the train anymore either," Crue tells me. He's lugging both kayaks back the same way he brought them here—by himself. Only, he's shirtless now.

Other girls are checking him out, their gazes glued to his abs like a five-year-old's craft project, and it's making me feel very volatile. I want to scream at them to stop eye-fucking my boyfriend. I want to rub stinky sand in their eyes, preventing them from ever eye-fucking him, or anyone, again.

Sadly, I do neither. I already drew enough attention to myself earlier calling out that witch in a straw hat. This is how it will be for us here—Crue and I constantly shrinking ourselves to avoid recognition. I've been watching him do it all afternoon, never making eye contact with strangers, never raising his voice, never causing a scene about anything.

On vacations, I would study other families, memorize how they'd behave. Each one was different, no obvious commonalities between them…except one. They were carefree. Some were loud and boisterous while others were quiet and lazy. But they all smiled. They all talked, laughed, interacted.

That's how the Brantleys were inside their house, but out here, they were anything but carefree. The three of them hardly spoke to each other louder than they would inside a library. They did everything they could not to draw attention to themselves, blending in with the sand almost as well as the crabs discreetly scuttling along the shoreline.

That's one reason why Crue was such a good bodyguard. He's proficient at trying to be invisible.

I used to think it was because of his scar. Now I know it's not *just* about the scar. It's about hiding his entire identity.

And his parents let him. They enable him. They join him. They had the opportunity to confront someone speaking poorly, not to mention incorrectly, about their son, but they didn't. They stayed silent, drawing in on themselves to make the family less noticeable as a whole.

I understand why they do it. It would be them against Sea Haven.

I just don't agree with it. Crue's willing to sacrifice so much for them, but they're not willing to make sacrifices for him.

Maybe that is their sacrifice. Maybe they had a loud life before that fateful night that forever changed two families. Yasmin's family lost her, but Crue's parents lost him, too. And maybe they lost themselves. Maybe Phoebe and Reid are doing all they're capable of to ensure Crue still feels loved, and has a home, a safe abditory to hide from the world in.

But he should have more. I want him to have more. I want him to have everything. Crue is worth the battle. He's worth a war.

He's also worth peace, something I'll never get knowing he chose me over his dreams. That's exactly what he's going to do. In the name of love, Crue will continue to let this town beat him down until there's nothing left. Pressure may make diamonds, but too much can vaporize them. I can't sit back and watch that happen. I love him too much. I'd rather sell my soul to the devil—

The devil… The very one in need of a soul right now. And funds to spare.

"What's that?" I ask. At the end of Crue's street is a stone pier. There's a bunch of wooden pillars sticking out of the water around it. It looks like it's supposed to be for boats but there aren't any moored to it. There's a couple holding hands, walking on it, otherwise it's kind of an eyesore honestly.

"This used to be a shipbuilding area. That's the old wharf. Nobody uses it anymore though."

It's certainly long enough. I'm just not sure about the width. As long as it has a twenty-five-foot diameter, it should work.

"Some people fish off it," Crue adds.

I tune back in to tease, "Like you?" His fishing story was very believable.

He gives an unconvincing, yet flirty, "Maybe."

"When's the last time you fished, son?" Reid asks, sparking a conversation about the one and only time the two of them went fishing together back when Crue was still in elementary school, before wrestling claimed all of his free time.

Diving into my thoughts again, I don't even realize we've made it back to the Brantleys' until Crue shouts my name. Looking up, I find myself in front of their neighbor's house, apparently having blown right by Crue's.

"Whoops," I say as I quickly backtrack a house.

"Don't worry about it. It happens all the time," Phoebe reassures me.

"The houses do sort of look alike." If I was paying attention, I could've looked for the purple door.

"Mom, Dad, Ever needs some statues out front so she can tell which house is ours."

"I don't," I tell Crue's parents with a headshake.

"Crue," Phoebe tsks before telling me, "Just look for the sailboat mailbox. That's ours."

I glance back at the mini sailboat replica made into a mailbox, the number 597 on it.

"It matches the keyrings."

Her keyring has yet another smaller sailboat replica on it.

"Sailboat. Got it."

Phoebe and Reid excuse themselves inside.

"You can dump the cooler in the flower beds, then meet me in the shower out back," Crue tells me on his way to the backyard to drop the kayaks by the side of the house.

"I didn't even get that wet," I point out. We didn't swim and I didn't capsize, so only the bottom halves of my legs got wet. I am sandy though.

"Not yet," Crue threatens, and I grin.

Bent down, almost finished scattering the ice under the hydrangeas, I hear voices and freeze. The manor's neighbors live too far away to overhear anything.

"Someone should tell her."

"Let someone else."

I strain my ears a little harder, hoping they'll spill more details than that.

"Excuse me."

My eyes wander around the bush as I wait to hear this.

"Excuse me? Miss?"

Glancing to the side, I jump when I notice someone behind me. I stand immediately and spin around to face the two older women, one on the sidewalk and one only a few feet away from me.

"Yes?"

"Do you know that boy's history?"

"Crue?"

"Mm-hm."

It's as if I can feel each and every one of my hackles rise. If I were a cat, my back would be bowed like a fishhook right now.

"Do you?" I counter.

"Yes—"

"Then you'll know he's no longer a boy. He's a man. You'll also know that he was never charged with anything, not driving under the influence, not manslaughter, and not anything else being said about him. If the law didn't persecute him, why the fuck do you think it's your job to?"

At my curse, I sense her hackles get raised as well.

Raise them. Raise them *all*. I'm not a Brantley. I'm a Munreaux and I'm not afraid to make a scene. I'm already on borrowed time as it is.

Tick.

Tock.

"What he did to that girl—"

"Was fabricated. He didn't hurt that girl. He would *never* hurt a girl."

The woman closest to me shoots her friend a look.

"I, however…" I close the distance so that when she turns back around, I'm nearly in her face. Luckily, she's short as well, so it has the effect I want. Crue thinks I'm creepy. Hopefully she does, too.

She rears back, clutching her throat as if she's seeking out her pearls. Or rosary.

"…have no such qualms. Speak poorly about anyone in the Brantley family again, and I will come to your house and prove it."

"You don't know where I live."

A swinging lighthouse on her keyring catches my eye and I decide to take a wild guess.

"The one with the lighthouse mailbox?"

Her eyes widen to near comical proportions, telling me I hit the bullseye.

What is with this neighborhood and their matching mailboxes and keyrings?

"And next time you see Crue, try smiling at him. It won't change anything in your life, but it might in his."

"I don't think so," she sneers with a fake smile.

Matching her energy, I say, "Then avoid using this street ever again or I'll pump water directly from the salt marsh in through your windows while you sleep."

Everyone in this neighborhood seems to keep their windows open all hours of the day, even at night, like none of them have air-conditioning. I know not everybody in the area does, but don't *any* of them? The manor had air-conditioning installed before I was born, so last night was my first time sleeping with an open window.

It wasn't terrible.

But I had Crue to protect me. This judgy bitch probably doesn't have anyone to keep her safe.

That both delights and saddens me. She might be nicer if she had someone to love her.

Another sneer in my direction, then she and her bestie are strolling away.

Or maybe she drives everyone away with her holier-than-thou attitude.

I flip off her back, then go in search of my boyfriend.

Standing just shy of the outdoor shower's overhead faucet, Crue's using the bottom spray to rinse his feet off. He looks up at my approach but I don't stop. I don't so much as slow down until my hands are grabbing his face and my lips are sealed to his.

He's still shirtless but has his pants on. I'm completely dressed. Yet his hands cup my ass and lift, then my back's touching siding,

Crue's erection caught between us as his hips pin me to the house, the shower streaming down over our bodies.

He tears his mouth from mine to ask, "You wet now?"

Biting his bottom lip, I nod before drawing him back to me.

Crue kisses me until I'm breathless and my pussy is aching to be filled.

I don't know how he does it but he reaches back to tickle my foot. I think he's going to put it over his shoulder, but he just focuses on my heel. His hands are also kneading my ass which…doesn't make any sense if he's playing with my—

I crack an eye to see a dog licking my foot.

"Oh my Goddess!"

Crue pulls back. "What?"

"There's a dog."

Without even investigating, he says, "That's just Zeus," before going in for another kiss. When I don't respond, he moves to my neck.

"He's licking me."

"Zeus, go away," gets muffled against my skin.

Zeus does not. Zeus sits right where he is and gives me literal puppy-dog eyes.

"Crue. Crue." I shove on his shoulders. "He won't stop."

"He's still licking you?"

"No, now he's looking at me."

"So what? He doesn't know."

"He knows."

"He doesn't."

"How do you know what he knows?"

"I don't…" Crue sighs, then shoos Zeus. "Go on. Get inside."

The only thing on the dog that moves are his eyebrows as he continues giving me sad, pleading eyes.

"Don't be mean to him."

"I'm not being mean to him. I promise. He just… He's… He's cock-blocking me right now and I need him to go inside so I can have sex with my girlfriend."

I roll my eyes. "We're not having sex out here."

"We were about to."

"Not anymore." One full-body wiggle, then I'm put back on my feet.

Zeus's tail goes into hyperdrive as he gets to all fours, coming right over to me to nuzzle everything he can reach.

The water shuts off behind me as I bend down to Zeus's level, my knees in the grass while his whiskers tickle my skin.

"What's he doing?" I ask through a giggle.

"You never had a dog sniff you before?"

"No."

"Your scent's new to him. He's just checking you out."

"Oh, yeah? How do I smell?" I ask Zeus, petting his floppy ears. His fur—hair?—is a beautiful shiny gold and wavy. I never understood people's desire to pet dogs until now. He's *so* soft, softer than Crue 2.0.

"Probably a lot like me."

"But he can tell the difference?"

"Yeah. Their sense of smell is supposed to be something like a hundred thousand times better than ours."

"Wow. You're amazing," I tell Zeus, earning myself a lick on the nose. And maybe up it? Yuck.

I keep a smile on my face though so I don't hurt his feelings.

"He likes you."

"How can you tell?" I ask.

"Because right now, my dog looks like what it feels like to be in love with you."

Zeus walks forward, causing me to fall back on my butt, more giggles erupting out of me, then next thing I know, I'm flat on my back and Zeus is standing over me, his entire body wagging as he licks my face.

"All right." Crue starts backing him up. "I get it, Zeus. Trust me, buddy. I get it. But she's mine."

With Zeus off me, Crue towers above me, holding his hand out to me, but I take a minute to stare up at him from down here.

"You're amazing, too."

"Is that your way of telling me you want me to lick your face?"

"No," I say, but Crue seems to take my ear-to-ear smile as an invitation to drop down on top of me and do it anyway.

The squeals that leave my mouth don't sound human whatsoever but apparently something dogs understand because Zeus's wet nose is suddenly in the mix again, trying to shove Crue's out of the way.

Between laughs, Crue sends his dog away again as he holds himself suspended over me.

"Let's get out of here."

I reach up to pull Crue closer by the back of his neck, wanting to stay just like this for as long as possible.

"Ever." He looks at our position. "We're disgusting."

"I know. Just…"

We're in the prickly, swampy grass that doesn't smell particularly good, probably what I imagine wet dog to smell like, and it feels itchy and gross and, yes, beyond disgusting. But this is one of those moments in life that are special in a way that's indescribable. It's a core memory in the making. How can I not stretch it just a little bit longer?

"There's nothing I wouldn't do for you," I promise him.

His response is immediate. "There's nothing you need to do for me. Whether you're up on your throne or down here in the mud, I love you the same…unconditionally."

I gaze into his eyes, only seeing pure, unequivocal love staring back at me.

"Thank you."

Grinning, he says, "You're welcome," in the same way we always do.

"No, I'm serious. Thank you for showing me what this kind of love feels like. I didn't think I'd ever experience it."

"I don't think most people experience love like this. If they did, the world would be a lot happier."

Focusing on the feeling of love, I picture my chest filling with warm air, thick like smoke but pink and cotton candy scented. It expands my rib cage until it bursts wide open in the middle, spilling out into the atmosphere in large drafts, larger than could fit in my body. I can almost see it spreading, searching for others to influence, to wrap up in security.

The reason why the world isn't happier is because love is a master of disguise. It's adaptable. It's adrenaline and fear and perseverance and trust. It's transformative, miraculous. It's…everything. Love is in everything and everyone, but it can be hard to identify, sometimes impossible. The subconscious love you have for yourself is what keeps you from stepping out into traffic, is what urges you to snuggle down into your coat on a cold day, is what scares you about jumping into another relationship after being hurt. Love is a watchdog on constant alert just to keep you safe, to keep you alive.

"I love you, Crue Brantley."

"I love you, Ever Brantley."

"I'm… Wha—"

"I'm manifesting that shit into existence right now. You're gonna be my wife *very* soon, so get used to the name."

Suddenly lifting my head up, I capture Crue's mouth with mine, breathing every last pink tendril I have into him, leaving it here, where it belongs.

Keep him safe.

Keep him alive.

Keep him perfect.

CHAPTER 52

Ever

KEEP EXPECTING PHOEBE TO KICK ME OUT OF THE KITCHEN while helping her with dinner, but her patience is limitless, and thankfully, she lets me stay the whole time, gently walking me through the steps to make fried flounder.

"So…Ever. What do you like to do?"

"Um. In what way?"

"Just in general. What are you passionate about?"

That's a first. If people aren't grilling me about Munreaux Motorcycles, they're talking about school. School and work are the Northeast's idea of small talk. After names are exchanged, they don't even touch on weather before jumping right into "What do you do?" and "Where'd you go to school?" Nobody's ever asked me what I'm passionate about before.

"I… Well…"

Despite having hobbies, I find myself struggling to answer right away. It's just such an unusual question.

It shouldn't be.

I start with the biggest one, telling her, "I was a cheerleader."

"Were? What happened?"

"Family obligations."

"That sounds complicated."

"Very."

"Mm."

She gives me time to expand on that but I don't want to, so we sit in an awkward silence until Crue calls from the living room, "Ever draws, too," making me blush. I didn't realize he could hear us. That means his father can, too. I don't have anything against Reid personally, but fathers are…not people I'm used to being open with.

"Do you really?"

"Yeah."

"What do you like to draw?"

"Me!" Crue yells.

Phoebe raises her eyebrows but gives a soft smile.

Not sensing any judgement, I nod. "Your egomaniac son is my favorite subject, yes."

Crue's and Reid's chuckles from the other room float into this one. They sound very similar, but I have Crue's memorized.

"I draw other things, too. Flowers, butterflies, bats…"

"Is that why Crue calls you little bat?"

That blush turns into an inferno.

"Um, I'm not sure why he calls me that," I try to say quietly.

"It's because she likes things dark and cold!"

I shake my head. "Not cold."

"Just dark?"

"I guess so." That's how my house has always been decorated. It used to scare me, but eventually, I adapted to it.

My father was right. He's been preparing me all along to adapt to daunting conditions. I just didn't realize it.

Phoebe's laugh interrupts my thoughts.

"Um, I also like collecting crystals, tarot cards, anything meta-physical really," I say out loud for the first time ever. Nobody in my life has ever cared to hear about the real me. Phoebe seems like she does.

"Ah, so you're a witch."

"No, not really."

"Well, you've certainly bewitched my son. We've never seen him so…happy."

I hear Crue say, "She enchanted me, all right."

Accustomed to her own environment, Phoebe simply rolls her eyes at her family's constant eavesdropping.

Meanwhile, I have to study the bubbling oil to keep from crying.

I can still make Crue happy. He will be. He will.

Crue's smile drops the second he sees me walk through his bedroom door.

"What's he doing here?" he asks from his bed, one hand behind his head, the other pointed to what's by my feet.

"Oh him?" I ask innocently before looking down. I don't know if dogs can smile, but I swear Zeus is grinning so smugly right now.

"He can't come in here."

I prop both hands on my hips. "You said he sleeps wherever he wants. He wants to sleep in here."

"Am I just supposed to let everybody sleep with my girlfriend that wants to?"

"He's your dog," I deadpan.

"He's a cock-block."

"He'll sleep on the floor and look at the wall," I say, despite knowing nothing about dogs' sleeping habits.

"He won't." Crue laughs. "He'll be on the bed, right between us..."

That's perfect actually.

"...snoring and farting and—"

"Sorry, Zeus," I say.

"Find Mom," Crue tells Zeus, causing the dog to forget all about me to go in search of Phoebe.

"I thought he loved me," I say morosely, watching his luscious tail disappear around the corner, not even getting a single look back.

"Don't take it personally. He loves anyone that gives him attention. Or treats."

Hm.

"What kind of treats does he like? Cookies?"

He chuckles. "No, dog treats."

"Do you have any?" I ask with as little interest in my voice as possible while closing the door behind me.

If Crue suspects anything, he doesn't let on.

"Yeah, we keep a bunch in the kitchen. As soon as Zeus hears the cabinet open, he comes running."

That'll be helpful.

"Come to bed so I can finish what you started earlier."

"Me? What did I do?"

"You seduced me in the backyard."

"I kissed you," I say as I slowly approach the end of the bed.

"It was a hell of a kiss."

Not as patient as his mother, Crue hinges forward, grabs a wrist, and yanks me on to the mattress.

We wrestle around for a few minutes, each of us fighting for control, before eventually Crue lets me mount him.

"That's a pin," I say, pressing both his shoulders down.

Through heavy lids, he says, "Good girl," the praise going straight to my core.

"I think you should. Go to college."

"I'm done with wrestling. I don't have the same passion for it that I used to."

"You can go for anything."

"Will you go with me?"

That's…an idea. Not a realistic one, but it's an idea.

"Not to Littoral," I say, humoring him.

"Fuck Littoral. Your strengths weren't being utilized there."

"Like wrestling?" I taunt with an eyebrow jump.

I'm suddenly on my back, looking up at Crue, my stomach following a moment later apparently, giving me a brief bout of nausea. Um…

"How did you…"

The brow lift he gives me is all arrogance. "*That's a pin.*"

"Good boy," I croon with a proud smile.

Those words like a blow horn in a race, Crue pushes to his knees, removing his shirt and shorts as quick as he can. Since I'm competitive, I do the same, kicking my panties down my legs just before Crue wedges himself between them, aligning our centers so his rigid length is nestled against my pussy.

I reach between us and guide him in one-handed, making both of us groan.

Needing him closer than what's physically possible, I cling to him, and plead, "Finish me."

"Finish…what you started?"

"No. Finish me. Make sure you're the only one I'll ever think about like this."

Crue gives me a questioning look. "If you're worried about fantasizing about someone else with me, tell me who it is and I'll be him for you. I want to be your everything, but I can be your everyone, too. If you're worried about doing this with someone else, don't bother because you won't. I'm the only one you're ever going to do this with, period. I wasn't just talking shit earlier, Ever. I'm going to marry you and make you mine forever. There will never be someone else. Not for me. And not for you. On my life, 'til death."

Two steady streams of hot tears flow from the corners of my eyes into my hairline.

"'Do us part'?" I quote with a shallow laugh.

Crue doesn't so much as crack a smile, only shakes his head once.

"No, butterfly. Not even death can part us."

He starts moving, slow and easy, dragging himself upward with each thrust to rub my clit.

"I love you," I tell him, repeatedly, empathetically. I tell him all the things I love about him, barely getting them out between ragged breaths.

When he comes, he doesn't just stop and hop off, he lets me

roll my hips from below, grinding my clit while he professes his own reasons for loving me. I come hard and long, biting his pec to keep from screaming out.

His body shakes over mine as he breathes, "Jesus, Ever. If you hadn't already ruined me, that would've done it."

I release his skin from between my teeth and kiss the imprint. "I'm sorry. I'm so sorry."

"It's all right, little bat. You didn't hurt me."

No…

But I'm about to.

CHAPTER 53

ITIPTOE INTO THE KITCHEN AND OPEN EACH AND EVERY CABINET. I know I found the right one when I hear the pitter-patter of paws. Gabbing a handful of treats out, I jiggle them at a very eager Zeus and step backward. He follows me easily enough, so I lead him to Crue's room, where I put the bone-shaped treats in a pile next to Crue. Zeus climbs onto the spot I just vacated and starts munching.

I kiss him on the head, then do the same to Crue.

I love you. I love you with all of my battered heart.

Out on the front porch, I make the call.

Despite the hour, he answers on the second ring.

"I'd like to revisit the terms of my contract," I say before he can get a word out.

"You are in no position to make demands."

"Tell me, Father, what other daughter will you get to do your bidding if I don't?"

"Yours."

I would sterilize myself just to keep that from happening. But since this is a negotiation, I go along with it.

"Eighteen years is an awfully long time to wait. Are you sure Munreaux Motorcycles has that kind of time?"

"What do you want?"

I'd let my lips curve if I had any feeling in them.

"Remember that million dollars you accused me of stealing? I want it. Upfront."

"Do you think I'm stupid? The second that money hits your account, you'll use it to run away."

"It's not going in my account."

"Whose account is it going in?"

Less than thirty minutes later, I watch as my father lands his helicopter on the old wharf, the wind creating angry ripples in the water below.

"The fucking help, Never?" is the first thing he says to me in the headset. "My God, you're a disappointment."

"I won't disappoint you in this, Father." I look over at him. "It's all I'm good for, after all."

After a condescending shake of his head, we're airborne.

I seek out that sailboat mailbox one final time.

Don't look for me.

CHAPTER 54

Crue

"How'd you get in here?" I grumble to Zeus, who I hear whining by the door.

Ever must've let him in sometime during the night but made the mistake of closing the door after. She's never had a pet. She doesn't know they gotta go out to pee.

I turn over to look at her.

"Butter—"

My head shoots off the bed.

Where's Ever? She's not beside me. She's not anywhere in this room.

Did she need to pee?

Pushing myself up, one of my palms lands in a bunch of brown crumbs on my sheet.

I groan.

She's never had a pet, I repeat to myself as I stumble down the hall, passing by the bathroom that's empty judging by the open door.

Mm. Don't love that. Where'd she go?

No sign of Ever in the kitchen either, I complete an entire circle in my spot. That's pretty much the whole house so…where is she?

"What are you looking for?" my dad asks from the table.

"My girlfriend. Have you seen her?"

"She wasn't in your room?"

"Nope."

"Did you check the bathroom?"

I give him a flat look. These are not helpful suggestions.

After an apologetic shrug, he unfolds his newspaper, letting the bottom half fall open. When he opens it, something inside makes his eyes bulge.

"I think I might know where she is."

"Where?" I ask, getting closer. Without waiting for an answer, I take the paper right out of his hands.

"I don't know how to tell you this, son…"

Staring up at me is a large black-and-white picture of Mallory Larson and tucked against his side is Ever.

"I recognize this picture," I say. "This was at a gala last month."

"Did you read the headline at the top of the page?"

My eyes find it, but my brain refuses to believe it.

"They're not… That's… She…"

"It says the wedding is today."

"No." I shake my head. Fuck no. She's not getting… Married? Today? To fucking Mallory?

"Ever?" I bellow and drop the paper. She's here. With me. She has to be.

"She didn't tell you she was engaged?"

"Dad!" I warn as I tear through the house, checking every nook and cranny, even behind the couch because if her mom made her play hours of hide-and-seek, she must be pretty good at it. That's all this is. She's just…hiding. Once I find her, I'm keeping her. She's mine.

She's…

Not here.

"Fuck!"

"What's going on?" my mom asks, rushing out of her bedroom with a towel wrapped around her head and wearing a robe.

My dad tilts the paper in her direction and I watch her eyes do the same thing his did.

"Mom, did you see Ever this morning?"

"No, but…honey…"

I put a hand up to silence her. No. No. It can't be real. This is an elaborate prank. Ever loves to get one over on me. She's just a funny girl, pulling a funny—

"She looks like she really loves him if that's any consolation," my mom says.

"What? She doesn't love *him*. She's not marrying *him*."

I stomp over and rip the paper out of my dad's hand a second time. I should've never given it back to him. I should've burned it. Thrown it in the fucking trash where trash belongs.

I can't help but examine the picture again, trying to see what my mom sees. I remember when this was being taken. Ever wasn't looking at Mallory at all. She was looking at me. She loves *me*. She's gonna marry *me*. I told her that.

"It'd be really smart if she did."

"Why's that?" I ask my dad, still staring at Ever's beautiful face, wishing I was looking at it in real life, not on a newspaper.

"The Larsons own Infinite Energy. If Munreaux Motorcycles plans to deliver on that promise they made back in November to roll out a line of electric motorcycles soon, it'd be extremely beneficial for them to partner with a hydrogen company."

"Partnering is one thing. This is…"

"Better."

I finally tear my eyes off Ever and pin them on my dad.

"The marriage would guarantee exclusivity," he explains. "Infinite Energy won't be able to supply hydrogen to any other motorcycle companies, making Munreaux Motorcycles miles ahead of the competition. No pun intended."

I didn't even think of that. Why didn't I think of that?

I can see Arthur doing that. But Ever? She wouldn't agree to that. Ever hates her father. She wouldn't agree to marry someone, sign her fucking life away, just to help Munreaux Motorcycles.

This doesn't make any sense.

Her bracelet. If she's still wearing it, I can track her. I send one last glance around the house before returning to my room to get my phone. On the screen is a notification of a large deposit into my bank account. Assuming it's just the one from Friday about my paycheck,

I flick it away with my thumb. My hand's shaking so bad though, I accidentally press it too long and it opens to that instead of my home screen.

"Shit." I don't care about that. I care about—

Wait. What the fuck? How are there so many zeroes? That's…

I count.

Then recount.

A million dollars?

I scroll through the history. A deposit of one million dollars was deposited into my account at 3:14 this morning.

How? It's the fucking weekend. Nothing in banking happens on the weekend.

Unlike the other payments that came via Munreaux Motorcycles, this one's from Arthur Munreaux himself.

Did he suddenly grow a heart and feel bad about stiffing me that million dollars I thought I was getting?

If I thought I wasn't exerting every muscle in my body to hold myself together right now, I'd laugh. I'd fucking howl with laughter.

That didn't happen. No way that fucking happened.

So then, what is it?

I don't care. That's not important. Finding Ever is.

I get the GPS app open and wait for it to update.

She's on Nantucket. Where the wedding is. Fuck!

I scour my room. I ransack the fucking thing, searching for any clue to explain what's going on, why Ever left to marry…Mallory, a guy who tried to rape her.

She's not marrying him.

The only thing out of place is Crue 2.0. He's missing.

That bear.

I check the newspaper again, scanning the article for the ceremony details. Today. Nantucket. Church.

Time.

Time.

Time.

Got it. Eleven a.m., with reception to follow.

It's eight thirty now. It'll take me at least two and a half hours to drive to the port, another hour on the ferry out to the island. I won't make it in time.

I won't fucking make it!

I crumple the newspaper up and throw it at the wall. It lands without a sound on the floor, so I kick it.

She was here. She was mine. Then, she disappeared right out of my fucking hands. Gone. Taken. Again. Just like in the corn maze.

How was she taken? Arthur's a fucking liar and has a helicopter somewhere. If that's how he picked Ever up at Hide and Keep, I'm willing to bet he used it this time, too.

If he can fly to Nantucket, so can I. I have over a million fucking dollars at my disposal.

I'm gonna make it.

Keeping my head low, I part from the helicopter I chartered to fly me here. I've never been on Nantucket, so I don't have the first clue where the fuck I'm going but I got an address and enough cash to get me there fast.

Right outside the tiny airport is a lane just for taxis. But it's empty. Every person getting picked up curbside is with family it looks like. No impersonal hired drivers awkwardly taking their luggage from them to throw it in the trunk.

Goddamn it.

I see a sign for car rentals and sprint over to the customer service counter, which only has three people waiting. With one representative though, it might take forever to get through the line.

"Excuse me, this is an emergency!" I announce. "Would anyone mind letting me cut in front of them?"

The last person in line shrugs, and says, "Sure. You can go ahead of me."

"Thanks," I mumble, stepping in front of them.

Two people. Two fucking people I still have to wait on.

It takes way longer than it should for me to get to the counter for my turn, and by the time I do, I'm sweating profusely, and not because of the temperature.

"I need a car. Any car. Right now."

"Okay, do you have a preference on—"

"Zero preferences. I will literally take any car you have available right this second. It's an emergency."

"Oh, gosh. I hope everything's okay," the attendant says while typing at a snail's pace.

"It's not," I tell her, hoping that speeds things up.

Apparently, she's a liar, too, and does not hope everything's okay because if she did, she wouldn't continue with the same exact lack of urgency as she did with the previous two customers.

Seventeen excruciating minutes later, I'm out the door, running to a blue Mini Cooper. Who the fuck's renting Mini Coopers?

Using my phone's GPS, I speed off toward the church Ever's wedding is taking place in…

I glance at the time on the dashboard.

Shit!

Now. She's getting married right fucking now.

My foot almost breaks through the floorboard as I lay on the gas, swerving around cars and fountains and people as fast as I can, but Jesus Christ, this place is small. And old. The roads are brick. Uneven brick that makes the Mini Cooper feel like a damn lawnmower with all the vibration.

I don't give a fuck. I have a wedding to crash.

Passing the church and the twenty cars packed in front of it like sardines, I'm forced to park four blocks down.

I'm bursting through the double doors less than a minute later, booming, "I object!"

"Sir, the time for objections has passed," the priest tries to inform me, but I ignore him because Ever, *my* woman, comes into view. In a white, lacy gown, a veil over her face, and a long train spread out behind her, she's the epitome of the perfect bride. Even spotting a frown under that veil, she manages to do that thing again—steal my breath right out of my lungs.

I point at her and say, "You promised." She said she'd never leave me to run into another man's arms. That motherfucker Mallory has both of his around her right now, cradling her like she's some precious ornament. And to him, she probably would be. An ornament. Not precious. If she was, he wouldn't have tried to stick his dick in her without her permission.

Fuck, I hate him.

Arthur stands to round on me coming up the aisle. "Mr. Brantley, you are—"

I don't skip a fucking beat to give him a right hook. I hate him, too.

"That's for slapping your daughter."

That very daughter demands, "What are you doing here?"

I spin and tell her point-blank, "Taking you home."

"You can't just steal my bride," Mallory says with a snooty scoff because he's a snooty piece of shit.

"I'm not stealing anything. I'm just taking back what's mine."

Turning to face me fully, Ever says, "Crue."

One of Mallory's hands drops, but he keeps the other on her. At her hip, to be exact.

Ever hisses and bends away from him.

Motherfucker's pinching her in the same spot Arthur does and he's doing it right in front of me, right in front of everybody.

Oh. He's fucking dead.

Climbing the steps to the altar two at a time, I wrap my arms around him from the side, then throw him over my back in a suplex. Suplexes are risky as shit because they can paralyze—or worse, kill— the person getting thrown to the ground on their head or neck. I'm hoping for worst-case scenario when I bring Mallory down as hard as I can. *Die, fucker.*

I pop back up on my feet without waiting to see if he did, and grab Ever's hand. Immediately, she tries to pull it out of mine. There's that funny girl of mine.

Ha-fucking-ha.

I snatch her hand again.

"Ever. Come on. We're leaving. You're not marrying this fucking loser."

"Excuse me! I'll have you know—"

I swing a glare around on Mallory's dad, whatever the fuck his name is again. "Shut the fuck up or I'll body-slam you, too, old man. You arranged a marriage for your rapist son with a woman that was already promised to someone else."

A collective gasp echoes through the crowd of wedding guests, but I'm not sure for which juicy tidbit. The abusive father? The arranged marriage? Or the rapist son? All three are pretty fucking disturbing in my opinion.

"Who?" Larson, Sr. and Arthur demand at the same time.

"Me."

Arthur points at Ever. "You better fix this."

"Crue." Ever tugs on me until I turn to her.

Her face is covered and I…hate it. Is that why she was always taking my hat off?

I remove the veil from her hair and throw it out to the side.

There's my beautiful bride. Mine. Not Mallory's.

Instead of vows, my bride whispers, "Just take the money."

"What money?"

She widens her eyes at me.

The million dollars.

"That was you?"

"You can get away. Move anywhere you want. Live out your dream."

"Are you fucking shitting me?" I use her own saying against her. "I would *never* choose travel or money or *anything* over you. You're my dream. You."

Instead of being happy at that, she only looks more miserable.

"I'll be your end, too."

"Then finish me." That's what she said last night, right? I didn't fully understand what she meant until now. She chose me to be her end. I'm choosing her to be mine. I drop to my knees at her feet and with my hands together in prayer, I beg, "Fucking finish me, Ever, because I'm yours no matter what, no matter where. Go to outer space and I'll still come find you."

She shakes her head, the pain inside her causing fissures in her makeup as it claws its way out and onto her features.

"Ever."

Tears run down her quivering cheeks. "I'm sorry."

"Don't be. You're—"

Mallory's moan beside us cuts me off. He starts thrashing around, making me instantly pissed he's still alive. And obviously not paralyzed.

Pressing the bottom of my shoe against his back, I kick him away from us.

"You're not marrying him. Not today. Not ever. You're going to be *my* wife and you're going to bear *my* children." I think. I don't know. We never talked about having kids before. "We're going to travel the world *together*, every single step of the way." I don't care how many jobs I have to suffer through to make that happen, or how many years it'll take to earn enough savings, but I'll do it. I'll do anything to keep Ever.

And I'll do it all without a fucking hat on. Anything to make her happy.

"It's my choice," she cries. "I'm choosing your life over mine."

"I have no life without you, Ever." Doesn't she fucking see that? She is my life now.

"I'm sorry. I'm so, *so* sorry. But I'm—"

Suddenly, she drops to her knees, too, and with my head blocking her from everyone's view, she whispers in a completely different tone, "There's a door out back."

"Can you run in that dress?"

"Faster than you."

"You're on, little bat."

"Try to keep—"

We both move at the same time, scrambling off the floor to run toward the back.

The back? That's so vague.

I'm forced to give Ever the lead just so I can follow her. That's okay though. I'll follow her anywhere.

Shouts go off behind us, one after the other, like explosions in a minefield, but we don't stop. We don't look back. With Ever with me, I don't have any reason to anyway.

CHAPTER 55

ESIDE ME, EVER PUSHES ALL HER FINGERTIPS TOGETHER until her fingers shake.

I grab one of her hands. "Are you ready?"

"No."

"You don't have to go in there. I can do it by myself if you want."

"And miss the look on his face when he hears the wonderful news?"

That's my petty girl.

After getting the passenger door for her, we pass the motorcycle statues, and go up the front steps together, hand in hand.

"Welcome back, Miss Munreaux," Edwin greets her, ignoring me altogether. I am breaking the law being here, but it's still rude as fuck.

"It's Mrs. Brantley now," she corrects him before I can. It sounds so much better when she says it.

"My apologies, Mrs. Brantley."

Edwin ushers us into Arthur's office, where a new door's already replaced the one I broke.

"The Brantleys, sir," he announces to his boss more apologetically than when he offered Ever his apologies.

The face on Arthur though? Priceless.

I can sense Ever's evil grin without needing to see it.

Now that Ever's married to me, Arthur can't sell her off as anyone else's bride. If he really believes what he told her, that a strategic marriage is all she's good for, then according to him, she's no longer of use to him. I rid her of the Munreaux name and burden all at once.

"The Brantleys? Never, what the fu—"

"Ever," I tell Arthur. "Her name is Ever."

"I know her name. She's my daughter."

"She's *my wife*," I snarl even though I swore I wouldn't lose my patience. But this is the first time seeing him since Ever and I ran out of her arranged wedding and it's harder than I thought not to jump across his desk and strangle him with his own tie. He was going to sell off the love of my life. "You will use her real name or you will not speak to her at all."

With a scathing look at me, he grits, "*Ever*," before swinging his gaze to my wife. "What the—"

I bring out the anchor from behind my back and drop it on his desk. "Do you know what that is?" I give a one-second pause for dramatic effect, then continue without his input. "It's a six-pound, stainless steel fluke anchor."

An anchor guide I found online suggested counting one pound of anchor for every foot of boat length, but I was being generous rounding up to six pounds despite Arthur not being six feet tall. I figured it was better to err on the side of caution here.

"If you touch my wife again… If you go near my wife again… If you so much as fucking *talk* to my wife again, I will tie this to your ankles and drop you in the middle of the goddamn Atlantic."

"You just said as long as I use her name, I can talk to her." He points at Ever, and I take a strategic step in front of her. That finger has caused her so much pain.

But it never will again.

"I lied. I just wanted Ever to hear you say her name correctly for once."

He studies me, her, then the anchor.

"Six pounds won't drown me."

"No, the ocean will do that just like it did to *your* wife. The anchor's just to keep your body from floating back up once it does because we never want to see your ugly ass again."

My wife and I turn to leave.

"Aren't you going to take this with you?"

"You keep it," I tell him without looking back. I may not be fuck-you rich like Arthur Munreaux but I do still have most of that million dollars and that's more than enough to buy another anchor. "Let it serve as a reminder."

"She's out of the will!" he calls after us like we care. Even if my account didn't currently have lots of zeroes in it, we wouldn't care. Nothing in our future requires the Munreaux fortune. It'll help, for sure, but we'd be happy without it, too.

I keep a hand at the small of Ever's back, pushing her forward. We need to get out of here before her father says something to make me snap and send him to that deep-sea grave right now.

Just as we make it to that new door though, Ever stops.

"And, Arthur?" She spins around to face him. "That goes for my future kids, too. Don't even *think* about contacting any of my children."

"I'm your father. And someday I'll be their grand—"

"No. You were never a father. You were just a plague I survived. Your rot will never touch my children. If I have to rid this planet of you myself to ensure it doesn't, I will. I already lost one biological parent off the back of the *Burning Rudder*, I won't hesitate to lose another the same way. And trust me, there will be *no* question as to whether it was accidental or not."

For once, Ever's rendered her father speechless. He says nothing. He does nothing. If I believed he had a heart, I'd think his daughter just broke it.

Since I know that's not true, I assume the motherfucker's just plotting.

He can plot. We got lives to start.

I wait until we're back in the car to voice my thoughts. "So…you do want kids?"

We've been a little busy these past couple days getting married and consummating that marriage. Lots of consummating. We wanted to be sure there was no chance for an annulment. If Arthur's willing to arrange a marriage for his daughter, he's archaic enough to challenge one.

Ever puts on her seat belt. "And a dog."

"Okay…" I gotta be honest, I did not see that coming. "No feeding the dog treats in bed though."

"That was just to lure Zeus into bed with you."

"Why'd you want Zeus in bed with me?"

"So you had someone to snuggle in my place."

My head starts shaking on its own accord. "I didn't snuggle… Zeus…" Wait. "…thinking it was…" Did I? "…you."

Ever cups her mouth, trying and pretty much failing to hold in a laugh.

I didn't notice she was gone until morning. And I almost always have at least one arm around her when we're sleeping.

Shit.

"It has to be a small dog," I declare, making her lose it entirely.

"Whatever you say, Major."

"We both know that's not true."

My wife's smile confirms I'm right.

Shit.

Here's to a lifetime of folding. And being ridiculously, sickeningly, *pathetically* happy about it.

EPILOGUE

KEEPING MY BODY SIDEWAYS, I SLOWLY MAKE MY WAY DOWN the steep incline, one hand up and behind me, tightly gripping Ever's as she follows my every step.

We've been on the move ever since we arrived in Mexico. After landing in Morelia, Michoacán, we've driven—in a car that wasn't much bigger than that damn Mini Cooper I stole my bride in—rode horses—that were *way* bigger than the Mini Cooper—and are now hiking.

All for butterflies.

All for *my* butterfly.

We've already spotted hundreds of monarchs during our travel to the preserve, swarms of them fluttering around our car, then on bushes we passed on horseback, but the forest we're in now currently holds over a hundred million monarchs keeping warm until the spring when they can start the first leg of their big migration.

The entire hike has been littered with dead orange-and-black bodies of butterflies. Everywhere you look basically are monarchs that didn't survive after the flight down here.

It's sad to think about—spending so much energy on reaching a destination, just to die when you get there. That's essentially what happened to Ever. Or *almost* happened to Ever. She escaped Arthur, was about to be free of him, until she got it in her head that sacrificing herself, her life, her happiness, was an even trade for mine.

It wasn't an even trade. It wasn't even a possible trade because my life's forever intwined with hers. Same with my happiness. And *our* life is just beginning.

Our guide, Vincente, stops us to point at the tree trunks.

"There. You see?"

I scan the trunks, noticing how textured they are compared to other trees.

The altitude up here has me out of breath as I ask, "They're fuzzy?"

He shakes his head and grins. "They're alive."

"Those are butterflies, Major."

I look again, this time at the movement of those textured trunks. They do look alive.

"Shouldn't they be orange?"

"The butterflies are so tightly packed together, all we're seeing are the tips of their wings. The black-and-white parts," Ever explains, not as affected by the altitude since she's well-traveled and I'm…not. Not yet anyway. We're working on it.

Ever and I both applied to some of the best cheerleading colleges in the country and were accepted to several. All of them highly ranked, we chose the cheapest. Now we live in Florida, where we spend our days either in class—going after degrees in natural resources conservation—or on the mat, together. After twenty-five years of doubting cheerleaders as athletes, I'm now one. But only for Ever. I couldn't let anyone else be my wife's base. Truthfully, I like cheer way more than I ever liked wrestling. Having a partner makes every win, no matter how big or small, that much sweeter. It just so happens, I have a pretty big winner for a partner. Nobody at our college calls her Zero, but she's definitely earned the title. Her precision inspires me to achieve my own, so even though this is my first year cheering, I work my ass off trying to match her skill level.

Every night, we walk along the beach—that doesn't smell like sulfur but something else we can't quite put our fingers on—then go home and fall asleep in each other's arms, grateful that nobody knows or cares who Crue and Ever Brantley are.

Now that I have a little bit of money, I know it's not what makes people good or bad. Money only provides more options. It's what you do with those options that determines what kind of person you are.

We've been smart with ours, stretching Arthur's inadvertent wedding gift out as long as possible. This trip is the first non-essential expense we've allowed ourselves. After visiting my parents for the holidays and checking on my dad's recovery from back surgery, we flew down here—in coach—before our practices increase in both quantity and intensity in preparation for Nationals in April.

With it only being the beginning of January, the preserve warned us it might be too cold for the butterflies to fly around. They said it might even snow. I'm really hoping it doesn't though and that the sun comes out so we get to see millions of monarchs take flight. A lot are flying around now, but most of them are sticking to the trunks and branches and leaves and—Holy shit, they're on everything.

There's a butterfly conservatory near where we live that we like to visit, but it doesn't compare to Ever's old one. A labor of love, hers was pure magic.

We don't know what happened to it after Ever left the manor, but we're optimistic the butterflies found their way out into the real world.

Mine did.

"Do you think any of your butterflies could be here?" I ask her.

"Doubtful."

A single monarch dances in front of her, so she puts her hand out for it to land on.

Fascination lights up her face as she considers the butterfly on her palm. She's seen hundreds, maybe thousands, of butterflies from the egg stage all the way through to adulthood, and she's still amazed at every one.

It's probably like when I look at Ever. From the first glimpse of her morning bed head to the last hint of her serene face next to me at night, I'm always captivated by her. Bewitched, as my mom put it.

"But…maybe their grandchildren."

"There's no way for you to tell? Like markings?"

"No. Only if there was a tag on it."

"You can tag a butterfly?"

With a smile, she peeks at me. "You did, didn't you?"

"I, uh, don't think…" The butterfly-covered trees become *very* interesting as I avoid Ever's general direction. I even point at one.

My wife's chuckle brings my attention back to her. She's just shaking her head.

"Yeah, I did," I admit.

Vincente's been pretending not to listen, but his eyes widening confirm he's hearing every word.

"How?"

"It was back at the manor. I put a microchip in a couple of your bracelets."

"The amethyst one?"

I jerk a nod. "And the tiger's eye." This shit's so embarrassing out of context. I almost explain to Vincente that I was Ever's personal protection agent, but don't in case he questions why she needed one in the first place. The Munreaux name has been dead to us for months. We don't so much as utter it anymore. I didn't even put my time there on my résumé. I'd rather let people think I was unemployed for that month than have Arthur Munreaux's name listed on anything of mine. It's not like he'd be a good reference anyway. I stole his daughter off her wedding altar, prevented his company from cornering the market on hydrogen-powered electric motorcycles, and threatened to sink him like a retired ship.

Damn. I'm as diabolical as Ever.

Bars of golden sunlight cut through the forest, slicing between leaves and branches to send warmth out around us.

It starts slowly, butterflies falling by the dozens, then more and more, until suddenly they're all cascading down off the trees like black, white, and orange waterfalls before catching air and taking flight.

Ever releases a quiet sob.

I shift my gaze to watch her instead. She's in awe, absolutely transfixed by the dreamlike spectacle, and all I can think of is how lucky I am that I get to witness *her* like this.

"Butterfly?"

"Yes?" she responds distractedly.

"Do you want to be kept?"

Her shimmering azure eyes find mine. "Only by you."

"Come on." I pull her over to a flat spot and place her in front of me, both of us facing forward.

"What are we doing?" she asks, already setting her feet apart as I grip her waist. I'm good enough now, she doesn't bat an eye at me throwing her places outside the gym.

"Double cupie."

I toss her straight up and she completes a double body spin before I catch both her feet with my right palm. Without a hat on, I can see every detail.

Her hands in a V above her, my wife tilts her head back to take in the view. We're surrounded by fluttering monarchs, both our bodies holding at least a dozen of the inquisitive insects each.

I'd do it all again. Arthur wasn't just holding Ever back. He was killing her. She's a flyer, meant to soar above us all. And I'm meant to keep her safe when she lands.

I'm meant to keep her safe.

I'm meant to keep her.

BOOKS BY
A. MARIE

Creekwood Series
Detour
Changing Lanes
Blind Spot
Roundabout

Lit U Series
Hide and Keep

Standalones
Let the Light Shine Through
The Comedown
Nothing Above

For more playlists, inspiration boards, and bonus content,
be sure to check out my website amarieauthor.com

www.ingramcontent.com/pod-product-compliance
Lightning Source LLC
Chambersburg PA
CBHW061030310726
48969CB00004B/909